The Mystery of a Hansom Cab

FERGUS W. HUME

BREESE
BOOKS
LONDON

First published in 1886 by
Kemp and Boyce, Melbourne, Australia.

Published in London in 1887 by
The Hansom Cab Publishing Company

With an introduction by H.R.F. Keating

ISBN: 0 947533 42 7

Typeset in 11/12pt Garamond and Prose Antique by
Ann Buchan (Typesetters), Middlesex
Printed and bound in Great Britain by
Itchen Printers Ltd, Southampton

Introduction

Read this book. Written as long ago as 1886, of course it creaks a bit here and there, in for instance the longish verbatim quotations from the inquest near the start. But even passages like that have their nostalgic charm, and they do move the story on. Because this is the point. Fergus Hume told a splendid unfolding story, making you want to know what will happen next, from the first discovery in a night street in Melbourne of a body in the hansom cab of the title to the final unravelling of the complex mystery.

It was a great piece of luck for readers down the years from the first extraordinary success of the book in Australia where Hume, who was born in England in 1859, was a barrister's clerk that he should have tried to make some extra money by writing. The first edition of the book went into three impressions in just a few months. In London, where it was published in the following year, 25,000 copies were printed each month for fourteen months in succession. After that the book was brought out in various editions and in various languages down the years, only to fade away somewhat in recent times.

The eagerness of its readers is easy to understand. The story has dozens of the ingredients of success. First there is that startling, read-on beginning. A hansom, one of the speedy, two-person cabs with the driver perched up behind, patented in London by one J.A. Hansom and later the frequently chosen vehicle of Sherlock Holmes, arrives at a police station with in it all alone a man who has been chloroformed to death. Soon the mystery begins to be explained by a delightful stolid detective who has as his 'Watson' — an authorial device yet to be developed — nothing else but his shaving mirror.

But Gorby, who also has a touch of Wilkie Collins's plain-man Sergeant Cuff, we discover, is not to be the hero of the whole tale.

Hume cunningly provides him with what he calls, using a popular Shakespearean reference of his day, 'another Richmond in the field'. This is his arch rival, the sleekly sharp Kilsip, who — I'm not spoiling the story — proves, like Sergeant Cuff, to be right in the end after all, despite all appearances. And there are other sleuths who play their parts: the lawyer, Mr Calton, a figure not unlike the persevering solicitor hero of Josephine Tey's 1948 classic *The Franchise Affair*, and, if not achieving very much, the playboy journalist, Felix Rolleston, a precursor surely of Nicholas Blake's Nigel Strangeways.

Rolleston is portrayed with some nice flicks of humour, and Hume's well-crafted comic scenes are another of the book's pleasures. It was Wilkie Collins, that great master, who once gave as the recipe for his books the maxim 'Make 'em laugh, make 'em weep, make 'em wait.' And Hume certainly follows that first injunction in his scenes with the book's two landladies. First Mrs Hableton with her strictures on men 'a callin' 'emselves lords of creation, as if women were made for nothin' but to earn money an' see 'em drink it, as my 'usband did, which 'is inside never seemed to 'ave enough beer'. And then Mrs Sampson, so dried up that 'it would do her good if she were soaked in water for a year', with her 'Not bein' a blue ribbing [The Blue Ribbon Army was a total abstinence organisation] all the same, and I never saw him the wuss for drink, 'e being allus able to use his latch key, an' take 'is boots off afore going to bed'.

And, if there are no passages that might make tears fall from unsentimental twentieth-century eyes, there are moments when we feel not a little sympathy for Hume's heroine, the millionaire's daughter, Madge Frettlby, whom her father has commanded to marry the book's unpleasant victim. This plot twist, one suspects, must have been in Conan Doyle's mind when he wrote 'The Boscombe Valley Mystery', also with its roots in Australia. It is as if Doyle were justifying his appropriation when he has Holmes subtly knock the hansom cab drama by saying 'Singularity is almost invariably a clue. The more featureless and commonplace a crime is, the more difficult it is to bring it home.'

But it is the difficulties that Hume concocts to come between us and his solution, the times that he makes us wait, that keep us reading. At one stage, too, he even gives us that staple of countless

Golden Age detective stories, complications with a clock and an alibi. Or, as Hume always prints it, an *alibi*. Because here, for us today, is another of the book's pleasures, its setting in a different age, an age where Latin origins had to be acknowledged and Latin quotations *Dulce est desipere in loco* (Sweet it is in places to forget wisdom) did not baffle. A different age and a different place. Time and again as one reads one is inclined to exclaim *Did they have that in Melbourne then?* Here is no settlement for convicts, but a flourishing nineteenth-century city. A city where 'evening clothes — which nine men out of ten are in the habit of wearing' are to be seen in all the best parts after dark. A city of much the same sort as London in which the occasional visitor from the British Isles, the 'squatter', easily took his place.

We get the whole fascinating picture of the city, from the elegant fashion parades of The Block and the rich luxuriousness of its gentlemen's clubs to the noise and squalor of its slums. And here is another of Hume's successes. He is one of the few authors of his time who can paint a low-life scene that has the ring of truth about it. Plainly he has read and absorbed his realist Zola, of whom Detective Gorby says 'if his novels are as bad as his reputation I shouldn't care to read them'. You might almost say Hume in his description of Mother Guttersnipe's den in the slums succeeds in foreshadowing the much-hailed *noir* writers of the late twentieth century.

Hume's ability to handle such scenes points to what one might call the core of steel that lies underneath the book's surface sensationalism. He may have been consciously imitating, as he admits in a preface he wrote for one of the later editions, the melodramatic French novels of Emile Gaboriau (spelt, oddly, Gaboreau in the pages) as well as taking tips from such bestsellers as Bulwer Lytton (*The Last Days of Pompeii* and the play *Richelieu*), Anna Katharine Green of *The Leavenworth Case* and Mrs Braddon, author of *Lady Audley's Secret*, but he acknowledges in his pages as well altogether tougher authors. George Eliot, De Quincey, Disraeli (referred to as Lord Beaconsfield) with his novel *Vivian Grey* and the ever-philosophical Edgar Allan Poe are all drawn on. This steel core means he can speak without frothy moralising about his young male characters' promiscuities and can deliver a sharp jab at people — there are plenty of them today — who, regardless of the actualities, 'make a point of coming forward as champions of those in trouble'. Or, when Madge Frettlby innocently exclaims that God will not permit such a judicial crime as the murder of an innocent man, he can have his lawyer sleuth say — something that still reverberates today — 'God has permitted it to take place before.'

So much going for the book. No wonder it had its great success. But here is the sad note. Hume never repeated his triumph. He came to England and wrote and wrote and wrote, altogether some 140 neglected other books. Professor Barrie Hayne, of St Michael's College, Toronto, claims, however, that at least twenty of them are 'eminently readable' but no other commentator seems to have tried them. Hume, however, did make a living with his unresting pen right up to his death in 1932, the year in which, bar one posthumous novel, his final book *The Last Straw* came out. But it seems that, *The Mystery of a Hansom Cab* apart, his huge output is destined now to do no more than rest undisturbed along some yards of the pristine shelves of the new British Library.

H.R.F. Keating

Contents

To

JAMES PAYN,

Novelist,

this story is dedicated,

in grateful acknowledgment of his kind

encouragement to the Author

I

What the *Argus* Said

The following report appeared in the *Argus* newspaper of Saturday, the 28th July, 18—:

'Truth is said to be stranger than fiction, and certainly the extraordinary murder which took place in Melbourne on Thursday night, or rather Friday morning, goes a long way towards verifying this saying. A crime has been committed by an unknown assassin, within a short distance of the principal streets of this great city, and is surrounded by an impenetrable mystery. Indeed, from the nature of the crime itself, the place where it was committed, and the fact that the assassin has escaped without leaving a trace behind him, it would seem as though the case itself had been taken bodily out of one of Gaboreau's novels, and that his famous detective Lecoq only would be able to unravel it. The facts of the case are simply these:

'On the twenty-seventh day of July, at the hour of twenty minutes to two o'clock in the morning, a hansom cab drove up to the police station, in Grey Street, St Kilda, and the driver made the startling statement that his cab contained the body of a man whom he had reason to believe had been murdered.

'Being taken into the presence of the Inspector, the cabman, who gave his name as Malcolm Royston, related the following strange story:

'At the hour of one o'clock in the morning, he was driving down Collins Street East, when as he was passing the Burke and Wills' monument he was hailed by a gentleman standing at the corner by the Scotch Church. He immediately drove up, and saw that the gentleman who hailed him was supporting the deceased, who appeared to be very intoxicated. Both were in evening dress, but the deceased had no overcoat on, while the other wore a short covert coat of a light fawn colour, which was open. As Royston drove up, the gentleman in the light coat said, "Look here, cabby, here's some fellow awfully tight, you'd better take him home!"

'Royston then asked him if the drunken man was his friend, but this the other denied, saying that he had just picked him up from the footpath, and did not know him from Adam. At this moment the deceased turned his face up to the light of the lamp under which both were standing, and the other seemed to recognise him, for he recoiled a pace, letting the drunken man fall in a heap on the pavement, and gasping out "You?" He turned on his heel, and walked rapidly away down Russell Street in the direction of Bourke Street.

'Royston was staring after him, and wondering at his strange conduct, when he was recalled to himself by the voice of the deceased, who had struggled to his feet, and was holding on to the lamp-post, swaying to and fro. "I wan' g'ome," he said in a thick voice, "St Kilda." He then tried to get into the cab, but was too drunk to do so, and finally sat down again on the pavement. Seeing this, Royston got down, and lifting him up, helped him into the cab with some considerable difficulty. The deceased fell back into the cab, and seemed to drop off to sleep; so, after closing the door, Royston turned to remount his driving-seat, when he found the gentleman in the light coat whom he had seen holding up the deceased, close to his elbow. Royston said, "Oh, you've come back," and the other answered, "Yes, I've changed my mind, and will see him home." As he said this he opened the door of the cab, stepped in beside the deceased, and told Royston to drive down to St Kilda. Royston, who was glad that the friend of the deceased had come to look after him, drove as he had been directed, but near the Church of England Grammar School, on the St Kilda Road, the gentleman in the light coat called out to him to stop. He did so, and the gentleman got out of the cab, closing the door after him.

' "He won't let me take him home," he said, "so I'll just walk back to the city, and you can drive him to St Kilda."

' "What street, sir?" asked Royston.

' "Grey Street, I fancy," said the other, "But my friend will direct you when you get to the Junction."

' "Ain't he too much on, sir?" said Royston, dubiously.

' "Oh, no! I think he'll be able to tell you where he lives — it's Grey Street or Acland Street, I fancy. I don't know which."

'He then opened the door of the cab and looked in. "Good

night, old man," he said — the other apparently did not answer, for the gentleman in the light coat, shrugging his shoulders, and muttering "sulky brute," closed the door again. He then gave Royston half a sovereign, lit a cigarette, and after making a few remarks about the beauty of the night, walked off quickly in the direction of Melbourne. Royston drove down to the Junction, and having stopped there, according to his instructions he asked his fare several times where he was to drive him to. Receiving no answer, and thinking that the deceased was too drunk to answer, he got down from his seat, opened the door of the cab, and found the deceased lying back in the corner with a handkerchief across his mouth. He put out his hand with the intention of rousing him, thinking that he had gone to sleep, when on touching him the deceased fell forward, and on examination, to his horror, he found that he was quite dead. Alarmed at what had taken place, and suspecting the gentleman in the light coat, he drove to the police station at St Kilda, and there made the above report. The body of the deceased was taken out of the cab and brought into the station, a doctor being sent for at once. On his arrival, however, he found that life was quite extinct, and also discovered that the handkerchief which was tied lightly over the mouth was saturated with chloroform. He had no hesitation in stating that from the way in which the handkerchief was placed, and the presence of chloroform, that a murder had been committed, and from all appearances the deceased died easily, and without a struggle. The deceased is a slender man, of medium height, with a dark complexion, and is dressed in evening dress, which will render identification difficult, as it is a costume which has not any distinctive mark to render it noticeable. There were no papers nor cards found on the deceased from which his name could be discovered, and the clothing was not marked in any way. The handkerchief, however, which was tied across his mouth, was of white silk, and marked in one of the corners with the letters "O.W." in red silk. The assassin, of course, may have used his own handkerchief to commit the crime, so that if the initials are those of his name they may ultimately lead to his detection. There will be an inquest held on the body of the deceased this morning, when, no doubt, some evidence may be elicited which may solve the mystery.'

In Monday morning's issue of the *Argus* the following article appeared with reference to the matter:

'The following additional evidence has been obtained which may throw some light on the mysterious murder in a hansom cab of which we gave a full description in Saturday's issue: "Another hansom cabman called at the police office, and gave a clue which will, no doubt, prove of value to the detectives in their search after the murderer. He states that he was driving up the St Kilda Road on Friday morning about half-past one o'clock, when he was hailed by a gentleman in a light coat, who stepped into the cab and told him to drive to Powlett Street, in East Melbourne. He did so, and, after paying him, the gentleman got out at the corner of Wellington Parade and Powlett Street and walked slowly up Powlett Street, while the cab drove back to town. Here all clues end, but there can be no doubt in the minds of our readers as to the identity of the man in the light coat who got out of Royston's cab on the St Kilda Road, with the one who entered the other cab and alighted therefrom at Powlett Street. There could have been no struggle, as the cabman Royston would surely have heard the noise had any taken place. The supposition is, therefore, that the deceased was too drunk to make any resistance, and the other, watching his opportunity, placed the handkerchief saturated with chloroform over the mouth of his victim, and after a few ineffectual struggles the latter would relapse into a state of stupor from such inhalation. The man in the light coat, judging from his conduct before getting into the cab, appears to have known the deceased, though from the circumstance of his walking away on recognition, and returning again, shows that his attitude towards the deceased was not altogether a friendly one.

'The difficulty is where to start from in the search after the author of what appears to be a deliberate murder, as the deceased seems to be unknown, and his presumed murderer has escaped. But it is impossible that the body can remain long without being identified by someone, as though Melbourne is a large city, yet it is neither Paris nor London, where a man can disappear in a crowd and never be heard of again. The first thing to be done is to establish the identity of the deceased, and then, no doubt, a clue will be obtained leading to the detection of the man in the light coat who appears to have been the perpetrator of the crime. It is of the utmost importance that the mystery in which the crime is shrouded should be cleared up, not only in the interests of justice, but also in those of the public — taking place as it did in a public conveyance, and in the public street. To think that the author of such a crime is at present at large, walking in our midst, and perhaps preparing for the committal of another, is enough to shake the strongest nerves. According to James Payn, the well-known novelist, fact is sometimes in the habit of poaching on the domain of fiction, and, curiously enough, this case is a proof of the truth of his saying. In one of Du Boisgobey's stories, entitled "An Omnibus Mystery," a murder closely resembling this tragedy takes place in an omnibus, but we question if even that author would have been daring enough to have written about a crime being committed in such an unlikely place as a hansom cab. Here is a great chance for some of our detectives to render themselves famous, and we feel sure that they will do their utmost to trace the author of this cowardly and daring murder.'

II
The Evidence at the Inquest

At the inquest held on the body found in the hansom cab the following articles taken from the deceased were placed on the table:

1. Two pounds ten shillings in gold and silver;
2. The white silk handkerchief which was saturated with chloroform, and was found tied across the mouth of the deceased, marked with the letters O.W. in red silk;
3. A cigarette case of Russian leather, half filled with Old Judge cigarettes;
4. A left-hand white glove of kid — rather soiled — with black seams down the back.

Samuel Gorby, of the detective office, was present in order to see if anything might be said by the witnesses likely to point to the cause or to the author of the crime.

The first witness called was Malcolm Royston, in whose cab the crime had been committed. He told the same story as had already appeared in the *Argus*, and the following facts were elicited by the coroner:

Q. Can you give a description of the gentleman in the light coat who was holding the deceased when you drove up?

A. I did not observe him very closely, as my attention was taken up by the deceased; and, besides, the gentleman in the light coat was in the shadow.

Q. Describe him from what you saw of him.

A. He was fair, I think, because I could see his moustache, rather tall, and in evening dress, with a light coat over it. I could not see his face very plainly, as he wore a soft felt hat, which was pulled down over his eyes.

Q. What kind of hat was it he wore — a wide-awake?

A. Yes. The brim was turned down, and I could only see his mouth and moustache.

Q. What did he say when you asked him if he knew the deceased?

A. He said he didn't; that he had just picked him up.

Q. And afterwards he seemed to recognise him?

A. Yes. When the deceased looked up he said 'You!' and let him fall on to the ground; then he walked away toward Bourke Street.

Q. Did he look back?

A. Not that I saw.

Q. How long were you looking after him?

A. About a minute.

Q. And when did you see him again?

A. After I put the deceased into the cab I turned round and found him at my elbow.

Q. And what did he say?

A. I said, 'Oh! You've come back,' and he said, 'Yes, I've changed my mind, and will see him home,' and then he got into the cab, and told me to drive to St Kilda.

Q. He spoke then as if he knew the deceased?

A. Yes. I thought that he only recognised him when he looked up, and perhaps having had a row with him walked away, but thought he'd come back.

Q. Did you see him coming back?

A. No, the first I saw of him was at my elbow when I turned.

Q. And when did he get out?

A. Just as I was turning down by the Grammar School on the St Kilda Road.

Q. Did you hear any sounds of fighting or struggling in the cab during the drive?

A. No. The road was rather rough, and the noise of the wheels going over the stones would have prevented me hearing anything.

Q. When the gentleman in the light coat got out did he appear disturbed?

A. No, he was perfectly calm.

Q. How could you tell that?

A. Because the moon had risen, and I could see plainly.

Q. Did you see his face then?

A. No, his hat was pulled down over it. I only saw as much as I did when he entered the cab in Collins Street.

Q. Were his clothes torn or disarranged in any way?

A. No, the only difference I saw in him was that his coat was buttoned.

Q. And was it open when he got in?

A. No, but it was when he was holding up the deceased.

Q. Then he buttoned it before he came back and got into the cab?

A. Yes. I suppose so.

Q. What did he say when he got out of the cab on the St Kilda Road?

A. He said that the deceased would not let him take him home, and that he would walk back to Melbourne.

Q. And you asked him where you were to drive the deceased to?

A. Yes, and he said that the deceased lived either in Grey Street or Ackland Street, St Kilda, but that the deceased would direct me at the Junction.

Q. Did you not think that the deceased was too drunk to direct you?

A. Yes, I did, but his friend said that the sleep and the shaking of the cab would sober him a bit by the time I got to the Junction.

Q. The gentleman in the light coat apparently did not know where the deceased lived?

A. No, he said it was either in Ackland Street or Grey Street.

Q. Did you not think that curious?

A. No, I thought he might be a club friend of the deceased.

Q. How long did the man in the light coat talk to you?

A. About five minutes.

Q. And during that time you heard no noise in the cab?

A. No, I thought the deceased had gone to sleep.

Q. And after the man in the light coat said goodnight to the deceased what happened?

A. He lit a cigarette, gave me a half sovereign, and walked off towards Melbourne.

Q. Did you observe if the gentleman in the light coat had his handkerchief with him?

A. Oh, yes, because he dusted his boots with it. The road was very dusty.

Q. Did you notice any striking peculiarity about him?

A. Well, no, except that he wore a diamond ring.

Q. What was there peculiar about that?

A. He wore it on the forefinger of the right hand, and I never saw it that way before.

Q. When did you notice this?

A. When he was lighting his cigarette.

Q. How often did you call to the deceased when you got to the Junction?

A. Three or four times. I then got down, and found he was quite dead.

Q. How was he lying?

A. He was doubled up in the far corner of the cab, very much in the same position as I left him when I put him in. His head was hanging on one side, and there was a handkerchief across his mouth. When I touched him he fell into the other corner of the cab, and then I found out he was dead. I immediately drove to the St Kilda police station and told the police.

At the conclusion of Royston's evidence, during which Gorby had been continually taking notes, Robert Chinston was called. He deposed:

I am a duly qualified medical practitioner, residing in Collins Street East. I made a *post mortem* examination of the body of the deceased on Friday.

Q. That was within a few hours after his death?

A. Yes. Seeing from the position of the handkerchief and the presence of chloroform that he had died through chloroform, and knowing how quickly that poison evaporates, I made the examination at once.

Coroner: Go on, sir.

Dr Chinston: Externally, the body was healthy-looking and well nourished. There were no marks of violence. The staining apparent at the back of the legs and trunk was due to *post mortem* congestion. Internally, the brain was hyperaemic, and there was a considerable amount of congestion, especially apparent in the superficial vessels. There was no brain disease. The lungs were healthy, but slightly congested. On opening the thorax there was a faint spirituous odour discernible. The stomach contained about a pint of completely digested food. The heart was flaccid. The right-heart contained a considerable quantity of dark, fluid blood. There was a tendency to fatty degeneration of that organ.

I am of the opinion that the deceased died from the inhalation of some such vapour as chloroform or methylene.

Q. You say there was a tendency to fatty degeneration of the heart? Would that have anything to do with the death of the deceased?

A. Not of itself. But chloroform administered while the heart was in such a state would have a decided tendency to accelerate the fatal result. At the same time, I may mention that the *post mortem* signs of poisoning by chloroform are mostly negative.

Dr Chinston was then permitted to retire, and Clement Rankin, another hansom cabman, was called. He deposed: I am a cabman, living in Collingwood, and usually drive a hansom cab. I remember Thursday last. I had driven a party down to St Kilda, and was returning about half-past one o'clock. A short distance past the Grammar School I was hailed by a gentleman in a light coat; he was smoking a cigarette, and told me to drive him to Powlett Street, East Melbourne. I did so, and he got out at the corner of Wellington Parade and Powlett Street. He paid me half a sovereign for my fare, and then walked up Powlett Street, while I drove back to town.

Q. What time was it you stopped at Powlett Street?

A. Two o'clock exactly.

Q. How do you know?

A. Because it was a still night, and I heard the Post Office clock strike two o'clock.

Q. Did you notice anything peculiar about the man in the light coat?

A. No! He looked just the same as anyone else. I thought he was some swell of the town out for a lark. His hat was pulled down over his eyes, and I could not see his face.

Q. Did you notice if he wore a ring?

A. Yes! I did. When he was handing me the half sovereign, I saw he had a diamond ring on the forefinger of his right hand.

Q. He did not say why he was on the St Kilda Road at such an hour?

A. No! He did not.

Clement Rankin was then ordered to stand down, and the Coroner then summed up in an address of half-an-hour's duration. There was, he pointed out, no doubt that the death of the deceased had resulted not from natural causes, but from the effects of poisoning. Only slight evidence had been obtained up to the present time regarding the circumstances of the case, but the only person who could be accused of committing the crime was the unknown man who entered the cab with the deceased on Friday morning at the corner of the Scotch Church, near the Burke and Wills' monument. It had been proved that the deceased, when he entered the cab, was, to all appearances, in good health, though in a state of intoxication, and the fact that he was found by the cabman Royston, after the man in the light coat had left the cab, with a handkerchief, saturated with chloroform, tied over his mouth, would seem to show that he had died through the inhalation of chloroform, which had been deliberately administered. All the obtainable evidence in the case was circumstantial, but, nevertheless, showed conclusively that a crime had been committed. Therefore, as the circumstances of the case pointed to one conclusion, the jury could not do otherwise than frame a verdict in accordance with that conclusion.

The jury retired at four o'clock, and, after an absence of a quarter of an hour, returned with the following verdict: 'That the deceased, whose name there was no evidence to show, died on the 27th day of July, from the effects of poison, namely, chloroform, feloniously administered by some person unknown; and the jury, on their oaths, say that the said unknown person feloniously, wilfully, and maliciously did murder the said deceased.'

III
One Hundred Pounds Reward

V.R.
MURDER
£100 REWARD

'Whereas, on Friday, the 27th day of July, the body of a man, name unknown, was found in a hansom cab. And whereas, at an inquest held at St Kilda, on the 30th day of July, a verdict of wilful murder, against some person unknown, was brought in by the jury. The deceased is of medium height, with a dark complexion, dark hair, clean shaved, has a mole on the left temple, and was dressed in evening dress. Notice is hereby given that a reward of £100 will be paid by the Government for such information as will lead to the conviction of the murderer, who is presumed to be a man who entered the hansom cab with the deceased at the corner of Collins and Russell Streets, on the morning of the 27th day of July.'

IV
Mr Gorby Makes a Start

'Well,' said Mr Gorby, addressing his reflection in the looking-glass, 'I've been finding out things these last twenty years, but this is a puzzler, and no mistake.'

Mr Gorby was shaving, and as was his usual custom conversed with his reflection. Being a detective, and of an extremely reticent disposition, he never talked outside about his business, or made a confidant of anyone. When he did want to unbosom himself, he retired to his bedroom and talked to his reflection in the mirror. This mode of proceeding was a safe one, and moreover, relieved his over-burdened mind of anything he wished to speak about, yet wanted to keep secret. The barber of Midas, when he found out what was under the royal crown of his master, fretted and chafed over his secret, until he stole one morning to the reeds by the river, and whispered 'Midas has ass's ears.' In the like manner Mr Gorby felt a necessity at times to let out his secret thoughts in talk, and as he did not care about chattering to the air, he made his mirror the confidant of his ideas, and liked to see his own jolly red face nodding gravely at him out of the shining glass, like a mandarin. If that cheap little looking-glass which Mr Gorby stared at every morning could only have spoken, what revelations there would have been of Melbourne secrets and Melbourne morals. But then, luckily for some people, we do not live in fairyland, and however sympathetic Mr Gorby found his mirror, it revealed nothing. This morning the detective was unusually animated in his talk with the looking-glass, and at times a puzzled expression passed over his face. The hansom cab murder had been put into his hands in order to clear up the mystery connected therewith, and he was trying to think of how to make a beginning.

'Hang it,' he said, thoughtfully stropping his razor, 'a thing with an end must have a start, and if I don't get the start how am I to get the end?'

As the mirror did not answer this question, Mr Gorby lathered his face, and started shaving in a somewhat mechanical fashion, for his thoughts were with the case, and ran on in this manner:

'Here's a man — well, say a gentleman — who gets drunk, and, therefore, don't know what he's up to. Another gent who is on the square comes up and sings out for a cab for him — first he says he don't know him, and then he shows plainly he does — he walks away in a temper, changes his mind, comes back and gets into the cab, after telling the cabby to drive down to St Kilda. Then he polishes the drunk one off with chloroform, gets out of the cab, jumps into another, and after getting out at Powlett Street, vanishes — that's the riddle I've got to find out, and I don't think the Sphinx ever had a harder one. There are three things to be discovered: First, who is the dead man? Second, what was he killed for? And third, who did it? Once I get hold of the first the other two won't be very hard to find out, for one can tell pretty well from a man's life whether it's to anyone's interest that he should be got off the books. The man that murdered that chap must have had some strong motive, and I must find out what that motive was. Love? No, it wasn't that — men in love don't go to such lengths in real life — they do in novels and plays, but I've never seen it occurring in my experience. Robbery? No, there was plenty of money in his pocket. Revenge? Now, really it might be that — it's a kind of thing that carries on most people further than they want to go. There was no violence used, for his clothes weren't torn, so he must have been taken sudden, and before he knew what the other chap was up to. By the way, I don't think I examined his clothes sufficiently; there might be something about them to give a clue; at any rate, it's worth looking after, so I'll start with his clothes.'

So Mr Gorby, after he had finished dressing and had his breakfast, walked quickly to the police station, where he asked for the clothes of the deceased to be shown to him. When he received them he went into a corner by himself, and started to examine them. There was nothing remarkable about the coat, as it was merely a well-cut and well-made dress coat, so with a grunt of dissatisfaction Mr Gorby threw it on one side, and picked up the waistcoat.

Here he found something which interested him very much, and that was a pocket made on the left-hand side of the waistcoat, and on the inside.

'Now, what the deuce is this for?' said Mr Gorby, scratching his head, 'it ain't usual for a dress waistcoat to have a pocket on its inside as I'm aware of, and,' continued the detective, greatly excited, 'this ain't tailor's work. He did it himself, and jolly badly he did it too. Now he must have taken the trouble to make this pocket himself, so that no one else would know anything about it, and it was made to carry something valuable — so valuable that he had to carry it with him even when he wore evening clothes. Ah! Here's a tear on the side nearest the outside of the waistcoat; something has been pulled out roughly. I begin to see now. The dead man possessed something which the other man wanted, and which he knew the dead one carried about with him. He sees him drunk, gets into the cab with him, and tries to get what he wants. The dead man resists, upon which the other kills him by means of the chloroform which he had with him, and being afraid that the cab will stop, and he will be found out, snatches what he wants out of the pocket so quickly that he tears the waistcoat, and then makes off. That's clear enough, but the question is, What was it he wanted? A case with jewels? No! It could not have been anything so bulky, or the dead man would never have carried it about inside his waistcoat. It was something flat, which could easily lie in the pocket — a paper — some valuable paper which the assassin wanted, and for which he killed the other.

'This is all very well,' said Mr Gorby, throwing down the waistcoat, and rising. 'I have found number two before number one.' The first question is: Who is the murdered man. He's a stranger in Melbourne, that's pretty clear, or else someone would be sure to have recognised him before now by the description given in the reward. Now, I wonder if he has any relations here? No, he can't, or else they would have made enquiries before this. Well, there's one thing certain, he must have had a landlady or landlord, unless he slept in the open air. He can't have lived in an hotel, as the landlord of any hotel in Melbourne would have recognised him from the description, especially when the whole place is ringing with the murder. Private lodgings more like, and a landlady who doesn't read the papers and doesn't gossip, or she'd have known all about it by this time. Now, if he did live, as I think, in private lodgings, and suddenly disappeared, his landlady wouldn't keep quiet. It's a whole week since the murder, and as the lodger has not been seen or heard of, the landlady will naturally make enquiries. If, however, as I surmise, the lodger is a stranger, she will not know where to enquire; therefore, under these circumstances, the most natural thing for her to do would be to advertise for him; so I'll have a look at the newspapers.

Mr Gorby got a file of the different newspapers, and looked carefully in the columns where missing friends and people who will hear something to their advantage are generally advertised for.

'He was murdered,' said Mr Gorby to himself, 'on a Friday morning, between one and two o'clock, so he might stay away till Monday without exciting any suspicion. On Monday, however, the landlady would begin to feel uneasy, and on Tuesday she would advertise for him. Therefore,' said Mr Gorby, running his fat finger down the column, 'Wednesday it is.'

It did not appear in Wednesday's paper, neither did it in

Thursday's, but in Friday's issue, exactly one week after the murder, Mr Gorby suddenly came on the following advertisement:

'If Mr Oliver Whyte does not return to Possum Villa, Grey Street, St Kilda, before the end of the week, his rooms will be let again — Rubina Hableton.'

'Oliver Whyte,' repeated Mr Gorby slowly, 'and the initials on the pocket handkerchief which was proved to have belonged to the deceased were, "O.W." So his name is Oliver Whyte, is it? Now, I wonder if Rubina Hableton knows anything about this matter. At any rate,' said Mr Gorby, putting on his hat, 'as I'm fond of sea breezes, I think I'll go down, and call at Possum Villa, Grey Street, St Kilda.'

V
Mrs Hableton Unbosoms Herself

Mrs Hableton was a lady with a grievance, as anybody who happened to become acquainted with her soon found out. It is Beaconsfield who says, in one of his novels, that no one is so interesting as when he is talking about himself; and, judging Mrs Hableton by this statement, she was an extremely fascinating individual, as she never by any chance talked upon any other subject. What was the threat of a Russian invasion to her as long as she had her special grievance — once let that be removed, and she would have time to attend to these minor details which affected the colony. The grievance Mrs Hableton complained of, was want of money; not an uncommon one by any means, but on being reminded of this, Mrs Hableton would reply snappishly, that she 'know'd that, but some people weren't like other people,' the meaning of which mystical remark was simply this: She had come out to the colonies in the early days, when there was not so much difficulty in making money as now, but owing to a bad husband, had failed to make any. The late Mr Hableton — for he had long since departed this life — was addicted to the intemperate use of the flowing bowl, and at the time when he should have been earning money, was generally to be found in a drinking shanty, spending his wife's earnings in standing treat for himself and his friends. The constant drinking, and the hot Victorian climate, soon carried him off, and when Mrs Hableton had seen him safely under the ground in the Melbourne Cemetery, she returned home to survey her position, and see how it could be bettered. She gathered together a little money from the wreck of her fortune, and land being cheap, purchased a small section at St Kilda, and built a house on it. She supported herself by going out charring, taking in sewing, and acting as a sick nurse. So, among this multiplicity of occupations, she managed to do fairly well, and even put a little money in the bank. But she was very bitter against the world for the treatment she had received, and often spoke of it. 'I ought to 'ave bin in my kerrige, and 'e in the 'Ouse,' she would say bitterly, 'if 'e 'adn't bin such a brute, but ye can't make a man out of a beast, whatever them Darwin folks say.'

And, indeed, it was a hard case, for just at the time when she should have been resting, and reaping the reward for her early industry, she had to toil for her daily bread, and all through no fault of her own. Depend upon it, that if Adam was angry at Eve for having eaten the apple and got them driven out of the pleasant garden, his descendants have amply revenged themselves on Eve's daughters for her sin. Mrs Hableton is only the type of many women who, hardworking and thrifty themselves, are married to men who are a curse both to their wives and families. Little wonder it was that Mrs Hableton should have condensed all her knowledge of the masculine gender in the one bitter aphorism, 'Men is brutes.' This she firmly believed in, and who can say she had not good grounds for saying so? 'They is brutes,' said Mrs Hableton, 'they marries a woman, and makes her a beast of burden while they sits at 'ome swillin' beer and calling themselves lords of creation.'

Possum Villa was an unpretentious-looking place with one bow window and a narrow verandah in front. It was surrounded with a small garden and a few sparse flowers in it which were Mrs Hableton's delight. When not otherwise engaged she tied an old handkerchief round her head and went out into the garden, where she dug and watered her flowers until they all gave up attempting to grow from sheer desperation at not being left alone. She was engaged in her favourite occupation about a week after her lodger had disappeared, and was wondering where he had gone.

'Lyin' drunk in a public 'ouse, I'll be bound,' she said, viciously pulling up a weed with an angry tug, 'a-spendin' 'is rent and a-spilin' 'is inside with beer — ah, men is brutes, drat 'em!'

Just as she said this, a shadow fell across the garden, and on looking up, she saw a man leaning over the fence, looking at her.

'Git out,' she said, sharply, rising from her knees and shaking her trowel at the intruder. 'I don't want no apples today, an' I don't care how cheap you sells 'em.'

Mrs Hableton evidently laboured under the delusion that the man was a hawker, but not seeing any handcart with him she changed her mind.

'You're takin' a plan of the 'ouse to rob it, are you?' she said. 'Well, you needn't, 'cause there ain't nothin' to rob, the silver spoons as belonged to my father's mother 'avin' gone down my 'usband's throat long ago, an' I ain't 'ad money to buy more. I'm a lone pusson as is put on by brutes like you, an' I'll thank you to leave the fence I bought with my own 'ard-earned money alone, and git out.'

Mrs Hableton stopped short for want of breath, and stood shaking her trowel, and gasping like a fish out of water.

'My dear lady,' said the man at the fence, mildly, 'are you—'

'No, I ain't,' retorted Mrs Hableton, fiercely, 'I ain't neither a member of the 'Ouse, nor a school teacher, to answer your questions. I'm a woman as pays my rates an' taxes, and don't gossip nor read yer rubbishin' newspapers, nor care for the Russings, no how, so git out.'

'Don't read the papers,' repeated the man, in a satisfied tone, 'ah! That accounts for it.'

Mrs Hableton stared suspiciously at the man who made such a peculiar remark. He was a burly-looking man, with a jovial red face, clean shaved, and sharp, shrewd-looking grey eyes which kept twinkling like two stars. He was well dressed in a suit of light clothes, and wore a stiffly starched white waistcoat, with a massive gold chain stretched across it. Altogether he gave Mrs Hableton the impression of being a well-do-do tradesman, and she mentally wondered what he wanted.

'What d'y want?' she asked, abruptly.

'Does Mr Oliver Whyte live here?' asked the stranger.

'He do, an' he don't,' answered Mrs Hableton, epigramatically.

'I ain't seen 'im for over a week, so I s'pose 'e's gone on the drink, like the rest of 'em, but I've put sumthin' in the paper as 'ill pull him up pretty sharp, and let 'im know I ain't a carpet to be trod on, an' if you're a friend of 'im, you can tell 'im from me 'e's a brute, an' it's no more but what I expected of 'im, 'e bein' a male.'

The stranger waited placidly during the outburst, and Mrs Hableton, having stopped for want of breath, he interposed, quietly—

'Can I speak to you for a few moments?'

'An' who's a-stoppin' of you?' said Mrs Hableton, defiantly. 'Go on with you, not as I expects the truth from a male, but go on.'

'Well, really,' said the other, looking up at the cloudless blue sky, and wiping his face with a gaudy red silk pocket-handkerchief, 'it is rather hot, you know, and—'

Mrs Hableton did not give him time to finish, but walking to the gate, opened it with a jerk.

'Use yer legs and walk in,' she said, and the stranger having done so, she led the way into the house, and into a small neat sitting room which seemed to overflow with antimacassars, wool mats, and wax flowers. There was also a row of emu eggs on the mantelpiece, a cutlass on the wall, and a grimy line of hard-looking little books, set in a stiff row on a shelf, presumably for ornament, as they looked too unpleasant to tempt anyone to read them. The furniture was of horsehair, and everything was hard and shiny, so when the stranger sat down in the slippery-looking armchair that Mrs Hableton pushed towards him, he could not help thinking it had been stuffed with stones, it felt so cold and hard. The lady herself sat opposite to him in another hard chair, and having taken the handkerchief off her head, folded it carefully, laid it on her lap, and then looked straight at her unexpected visitor.

'Now then,' she said, letting her mouth fly open so rapidly that it gave one the impression that it was moved by strings like a marionette, 'Who are you? What are you? And what do you want?'

The stranger put his red silk handkerchief into his hat, placed it on the table, and answered deliberately—

'My name is Gorby. I am a detective. I want Mr Oliver Whyte.'

'He ain't here,' said Mrs Hableton, thinking that Whyte had got into trouble, and was going to be arrested.

'I know that,' answered Mr Gorby.

'Then where is 'e?'

Mr Gorby answered abruptly, and watched the effect of his words.

'He is dead.'

Mrs Hableton got quite pale, and pushed back her chair. 'No,' she cried, 'he never killed 'im, did 'e?'

'Who never killed him?' queried Mr Gorby, sharply.

Mrs Hableton evidently knew more than she intended to tell, for, recovering herself with a violent effort, she answered evasively—

'He never killed himself.'

Mr Gorby looked at her keenly, and she returned his gaze with a defiant stare.

'Clever,' muttered the detective to himself; 'knows something more than she chooses to tell, but I'll get it out of her.' He paused a moment, and then went on smoothly, 'Oh, no! He did not commit suicide; what makes you think so?'

Mrs Hableton did not answer, but, rising from her seat, went over to a hard and shiny-looking sideboard, from whence she took a bottle of brandy and a small wine-glass. Half filling the glass, she drank it off, and returned to her seat. 'I don't take much of that stuff,' she said, seeing the detective's eyes fixed curiously on her, 'but you 'ave given me such a turn that I 'ad to take something to steady my nerves; what do you want me to do?'

'Tell me all you know,' said Mr Gorby, keeping his eyes fixed on her face, which thereupon changed, and grew a shade paler.

'Where was Mr Whyte killed?' she asked.

'He was murdered in a hansom cab on the St Kilda Road.'

'In the open street?' she asked, in a startled tone.

'Yes, in the open street.'

'Ah!' She drew a long breath, and closed her lips firmly.

Mr Gorby said nothing as he saw that she was deliberating whether to tell or not, and a word from him might seal her lips, so, like a wise man, he kept silent. He obtained his reward sooner than he expected.

'Mr Gorby,' she said at length, 'I 'ave 'ad a 'ard struggle all my life which it came along of a bad husband, who was a brute and a drunkard, so, God knows, I ain't got much inducement to think well of the lot of you, but — murder,' she shivered slightly, though the room was quite warm, 'I didn't think of that.'

'In connection with whom?'

'Mr Whyte, of course,' she answered, hurriedly.

'And who else?'

'I don't know.'

'Then there is nobody else?'

'Well, I don't know — I'm not sure.'

The detective was puzzled.

'What do you mean?' he asked.

'I will tell you all I know,' said Mrs Hableton, 'an' if 'e's innocent, God will 'elp 'im.'

'If who is innocent?'

'I'll tell you everythin' from the start,' said Mrs Hableton, 'an' you can judge for yourself.'

Mr Gorby assented, and she began:

'It's only two months ago since I decided to take in lodgers; but charin's 'ard work, and sewin's tryin' for the eyes. So, bein' a lone woman, 'avin' bin badly treated by a brute, who is now dead, which I was allays a good wife to 'im, I thought lodgers 'ud 'elp me a little, so I put a notice in the paper, an' Mr Oliver Whyte took the rooms two months ago.'

'What was he like?'

'Not very tall, dark face, no whiskers nor moustache, an' quite the gentleman.'

'Anything peculiar about him?'

Mrs Hableton thought for a moment.

'Well,' she said at length, 'he 'ad a mole on his left temple, but it was covered with 'is 'air, an' few people 'ud 'ave seen it.'

'The very man,' said Gorby to himself, 'I'm on the right path.'

'Mr Whyte said 'e 'ad just come from England,' went on the woman.

'Which,' murmured Mr Gorby, 'accounts for the corpse not being recognised by friends.'

'He took the rooms, an' said 'e'd stay with me for six months, an' paid a week's rent in advance, an' 'e allays paid up reg'ler like a respectable man, tho' I don't believe in 'em myself. He said 'e'd lots of friends, an' used to go out every night.'

'Who were his friends?'

'That I can't tell you, for 'e were very close, an' when 'e went out of doors I never know'd where 'e went, which is jest like 'em; for they ses they're goin' to work, an' you finds 'em in the beershop. Mr Whyte told me 'e was a-goin' to marry a heiress, 'e was.'

'Ah!' interjected Mr Gorby, sapiently.

'He 'ad only one friend as I ever saw — a Mr Moreland — who comed 'ere with 'im, an' was allays with 'im — brother-like.'

'What like is this Mr Moreland?'

'Good-lookin' enough,' said Mrs Hableton sourly, 'but 'is 'abits weren't as good as 'is face — 'andsome is as 'andsome does, is what I ses.'

'I wonder if he knows anything about this affair,' muttered Gorby to himself. 'Where is Mr Moreland to be found?' he asked aloud.

'Not knowin', can't tell,' retorted the landlady, ' 'e used to be 'ere reg'ler, but I ain't seen 'im for over a week.'

'Strange! Very!' thought Gorby, shaking his head. 'I should like to see this Mr Moreland. I suppose it's probable he'll call again?' he remarked, aloud.

' 'Abit bein' second nature I s'pose he will,' answered the woman, ' 'e might call at any time, mostly 'avin' called at night.'

'Ah! Then I'll come down this evening on chance of seeing him,' replied the detective. 'Coincidences happen in real life as well as in novels, and the gentleman in question may turn up in the nick of time. Now, what else about Mr Whyte?'

'About two weeks ago, or three, I'm not cert'in which, a gentleman called to see Mr Whyte; 'e was very tall, and wore a light coat.'

'Ah! A morning coat?'

'No! 'e was in evenin' dress, and wore a light coat over it, an' a soft 'at.'

'The very man,' said the detective below his breath, 'Go on.'

'He went into Mr Whyte's room, an' shut the door. I don't know how long they were talkin' together; but I was sittin' in this very room and heard their voices git angry, and they were a-swearin' at one another, which is the way with men, the brutes. I got up and went into the passage in order to ask 'em not to make such a noise, when Mr Whyte's door opens, an' the gentleman in the light coat comes out, and bangs along to the door. Mr Whyte

’e comes to the door of ’is room, an’ ’e ’ollers out “She is mine; you can’t do anything,” an’ the other turns with ’is ’and on the door an’ says, “I can kill you, an’ if you marry ’er I’ll do it, even in the open street”.’

‘Ah!’ said Mr Gorby, drawing a long breath, ‘and then?’

‘Then he bangs the door to, which it’s never shut easy since, an’ I ain’t got no money to get it put right, an’ Mr Whyte walks back to his room, laughing?’

‘Did he make any remark to you?’

‘No; except he’d bin worried by a loonatic.’

‘And what was the stranger’s name?’

‘That I can’t tell you, as Mr Whyte never told me. He was very tall, with a fair moustache, an’ dressed as I told you.’

Mr Gorby was satisfied.

‘That is the man,’ he said to himself, ‘who got into the hansom cab, and murdered Whyte; there’s no doubt of it! Whyte and he were rivals for the heiress.’

‘What d’y think of it?’ said Mrs Hableton curiously.

‘I think,’ said Mr Gorby slowly, with his eyes fixed on her, ‘I think that there is a woman at the bottom of this crime.’

VI
Mr Gorby Makes Further Discoveries

When Mr Gorby left Possum Villa no doubt remained in his mind as to who had committed the murder. The gentleman in the light coat had threatened to murder Whyte, even in the open street — these last words being especially significant — and there was no doubt that he had carried out his threat. The committal of the crime was merely the fulfilment of the words uttered in anger. What the detective had now to do was to find who the gentleman in the light coat was, where he lived, and, having found out these facts, ascertain his doings on the night of the murder. Mrs Hableton had described him, but was ignorant of his name, and her very vague description might apply to dozens of young men in Melbourne. There was only one person who, in Mr Gorby’s opinion, could tell the name of the gentleman in the light coat, and that was Moreland, the intimate friend of the dead man. They appeared, from the landlady's description, to have been so friendly that it was more than likely Whyte would have told Moreland all about his angry visitor. Besides, Moreland's knowledge of his dead friend's life and habits might be able to supply the answer as to whom Whyte's death would have been a gain, and whom the heiress was the deceased boasted he was going to marry. What puzzled the detective was that Moreland should be ignorant of his friend's tragic death, seeing that the papers were full of the murder, and that the reward gave an excellent description of the personal appearance of the deceased. The only way in which Gorby could account for Moreland's extraordinary silence was that he was out of town, and had neither seen the papers nor heard anyone talking about the murder. If this was the case he might either stay away for an indefinite time or might come back after a few days. At all events it was worth while going down to St Kilda in the evening on the chance that Moreland might have returned to town, and would call to see his friend. So, after his tea, Mr Gorby put on his hat, and went down to Possum Villa, on what he could not help acknowledging to himself was a very slender possibility.

Mrs Hableton opened the door for him, and in silence led the way, not into her own sitting-room, but into a much more luxuriously furnished apartment, which Gorby guessed at once was that of Whyte's. He looked keenly round the room, and his estimate of the dead man's character was formed at once.

'Fast,' he said to himself, 'and a spendthrift. A man who would have friends, and possibly enemies, among a very shady lot of people.'

What led Mr Gorby to this belief was the evidences which surrounded him of Whyte's mode of life. The room was well furnished, the furniture being covered with dark-red velvet, while the curtains on the windows and the carpet were all of the same somewhat sombre hue.

'I did the thing properly,' observed Mrs Hableton, with a satisfactory smile on her hard face. 'When you wants young men to stop with you, the rooms must be well furnished, an' Mr Whyte paid well, tho' 'e was rather pertickler about 'is food, which I'm only a plain cook, an' can't make them French things which spile the stomach.'

The globes of the gas lamps were of a pale pink colour, and Mrs Hableton having lit the gas in expectation of Mr Gorby's arrival, there was a soft roseate hue through all the room like the first faint flush of the early dawn. Mr Gorby put his hands in his capacious pockets, and strolled leisurely through the room, examining everything with a curious eye. The walls were covered with pictures of celebrated horses and famous jockeys. Alternating with these were photographs of ladies of the stage, mostly London actresses, Nellie Farren, Kate Vaughan, and other burlesque stars, evidently being the objects of the late Mr Whyte's adoration. Over the mantelpiece hung a rack of pipes, above which were two crossed foils, and under these a number of plush frames of all colours, with pretty faces smiling out of them; a remarkable fact being, that all the photographs were of ladies, and not a single male face was to be seen, either on the walls or in the plush frames.

'Fond of the ladies, I see,' said Mr Gorby, nodding his head towards the mantelpiece.

'A set of hussies,' said Mrs Hableton grimly, closing her lips tightly. 'I feel that ashamed when I dusts 'em as never was — I don't believe in gals gettin' their picters taken with 'ardly any clothes on, as if they just got out of bed, but Mr Whyte seems to like 'em.'

'Most young men do,' answered Mr Gorby dryly, going over to the bookcase.

'Brutes,' said the lady of the house. 'I'd drown 'em in the Yarrer, I would, a settin' 'emselves and a callin' 'emselves lords of creation, as if women were made for nothin' but to earn money an' see 'em drink it, as my 'usband did, which 'is inside never seemed to 'ave enough beer, an' me a poor lone woman with no family, thank God, or they'd 'ave taken arter their father in 'is drinkin' 'abits.'

Mr Gorby took no notice of this tirade against men, but stood looking at Mr Whyte's library, which seemed to consist mostly of French novels and sporting newspapers.

'Zola,' said Mr Gorby, thoughtfully, taking down a flimsy yellow book rather tattered. 'I've heard of him; if his novels are as bad as his reputation I shouldn't care to read them.'

Here a knock came at the front door, loud and decisive, on hearing which Mrs Hableton sprang hastily to her feet. 'That may be Mr Moreland,' she said, as the detective quickly replaced Zola in the bookcase. 'I never 'ave visitors in the evenin' bein' a lone widder, and if it is 'im I'll bring 'im in 'ere.'

She went out, and presently Gorby, who was listening intently, heard a man's voice ask if Mr Whyte was at home. 'No, sir, he ain't,' answered the landlady, 'but there's a gentleman in his room askin' after 'im. Won't you come in, sir?'

'For a rest, yes,' returned the visitor, and immediately afterwards Mrs Hableton appeared, ushering in the late Oliver Whyte's most intimate friend. He was a tall, slender man, with a pink and white complexion, curly fair hair, and a drooping straw-coloured moustache — altogether a strikingly aristocratic individual. He was well-dressed in a fashionable suit of check, and had a cool, nonchalant air about him.

'And where is Mr Whyte tonight?' he asked, sinking into a chair, and taking no more notice of the detective than if he had been an article of furniture.

'Haven't you seen him lately?' asked the detective quickly. Mr Moreland stared in an insolent manner at his questioner for a few moments, as if he were debating the advisability of answering or not. At last he apparently decided that he would, for slowly pulling off one glove he leaned back in his chair.

'No, I have not,' he said, with a yawn. 'I have been up the country for a few days, and only arrived back this evening, so I have not seen him for over a week. Why do you ask?'

The detective did not answer, but stood looking at the young man before him in a thoughtful manner.

'I hope,' said Mr Moreland, nonchalantly, 'I hope you will know me again, my friend, but I didn't know Whyte had started a lunatic asylum during my absence. Who are you?'

Mr Gorby came forward and stood under the gas light. 'My name is Gorby, sir, and I am a detective,' he said quietly.

'Ah! Indeed,' said Moreland, coolly looking him up and down. 'What has Whyte been doing, running away with someone's wife, eh? I know he has little weaknesses of that sort.'

Gorby shook his head.

'Do you know where Mr Whyte is to be found?' he asked, cautiously.

Moreland laughed.

'Not I, my friend,' said he, lightly. 'I presume he is somewhere about here, as these are his headquarters. What's he been doing? Nothing that can surprise me, I assure you — he was always an erratic individual, and—'

'He paid reg'ler,' interrupted Mrs Hableton, pursing up her lips.

'A most enviable reputation to possess,' answered the other with a sneer, 'and one I'm afraid I'll never enjoy. But why all this questioning about Whyte? What's the matter with him?'

'He's dead!' said Gorby, abruptly.

All Moreland's nonchalance vanished on hearing this, and he started up out of his chair.

'Dead,' he repeated mechanically. 'What do you mean?'

'I mean that Mr Oliver Whyte was murdered in a hansom cab.'

Moreland stared at the detective in a puzzled sort of way, and passed his hand across his forehead.

'Excuse me, my head is in a whirl,' he said, as he sat down again. 'Whyte murdered! He was all right when I left him nearly two weeks ago.'

'Haven't you seen the papers?' asked Gorby.

'Not for the last two weeks,' replied Moreland. 'I have been up country, and it was only on arriving back in town tonight that I heard about the murder at all, as my landlady gave me a garbled account of it, but I never for a moment connected it with Whyte, and came down here to see him, as I had agreed to do when I left. Poor fellow! Poor fellow! Poor fellow!' and much overcome, he buried his face in his hands.

Mr Gorby was touched by his evident distress, and even Mrs Hableton permitted a small tear to roll down one hard cheek as a tribute of sorrow and sympathy. Presently Moreland raised his head, and spoke to Gorby in a husky tone.

'Tell me all abut it,' he said, leaning his cheek on his hand. 'Everything you know.'

He placed his elbows on the table, and buried his face in his hands again, while the detective sat down and related all that he knew about Whyte's murder. When it was done he lifted up his head, and looked sadly at the detective.

'If I had been in town,' he said, 'this would not have happened, for I was always beside Whyte.'

'You knew him very well, sir?' said the detective, in a sympathetic tone.

'We were like brothers,' replied Moreland, mournfully. 'I came out from England in the same steamer with him, and used to visit him constantly here.'

Mrs Hableton nodded her head to imply that such was the case.

'In fact,' said Mr Moreland, after a moment's thought, 'I believe I was with him the night he was murdered.'

Mrs Hableton gave a slight scream, and threw her apron over her face, but the detective sat unmoved, though Moreland's last remark had considerably startled him.

'What's the matter?' said Moreland, turning to Mrs Hableton. 'Don't be afraid; I didn't kill him — no — but I met him last Thursday week, and I left for the country on Friday morning at half-past six.'

'And what time did you meet Whyte on Thursday night?' asked Gorby.

'Let me see,' said Moreland, crossing his legs and looking thoughtfully up to the ceiling, 'it was about half-past nine o'clock. I was in the Orient Hotel, in Bourke Street. We had a drink together, and then went up the street to an hotel in Russell Street, where we had another. In fact,' said Moreland, coolly, 'we had several other drinks.'

'Brutes!' muttered Mrs Hableton, below her breath.

'Yes,' said Gorby, placidly. 'Go on.'

'Well of — it's hardly the thing to confess it,' said Moreland, looking from one to the other with a pleasant smile, 'but in a case like this, I feel it my duty to throw all social scruples aside. We both got very drunk.'

'Ah! Whyte was, as we know, drunk when he got into the cab — and you—?'

'Was not quite so bad as Whyte,' answered the other. 'I had my senses about me. I fancy he left the hotel some minutes before one o'clock on Friday morning.'

'And what did you do?'

'I remained in the hotel. He left his overcoat behind him, and I picked it up and followed him shortly afterwards, to return it. I was too drunk to see which direction he had gone in, and stood leaning against the hotel door in Bourke Street with the coat in my hand. Then someone came up, and, snatching the coat out of my hand, made off with it, and the last thing I remember was shouting out: "Stop, thief!" Then I must have fallen down, for next morning I was in bed with all my clothes on, and they were very muddy. I got up and left town for the country by the six-thirty train, so I knew nothing about the matter until I came back to Melbourne tonight. That's all I know.'

'And you had no impression that Whyte was watched that night?'

'No, I had not,' answered Moreland, frankly. 'He was in pretty good spirits, though he was put out at first.'

'What was the cause of his being put out?'

Moreland arose, and going to a side-table, brought Whyte's album, which he laid on the table and opened in silence. The contents were very much the same as the photographs in the room, burlesque actresses and ladies of the ballet predominating; but Mr Moreland turned over the pages till nearly the end, when he stopped at a large cabinet photograph, and pushed the album towards Mr Gorby.

'That was the cause,' he said.

It was the portrait of a charmingly pretty girl, dressed in white, with a sailor hat on her fair hair, and holding a lawn-tennis racket. She was bending half forward, with a winning smile, and in the background was a mass of some tropical plants. Mrs Hableton gave a cry of surprise at seeing this.

'Why, it's Miss Frettlby,' she said. 'How did he know her?'

'Knew her father — letter of introduction, and all that sort of thing,' said Mr Moreland, glibly.

'Ah! Indeed,' said Mr Gorby, slowly. 'So Mr Whyte knew Mark Frettlby, the millionaire; but how did he obtain a photograph of the daughter?'

'She gave it to him,' said Moreland. 'The fact is, Whyte was very much in love with Miss Frettlby.'

'And she—'

'Was in love with someone else,' finished Moreland. 'Exactly! Yes, she loved a Mr Brian Fitzgerald, to whom she is now engaged. He was mad on her, and Whyte and he used to quarrel over the young lady desperately.'

Indeed!' said Mr Gorby. 'And do you know this Mr Fitzgerald?'

'Oh dear no!' answered the other, coolly. 'Whyte's friends were not mine. He was a rich young man who had good introductions. I am only a poor devil on the outskirts of society, trying to push my way in the world.'

'You know his personal appearance, of course?' observed Mr Gorby.

'Oh, yes, I can tell you that,' said Moreland. 'In fact, he's not at all unlike me, which I take to be rather a compliment, as he is said to be good-looking. He is tall, rather fair, talks in a bored sort of manner, and is altogether what one would call a heavy swell; but you must have seen him,' he went on, turning to Mrs Hableton, 'he was here three or four weeks ago, Whyte told me.'

'Oh, that was Mr Fitzgerald, was it?' said Mrs Hableton, in surprise. 'Yes, he was rather like you; and so the lady they quarrelled over must have been Miss Frettlby.'

'Very likely,' said Moreland, rising. 'Well, I'm off; here's my address,' putting a card in Gorby's hand. 'I'm glad to be of any use to you in this matter, as Whyte was my dearest friend, and I'll do all in my power to help you to find out the murderer.'

'I don't think that is a very difficult matter,' said Mr Gorby, slowly.

'Oh, you have your suspicions?' said Moreland, looking at him.

'I have.'

'Then who do you think murdered Whyte?'

Mr Gorby paused a moment, and then said deliberately: 'I have an idea — but I am not certain — when I am certain, I'll speak.'

'You think Fitzgerald killed my friend,' said Moreland. 'I see it in your face.'

Mr Gorby smiled. 'Perhaps,' he said, ambiguously. 'Wait till I'm certain.'

VII
A Wool King

The old Greek story of Midas, who turned everything he touched into gold, is truer than most people suppose. Medieval superstition changed the human being who possessed such a power into the philosopher's stone, after which so many alchemists went hunting in the dark ages, but we of the nineteenth century have given the miracle of changing everything into gold by the touch, back to its human possessor. We, however, do not ascribe it either to Greek deity or medieval superstition, but simply call it luck; and he who possesses luck is a happy man, or, at least, he ought to be. Wiseacres who may read this will, of course, repeat the stale proverb that 'Riches do not bring happiness.' But luck means more than riches — it means happiness in everything which the fortunate possessor may choose to go in for. If he goes into a speculation, it turns out well, if he marries a wife, she is sure to be everything that can be desired; if he aspires to a position, social or political, he attains it with ease — worldly wealth, domestic happiness, and good position, all these belong to the men who have luck. Mark Frettlby was one of these fortunate individuals, and his luck was proverbial throughout Australia. If there was any speculation for which Mark Frettlby went in, other men would be sure to follow, and in every case the result turned out as well, and in many cases even better than they expected. He had come out in the early days of the colony with comparatively little money, but his great perseverance and never failing luck had soon changed his hundreds into thousands, and now at the age of fifty-five he did not himself know the extent of his income. He had large stations scattered all over the colony of Victoria, which brought him in a splendid income; a charming country house, where at certain seasons of the year he dispensed hospitality to his friends, like the lord of an English manor, and a magnificent town house down in St Kilda, which would not have been unworthy of Park Lane.

Nor were his domestic relations less happy — he had a charming wife, who was one of the best known and most popular ladies of Melbourne, and an equally charming daughter, who, being both pretty and an heiress, naturally attracted crowds of suitors. But Madge Frettlby was capricious, and refused innumerable offers. Being an extremely independent young person, with a mind of her own, as she had not yet seen anyone she could love, she decided to remain single, and with her mother continued to dispense the hospitality of the mansion at St Kilda. But the fairy prince comes to every woman, even if she has to wait a hundred years like the Sleeping Beauty, and in this case he arrived at the appointed time. Ah! What a delightful prince he was, tall, handsome, and fair-haired, who came from Ireland, and answered to the name of Brian Fitzgerald. He had left behind him in the old country a ruined castle and a few acres of barren land, inhabited by discontented tenants who refused to pay the rent, and talked darkly about the Land League and other agreeable things. Under these circumstances, with no rent coming in, and no prospect of doing anything in the future, Brian had left the castle of his forefathers to the rats and the family Banshee, and came out to Australia to make his fortune. He brought letters of introduction to Mark Frettlby, and that gentleman, having taken a fancy to him, assisted him by every means in his power. Under Frettlby's advice Brian bought a station, and, to his astonishment, in a few years found himself growing rich. The Fitzgeralds had always been more famous for spending than for saving, and it was an agreeable surprise to their latest representative to find the money rolling in instead of out. He began to indulge in castles in the air concerning that other castle in Ireland, with the barren acres and discontented tenants. In his mind's-eye he saw the old place rise up in all its pristine splendour out of its ruins; he saw the barren acres well cultivated, and the tenants happy and content — he was rather doubtful on this latter point, but, with the rash confidence of eight and twenty, determined to do his best to perform even the impossible. Having built and furnished his castle in the air, Brian naturally thought of giving it a mistress, and this time actual appearance took the place of vision. He fell in love with Madge Frettlby, and having decided in his own mind that she and none other was fitted to grace the visionary halls of his renovated castle, he watched his opportunity, and declared himself. She, womanlike, coquetted with him for some time, but at last, unable to withstand the impetuosity of her Irish lover, confessed in a low voice, with a pretty smile on her face, that she could not live without him. Whereupon — well — lovers being of a conservative turn of mind, and accustomed to observe the traditional forms of wooing, the result can easily be guessed. Brian hunted all over the jewellers' shops in Melbourne with lover-like assiduity, and having obtained a ring wherein were set some turquoise stones, as blue as his own eyes, he placed it on her slender finger, and at last felt that his engagement was an accomplished fact. This being satisfactorily arranged, he next proceeded to interview the father, and had just screwed his courage up to the awful ordeal, when something occurred which postponed the interview indefinitely. Mrs Frettlby was out driving, when the horses took fright and bolted. The coachman and groom both escaped unhurt, but Mrs Frettlby was thrown out and killed instantaneously. This was the first really great trouble which had fallen on Mark Frettlby, and he seemed to be stunned by it. Shutting himself up in his room he refused to see anyone, even his daughter, and appeared at the funeral with a white and haggard face, which shocked everyone. When everything was over, and the body of the late Mrs Frettlby was consigned to the earth, with all the pomp and ceremony which money could give, the bereaved husband rode home, and resumed his old life. But he was never the same again. His face, which had always been so genial and bright, became stern and sad. He seldom smiled, and when he did, it was a faint, wintry smile, which seemed mechanical. His whole heart seemed centred in his daughter. She became the sole mistress of the St Kilda mansion, and her father idolised her. She seemed to be the one thing left to him which gave him an interest in life, and had it not been for her bright presence constantly near him, Mark Frettlby would have wished himself lying beside his dead wife in the quiet graveyard, wherein there is no trouble or care. After a time had elapsed, Brian again resolved to ask Mr Frettlby for the hand of his daughter, when for the second time fate interposed. This time it was a rival suitor who made his appearance, and Brian's hot Irish temper rose when he saw another Richmond in the field. The gentleman in question was a Mr Oliver Whyte, who had come out from England a few months previously, and brought a letter of introduction to Mr Frettlby, who received him hospitably, as was his custom, and Whyte soon made himself perfectly at home in the St Kilda mansion.

Brian took a dislike to the newcomer the first time he saw him, for Mr Fitzgerald was a student of Lavater, and prided himself on his reading of character. His opinion of Whyte was anything but flattering to that gentleman, for, in spite of his handsome face and suave manners, both Brian and Madge felt the same repulsion towards him as they would have to a snake. Mr Whyte, however, with true diplomacy, affected not to notice the cold way in which

Madge received him, and began to pay marked attention to her, much to Brian's disgust. At last he asked her to be his wife, and notwithstanding her prompt refusal, spoke to Mr Frettlby on the subject. Much to the daughter's astonishment, that gentleman consented to Whyte's paying his addresses to Madge, and told her that he wished her to consider the young man's proposal favourably. In spite of all Madge could say, he refused to alter his decision, and Whyte, feeling himself safe, began to treat Brian with an insolence which was highly galling to Fitzgerald's proud nature. He called on Whyte at his lodgings, and after a violent quarrel with him had left the house, vowing to kill Whyte, should he marry Madge Frettlby. Fitzgerald went along to Mr Frettlby that same night, and had an interview with him. He confessed that he loved Madge, and that his love was returned. So, when Madge added her entreaties to Brian's, Mr Frettlby found himself unable to withstand the combined forces, and gave his consent to their engagement. Whyte was absent in the country for the next few days after his stormy interview with Brian, and it was only on his return that he learnt that Madge was engaged to his rival. He saw Mr Frettlby on the subject, and having learnt from his own lips that such was the case, he left the house at once, and swore that he would never enter it again. He little knew how prophetic his words were, for on that same night he met his death in the hansom cab. He had passed out of the life of both the lovers, and they, glad that he troubled them no more, never suspected for a moment that the body of the unknown man found in Royston's cab was that of Oliver Whyte.

About two weeks after Whyte's disappearance, Mr Frettlby gave a dinner party in honour of his daughter's birthday. It was a delightful evening, and the wide French windows which led on to the verandah were open, letting in a gentle breeze, blowing with a fresh salt odour, from the ocean. Outside there was a kind of screen of tropical plants, and through the tangle of the boughs the guests, seated at the table, could just see the waters of the bay glittering like silver in the pale moonlight. Brian was seated opposite to Madge, and every now and then he caught a glimpse of her bright face behind the great silver epergne, filled with fruit and flowers, which stood in the centre of the table. Mark Frettlby was at the head of the table, and appeared in very good spirits, for his stern features were somewhat relaxed, and he drank more wine than usual. The soup had just been removed when someone, who was late, entered with apologies and took his seat. Someone in this case was Mr Felix Rolleston, one of the best known young men in Melbourne. He had an income of his own, scribbled a little for the papers, was to be seen at every house of any pretensions to fashion in Melbourne, and was always bright, happy, and full of news. Whenever any scandal occurred, Felix Rolleston was sure to know it first, and could tell more about it than anyone else. He knew everything that was going on, both at home and abroad. His knowledge, if not very accurate, was at least extensive, and his conversation was piquant and witty. As Calton, one of the leading lawyers of the city, said: 'Rolleston put him in mind of what Beaconsfield said of one of his characters in Lothair, "He wasn't an intellectual Croesus, but his pockets were always full of sixpences." ' There was a good deal of truth in Calton's remark, and Felix always distributed his sixpences freely. The conversation had been dull for the last few minutes at the Frettlby dinner-table; consequently, when Felix arrived, everybody brightened up, as they felt certain now that the conversation would be amusing.

'So awfully sorry, don't you know,' said Felix, as he slipped into a seat by Madge; 'but a fellow like me has got to be careful of his time — so many calls on it.'

'So many calls in it, you mean,' retorted Madge, with a disbelieving smile. 'Confess, now, you have been paying a round of visits.'

'Well, yes,' assented Mr Rolleston; 'that's the disadvantage of having a large circle of acquaintances. They give you weak tea and thin bread and butter, whereas—'

'You would rather have a B and S and some devilled kidneys,' finished Brian.

There was a laugh at this, but Mr Rolleston disdained to notice the interruption.

'The only advantage of five o'clock tea,' he went on, 'is, that it brings people together, and one hears what's going on.'

'Ah, yes, Rolleston,' said Mr Frettlby, who was looking at him with an amused smile. 'What news have you?'

'Good news, bad news, and such news as you have never heard

of,' quoted Rolleston, gravely. 'Yes, I have a bit of news — haven't you heard it?'

As no one knew what the news was they could not very well say that they had, so Rolleston was happy, having found out that he could make a sensation.

'Well, do you know,' he said, gravely fixing in his eyeglass, 'they have found out the name of the fellow that was murdered in the hansom cab.'

'Never!' cried everyone eagerly.

'Yes,' went on Rolleston, 'and what's more, you all know him.'

'It's never Whyte?' said Brian, in a horrified tone.

'Hang it, how did you know?' said Rolleston, rather annoyed at being forestalled. 'Why, I just heard it at the St Kilda station.'

'Oh, easily enough,' said Brian, rather confused. 'I used to see Whyte constantly, and as I had not set eyes on him for the last two weeks, I thought it might be him.'

'How did they find out who it was?' asked Mr Frettlby, idly toying with his wine-glass.

'Oh, one of those detective fellows, you know,' answered Felix. 'They know everything.'

'I'm sorry to hear it,' said Frettlby, referring to the fact that Whyte was murdered. 'He had a letter of introduction to me, and seemed a clever, pushing young fellow.'

'A confounded cad,' muttered Felix, under his breath; and Brian, who overheard him, seemed inclined to assent.

For the rest of the meal nothing was talked about but the murder, and the mystery in which it was shrouded. When the ladies retired they chatted about it in the drawing-room, but finally dropped it for more agreeable subjects. The gentlemen, however, when the cloth had been removed, filled their glasses, and continued the discussion with unabated vigour. Brian alone did not take part in the conversation. He sat moodily staring at his untasted wine, and wrapped in a brown study.

'What I can't make out,' observed Rolleston, who was amusing himself with cracking nuts, 'is how they did not find out who he was before.'

'That is not hard to answer,' said Frettlby, filling his glass; 'he was comparatively little known here, as he had been out from England such a short time, and I fancy that this was the only house he visited at.'

'And look here, Rolleston,' said Calton, who was sitting near him, 'if you were to find a man dead in a hansom cab, dressed in evening clothes — which nine men out of ten are in the habit of wearing in the evening — no cards in his pockets, and no name on his linen, I rather think you would find it hard to discover who he was. I consider it reflects great credit on the police for finding out so quickly.'

'Puts one in mind of "The Leavenworth Case," and all that sort of thing,' said Felix, whose reading was of the lightest description. 'Awfully exciting, like putting a Chinese puzzle together. Gad, I wouldn't mind being a detective myself.'

'I'm afraid if that was the case,' said Mr Frettlby, with an amused smile, 'criminals would be pretty safe.'

'Oh, I don't know so much about that,' answered Felix, shrewdly; 'some fellows are like trifle at a party — froth on top, but something better underneath.'

'What a greedy simile,' said Calton, sipping his wine; 'but I'm afraid the police will have a more difficult task in discovering the man who committed the crime. In my opinion he's a deuced clever fellow.'

'Then you don't think he will be discovered,' asked Brian, rousing himself out of his brown study.

'Well, I don't go as far as that,' rejoined Calton; 'but he has certainly left no trace behind him, and even the Red Indian, in whom instinct for tracking is so highly developed, needs some sort of a trail to find out his enemies. Depend upon it,' went on Calton, warming to his subject, 'the man who murdered Whyte is no ordinary criminal; the place he chose for the committal of the crime was such a safe one.'

'Do you think so?' said Rolleston. 'Why, I should think that a hansom cab in a public street would be very unsafe.'

'It is that very fact that makes it safer,' replied Mr Calton, epigrammatically. 'You read De Quincey's account of the Marr murders in London, and you will see that the more public the place the less risk there is of detection. There was nothing about the gentleman in the light coat who murdered Whyte to excite Royston's suspicions. He got into the cab with Whyte, no noise or anything likely to attract attention was heard, and then he got out. Naturally enough, Royston drove down to St Kilda, and never suspected Whyte was dead till he looked inside and touched him. As to the man in the light coat, he doesn't live in Powlett Street — no — nor in East Melbourne either.'

'Why not?' asked Frettlby.

'Because he wouldn't have been such a fool as to leave a trail to his own door; he did what the fox often does — he doubled. My opinion is that he either went right through East Melbourne to Fitzroy, or he walked back through the Fitzroy Gardens into town. There was no one about at that time of the morning, and he could walk home to his lodgings, hotel, or wherever it was, with impunity. Of course, this is a theory that may be wrong; but from what insight into human nature my profession has given me, I think that my idea is a correct one.'

All present agreed with Mr Calton's idea, as it really did seem the most natural thing that would be done by a man desirous of escaping detection.

'Tell you what,' said Felix to Brian, as they were on their way to the drawing-room, 'if the fellow that committed the crime is found out, by gad, he ought to get Calton to defend him.'

VIII
Brian Takes a Walk and a Drive

When the gentlemen entered the drawing-room a young lady was engaged in playing one of those detestable pieces of music called *Morceau de Salon*, in which an unoffending air is taken and variations embroidered on it till it becomes a perfect agony to distinguish the tune amid the perpetual rattle of quavers and demi-semi-quavers. The air in this case was 'Over the Garden Wall,' with variations by Signor Thumpanini, and the young lady who played it was a pupil of that celebrated Italian musician. When the male portion of the guests entered the air was being played in the bass with a great deal of power (that is, the loud pedal was down), and with a perpetual rattle of treble notes trying with all their shrill power to drown the tune.

'Gad! It's getting over the garden wall in a hailstorm,' said Felix, as he strolled over to the piano, for he saw that the musician was Dora Featherweight, an heiress to whom he was then paying attention, in the hopes that she might be induced to take the name of Rolleston, together with the present owner of the same. So, when the fair Dora had paralysed her audience with one final bang and rattle, as if the gentleman going over the garden wall had tumbled into the cucumber frame, Felix was loud in his expressions of delight.

'Such power, you know, Miss Featherweight,' he said, sinking into a chair, and mentally wondering if any of the piano strings had given way at that last crash. 'You put your heart into it — and all your muscle, too, by gad,' he added mentally.

'It's nothing but practice,' answered Miss Featherweight, with a modest blush; 'I am at the piano four hours every day.'

'Oh, Lord,' groaned Felix, 'what a time the family must have of it,' but he kept this remark to himself, and, screwing his eye-glass into his left organ of vision, merely ejaculated, 'Lucky piano.'

Miss Featherweight, not being able to think of any answer to this, looked down and blushed, while the ingenuous Felix looked up and sighed.

Madge and Brian were in one corner of the room talking together about Whyte's death.

'I never did like him,' she said, 'but it was horrible to think of him dying like that.'

'I don't know,' answered Brian, gloomily; 'from all I can hear chloroform is a very easy death.'

'Death can never be easy,' replied Madge, 'especially to a young man so full of health and spirits as Mr Whyte was.'

'I believe you are sorry he's dead,' said Brian, jealously.

'Aren't you?' she asked in some surprise.

'*De mortius nil nisi bonum*,' quoted Fitzgerald, 'but as I detested him when alive you can't expect me to regret his end.'

Madge did not answer him, but glanced quickly at his face, and for the first time it struck her that he looked ill.

'What is the matter with you, dear?' she asked, placing her hand on his arm. 'You are not looking well.'

'Nothing — nothing,' he answered hurriedly. 'I've been a little worried about business lately — but come,' he said, rising, 'let us go outside, for I see your father has got that girl with the steam-whistle voice to sing.'

The girl with the steam-whistle voice was Julia Featherweight, the sister of Rolleston's inamorata, and Madge stifled a laugh as she went on to the verandah with Fitzgerald.

'What a shame of you,' she said, bursting into a laugh when they were safely outside; 'she's been taught by the best masters.'

'How I pity them,' retorted Brian, grimly, as Julia wailed out, 'Meet me once again,' with an ear-piercing shrillness. 'I'd much rather listen to our ancestral Banshee, and as to meeting her again, one interview would be more than enough.'

Madge did not answer, but leaning lightly over the high rail of the verandah looked out into the beautiful moonlight night. There were a number of people passing along the Esplanade, some of whom stopped and listened to Julia's shrill notes, which, being mellowed by distance, must have sounded rather nice. One man in particular seemed to have a taste for music, for he persistently stared over the fence at the house. Brian and Madge talked of all sorts of things, but every time Madge looked up she saw the man watching the house.

'What does that man want, Brian?' she asked.

'What man?' asked Brian, starting. 'Oh,' he went on indifferently, as the man moved away from the gate and crossed the road on to the footpath, 'he's taken up with the music, I suppose; that's all.'

Madge did not say anything, but could not help thinking there was more in it than the music. Presently Julia ceased, and she proposed to go in.

'Why?' asked Brian, who was lying back in a comfortable seat, smoking a cigarette. 'It's nice enough here.'

'I must attend to my guests,' she answered, rising. 'You stop here and finish your cigarette,' and with a gay laugh she flitted into the house like a shadow.

Brian sat and smoked, staring out into the moonlight meanwhile. Yes, the man was certainly watching the house, for he sat on one of the seats, and kept his eyes fixed on the brilliantly-lighted windows. Brian threw away his cigarette and shivered slightly.

'Could anyone have seen me?' he muttered, rising uneasily. 'Pshaw, of course not, and the cabman would never recognise me again. Curse Whyte, I wish I'd never set eyes upon him.'

He gave one glance at the dark figure on the seat, and then, with a shiver, passed into the warm, well-lighted room. He did not feel easy in his mind, and he would have felt still less so had he known that the man on the seat was one of the cleverest of the Melbourne detectives.

Mr Gorby had been watching the Frettlby mansion the whole evening, and was getting rather annoyed. Moreland did not know where Fitzgerald lived, and as the detective wanted to find out, he determined to watch Brian's movements and trace him home.

'If he's that pretty girl's lover, I'll wait till he leaves the house,' argued Mr Gorby to himself, when he first took his seat on the Esplanade. 'He won't stay long away from her, and once he leaves the house, I'll follow him up till I find out where he lives.'

When Brian made his appearance early in the evening on his way to Mark Frettlby's mansion, he was in evening dress, with a light coat over it, and also had on a soft hat.

'Well, I'm dashed!' ejaculated Mr Gorby, when he saw Fitzgerald disappear; 'if he isn't a fool I don't know who is, to go about in the very clothes he wore when he polished Whyte off, and think he won't be recognised. Melbourne ain't Paris or London, that he can afford to be so careless, and when I put the darbies on him he will be astonished. Ah, well,' he went on, lighting his pipe and taking a seat on the Esplanade, 'I suppose I'll have to wait here till he comes out.'

Mr Gorby's patience was pretty severely tried, for hour after hour passed, and no one appeared. He smoked several pipes, and watched the people strolling along in the soft silver moonlight. A bevy of girls passed by with their arms round one another's waists, and were giggling to one another. Then a young man and woman came walking slowly along, evidently lovers, for they sat down by Mr Gorby, and looked hard at him, just to hint that he need not stay. But the detective took no notice of their appealing glances, but kept his eyes steadily on the great house opposite to him, so the lovers took themselves off with a very bad grace. Then he saw Madge and Brian come out on to the verandah, and heard Miss Featherweight's shrill voice singing, which sounded weird and unearthly in the stillness of the night. He saw Madge go in, and then Brian, the latter turning and staring at him for a minute or so.

'Ah!' said Gorby to himself, relighting his pipe, 'your conscience is a-smiting you, is it? Wait till you're in gaol.'

Then the guests came out of the house and disappeared one by one, black figures in the moonlight, after kisses and handshaking. Shortly afterwards Brian came down the path with Frettlby by his side, and Madge hanging on to her father's arm. Frettlby opened the gate, and held out his hand.

'Goodnight, Fitzgerald,' he said, in a hearty voice; 'come down soon again.'

'Goodnight, Brian, dearest,' said Madge, kissing him, 'and don't forget tomorrow.'

Then father and daughter closed the gate, leaving Brian outside, and walked back to the house.

'Ah!' said Mr Gorby to himself, 'if you only knew what I know, you wouldn't be so precious kind to him.'

Brian walked, strolled along the Esplanade, and then crossing over, passed by Gorby and walked on till he was opposite the Esplanade Hotel. Then he leaned his arms on the fence, and, taking off his hat, enjoyed the calm beauty of the hour.

'What a good-looking fellow,' murmured Mr Gorby, in a regretful tone. 'I can hardly believe it of him, but the proofs are too clear.'

Such a still night, not a breath of wind stirring, for the breeze had long since died away, and Brian could see the white waves breaking on the yellow sands, the long narrow pier running out like a black thread into the sheet of gleaming silver, and away in the distance the long line of the Williamstown lights like a fairy illumination. Over all this fantastic scene of land and water was a sky such as Doré loved — great heavy masses of rain clouds heaped one on top of the other like the rocks the Titans piled to reach Olympus. Then a break in the white woof, and a bit of dark blue sky could be seen glittering with stars, in the midst of which sailed the serene moon shedding down her cold light on the fantastical cloudland beneath, and giving to every one a silver lining. Such a weird *bizarre* sort of sky that Brian gazed up at it for several minutes, admiring the wonderful beauty of the broken masses of light and shadow, much to the annoyance of Mr Gorby, who had no eye for the picturesque. At last, with a sigh, Mr Fitzgerald withdrew his eyes from the contemplation of the marvellous, and, lighting a cigarette, walked down the steps on to the pier.

'Suicide, is it?' muttered Mr Gorby to himself, as he saw the tall, black figure striding resolutely on, a long way ahead. 'Not if I can help it.' So he lighted his pipe, and strolled down the pier in an apparently aimless manner.

He found Brian leaning over the parapet at the end of the pier, and looking at the glittering waters beneath, which kept rising and falling in a dreamy rhythm, that soothed and charmed the ear. 'Poor girl! Poor girl!' the detective heard him mutter as he came up. 'If she only knew all! If she—'

At this moment he heard the approaching step, and turned round sharply. The detective saw that his face was ghastly pale in the moonlight, and his brows wrinkled angrily.

'What the devil do you want?' he burst out, as Gorby paused. 'What do you mean by following me all over the place.'

'Saw me watching the house,' said Gorby to himself. 'I'm not following you, sir,' he said aloud. 'I suppose the pier ain't private property. I only came down here for a breath of fresh air.'

Fitzgerald did not answer, but turned sharply on his heel, and walked quickly up the pier, leaving Gorby staring after him.

'He's getting frightened,' soliloquised the detective to himself, as he strolled easily along, keeping the black figure in front well in view. 'I'll have to keep a sharp eye on him or he'll be clearing out of Victoria.'

Brian walked quickly up to the St Kilda station, for on looking at his watch he found that he would just have time to catch the last train. He arrived a few minutes before it started, so, getting into the smoking carriage at the near end of the platform, he lit a cigarette, and, leaning back in his seat, watched latecomers hurrying into the station. Just as the last bell rang he saw a man rush along, who seemed likely to miss the train. It was the same man who had been watching him the whole evening, and Brian felt confident that he was following him. He comforted himself, however, with the thought that this pertinacious follower would lose the train, and, being in the last carriage himself, he kept a lookout along the platform, expecting to see his friend of the Esplanade standing disappointed on it. There was no appearance of him, however, so Brian, sinking back into his seat, cursed his ill-luck in not having shaken off this man who kept him under such strict surveillance.

'D— him!' he muttered softly. 'I expect he will follow me to East Melbourne, and find out where I live, but he shan't if I can help it.'

There was no one in the carriage except himself, on which he felt a sense of relief, for he was in that humour which comes on men sometimes of talking aloud to himself.

'Murdered in a cab,' he said, lighting a fresh cigarette, and blowing a cloud of smoke. 'A romance in real life, which beats Miss Braddon hollow. There is one thing certain, he won't come between Madge and me again. Poor Madge!' with an impatient sigh. 'If she only knew all, there would not be much chance of our marriage; but she can never find out, and I don't suppose anyone else ever will.'

Here a sudden thought struck him, and rising out of his seat, he walked to the other end of the carriage, and threw himself on the cushions, as if desirous of escape from himself.

'What grounds can that man have for suspecting me?' he said aloud. 'No one knows I was with Whyte on that night, and the police can't possibly bring forward any evidence to show that I was. Pshaw!' he went on, impatiently buttoning up his coat. 'I am like a child, afraid of my shadow — the fellow on the pier is only someone out for a breath of fresh air, as he said himself — I am quite safe.'

All the same he did not feel easy in his mind, and when the train arrived at the Melbourne station he stepped out on to the platform with a shiver and a quick look round, as if he expected to feel the detective's hand on his shoulder. He saw no one, however, at all like the man he had met on the St Kilda Pier, and, with a sigh of relief, left the station. Mr Gorby, however, was on the watch, and followed him at a safe distance along the platform. Brian left the station and walked slowly along Flinders Street, apparently in deep thought. When he got to Russell Street he turned up there, and did not stop until he came close to the Burke and Wills' monument, in the very place where the cab had stopped on the night of Whyte's murder.

'Ah!' said the detective to himself, as he stood in the shadow on the opposite side of the street. 'You're going to have a look at it, are you? — I wouldn't, if I were you — it's dangerous.'

Fitzgerald stood for a few minutes at the corner, and then walked up Collins Street. When he got to the cab-stand, opposite the Melbourne Club, still suspecting he was followed, he hailed a hansom, and drove away in the direction of Spring Street. Gorby was rather perplexed at this sudden move, but without delay, he hailed another cab, and told the driver to follow the first till it stopped.

'Two can play at that game,' he said, settling himself back in the cab, 'and I'll get the better of you, clever as you are — and you are clever,' he went on in a tone of admiration, as he looked round the luxurious hansom, 'to choose such a convenient place for a murder; no disturbance and plenty of time for escape after you had finished; it's a pleasure going after a chap like you, instead of men who tumble down like ripe fruit, and ain't got any brains to keep their crime quiet.'

While the detective thus soliloquised, his cab, following on the trail of the other, had turned down Spring Street, and was being driven rapidly along the Wellington Parade, in the direction of East Melbourne. It then turned up Powlett Street, at which Mr Gorby exulted.

'Ain't so clever as I thought,' he said to himself. 'Shows his nest right off, without any attempt to hide it.'

The detective, however, had reckoned without his host, for the cab in front kept driving on, through an interminable maze of streets, until it seemed as if Brian was determined never to stop the whole night.

'Look 'ere, sir!' cried Gorby's cabman, looking through his trap-door in the roof of the hansom, ' 'ow long's this 'ere game agoin' to larst? My 'oss is knocked up, 'e is, and 'is blessed old legs is agivin' way under 'im!'

'Go on! Go on!' answered the detective, impatiently; 'I'll pay you well.'

The cabman's spirits were raised by this, and by dint of coaxing and a liberal use of the silk, he managed to get his jaded horse up to a pretty good pace. They were in Fitzroy by this time, and then both cabs turned out of Gertrude Street into Nicholson Street; thence passed on to Evelyn Street and along Spring Street, until Brian's cab stopped at the corner of Collins Street, and Gorby saw him alight and dismiss his cabman. He then walked down the street and disappeared into the Treasury Gardens.

'Confound it,' said the detective, as he got out and paid his fare, which was not by any means a light one, but over which he had no time to argue, 'we've come in a circle, and I do believe he lives in Powlett Street after all.'

He went into the gardens, and saw Brian some distance ahead of him, walking rapidly. It was bright moonlight, and he could easily distinguish Fitzgerald by his light coat. He went along that noble avenue of elms, which were in their winter dress, and the moon shining through their branches wrought fantastic tracery on the smooth asphalt beneath. And on either side Gorby could see the dim white forms of the old Greek gods and goddesses — Venus Victrix, with the apple in her hand (which Mr Gorby, in his happy ignorance of heathen mythology, took for Eve offering Adam the forbidden fruit); Diana, with the hound at her feet, and Bacchus and Ariadne (which the detective imagined were the Babes in the Wood). He knew that each of the statues had queer names, but thought they were merely allegorical. Passing over the bridge, with the water rippling quietly underneath, Brian went up the smooth yellow path to where the statue of Hebe, holding the cup, seems instinct with life, and almost stepping of the pedestal, and turning down the path to the right, he left the gardens by the end gate, near which stands the statue of the Dancing Faun, with the great bush of scarlet geranium burning like an altar before it. Then he went along the Wellington Parade, and turned up Powlett Street, where he stopped at a house near Cairns' Memorial Church, much to Mr Gorby's relief, who, being like Hamlet, 'fat and scant of breath,' found himself rather exhausted. He kept well in the shadow, however, and saw Fitzgerald give one final look round before he disappeared into the house. Then Mr Gorby, like the Robber Captain in Ali Baba, took careful stock of the house, and fixed its locality and appearance well in his mind, as he intended to call at it on the morrow.

'What I'm going to do,' he said, as he walked slowly back to Melbourne, 'is to see his landlady when he's out, and find out what time he came in on the night of the murder. If it fits into the time he got out of Rankin's cab I'll get out a warrant, and arrest him straight off.'

IX
Mr Gorby is Satisfied at Last

In spite of his long walk, and still longer drive, Brian did not sleep well that night. He kept tossing and turning, or else lying on his back, wide awake, looking into the darkness, and thinking of Whyte. Towards dawn, when the first faint glimmer of morning came through the venetian blinds, he fell into a sort of uneasy doze, haunted by horrible dreams. He thought he was driving in a hansom, when suddenly he found Whyte by his side, clad in white cerements, grinning and gibbering at him with ghastly merriment. Then the cab went over a precipice, and he fell from a great height, down, down, with the mocking laughter still sounding in his ears, until he woke with a loud cry, and found it was broad daylight, and that drops of perspiration were standing on his brow. It was no good trying to sleep any longer, so, with a weary sigh, he arose and went for his tub, feeling jaded and worn out by worry and want of sleep. His bath did him some good, as the cold water brightened him up and pulled him together. Still he could not help giving a start of surprise when he saw his face looking at him from the mirror, old and haggard-looking, with dark circles round the eyes.

'A pleasant life I'm going to have of it if this sort of thing goes on,' he said bitterly. 'I wish to G— I had never seen or heard of Whyte.'

He dressed himself carefully, however, for Brian was a man who never neglected his toilet, however worried and out of sorts he might feel. Yet, notwithstanding his efforts to throw off his gloom and feel cheerful, his landlady was startled when she saw how haggard and worn his handsome face looked in the searching morning light.

She was a small, dried-up little woman, with a wrinkled, yellow face, and looked so parched and brittle that strangers could not help thinking it would do her good if she were soaked in water for a year, in order to soften her a little. Whenever she moved she crackled, and one was in constant dread of seeing one of her wizen-looking limbs break off short, like the branch of a dead tree. When she spoke it was in a hard, shrill voice, like a cricket;

and being dressed in a faded brown silk, what with her voice and attenuated body, she was not unlike that noisy insect. She crackled into Brian's sitting-room with the *Argus* and coffee, and a look of dismay came over her stony little face as she saw his altered looks.

'Dear me, sir,' she chirped out in her shrill voice, as she placed her burden on the table, 'are you took bad?'

Brian shook his head.

'Want of sleep, that's all, Mrs Sampson,' he answered, unfolding the *Argus*.

'Ah! That's because ye ain't got enough blood in yer 'ead,' said Mrs Sampson, wisely, for she had her own ideas on the subject of health. 'If you ain't got blood you ain't got sleep.'

Brian looked at her as she said this, for there seemed such an obvious want of blood in her veins that he wondered if she had ever slept in all her life.

'There was my father's brother, which, of course, makes 'im my uncle,' went on the landlady, pouring out a cup of coffee for Brian, 'an' the blood 'e 'ad was somethin' astoundin', which it made 'im sleep that long as they 'ad to draw pints from 'im afore 'e'd wake in the mornin'.'

Brian had the *Argus* before his face, and under its friendly cover laughed quietly to himself at the very tall story Mrs Sampson was telling.

'His blood poured out like a river,' went on the landlady, still drawing from the rich stores of her imagination, 'and the doctor was struck dumb with astonishment at seein' the Nigagerer which burst from 'im — but I'm not so full-blooded myself.'

Fitzgerald again stifled a laugh, and wondered that Mrs Sampson was not afraid of being treated in the same manner as Ananias and Sapphira. However, he said nothing, but merely intimated that if she would leave the room he would take his breakfast.

'An' if you wants anythin' else, Mr Fitzgerald,' she said, going to the door, 'you knows your way to the bell as easily as I do to the kitching,' and, with a final chirrup, she crackled out of the room.

As soon as the door was closed Brian put down his paper and roared, in spite of the worry he was in. He had that extraordinary vivacious Irish temperament, by which a man can put all trouble behind his back, and thoroughly enjoy the present. His landlady, with her Arabian Night-like romances, was a source of great amusement to him, and he felt considerably cheered by the odd turn her humour had taken this morning. After a time, however, his laughter ceased, and all his troubles came crowding on him again. He drank his coffee, but pushed away the food which was before him, and then looked through the *Argus*, to see the latest report about the murder case. What he read made his cheek even turn paler than it was, and he could feel his heart beating loudly.

'They've found a clue, have they?' he muttered, rising and pacing restlessly up and down. 'I wonder what it can be? I threw that man off the scent last night, but if he suspects me, there will be no difficulty in him finding out where I live. Bah! What nonsense I am talking. I am the victim of my own morbid imagination. There is nothing to connect me with the crime, so I need not be afraid of my shadow. I've a good mind to leave town for a time, but if I am suspected that would excite suspicion. Oh, Madge! My darling,' he cried, passionately, 'if you only know what I suffer, I know that you would pity me — but you must never know the truth — never! Never!' and sinking into a chair by the window, he covered his face with his hands. After remaining in this position for some minutes, occupied with his own gloomy thoughts, he arose and rang the bell. A faint crackle in the distance announced that Mrs Sampson had heard it, and she soon came into the room, looking more like a cricket than ever. Brian had gone into his bedroom, and called out to her from there—

'I am going down to St Kilda, Mrs Sampson,' he said, 'and, probably, will not be back all day.'

'Which I 'opes it 'ull do you good,' answered the cricket, 'for you've eaten nothin', an' the sea breezes is miraculous for makin' you take to your victuals. My mother's brother, bein' a sailor, an' wonderful for 'is stomach, which, when 'e 'ad done a meal, the table looked as if a low-cuss 'ad gone over it.'

'A what?' asked Fitzgerald, buttoning his gloves.

'A low-cuss!' replied the landlady, in surprise at his ignorance, 'as I've read in 'Oly Writ, as 'ow John the Baptist was partial to 'em, not that I think they'd be very fillin', tho', to be sure, 'e 'ad a sweet tooth, and ate 'oney with 'em.'

'Oh, you mean locusts,' said Brian, now enlightened.

'An' what else?' asked Mrs Sampson, indignantly; 'which, tho' not bein' a scholar'd, I speaks English I 'opes, my mother's second cousin 'avin' 'ad first prize at a spellin' bee, tho' 'e died early through brain fever, 'avin' crowded 'is 'ead over much with the dictionary.'

'Dear me,' answered Brian, mechanically. 'How unfortunate.' He was not listening to Mrs Sampson's remarks, but was thinking of an arrangement which Madge had made, and which he had forgotten till now.

'Mrs Sampson,' he said, turning round at the door, 'I am going to bring Mr Frettlby and his daughter to have a cup of afternoon tea here, so you might have some ready.'

'You 'ave only to ask and to 'ave,' answered Mrs Sampson, hospitably, with a gratified crackle of all her joints. 'I'll make the tea, sir, an' also some of my own perticler cakes, bein' a special kind I 'ave, which my mother showed me 'ow to make, 'avin' been taught by a lady as she nussed thro' the scarlet fever, tho' bein' of a weak constitootion, she died soon arter, bein' in the 'abit of contractin' any disease she might chance on.'

As Brian did not care about a connection between cooking and scarlet fever, he hurried away, lest Mrs Sampson should bring out more charnel-house horrors, for which she had a Poe-like appreciation. Indeed, at one period of her life, the little woman having been a nurse, she had frightened one of her patients into convulsions during the night by narrating to her the history of all the corpses she had laid out. This ghoul-like tendency having been discovered, she never obtained any more patients to nurse, as they objected when in a weak state to hear such grotesque horrors.

As soon as Fitzgerald had gone, she went over to the window and watched him as he walked slowly down the street — a tall, handsome man, of whom any woman would be proud.

'What an awful thing it are to think 'e'll be a corpse some day,' she chirped cheerily to herself, 'tho' of course bein' a great swell in 'is own place, 'e'll 'ave a nice airy vault, which 'ud be far more comfortable than a close, stuffy grave, even tho' it 'as a tombstone an' vi'lets over it. Ah, now! Who are you, impertinence?' she broke off, as a stout man in a light suit of clothes crossed the road and rang the bell, 'a-pullin' at the bell as if it were a pump 'andle.'

As the gentleman at the door, who was none other than Mr Gorby, did not hear her, he of course did not reply, so she hurried down the stairs, crackling with anger at the rough usage her bell had received.

Mr Gorby had seen Brian go out, and deeming it a good opportunity to prosecute enquiries, had lost no time in making a start.

'You nearly tored the bell down,' said the fiery cricket, as she presented her thin body and wrinkled face to the view of the detective.

'I'm very sorry,' answered Gorby, meekly. 'I'll knock next time.'

'Oh, no you won't,' said the landlady, tossing her head, 'me not 'avin' a knocker, an' your 'and a-scratchin' the paint off the door, which it ain't been done over six months by my sister-in-law's cousin, which 'e is a painter, with a shop in Fitzroy, an' a wonderful heye to colour.'

'Does Mr Fitzgerald live here?' asked Mr Gorby, quietly.

'He do,' replied Mrs Sampson, 'but 'e's gone out, an' won't be back till the arternoon, which any messige 'ull be delivered to 'im punctual on 'is arrival.'

'I'm glad he's not in,' said Mr Gorby. 'Would you allow me to have a few moments' conversation?'

'What is it?' asked the cricket, her curiosity being roused.

'I'll tell you when we get inside,' answered Mr Gorby.

The cricket looked at him with her sharp little eyes, and seeing nothing disreputable in him, led the way upstairs, crackling loudly the whole time. This so astonished Mr Gorby that he cast about in his own mind for an explanation of the phenomenon.

'Wants oiling about the joints,' was his conclusion, 'but I never heard anything like it, and she looks as if she'd snap in two, she's that brittle.'

Mrs Sampson took Gorby into Brian's sitting-room, and having closed the door, sat down and prepared to hear what he had to say for himself.

'I 'ope it ain't bills,' she said. 'Mr Fitzgerald 'avin' money in the bank, and everythin' respectable like a gentleman as 'e is, tho', to be sure, your bill might come down on him unbeknown, 'e not 'avin' kept it in mind, which it ain't everybody as 'ave sich a good memory as my aunt on my mother's side, she 'avin' bin famous for 'er dates like a 'istory, not to speak of 'er multiplication tables and the numbers of people's 'ouses.'

'It's not bills,' answered Mr Gorby, who, having vainly attempted to stem the shrill torrent of words, had given in, and waited mildly until she had finished; 'I only want to know a little about Mr Fitzgerald's habits.'

'And what for?' asked Mrs Sampson, with an indignant cackle. 'Are you a noospaper a-puttin' in articles about people who don't want to see 'emselves in print, which I knows your 'abits, my late 'usband 'avin' bin a printer on a paper which bust up, not 'avin' the money to pay wages, thro' which, there was doo to him the sum of one pound seven and sixpence half-penny, which I, bein' 'is widder, ought to 'ave, not that I expects to see it on this side of the grave — oh, dear, no!' and she gave a shrill, elfish laugh.

Mr Gorby, seeing that unless he took the bull by the horns, he would never be able to get what he wanted, grew desperate, and plunged in *medias res.*

'I am an insurance agent,' he said, rapidly, so as to prevent any interruption by the cricket; 'and Mr Fitzgerald wants to insure his life in our company. Before doing so, I want to find out if he is a good life to insure; does he live temperately? Keep early hours? And, in fact, all about him.'

'I shall be 'appy to answer any inquiries which may be of use to you, sir,' replied Mrs Sampson; 'knowin' as I do, 'ow good a insurance is to a family, should the 'ead of it be taken off unexpected, leavin' a widder, which, as I know, Mr Fitzgerald is a-goin' to be married soon, an' I 'opes 'e'll be 'appy, tho' thro' it I loses a lodger as 'as allays paid regler, an' be'aved like a gentleman.'

'So he is a temperate man?' said Mr Gorby, feeling his way cautiously.

'Not bein' a blue ribbing all the same,' answered Mrs Sampson; 'and I never saw him the wuss for drink, 'e being allays able to use his latch key, and take 'is boots off afore going to bed, which is no more than a woman ought to expect from a lodger, she 'avin' to do 'er own washin'.'

'And he keeps good hours?'

'Allays in afore the clock strikes twelve,' answered the landlady; 'tho, to be sure, I uses it as a figger of speech, none of the clocks in the 'ouse strikin' but one, which is bein' mended, 'avin' broke through overwindin'.'

‘Is he always in before twelve?’ asked Mr Gorby, keenly disappointed at this answer.

Mrs Sampson eyed him waggishly, and a smile crept over her wrinkled little face.

‘Young men, not bein’ old men,’ she replied, cautiously, ‘and sinners not bein’ saints, it’s not nattral as latch keys should be made for ornament instead of use, and Mr Fitzgerald bein’ one of the ’andsomest men in Melbourne, it ain’t to be expected as ’e should let ’is latch key git rusty, tho’, ’avin’ a good moral character, ’e uses it with moderation.’

‘But I suppose you are generally asleep when he comes in late?’ said the detective; ‘so you can’t tell what hour he comes home?’

‘Not as a rule,’ assented Mrs Sampson; ‘bein’ a ’eavy sleeper, and much disposed for bed, but I ’ave ’eard ’im come in arter twelve, the last time bein’ Thursday week.’

‘Ah!’ Mr Gorby drew a long breath, for Thursday week was the night when the murder was committed.

‘Bein’ troubled with my ’ead,’ said Mrs Sampson, ‘thro’ ’avin’ been out in the sun all day a-washin’, I did not feel so partial to my bed that night as in general, so went down to the kitching with the intent of getting a linseed poultice to put at the back of my ’ead, it being calculated to remove pain, as was told to me, when a nuss, by a doctor in the horspital, ’e now bein’ in business for hisself, at Geelong, with a large family, ’avin’ married early. Just as I was leavin’ the kitching I ’eard Mr Fitzgerald a-comin’ in, and, turnin’ round, looked at the clock, that ’avin’ been my custom when my late ’usband came in, in the early mornin’, I bein’ a-preparin’ ’is meal.’

‘And the time was?’ asked Mr Gorby, breathlessly.

‘Five minutes to two o’clock,’ replied Mrs Sampson.

Mr Gorby thought for a moment.

‘Cab was hailed at one o’clock — started for St Kilda at about ten minutes past — reached Grammar School, say, at twenty-five minutes past — Fitzgerald talks five minutes to cabman, making it half-past — say, he waited ten minutes for other cab to turn up, makes it twenty minutes to two — it would take another twenty minutes to get to East Melbourne — and five minutes to walk up here — that makes it five minutes past two instead of before — confound it. “Was your clock in the kitchen right?” ’ he asked, aloud.

'Well, I think so,' answered Mrs Sampson. 'It does get a little slow sometimes, not 'avin' bin cleaned for some time, which my nevy bein' a watchmaker I allays 'ands it over to 'im.'

'Of course it was slow on that night,' said Gorby, triumphantly. 'He must have come in at five minutes past two — which makes it right.'

'Makes what right?' asked the landlady, sharply. 'And 'ow do you know my clock was ten minutes wrong?'

'Oh, it was, was it?' asked Gorby, eagerly.

'I'm not denyin' that it wasn't,' replied Mrs Sampson; 'clocks ain't allays to be relied on more than men an' women — but it won't be anythin' agin 'is insurance, will it, as in general 'e's in afore twelve?'

'Oh, all that will be quite safe,' answered the detective, delighted at having obtained the required information. 'Is this Mr Fitzgerald's room?'

'Yes, it is,' replied the landlady; 'but 'e furnished it 'imself, bein' of a luxurus turn of mind, not but what 'is taste is good, tho' far be it from me to deny I 'elped 'im to select; but 'avin' another room of the same to let, any friends as you might 'ave in search of a 'ome 'ud be well looked arter, my references bein' very 'igh, an' my cookin' tasty — an' if —'

Here a ring at the front door bell called Mrs Sampson away, so with a hurried word to Gorby she crackled downstairs. Left to himself, Mr Gorby arose and looked round the room. It was excellently furnished, and the pictures on the wall were all in good taste. There was a writing table at one end of the room under the window, which was covered with papers.

'It's no good looking for the papers he took out of Whyte's pocket, I suppose,' said the detective to himself, as he turned over some letters, 'as I don't know what they are, and couldn't tell them if I saw them; but I'd like to find that missing glove and the bottle that held the chloroform — unless he's done away with them. There doesn't seem any sign of them here, so I'll have a look in his bedroom.'

There was no time to lose, as Mrs Sampson might return at any moment, so Mr Gorby walked quickly into the bedroom, which opened off the sitting-room. The first thing that caught the detective's eye was a large photograph of Madge Frettlby in a plush frame, which stood on the dressing table. It was the same kind as he had already seen in Whyte's album, and he took it up with a laugh.

'You're a pretty girl,' he said, apostrophising the picture, 'but you give your photograph to two young men, both in love with you, and both hot-tempered. The result is that one is dead, and the other won't survive him long. That's what you've done.'

He put it down again, and looking round the room, caught sight of a light covert coat hanging behind the door, and also a soft hat.

'Ah,' said the detective, going up to the door, 'here is the very coat you wore when you killed that poor fellow. I wonder what you have in the pockets,' and he plunged his hand into them in turn. There was an old theatre programme and a pair of brown gloves in one, but in the second pocket Mr Gorby made a discovery — none other than that of the missing glove. There it was — a soiled white glove for the right hand, with black bands down the back; and the detective smiled in a gratified manner as he put it carefully in his pocket.

'My morning has not been wasted,' he said to himself. 'I've found out that he came in at a time which corresponds to all his movements after one o'clock on Thursday night, and this is the missing glove, which clearly belonged to Whyte. If I could only get a hold of the chloroform bottle I'd be satisfied.'

But the chloroform bottle was not to be found, though he searched most carefully for it. At last, hearing Mrs Sampson coming upstairs again, he desisted from his search, and came back to the sitting-room.

'Threw it away, I expect,' he said, as he sat down in his old place; 'but it doesn't matter. I think I can form a chain of evidence, from what I have discovered, which will be sufficient to convict him. Besides, I expect when he is arrested he will confess everything; he seems to have such a lot of remorse for what he has done.'

The door opened, and Mrs Sampson crackled into the room in a state of indignation.

'One of them Chinese 'awkers,' she explained; ' 'e's bin a-tryin' to git the better of me over carrots — as if I didn't know what carrots was — and 'im a-talkin' about a shillin' in his gibberish, as if 'e 'adn't been brought up in a place where they don't know what a shillin' is. But I never could abide furreigners ever since a Frenchman, as taught me 'is language, made orf with my mother's silver teapot, unbeknown to 'er, it being set out on the sideboard for company.'

Mr Gorby interrupted these domestic reminiscences of Mrs Sampson's by stating that, now she had given him all necessary information, he would take his departure.

'An' I 'opes,' said Mrs Sampson, as she opened the door for him, 'as I'll 'ave the pleasure of seein' you again should any business on be'alf of Mr Fitzgerald require it.'

'Oh, I'll see you again,' said Mr Gorby, with heavy jocularity, 'and in a way you won't like, as you'll be called as a witness,' he added, mentally. 'Did I understand you to say, Mrs Sampson,' he went on, 'that Mr Fitzgerald would be at home this afternoon?'

'Oh yes, sir, 'e will,' answered Mrs Sampson, 'a drinkin' tea with his young lady, who is Miss Frettlby, and 'as got no end of money, not but what I mightn't 'ave 'ad the same 'ad I been born in a higher spear.'

'You need not tell Mr Fitzgerald I have been here,' said Gorby, closing the gate; 'I'll probably call and see him myself this afternoon.'

'What a stout person 'e are,' said Mrs Sampson to herself, as the detective walked away, 'just like my late father, who was allays fleshy, being a great eater, and fond of 'is glass, but I took arter my mother's family, they bein' thin-like, and proud of keeping 'emselves so, as the vinegar they drank could testify, not that I indulge in it myself.'

She shut the door, and went upstairs to take away the breakfast things, while Gorby was being driven along at a good pace to the police office, in order to get a warrant for Brian's arrest, on a charge of wilful murder.

X
In the Queen's Name

It was a broiling hot day — one of those cloudless days, with the blazing sun beating down on the arid streets, and casting deep, black shadows. By rights it was a December day, but the clerk of the weather had evidently got a little mixed, and popped it into the middle of August by mistake. The previous week, however, had been a little chilly, and this delightfully hot day had come as a pleasant surprise and a forecast of summer. It was Saturday morning, and of course all fashionable Melbourne was doing the Block. With regard to its 'Block,' Collins Street corresponds to New York's Broadway, London's Regent Street and Rotten Row, and to the Boulevards of Paris. It is on the Block that people show off their new dresses, bow to their friends, cut their enemies, and chatter small talk. The same thing no doubt occurred in the Appian Way, the fashionable street of Imperial Rome, when Catullus talked gay nonsense to Lesbia, and Horace received the congratulations of his friends over his new volume of society verses. History repeats itself, and every city is bound by all the laws of civilisation to have one special street, wherein the votaries of fashion can congregate. Collins Street is not, of course, such a grand thoroughfare as those above mentioned, but the people who stroll up and down the broad pavement are quite as charmingly dressed, and as pleasant as any of the peripatetics of those famous cities. As the sun brings out bright flowers, so the seductive influence of the hot weather had brought out all the ladies in gay dresses of innumerable colours, which made the long street look like a restless rainbow. Carriages were bowling smoothly along, their occupants smiling and bowing as they recognised their friends on the side walk; lawyers, their legal quibble finished for the week, were strolling leisurely along, with their black bags in their hands; portly merchants, forgetting Flinder's Lane and incoming ships, were walking beside their pretty daughters; and the representatives of swelldom were stalking along in their customary apparel of curly hats, high collars, and masher suits. Altogether, it was a very pleasant and animated scene, and would have delighted the heart of anyone who was not dyspeptic, nor in love — dyspeptic people and lovers (disappointed ones, of course, being accustomed to survey the world in a cynical vein.

Madge Frettlby was engaged in that pleasant occupation so dear to every female heart, of shopping. She was in Moubray, Rowan and Hicks', turning over ribbons and laces, while the faithful Brian waited for her outside, and amused himself by looking at the human stream which flowed along the pavement. If there is one thing above another which is dreaded by men it is shopping with ladies, for then a few minutes with them becomes hours, and the weary husband pensively smoking cigarettes outside, while his better half worries the young man at the counter about the last new shade, wonders, 'What the doose can be keeping Maris,' until that estimable lady makes her appearance, followed by a shopman bending like Atlas under his load of boxes and parcels. Brian disliked shopping quite as much as the rest of his sex, but, being a lover, of course it was his duty to be martyrised, though he could not help thinking of his pleasant club, where he could have been reading and smoking with something cool in a glass beside him. After Madge had purchased a dozen articles she did not want, and had interviewed her dressmaker on the momentous subject of a new dress, she remembered that Brian was waiting for her, and hurried quickly to the door.

'I haven't been many minutes, have I, dear?' she said, touching him lightly on the arm.

'Oh dear, no,' answered Brian, looking at his watch, 'only thirty — a mere nothing, considering a new dress was being discussed.'

'I thought I had been longer,' said Madge, her brow clearing; 'but still I am sure you feel a martyr.'

'Not at all,' replied Fitzgerald, handing her into the carriage; 'I enjoyed myself very much.'

'Nonsense,' she laughed, opening her sunshade, while Brian took his seat beside her; 'that's one of those social stories — which everyone considers themselves bound to tell from a sense of duty. I'm afraid I did keep you waiting — though, after all,' she went on, with a true feminine idea as to the flight of time, 'I was only a few minutes.'

'And the rest,' said Brian, quizzically looking at her pretty face, so charmingly flushed under her great white hat.

Madge disdained to notice this interruption.

'James,' she cried to the coachman, 'drive to the Melbourne Club. Papa will be there, you know,' she said to Brian, 'and we'll take him off to have afternoon tea with us.'

'But it's only one o'clock,' said Brian, as the Town Hall clock came in sight. 'Mrs Sampson won't be ready.'

'Oh, anything will do,' replied Madge, 'a cup of tea and some thin bread and butter isn't hard to prepare. I don't feel like lunch, and papa eats so little in the middle of the day, and you—'

'Eat a great deal at all times,' finished Brian, with a laugh. Madge went on chattering in her usual lively manner, and Brian listened to her with delight. It was very pleasant, he thought, lying back among the soft cushions of the carriage, with a pretty girl talking so gaily. He felt like Saul must have done when he heard the harp of David, and Madge, with her pleasant talk, drove away the evil spirit which had been with him for the last three weeks. Suddenly Madge made an observation as they were passing the Burke and Wills' monument, which startled him.

'Isn't that the place where Mr Whyte got into the cab?' she asked, looking at the corner near the Scotch Church, where a vagrant of musical tendencies was playing 'Just before the Battle, Mother,' on a battered old concertina in a most dismal manner.

'So the papers say,' answered Brian, listlessly, without turning his head.

'I wonder who the gentleman in the light coat could have been,' said Madge, as she settled herself again.

'No one seems to know,' he replied, evasively.

'Ah, but they've got a clue,' she said. 'Do you know, Brian,' she went on, 'that he was dressed just like you, in a light overcoat and soft hat?'

'How remarkable,' said Fitzgerald, speaking in a slightly sarcastic tone, and as calmly as he was able. 'He was dressed in the same manner as nine out of every ten young fellows in Melbourne.'

Madge looked at him in surprise at the tone in which he spoke, so different from his usual nonchalant way of speaking, and was about to answer when the carriage stopped at the door of the Melbourne Club. Brian, anxious to escape any more remarks about the murder, sprang quickly out, and ran up the steps into the building. He found Mr Frettlby smoking complacently, and reading the *Age*. As Fitzgerald entered he looked up, and putting down the paper held out his hand, which the other took.

'Ah! Fitzgerald,' he said, 'have you left the attractions of Collins Street for the still greater ones of Clubland?'

'Not I,' answered Brian. 'I've come to carry you off to afternoon tea with Madge and myself.'

'I don't mind,' answered Mr Frettlby, rising; 'but isn't afternoon tea at half-past one rather an anomaly?'

'What's in a name?' said Fitzgerald, absently, as they left the room. 'What have you been doing all morning?'

'I've been in here for the last half-hour reading,' answered the other, carelessly.

'Wool market, I suppose?'

'No, the hansom cab murder.'

'Oh, d— that thing!' said Brian, hastily; then, seeing his companion looking at him in surprise, he apologised. 'But, indeed,' he went on, 'I'm nearly worried to death by people asking all about Whyte, as if I knew all about him, whereas I know nothing.'

'Just as well you didn't,' answered Mr Frettlby, as they descended the steps together; 'he was not a very desirable companion.'

It was on the tip of Brian's tongue to say, 'And yet you wanted him to marry your daughter,' but he wisely refrained, and they reached the carriage in silence.

'Now then, papa,' said Madge, when they were all settled in the carriage, and it was rolling along smoothly in the direction of East Melbourne, 'what have you been doing?'

'Enjoying myself,' answered her father, 'until you and Brian came, and dragged me out into this blazing sunshine.'

'Well, Brian has been so good of late,' said Madge, 'that I had to reward him, so I knew that nothing would please him better than to play host.'

'Certainly not,' said Brian, rousing himself out of a fit of abstraction, 'especially when one has such charming visitors.'

Madge laughed at this, and made a little grimace.

'If your tea is only equal to your compliments,' she said lightly, 'I'm sure papa will forgive us for dragging him away from his club.'

'Papa will forgive anything,' murmured Mr Frettlby, tilting his hat over his eyes, 'as long as he gets somewhere out of the sun. I can't say I care about playing the parts of Shadrach, Meshach, and Abednego in the fiery furnace of a Melbourne hot day.'

'There now, papa is quite a host in himself,' said Madge mischievously, as the carriage drew up at Mrs Sampson's door.

'No, you are wrong,' said Brian, as he alighted and helped her out of the carriage; 'I am the host in myself this time.'

'If there is one thing I hate above another,' observed Miss Frettlby, calmly, 'it's puns, and especially bad ones.'

Mrs Sampson was very much astonished at the early arrival of her lodger's guests, and expressed her surprise in shrill tones.

'Bein' taken by surprise,' she said, with an apologetic cackle, 'it ain't to be suppose as miraculs can be performed with regard to cookin', the fire havin' gone out, not bein' kept alight on account of the 'eat of the day, which was that 'ot as never was, tho', to be sure, bein' a child in the early days, I remember it were that 'ot as my sister's aunt was in the 'abit of roastin' her jints in the sun.'

After telling this last romance, and leaving her visitors in doubt whether the joints referred to belonged to an animal or to her sister's aunt or herself, Mrs Sampson crackled away downstairs to get things ready.

'What a curious thing that landlady of yours is, Brian,' said Madge, from the depths of a huge armchair. 'I believe she's a grasshopper from the Fitzroy Gardens.'

'Oh, no, she's a woman,' said Mr Frettlby, cynically. 'You can tell that by the length of her tongue.'

'A popular error, papa,' retorted Madge, sharply. 'I know plenty of men who talk far more than any woman.'

'I hope I'll never meet them, then,' said Mr Frettlby, 'for if I did I would be inclined to agree with De Quincy's essay on murder as one of the fine arts.'

Brian shivered at this, and looked apprehensively at Madge, and saw with relief that she was not paying attention to her father, but was listening intently.

'There she is,' as a faint rustle at the door announced the arrival of Mrs Sampson and the tea-tray. 'I wonder, Brian, you don't think the house is on fire with that queer noise always going on — she wants oil!'

'Yes, St Jacob's oil,' laughed Brian, as Mrs Sampson entered, and placed her burden on the table.

'Not 'avin' any cake,' said the lady, 'thro' not being forewarned as to the time of arrival — tho' it's not ofting I'm taken by surprise — except as to a 'eadache, which, of course, is accidental to every pusson — I ain't got nothin' but bread and butter, the baker and grocer, both bein' all that could be desired, except in the way of worryin' for their money, which they thinks as 'ow I keeps the bank in the 'ouse, like Allading's cave, 'as I've 'eard tell in the Arabian Nights, me 'avin' gained it as a prize for English in my early girl'ood, bein' then considered a scolard an' industrus.'

Mrs Sampson's shrill apologies for the absence of cake having been received, she hopped out of the room, and Madge made the tea. The service was a quaint Chinese one which Brian had picked up in his wanderings, and used for gatherings like these. As he watched her he could not help thinking how pretty she looked, with her hands moving deftly among the cups and saucers, so bizarre-looking with their sprawling dragons of yellow and green. He half smiled to himself as he thought, 'If they knew all, I wonder if they would sit with me as cool and unconcerned?' Mr Frettlby, too, as he looked at his daughter, thought of his dead wife, and sighed.

'Well,' said Madge, as she handed them their tea, and helped herself to some thin bread and butter, 'you two gentlemen are most delightful company — papa is sighing like a furnace, and Brian is staring at me with his eyes like blue china saucers. You ought both to be turned forth to funerals like melancholy.'

'Why like melancholy?' queried Brian, lazily.

'I'm afraid, Mr Fitzgerald,' said the young lady, with a smile on her pretty black eyes, 'that you are not a student of "A Midsummer Night's Dream." '

'Very likely not,' answered Brian; 'midsummer out here is so hot that one gets no sleep, and, consequently, no dreams; depend upon it, if the four lovers whom Puck treated so badly had lived in Australia they wouldn't have been able to sleep for the mosquitos.'

'What nonsense you two young people do talk,' said Mr Frettlby, with an amused smile, as he stirred his tea.

'*Dulce est desipere in loco*,' observed Brian, gravely, 'a man who can't carry out that observation is sure not to be up to much.'

'I don't like Latin,' said Miss Frettlby, shaking her pretty head.

'I agree with Heine's remark, that if the Romans had had to learn it they would not have found time to conquer the world.'

'Which was a much more agreeable task,' said Brian.

'And more profitable,' finished Mr Frettlby.

They went on chattering in this desultory fashion for a considerable time, till at last Madge arose and said they must go. Brian proposed to dine with them at St Kilda, and then they would all go to the theatre. Madge consented to this, and she was just pulling on her gloves when suddenly they heard a ring at the front door, and presently heard Mrs Sampson talking in an excited manner at the pitch of her voice.

'You shan't come in, I tell you,' they heard her say, shrilly, 'so it's no good trying, which I've allays 'eard as an Englishman's 'ouse is 'is castle, an' your a-breakin' the law, as well as a-spilin' the carpets, which 'as bin newly put down.'

Someone made a reply; then the door of Brian's room was thrown open, and Gorby walked in, followed by another man. Fitzgerald turned as white as a sheet, for he felt instinctively that they had come for him. However, pulling himself together, he demanded, in a haughty tone, the reason of the intrusion. Mr Gorby walked straight over to where Brian was standing, and placed his hand on the young man's shoulder.

'Brian Fitzgerald,' he said, in a clear voice, 'I arrest you in the Queen's name.'

'For what?' asked Brian, steadily.

'The murder of Oliver Whyte.'

At this Madge gave a cry.

'It is not true!' she said, wildly. 'My God, it's not true.'

Brian did not answer, but, ghastly pale, held out his hands. Gorby slipped the hand-cuffs on to his wrists with a feeling of compunction, in spite of his joy in running his man down. This done, Fitzgerald turned round to where Madge was standing, pale and still, as if she had turned into stone.

'Madge,' he said, in a clear, low voice, 'I am going to prison — perhaps to death; but I swear to you, by all that I hold most sacred, that I am innocent of this murder.'

'My darling!' She made a step forward, but her father stepped before her.

'Keep back,' he said, in a hard voice; 'there is nothing between you and that man now.'

She turned round with an ashen face, but with a proud look in her clear eyes.

'You are wrong,' she answered, with a touch of scorn in her voice. 'I love him more now than I did before.' Then, before her father could stop her, she placed her arms round her lover's neck, and kissed him wildly on the cheek.

'My darling,' she said, with the tears streaming down her white cheeks, 'whatever the world may say, you are always dearest of all to me.'

Brian kissed her passionately, and then moved away, while Madge fell down at her father's feet in a dead faint.

XI
Counsel for the Prisoner

Brian Fitzgerald was arrested a few minutes past three o'clock, and by five all Melbourne was ringing with the news that the perpetrator of the now famous hansom cab murder had been caught. The evening papers were full of the affair, and the *Herald* went through several editions, the demand being far in the excess of the supply. Such a crime had not been committed in Melbourne since the Greer shooting case in the Opera House, and the mystery which surrounded it made it even more sensational. The committal of the crime in such an extraordinary place as a hansom cab had been startling enough, but the discovery that the assassin was one of the most fashionable young men in Melbourne was still more so. Brian Fitzgerald being well known in society as a wealthy squatter, and the future husband of one of the richest and prettiest girls in Victoria, it was no wonder that his arrest caused quite a sensation. The *Herald*, which was fortunate enough to obtain the earliest information about the arrest, made the best use of it, and published a flaming article in its most sensational type, somewhat after this fashion:

HANSOM CAB TRAGEDY

ARREST OF THE SUPPOSED MURDERER

STARTLING REVELATIONS IN HIGH LIFE

It is needless to say that some of the reporters had painted the lily pretty freely, but the public believed everything that came out in the papers to be gospel truth.

Mr Frettlby, the day after Brian's arrest, had a long conversation with his daughter, and wanted her to go up to Yabba Yallook Station until the public excitement had somewhat subsided. But this Madge flatly refused to do.

'I'm not going to desert him when he most needs me,' she said, resolutely; 'everybody has turned against him, even before they have heard the facts of the case. He says he is not guilty, and I believe him.'

'Then let him prove his innocence,' said her father, who was pacing slowly up and down the room; 'if he did not get into the cab with Whyte he must have been somewhere else, so he ought to set up the defence of an *alibi*.'

'He can easily do that,' said Madge, with a ray of hope lighting up her sad face; 'he was here till eleven o'clock on Thursday night.'

'Very probably,' returned her father dryly; 'but where was he at one o'clock on Friday morning?'

'Besides, Mr Whyte left the house long before Brian did,' she went on rapidly. 'You must remember — it was when you quarrelled with Mr Whyte.'

'My dear Madge,' said Frettlby, stopping in front of her with a displeased look, 'you are incorrect — Whyte and myself did not quarrel. He asked me if it were true that Fitzgerald was engaged to you, and I answered yes. That was all, and then he left the house.'

'Yes, and Brian didn't go until two hours after,' said Madge, triumphantly. 'He never saw Mr Whyte the whole night.'

'So he says,' replied Mr Frettlby, significantly.

'I believe Brian before any one else in the world,' said his daughter, hotly, with flushed cheeks and flashing eyes.

'Ah! But will a jury?' queried her father.

'You have turned against him, too,' answered Madge, her eyes filling with tears. 'You believe him guilty.'

'I am not prepared either to deny or confirm his guilt,' said Mr Frettlby, coldly. 'I have done what I could to help him — I have engaged Calton to defend him, and, if eloquence and skill can save him, you may set your mind at rest.'

'My dear father,' said Madge, throwing her arms round his neck, 'I knew you would not desert him altogether, for my sake.'

'My darling,' replied her father, in a faltering voice, as he kissed her, 'there is nothing in the world I would not do for your sake.'

Meanwhile Brian was sitting in his cell in the Melbourne Jail, thinking sadly enough about his position. He saw no hope of escape except one, and that he did not intend to take advantage of.

'It would kill her; it would kill her,' he said, feverishly, as he paced to and fro over the echoing stones. 'Better that the last of the Fitzgeralds should perish like a common thief than that she should know the bitter truth. If I engage a lawyer to defend me,' he went on, 'the first question he will ask me will be where was I on that night, and if I tell him all will be discovered, and then — no — no — I cannot do it; it would kill her, my darling,' and throwing himself down on the bed, he covered his face with his hands.

He was roused by the opening of the door of his cell, and on looking up saw that it was Calton who entered. He was a great friend of Fitzgerald's, and Brian was deeply touched by his kindness in coming to see him. Duncan Calton had a kindly heart, and was anxious to help Brian, but there was also a touch of self-interest in the matter. He had received a note from Mr Frettlby, asking him to defend Fitzgerald, which he agreed to do with avidity, as he foresaw in this case an opportunity for his name becoming known throughout the Australian colonies. It is true that he was already a celebrated lawyer, but his reputation was purely a local one, and as he foresaw that Fitzgerald's trial for murder would cause a great sensation throughout Australia and New Zealand, therefore determined to take advantage of it as another step in the ladder which led to fame, wealth, and position. So this tall, keen-eyed man, with the clean-shaven face and expressive mouth, advanced into the cell, and took Brian by the hand.

'It is very kind of you to come and see me,' said Fitzgerald; 'it is at a time like this that one appreciates friendship.'

'Yes, of course,' answered the lawyer, fixing his keen eyes on the other's haggard face, as if he would read his innermost thoughts. 'I came partly on my own account, and partly because Frettlby asked me to see you as to your defence.'

'Mr Frettlby?' said Brian, in a mechanical way. 'He is very kind; I thought he believed me guilty.'

'No man is considered guilty until he has been proved so,' answered Calton, evasively.

Brian noticed how guarded the answer was, for he heaved an impatient sigh.

'And Miss Frettlby?' he asked, in a hesitating manner. This time he got a decided answer.

'She declines to believe you guilty, and will not hear a word said against you.'

'God bless her,' said Brian, fervently, 'she is a true woman. I suppose I am pretty well canvassed?' he added, bitterly.

'Nothing else talked about,' answered Calton, calmly. 'Your arrest has for the present suspended all interest in theatres, cricket matches, and balls, and you are at the present moment being discussed threadbare in clubs and drawing-rooms.'

Fitzgerald writhed. He was a singularly proud man, and there was something inexpressibly galling in this unpleasant publicity.

'But this is all idle chatter,' said Calton, taking a seat. 'We must get to business. Of course, you will accept me as your counsel.'

'It's no good my doing so,' replied Brian, gloomily. 'The rope is already round my neck.'

'Nonsense,' replied the lawyer, cheerfully, 'the rope is round no man's neck until he is on the scaffold. Now, you need not say a word,' he went on, holding up his hand as Brian was about to speak; 'I am going to defend you in this case, whether you like it or not. I do not know all the facts, except what the papers have stated, and they exaggerate so much that one can place no reliance on them. At all events, I believe from my heart that you are innocent, and you must walk out of the prisoner's dock a free man, if only for the sake of that noble girl who loves you.'

Brian did not answer, but put out his hand, which the other grasped warmly.

'I will not deny,' went on Calton, 'that there is a little bit of professional curiosity about me. This case is such an extraordinary one, that I feel as if I were unable to let slip an opportunity of doing something with it. I don't care for your humdrum murders with the poker, and all that sort of thing, but this is something clever, and therefore interesting. When you are safe we will together look for the real criminal, and the pleasure of the search will be proportionate to the excitement when we find him out.'

'I agree with everything you say,' said Fitzgerald, calmly, 'but I have no defence to make.'

'No defence? You are not going to confess you killed him?'

'No,' with an angry flush, 'but there are certain circumstances which prevent me from defending myself.'

'What nonsense,' retorted Calton, sharply, 'as if any circumstances should prevent a man from saving his own life. But never mind, I like these objections, they make the nut harder to crack — but the kernel must be worth getting at. Now, you have to answer me certain questions.'

'I won't promise.'

'Well, we shall see,' said the lawyer, cheerfully, taking out his note-book, and resting it on his knee. 'First, where were you on the Thursday night preceding the murder?'

'I can't tell you.'

'Oh, yes, you can, my friend. You left St Kilda, and came up to town by the eleven o'clock train.'

'Eleven twenty,' corrected Brian.

Calton smiled in a gratified manner as he noted this down. 'A little diplomacy is all that's required,' he said, mentally. 'And where did you go then?' he added, aloud.

'I met Rolleston in the train, and we took a cab from the Flinders Street station up to the Club.'

'What Club?'

'The Melbourne Club.'

'Yes?' interrogatively.

'Rolleston went home, and I went into the Club and played cards for a time.'

'When did you leave the Club?'

'A few minutes to one o'clock in the morning.'

'And then, I suppose, you went home?'

'No, I did not.'

'Then where did you go?'

'Down the street.'

'Rather vague. I presume you mean Collins Street?'

'Yes.'

'You were going to meet someone, I suppose?'

'I never said so.'

'Probably not; but young men don't wander about the streets at night without some object.'

'I was restless, and wanted a walk.'

'Indeed! How curious you should prefer going into the heart of the dusty town for a walk to strolling through the Fitzroy Gardens, which were on your way home! It won't do; you had an appointment to meet someone.'

'Well — er — yes.'

'I thought as much. Man or woman?'

'I cannot tell you.'

'Then I must find out for myself.'

'You can't.'

'Indeed! Why not?'

'You don't know where to look for her.'

'Her,' cried Calton, delighted at the success of his craftily-put question. 'I knew it was a woman.'

Brian did not answer, but sat biting his lips with vexation.

'Now, who is this woman?'

No answer.

'Come now, Fitzgerald, I know that young men will be young men, and of course you don't like these things talked about; but in this case your character must be sacrificed to save your neck. What is her name?'

'I can't tell you.'

'Oh! You know it, then?'

'Well, yes.'

'And you won't tell me?'

'No!'

Calton, however, had found out two things that pleased him; first, that Fitzgerald had an appointment, and, second, it was with a woman. He went on another line.

'When did you last see Whyte?'

Brian answered with great reluctance, 'I saw him drunk by the Scotch Church.'

'What! You were the man who hailed the hansom?'

'Yes,' assented the other, hesitating slightly, 'I was!'

The thought flashed through Calton's brain as to whether the young man before him was guilty or not, and he was obliged to confess things looked very black against him.

'Then what the newspapers said was correct?'

'Partly.'

'Ah!' Calton drew a long breath — here was a ray of hope.

'You did not know it was Whyte when you found him lying drunk near the Scotch Church?'

'No, I did not. Had I known it was he I would not have picked him up.'

'Of course you recognised him afterwards?'

'Yes, I did. And, as the paper stated, dropped him and walked away.'

'Why did you leave him so abruptly?'

Brian looked at his questioner in some surprise.

'Because I detested him,' he said, shortly.

'Why did you detest him?'

No answer.

'Was it because he had admired Miss Frettlby, and from all appearances, was going to marry her?'

'Well, yes,' sullenly.

'And now,' said Calton, impressively, 'this is the whole point upon which the case turns — why did you get into the cab with him?'

'I did not get into the cab.'

'The cabman declares that you did.'

'He is wrong. I never came back after I recognised Whyte.'

'Then who was the man who got into the cab with Whyte?'

'I don't know.'

'You have no idea?'

'Not the least.'

'You are certain?'

'Yes, perfectly certain.'

'He seems to have been dressed exactly like you.'

'Very probably. I could name at least a dozen of my acquaintances who wear light coats over their evening dress, and soft hats.'

'Do you know if Whyte had any enemies?'

'No, I don't; I know nothing about him, beyond that he came from England a short time ago with a letter of introduction to Mr Frettlby, and had the impertinence to ask Madge to marry him.'

'Where did Whyte live?'

'Down in St Kilda, at the end of Grey Street.'

'How do you know?'

'It was in the papers, and — and —' hesitatingly, 'I called on him.'

'Why?'

'To see if he would drop asking Madge to marry him, and to tell him that she was engaged to me.'

'And what did he say?'

'Laughed at me. Curse him.'

'You had high words, evidently?'

Brian laughed bitterly.

'Yes, we had.'

'Did anyone hear you?'

'The landlady did, I think. I saw her in the passage as I left the house.'

'The prosecution will bring her forward as a witness.'

'Very likely,' indifferently.

'Did you say anything likely to criminate yourself?'

Fitzgerald turned away his head.

'Yes,' he answered in a low voice, 'I spoke very wildly — indeed, I did not know at the time what I said.'

'Did you threaten him?'

'Yes, I did. I told him I would kill him if he persisted in his plan of marrying Madge.'

'Ah! If the landlady can swear that she heard you say so, it will form a strong piece of evidence against you. As far as I can see, there is only one defence, and that is an easy one — you must prove an *alibi*.'

No answer.

'You say you did not come back and get into the cab?' said Calton, watching the face of the other closely.

'No, it was someone else dressed like me.'

'And you have no idea who it was?'

'No, I have not.'

'Then, after you left Whyte, and walked along Russell Street, where did you go?'

'I can't tell you.'

'Were you intoxicated?'

'No!' indignantly.

'Then you remember?'
'Yes.'
'And where were you?'
'I can't tell you.'
'You refuse?'
'Yes, I do.'
'Take time to consider. You may have to pay a heavy price for your refusal.'
'If necessary, I will pay it.'
'And you won't tell me where you were?'
'No, I won't.'
Calton was beginning to feel annoyed.
'You're very foolish,' he said, 'sacrificing your life to some feeling of false modesty. You must prove an *alibi*.'
No answer.
'What time did you get home?'
'About two o'clock in the morning.'
'Did you walk home?'
'Yes — through the Fitzroy Gardens.'
'Did you see anyone on your way home?'
'I don't know. I wasn't paying attention.'
'Did anyone see you?'
'Not that I know of.'
'Then you refuse to tell me where you were between one and two o'clock on Friday morning?'
'Absolutely!'
Calton thought for a moment, to consider his next move.
'Do you know that Whyte carried valuable papers about with him?'
Fitzgerald hesitated, and turned pale.
'No! I did not know,' he said, reluctantly.
The lawyer made a master stroke.
'Then why did you take them from him?'
'What! Had he it with him?'
Calton saw his advantage, and seized it at once.
'Yes, he had it with him. Why did you take it?'
'I did not take it. I didn't even know he had it with him.'
'Indeed! Will you kindly tell me what "it" is?'
Brian saw the trap into which he had fallen.

'No! I will not,' he answered steadily.

'Was it a jewel?'

'No!'

'Was it an important paper?'

'I don't know.'

'Ah! It was a paper. I can see it in your face. And was that paper of importance to you?'

'Why do you ask?'

Calton fixed his keen grey eyes steadily on Brian's face.

'Because,' he answered slowly, 'the man to whom that paper was of such value murdered Whyte.'

Brian started up, ghastly pale.

'My God!' he almost shrieked, stretching out his hands, 'it is true after all,' and he fell down on the stone pavement in a dead faint.

Calton, alarmed, summoned the gaoler, and between them they placed him on the bed, and dashed some cold water over his face. He recovered, and moaned feebly, while Calton, seeing that he was unfit to be spoken to, left the prison. When he got outside he stopped for a moment and looked back on the grim grey walls.

'Brian Fitzgerald,' he said to himself, 'you did not commit the murder yourself, but you know who did.'

XII
She was a True Woman

Melbourne society was greatly agitated over the hansom cab murder. Before the assassin had been discovered it had been merely looked upon as a common murder, and one that society need take no cognisance of beyond the fact that it was something new to talk about. But now the affair was assuming gigantic proportions, since the assassin had been discovered to be one of the most fashionable young men in Melbourne. Mrs Grundy was shocked, and openly talked about having nourished a viper in her bosom, which had turned unexpectedly and stung her. In Toorak drawing-rooms and Melbourne clubs the matter was talked about morn, noon, and night, and Mrs Grundy declared positively that she never heard of such a thing. Here was a young man, well born — 'the Fitzgeralds, my dear, an Irish family, with royal blood in their veins' — well-bred — 'most charming manners, I assure you, and so very good-looking' and engaged to one of the richest girls in Melbourne — 'pretty enough, madam, no doubt, but he wanted her money, sly dog.' And this young man, who had been petted by the ladies, voted a good fellow by the men, and was universally popular, both in drawing-room and club, had committed a vulgar murder — it was truly shocking. What was the world coming to, and what were gaols and lunatic asylums built for if men of young Fitzgerald's calibre were not put in them, and kept from killing people? And then, of course, everybody kept asking everybody else who Whyte was, and why he had never been heard of before. All people who had met Mr Whyte were worried to death with questions about him, and underwent a species of social martyrdom as to who he was, what he was like, why he was killed, and all the rest of the insane questions which some people will ask. It was talked about everywhere — in fashionable drawing-rooms at five o'clock tea, over thin bread and butter and souchong; at clubs, over brandies and sodas and cigarettes; by working men over their mid-day pint, and by their wives in the congenial atmosphere of the back yard over the wash-tub. The papers were full of paragraphs about the famous murder, and the society papers gave an interview with the prisoner by their special reporters, and which had been composed by those gentlemen out of the floating rumours which they heard around, and their own fertile imagination. In fact, one young man of literary tendencies had been so struck by the dramatic capabilities of the affair that he thought of writing a five-act drama on it — with a sensation scene of the hanging of Fitzgerald — and had an idea of offering it to Williamson for production at the Theatre Royal. But that astute manager refused to entertain the idea, with the dry remark that as the fifth act had not been played out in real life, he did not see how the dramatist could end it satisfactorily. As to the prisoner's guilt, everyone was certain of that. The cabman Royston had sworn that Fitzgerald had got into the cab with Whyte, and when he got out Whyte was dead. There could be no stronger proof than that, and the general opinion was that the prisoner would put in no defence, but would throw himself on the mercy of the court. Even the church caught the contagion, and ministers — Anglican, Roman Catholic, and Presbyterian, together with the lesser lights of minor denominations — took the hansom cab murder as a text whereon to preach sermons on the profligacy of the age, and to point out that the only ark which could save men from the rising flood of infidelity and immorality was their own particular church. 'Gad,' as Calton remarked, after hearing five or six ministers each claim their own church as the one special vessel of safety, 'there seems to be a whole fleet of arks!'

As to Mr Felix Rolleston, it was a time of great joy to him, knowing as he did all the circumstances of the case, and the *dramatis personae.* When any new evidence came to light, Rolleston was the first to know all about it, and would go round to his friends and relate it with certain additions of his own, which rendered it more piquant and dramatic. But when asked his opinion as to the guilt of the accused he would shake his head sagaciously, and hint that both he and his dear friend Calton — he knew Calton to nod to — could not make up their minds upon the matter.

'Fact is, don't you know,' observed Mr Rolleston, wisely, 'there's more in this than meets the eye, and all that sort of thing — think 'tective fellers wrong myself — don't think Fitz killed Whyte; jolly well sure he didn't.'

Then, of course, after such an observation, a chorus, chiefly feminine, would arise: 'Then who killed him?'

'Aha,' Felix would retort, putting his head on one side, like a meditative sparrow; ''tective fellers can't find out; that's the difficulty. Good mind to go on the prowl myself, by Jove.'

'But do you know anything of the detective business?' someone would ask.

'Oh, dear, yes,' with an airy wave of his hand; 'I've read Gaboreau, you know; awfully jolly life, 'tectives.'

Mr Rolleston, however, in spite of his asseverations, had no grounds for his belief that Fitzgerald was innocent, and in his heart of hearts thought him guilty. But then he was one of those people who, having either tender hearts or obstinate natures — more particularly the latter — always make a point of coming forward as champions of those in trouble with the world at large. There are, no doubt, many people who think that Nero was a pleasant young man, whose cruelties were merely an overflow of high spirits; and who regard Henry VIII as a henpecked husband, who was unfortunate in having six wives. It is these kind of people who delight in sympathising with great criminals of the Ned Kelly sort, and look upon them as embodiments of heroism, badly treated by the narrow understanding of the law. There is a proverb to the effect that the world kicks a man when he is down; but if one half of the world does act in such a brutal manner, the other consoles the prostrate individual with half-pence. So, taking things as a whole, though the weight of public opinion was dead against the innocence of Fitzgerald, still he had his friends and sympathisers, who stood up for him and declared that he had been wrongly accused.

The opinions of these kindly individuals were told to Madge, and she was much comforted thereby. Other people thought him innocent, and she was firmly convinced that they were right. If the whole of Melbourne had unanimously condemned Brian she would have still believed in his innocence. But then women are so singularly illogical — the world may be against a man, but the woman who loves him will stand boldly forth as his champion. No matter how low, how vile a man may be, if a woman loves him she exalts him to the rank of a demi-god, and refuses to see the clay feet of her idol. When all others forsake she clings to him, when all others frown she smiles on him, and when he dies she reverences his memory as that of a saint and a martyr. Young men of the present day are very fond of running down women, and think it a manly thing to sneer at them for their failings; but God help the man who, in time of trouble, has not a woman to stand by his side with cheering words and loving smiles to help him in the battle of life. And so Madge Frettlby, true woman as she was, had nailed her colours to the mast, and refused to surrender to anyone, whatever arguments they brought against her. He was innocent, and his innocence would be proved, for she had an intuitive feeling that he would be saved at the eleventh hour. How, she knew not; but she was certain that it would be so. She would have gone and seen Brian in prison, but that her father absolutely forbade her doing so, and she was dependent upon Calton for all the news respecting him, and any message which she wished conveyed.

Calton was very much annoyed at Brian's persistent refusal to set up the defence of an *alibi*, and, as he felt sure that the young man could do so, he was anxious to find out the reason why he would not do so.

'If it's for the sake of a woman,' he said to Brian, 'I don't care who she is, it's absurdly Quixotic. Self-preservation is the first law of nature, and if my neck was in danger I'd spare neither man, woman, nor child to save it.'

'I dare say,' answered Brian; 'but if you had my reasons you might think differently.'

In his own mind the lawyer had a theory which sufficiently accounted for Brian's refusal to answer for his doings on that night. Fitzgerald had admitted that he had an appointment on that night, and that it was with a woman. He was a handsome fellow, and probably his morals were no better than those of other young men, so Calton thought that Brian had some intrigue with a married woman, and had been with her on the night in question; hence his refusal to speak. If he did so her name would be brought into the matter; the outraged husband, whosoever he might be, would interpose, and the whole affair would probably end in the Divorce Court.

'It's better for him to lose his character than his life,' argued Calton, 'and that woman ought to speak — it would be hard on her, I admit, but when a man's neck is in danger she ought to risk anything rather than see him hanged.'

Full of these perplexing thoughts, Calton went down to St Kilda to have a talk with Madge over the matter, and also to see if she would help him to obtain the information he wanted. He had a great respect for Madge, knowing what a clever woman she was, and thought that, seeing Brian was so deeply in love with her, if she saw him about the matter he might be induced to confess everything.

The lawyer found Madge waiting anxiously to see him, and when he entered she sprang forward with a cry of delight.

'Oh, where have you been all this time?' she said, anxiously, as they sat down. 'I have been counting every moment since I saw you last. How is he — my poor darling?'

'Just the same,' answered Calton, taking off his gloves, 'still obstinately refusing to save his own life. Where's your father?' he asked, suddenly.

'Out of town,' she answered, impatiently. 'He will not be back for a week — but what do you mean that he won't save his own life?'

Calton leaned forward, and took her hand.

'Do you want to save his life?' he asked.

'Save his life,' she reiterated, starting up out of her chair with a cry; 'God knows, I would die to save him.'

'Pish,' murmured Calton to himself, as he looked at her glowing face and outstretched hands, 'these women are always in extremes. The fact is,' he said aloud, 'Fitzgerald is able to prove an *alibi*, and he refuses to do so.'

'But why?'

Calton shrugged his shoulders.

'That is best known to himself — some Quixotic idea of honour, I fancy. Now, he refuses to tell me where he was on that night; perhaps he won't refuse to tell you — so you must come up and see him with me, and perhaps he will recover his senses, and confess.'

'But my father,' she faltered.

'Did you not say he was out of town?' asked Calton.

'Yes,' hesitated Madge. 'But he told me not to go.'

'In that case,' said Calton, rising and taking up his hat and gloves, 'I won't ask you.'

She laid her hand on his arm.

'Stop! Will it do any good?'

Calton hesitated a moment, for he thought that if the reason of Brian's silence was, as he surmised, an intrigue with a married woman, he would certainly not tell the girl he was engaged to about it — but, on the other hand, there might be some other reason, and Calton trusted to Madge to find it out. With these thoughts in his mind he turned round.

'Yes,' he answered, boldly, 'it may save his life.'

'Then I will go,' she answered recklessly. 'He is more to me than my father, and if I can save him, I will. Wait,' and she ran out of the room.

'An uncommonly plucky girl,' murmured the lawyer, as he looked out of the window. 'If Fitzgerald is not a fool he will certainly tell her all — that is, of course, if he is able to — queer things these women are — I quite agree with Balzac's saying that no wonder man couldn't understand woman, seeing that God who created her failed to do so.'

Madge came back dressed to go out, with a heavy veil over her face.

'Shall I order the carriage?' she asked, pulling on her gloves with trembling fingers.

'Hardly,' answered Calton dryly, 'unless you want to see a paragraph in the society papers to the effect that Miss Madge Frettlby visited Mr Fitzgerald in gaol — no — no — we'll get a cab. Come, my dear,' and taking her arm he led her away.

They reached the station, and caught a train just as it started, yet notwithstanding this Madge was in a fever of impatience.

'How slow it goes,' she said, fretfully.

'Hush, my dear,' said Calton, laying his hand on her arm. 'You will betray yourself — we'll arrive soon — and save him.'

'Oh, God grant we may,' she said with a low cry, clasping her hands tightly together, while Calton could see the tears falling from under her thick veil.

'This is not the way to do so,' he said, almost roughly, 'you'll go into hysterics soon — control yourself for his sake.'

'For his sake,' she muttered, and with a powerful effort of will, calmed herself. They soon arrived in Melbourne, and, getting a hansom, drove up quickly to the gaol. After going through the usual formula, they entered the cell where Brian was, and, when the warder who accompanied them opened the door, found the young man seated on his bed, with his face buried in his hands. He looked up, and, on seeing Madge, rose and held out his hands with a cry of delight. She ran forward, and threw herself on his breast with a stifled sob. For a short time no one spoke — Calton being at the other end of the cell, busy with some notes which he had taken from his pocket, and the warder having retired.

'My poor darling,' said Madge, stroking back the soft, fair hair from his flushed forehead, 'how ill you look.'

'Yes!' answered Fitzgerald, with a hard laugh. 'Prison does not improve a man — does it?'

'Don't speak in that tone, Brian,' she said; 'it is not like you — let us sit down and talk calmly over the matter.'

'I don't see what good that will do,' he answered, wearily, as they sat down hand-in-hand. 'I have talked about it to Calton till my head aches, and it is no good.'

'Of course not,' retorted the lawyer, sharply, as he also sat down. 'Nor will it be any good until you come to your senses, and tell us where you were on that night.'

'I tell you I cannot.'

'Brian, dear,' said Madge, softly, taking his hand, 'you must tell all — for my sake.'

Fitzgerald sighed — this was the hardest temptation he had yet been subjected to — he felt half inclined to yield, and chance the result — but one look at Madge's pure face steeled him against doing so. What could his confession bring but sorrow and regret to one whom he loved better than his life.

'Madge!' he answered, gravely, taking her hand again, 'you do not know what you ask.'

'Yes, I do!' she replied, quickly. 'I ask you to save yourself — to prove that you are not guilty of this terrible crime, and not to sacrifice your life for the sake of — of —'

Here she stopped, and looked helplessly at Calton, for she had no idea of the reason of Fitzgerald's refusal to speak.

'For the sake of a woman,' finished Calton, bluntly.

'A woman!' she faltered, still holding her lover's hand. 'Is — is — is that the reason?'

Brian averted his face.

'Yes!' he said, in a low, rough voice.

A sharp expression of anguish crossed her pale face, and, sinking her head on her hands, she wept bitterly. Brian looked at her in a dogged kind of way, and Calton stared grimly at them both.

'Look here,' he said, at length, to Brian, in an angry voice; 'if you want my opinion of your conduct, I think you're an infernal scoundrel — begging your pardon, my dear, for the expression. Here is this noble girl, who loves you with her whole heart, and is ready to sacrifice everything for your sake, comes to implore you to save your life, and you coolly turn round, and acknowledge that you love another woman.'

Brian lifted his head haughtily, and his face flushed.

'You are wrong,' he said, turning round sharply; 'there is the woman for whose sake I keep silence;' and, rising up from the bed, he pointed to Madge, as she sobbed bitterly on it.

She lifted up her haggard face with an air of surprise.

'For my sake!' she cried, in a startled voice.

'Oh, he's mad,' said Calton, shrugging his shoulders; 'I will put in a defence of insanity.'

'No, I am not mad,' cried Fitzgerald, wildly, as he caught Madge in his arms. 'My darling! My darling! It is for your sake that I keep silence, and will do so though my life pays the penalty. I could tell you where I was on that night and save myself; but if I did, you would learn a secret which would curse your life, and I dare not speak — I dare not.'

Madge looked up into his face with a pitiful smile as her tears fell fast.

'Dearest!' she said, softly. 'Do not think of me, but only of yourself; better that I should endure misery than that you should die. I do not know what the secret can be, but if the telling of it will save your life, do not hesitate. See,' she cried, falling on her knees, 'I am at your feet — I implore you by all the love you ever had for me, save yourself, whatever the consequences may be to me.'

'Madge,' said Fitzgerald, as he raised her in his arms, 'at one time I might have done so, but now it is too late. There is another and stronger reason for my silence, which I have only found out since my arrest. I know that I am closing up the one way of escape from this charge of murder, of which I am innocent; but as there is a God in heaven, I swear that I will not speak.'

There was a silence in the cell, only broken by Madge's convulsive sobs, and even Calton, cynical man of the world though he was, felt his eyes grow wet. Brian led Madge over to him, and placed her in his arms.

'Take her away,' he said, in a broken voice, 'or I shall forget I am a man;' and turning away he threw himself on his bed, and covered his face with his hands. Calton did not answer him, but summoned the warder, and tried to lead Madge away. But just as they reached the door she broke away from him, and, running back, flung herself on her lover's breast.

'My darling! My darling!' she sobbed, kissing him, 'you shall not die. I will save you in spite of yourself;' and, as if afraid to trust herself any longer, she ran out of the cell, followed by the barrister.

XIII
Madge Makes a Discovery

Madge stepped into the cab, and Calton paused a moment to tell the cabman to drive to the railway station, when she stopped him.

'Tell him to drive to Brian's lodgings in Powlett Street,' she said, laying her hand on Calton's arm.

'What for?' asked the lawyer, in astonishment.

'And also to go past the Melbourne Club, as I want to stop there.'

'What the deuce does she mean?' muttered Calton, as he gave the necessary orders, and stepped into the cab.

'And now,' he asked, looking at his companion, who had let down her veil, while the cab rattled quickly down the street, 'what do you intend to do?'

She threw back her veil, and he was astonished to see the sudden change which had come over her. There were no tears now, and her eyes were hard and glittering, while her mouth was firmly closed. She looked like a woman who had determined to do a certain thing, and would carry out her intentions at whatever cost.

'I am going to save Brian in spite of himself,' she said, very distinctly.

'But how?'

'Ah, you think that, being a woman, I can do nothing,' she said, bitterly. 'Well, you shall see.'

'I beg your pardon,' retorted Calton, with a grim smile, 'my opinion of your sex has always been an excellent one — every lawyer's is; stands to reason that it should be so, seeing that a woman is at the bottom of nine cases out of ten.'

'The old cry.'

'Nevertheless a true one,' answered Calton. 'Ever since the time of Father Adam it has been acknowledged that women influence the world either for good or evil more than men. But this is not the point,' he went on, rather impatiently. 'What do you propose to do?'

'Simply this,' she answered. 'In the first place, I may tell you that I do not understand Brian's statement that he keeps silence for my sake, as there are no secrets in my life that can justify him saying so, but the facts of the case are simply these: Brian, on the night in question, left our place, at St Kilda, at eleven o'clock. He told me he would call at the Club to see if there were any letters for him, and then go straight home.'

'But he might have said that merely as a blind.'

Madge shook her head.

'No, I don't think so. I never asked him where he was going, and he told me quite spontaneously. I know Brian's character, and he would not go and tell a deliberate lie, especially when there was no necessity for it. I am quite certain that he intended to do as he said, and go straight home. When he got to the Club, he found a letter there, which caused him to alter his mind.'

'But who did he receive the letter from?'

'Can't you guess?' she said impatiently. 'From the person, man or woman, who wanted to see him and reveal this secret about me, whatever it is. He got the letter at his Club, and went down Collins Street to meet the writer. At the corner of the Scotch Church he found Mr Whyte, and on recognising him, left in disgust, and walked down Russell Street to keep his appointment.'

'Then you don't think he came back.'

'I am certain he did not, for, as Brian told you, there are plenty of young men who wear the same kind of coat and hat as he does. Who the second man who got into the cab was I do not know, but I will swear that it was not Brian.'

'And you are going to look for that letter?'

'Yes, in Brian's lodgings.'

'He might have burnt it.'

'He might have done a thousand things, but he did not,' she answered. 'Brian is the most careless man in the world; he would put the letter into his pocket, or throw it into the waste paper basket, and never think of it again.'

'In this case he did, however.'

'Yes, he thought of the conversation he had with the writer, but not of the letter itself. Depend upon it, we will find it in his desk, or in one of the pockets of the clothes he wore that night.'

'Then there's another thing,' said Calton, thoughtfully. 'The letter might have been delivered to him between the Elizabeth Street Railway Station and the Club.'

'We can soon find out about that,' answered Madge; 'for Mr Rolleston was with him at that time.'

'So he was,' answered Calton; 'and here is Rolleston coming down the street. We'll ask him now.'

The cab was just passing the Burke and Wills' monument, and Calton's quick eye had caught a glimpse of Rolleston coming down the street on the left-hand side. What first attracted Calton's attention was the glittering appearance of Felix. His well-brushed top-hat glittered, his varnished boots glittered, and his diamond rings and scarf-pin glittered; in fact, so resplendent was his appearance that he looked like an animated diamond coming along in the blazing sunshine. The cab drove up to the kerbing, and Rolleston stopped short, as Calton sprang out directly in front of him. Madge lay back in the cab and pulled down her veil, not wishing to be recognised by Felix, as she knew that if he did it would soon be all over the town.

'Hallo, old chap!' said Rolleston, in considerable astonishment. 'Where did you spring from?'

'From the cab, of course,' answered Calton, with a laugh.

'A kind of *Deus ex machina*,' replied Rolleston, attempting a bad pun.

'Exactly,' said Calton. 'Look here, Rolleston, do you remember the night of Whyte's murder — you met Fitzgerald at the Railway Station.'

'In the train,' corrected Felix.

'Well, well, no matter, you came up with him to the Club.'

'Yes, and left him there.'

'Did you notice if he received any message while he was with you?'

'Any message?' repeated Felix. 'No, he did not; we were talking together the whole time, and he spoke to no one but me.'

'Was he in good spirits?'

'Excellent, made me laugh awfully — but why all this thusness?'

'Oh, nothing,' answered Calton, getting back into the cab. 'I wanted a little information from you; I'll explain next time I see you! — Goodbye.'

'But I say,' began Felix, but the cab had already rattled away, so Mr Rolleston turned angrily away.

'I never saw anything like these lawyers,' he said to himself. 'Calton's a perfect whirlwind, by Jove.'

Meanwhile Calton was talking to Madge.

'You were right,' he said, 'there must have been a message for him at the Club, for he got none from the time he left your place.'

'And what shall we do now?' asked Madge, who, having heard all the conversation, did not trouble about questioning the lawyer about it.

'Find out at the Club if any letter was waiting for him on that night,' said Calton, as the cab stopped at the door of the Melbourne Club. 'Here we are,' and with a hasty word to Madge, he ran up the steps.

He went to the office of the Club to find out if any letters had been waiting for Fitzgerald, and found there a waiter with whom he was pretty well acquainted.

'Look here, Brown,' said the lawyer, 'do you remember on that Thursday night when the hansom cab murder took place if any letters were waiting here for Mr Fitzgerald?'

'Well, really, sir,' hesitated Brown, 'it's so long ago that I almost forget.'

Calton gave him a sovereign.

'Oh! It's not that, Mr Calton,' said the waiter, pocketing the coin, nevertheless. 'But I really do forget.'

'Try and remember,' said Calton, shortly.

Brown made a tremendous effort of memory, and at last gave a satisfactory answer.

'No, sir, there were none!'

'Are you sure?' said Calton, feeling a thrill of disappointment.

'Quite sure, sir,' replied the other, confidently, 'I went to the letter rack several times that night, and I am sure there were none for Mr Fitzgerald.'

'Ah! I thought as much,' said Calton, heaving a sigh.

'Stop!' said Brown, as though struck with a sudden idea. 'Though there was no letter came by post, sir, there was one brought to him on that night.'

'Ah!' said Calton, turning sharply. 'At what time?'

'Just before twelve o'clock, sir.'

'Who brought it?'

'A young woman, sir,' said Brown, in a tone of disgust.

'A bold thing, beggin' your pardon, sir; and no better than she should be. She bounced in at the door as bold as brass, and sings out, “Is he in?” “Get out,” I says, “or I’ll call the perlice.” “Oh no you won’t,” says she. “You’ll give him that,” and she shoves a letter into my hands. “Who’s him!” I asks. “I dunno,” she answers. “It’s written there, and I can’t read; give it him at once.” And then she clears out before I could stop her.’

‘And the letter was for Mr Fitzgerald?’

‘Yes, sir; and a precious dirty letter it was, too.’

‘You gave it to him, of course?’

‘I did, sir. He was playing cards, and he put it in his pocket, after having looked at the outside of it, and went on with his game.’

‘Didn’t he open it?’

‘Not then, sir; but he did later on, about a quarter to one o’clock. I was in the room, and he opens it and reads it. Then he says to himself “What d——d impertinence,” and puts it into his pocket.’

‘Was he disturbed?’

‘Well, sir, he looked angry like, and put his coat and hat on, and walked out about five minutes to one.’

‘Ah! And he met Whyte at one,’ muttered Calton. ‘There’s no doubt about it. The letter was an appointment, and he was going to keep it. What kind of a letter was it?’ he asked.

‘Very dirty, sir, in a square envelope; but the paper was good, and so was the writing.’

‘That will do,’ said Calton; ‘I am much obliged to you,’ and he hurried down to where Madge awaited him in the cab.

‘You were right,’ he said to her, when the cab was once more in motion. ‘He got a letter on that night, and went to keep his appointment at the time he met Whyte.’

‘I knew it,’ cried Madge, with delight. ‘You see, we will find it in his lodgings.’

‘I hope so,’ answered Calton; ‘but we must not be too sanguine; he may have destroyed it.’

‘No, he has not,’ she replied. ‘I am convinced it is there.’

‘Well,’ answered Calton, looking at her, ‘I won’t contradict you, for your feminine instincts have done more to discover the truth than my reasonings; but that is often the case with women — they jump in the dark where a man would hesitate, and in nine cases out of ten land safely.’

'Alas for the tenth!' said Miss Frettlby. 'She has to be the one exception to prove the rule.'

She had in a great measure recovered her spirits, and seemed confident that she would save her lover. But Mr Calton saw that her nerves were strung up to the highest pitch, and that it was only her strong will that kept her from breaking down altogether.

'By Jove,' he muttered, in an admiring tone, as he watched her. 'She's a plucky girl, and Fitzgerald is a lucky man to have a woman like that in love with him.'

They soon arrived at Brian's lodgings, and the door was opened by Mrs Sampson, who looked very disconsolate indeed. The poor cricket had been blaming herself severely for the information she had given to the false insurance agent, and the floods of tears which she had wept had apparently had an effect on her physical condition, for she crackled less loudly than usual, though her voice was as shrill as ever.

'That sich a thing should 'ave 'appened to 'im,' she wailed, in her thin, high voice. 'An' me that proud of 'im, not 'avin' any family of my own, except one as died and went up to 'eaving arter 'is father, which I 'opes as they both are now angels, an' friendly, as 'is nature 'ad not developed in this valley of the shadder to determine 'is feelin's towards 'is father when 'e died, bein' carried off by a chill, caused by the change from 'ot to cold, the weather bein' that contrary.'

They had arrived in Brian's sitting-room by this time, and Madge sank into a chair, while Calton, anxious to begin the search, hinted to Mrs Sampson that she could go.

'I'm departin', sir,' piped the cricket, with a sad shake of her head, as she opened the door; 'knowin', as I do, as 'e's as innocent as an unborn babe, an' to think of me 'avin' told that 'orrid pusson who 'ad no regard for the truth all about 'im as is now in a cold cell, not as what the weather ain't warm, an' 'e won't want a fire as long as they allows 'im blankets.'

'What did you tell him?' asked Calton, sharply.

'Ah! You may well say that,' lamented Mrs Sampson, rolling her dingy handkerchief into a ball, and dabbing at her red-rimmed eyes, which had quite a bacchanalian look about them, though, poor soul, it was owing to grief, and not to liquor. ' 'Avin' bin beguiled by that serping in light clothes as wanted to know if 'e allays come 'ome afore twelve, which I said 'e was in the 'abit of doin', tho', to be sure, 'e did sometimes use 'is latch-key.'

'The night of the murder, for instance.'

'Oh! Don't say that, sir,' said Mrs Sampson, with a terrified crackle. 'Me bein' weak an' ailin', tho' comin' of a strong family, as allays lived to a good age, thro' being in the 'abit of wearin' flannels, which my mother's father thought better nor a-spilin' the inside with chemistry.'

'Clever man, that detective,' murmured Calton to himself; 'he got out of her by strategy what he never would have done by force. It's a strong piece of evidence against Fitzgerald, but it does not matter much if he can prove an *alibi*. You'll likely be called as a witness for the prosecution,' he said aloud.

'Me, sir!' squeaked Mrs Sampson, trembling violently, and thereby producing a subdued rustle, as of wind in the trees. 'As I've never bin in the court, 'cept the time as father tooked me for a treat, to 'ear a murder, which there's no denyin' is as good as a play, 'e bein' 'ung, 'avin' 'it 'is wife over the 'ead with the poker when she weren't lookin', and a-berryin' 'er corpse in a back garding, without even a stone to mark the place, let alone a line from the Psalms and a remuneration of 'er virtues.'

'Well, well,' said Calton, rather impatiently, as he opened the door for her. 'Leave us for a short time, there's a good soul; Miss Frettlby and I want to have a rest, and we will ring for you when we are going.'

'Thank you, sir,' said the alachrymose landlady, 'an' I 'opes they won't 'ang 'im, which is sich a choky way of dyin'; but in life we are in death,' she went on, rather incoherently, 'as is well known to them as 'as diseases, an' may be corpsed at any minute, and as —'

Here Calton, unable to restrain his impatience any longer, shut the door, and they heard Mrs Sampson's shrill voice and subdued cracklings die away in the distance.

'Now then,' he said, 'now that we have got rid of that woman and her tongue, where are we to begin?'

'The desk,' replied Madge, going over to it; 'it's the most likely place.'

'Don't think so,' said Calton, shaking his head. 'If, as you say, Fitzgerald is a careless man, he would not have troubled to put it there. However, perhaps we'd better look.'

The desk was very untidy ('Just like Brian,' as Madge remarked) — full of paid and unpaid bills, old letters, playbills, ball-programmes, and several withered flowers. 'Reminiscences of former flirtations,' said Calton, with a laugh, pointing to these.

'I should not wonder,' retorted Miss Frettlby, coolly. 'Brian always was in love with someone or other; but you know what Lytton says, "There are many counterfeits, but only one Eros," so I can afford to forget these things.'

The letter, however, was not to be found in the desk, nor was it in the sitting-room; they tried the bedroom, but with no better result; so Madge was nearly giving up the search in despair, when suddenly Calton's eye fell on the waste-paper basket, which, by some unaccountable reason, they had overlooked in their search. The basket was half full, in fact, more than half, and, on looking at it, a sudden thought struck the lawyer. He rang the bell, and presently Mrs Sampson made her appearance.

'How long has that waste-paper basket been standing like that?' he asked, pointing to it.

'It bein' the only fault I 'ad to find with 'im,' said Mrs Sampson, ''e bein' that untidy that 'e a never let me clean it out until 'e told me pussonlly. 'E said as 'ow 'e throwed things into it as 'e might 'ave to look up again; an' I 'aven't touched it for more nor six weeks, 'opin' you won't think me a bad 'ousekeeper, it bein' 'is own wish — bein' fond of litter an' sich like.'

'Six weeks,' repeated Calton, with a look at Madge. 'Ah, and he got the letter four weeks ago. Depend upon it, we shall find it there.'

Madge gave a cry and, falling on her knees, emptied the basket out on the floor, and both she and Calton were soon as busy among the fragments of paper as though they were rag-pickers.

' 'Opin' they ain't orf their 'eads,' murmured Mrs Sampson, as she went to the door, 'but it looks like it, they bein' —'

Suddenly a cry broke from Madge, as she drew out of the mass of paper a half-burnt letter, written on thick and creamy-looking paper.

'At last,' she cried, rising off her knees, and smoothing it out; 'I knew he had not destroyed it.'

'Pretty nearly, however,' said Calton, as his eye glanced rapidly over it; 'it's almost useless as it is, seeing there's no name to it.'

He took it over to the window and spread it out upon the table. It was dirty, and half burnt, but still it was a clue. The following is a *fac simile* of the letter:

OT VILLA
OORAK
July 26th
Mr Fitzgerald is requeste
on a dying woma
who wants to tell
concerns it
bearer who will
Bourke Street and
street, do not dela

'There is not much to be gained from that, I'm afraid,' said Madge, sadly. 'It shows that he had an appointment — but where?'

Calton did not answer, but, leaning his head on his hands, stared hard at the paper. At last he jumped up with a cry —

'I have it,' he said, in an excited tone. 'Look at that paper; see how creamy and white it is, and, above all, look at the printing in the corner — "OT VILLA, TOORAK." '

'Then he went down to Toorak?'

'In an hour, and back again — hardly.'

'Then it was not written from Toorak?'

'No, it was written in one of the Melbourne back slums.'

'How do you know?'

'Look at the girl who brought it,' said Calton, quickly. 'A disreputable woman, one far more likely to come from the back slums than Toorak. As to the paper, three months ago there was a robbery at Toorak, and this is some of the paper that was stolen by the thieves.'

Madge said nothing, but her sparkling eyes and nervous trembling of the hands showed her excitement.

'I will see a detective this evening,' said Calton, exultingly, 'find out where this letter came from, and go and see who wrote it. We'll save him yet,' he said, placing the precious letter carefully in his pocket-book.

'You think that you will be able to find the woman who wrote that?'

'Hum,' said the lawyer, looking thoughtful, 'she may be dead, as the letter says she is in a dying condition. However, if I can find the woman who delivered the letter at the Club, and who waited for Fitzgerald at the corner of Bourke and Russell Streets, that will be sufficient. All I want to prove is that he was not in the hansom cab with Whyte.'

'And do you think you can do that?'

'Depends upon this letter,' said Calton, enigmatically tapping his pocket-book with his finger. 'I'll tell you tomorrow.'

Shortly afterwards they left the house, and when Calton put Madge safely into the St Kilda train, her heart felt lighter than it had done since Fitzgerald's arrest.

XIV
Another Richmond in the Field

There is an old adage that 'like draws to like,' and the antithesis of this would probably be that unlike keeps as far away from unlike as it possibly can. Sometimes, however, Fate, who seems to take a malignant pleasure in worrying humanity, throws them together, and the result is an eternal conflict between the uncongenial elements. Mr Gorby was a very clever detective, and got on well with every one with the exception of Kilsip. The latter, on the other hand, was equally as clever in his own way, and was a favourite with every one but Gorby. One was fire and the other water, so when they came together there was sure to be trouble. Kilsip, in his outward appearance, was quite different from Gorby, being tall and slender, whereas the other was short and stout. Kilsip was dark and clever-looking, Gorby was not, his face wearing a complacent and satisfied smile, which one would not expect to find on the features of a man who was looked upon as such a clever detective. But it was this very smile that was Mr Gorby's greatest aid in getting information, as people were more ready to tell a kindly and apparently simple man like him all they knew than a sharp-looking fellow like Kilsip, whose ears and eyes seemed always on the alert. The hearts of all went forth to Gorby's sweet smile and insinuating manner, but when Kilsip appeared everyone shut up like an oyster, and each retired promptly into his or her shell like an alarmed snail. The face is not always the index of the mind, in spite of the saying to that effect, and the student of Lavater is not invariably right in his readings of character by means of the features. The only thing sharp about Mr Gorby's appearance was his keen little grey eyes, which he knew how to use so well, and a glance from which startled any unsuspecting person who had been beguiled by the complacent smile and sweet manner. Kilsip, on the contrary, had one of those hawk-like faces, which always seem seeking for prey, with brilliant black eyes, hooked nose, and small, thin-lipped mouth. His complexion was quite colourless, and his hair jet black, so that with his tall slender figure and snake-like movements he was hardly a pleasant object to look upon. He also possessed in a great measure the craft and cunning of the snake, and as long as he conducted his movements in secret was successful, but once he appeared personally on the scene his strange looks seemed to warn people that they might be too communicative. So, taking things all round, although Kilsip was the most clever of the two, yet Gorby, owing to his physical advantages, was the most successful. They each had their followers and admirers, but both men cordially detested one another, seldom meeting without a quarrel. When Gorby, therefore, had the hansom cab murder case put into his hands, the soul of Kilsip was smitten with envy, and when Fitzgerald was arrested, and all the evidence collected by Gorby seemed to point so conclusively to his guilt, Kilsip writhed in secret over the triumph of his enemy. Though he would only have been too glad to have said Gorby had got hold of the wrong man, yet the evidence was so conclusive that such a thought had never entered his head until he received a note from Mr Calton, asking him to call at his office that evening at eight o'clock, with reference to the hansom cab murder. Kilsip knew that Calton was counsel for the prisoner, and instantly guessed that a clue had been discovered, which he was wanted to follow up, and which might prove the prisoner's innocence. Full of this idea, he had determined to devote himself, heart and soul, to whatever Calton wanted him to do, and if he only could prove Gorby wrong, what a triumph it would be. He was so pleased with the possibility of such a thing that, accidentally meeting his rival, he asked him to have a glass. As such a thing had not occurred before, Gorby was somewhat suspicious of such sudden hospitality, but as he flattered himself that he was more than a match for Kilsip, both mentally and physically, he accepted the invitation.

'Ah!' said Kilsip, in his soft, low voice, rubbing his lean white hands together, as they sat over their drinks; 'you are a lucky man to have laid your hands on that hansom cab murderer so quickly.'

'Yes; I flatter myself I did manage it pretty well,' said Gorby, lighting his pipe. 'I had no idea that it would be so simple — though, mind you, it required a lot of thought before I got a proper start.'

'I suppose you're pretty sure he's the man you want?' pursued Kilsip, softly, with a brilliant flash of his black eyes.

'Pretty sure, indeed!' retorted Mr Gorby, scornfully, 'there ain't no pretty sure about it. I'd take my Bible oath he's the man. He and Whyte hated one another. He says to Whyte, "I'll kill you, if I've got to do it in the open street." He meets Whyte drunk, a fact which he acknowledges himself; he clears out, and the cabman swears he comes back; then he gets into the cab with a living man, and when he comes out leaves a dead one; he drives to East Melbourne and gets into the house at a time which his landlady can prove — just the time that a cab would take to drive from the Grammar School on the St Kilda Road. If you ain't a fool, Kilsip, you'll see as there's no doubt about it.'

'It looks all square enough,' said Kilsip, who wondered what evidence Calton could have found to contradict such a plain statement. 'And what's his defence?'

'Mr Calton's the only man as knows that,' answered Gorby, finishing his drink; 'but, clever and all as he is, he can't put anything in that can go against my evidence.'

'Don't you be too sure of that,' sneered Kilsip, whose soul was devoured with envy.

'Oh, but I am,' retorted Gorby, getting as red as a turkey-cock at the sneer. 'You're jealous, you are, because you haven't got a finger in the pie?'

'Ah, but I may have yet.'

'Going a-hunting yourself, are you?' said Gorby, with an indignant snort. 'A-hunting for what — for a man as is already caught?'

'I don't believe you've got the right man,' remarked Kilsip, deliberately.

Mr Gorby looked upon him with a smile of pity.

'No! Of course you don't, just because I've caught him; perhaps, when you see him hanged, you'll believe it then?'

'You're a smart man, you are,' retorted Kilsip; 'but you ain't the Pope to be infallible.'

'And what grounds have you for saying he's not the right man?' demanded Gorby.

Kilsip smiled, and stole softly across the room like a cat.

'I'm not going to tell you all I know, but you ain't so safe nor clever as you think,' and, with another irritating smile, he went out.

Mr Gorby started after him in indignant surprise. The fact is, Kilsip had believed firmly that Fitzgerald was the right man, but a doubt having been put into his mind by Calton, he thought he would irritate Gorby by these insinuations, though he himself knew nothing that could justify them.

'He's a cat and a snake,' said Gorby, to himself, when the door had closed on his brother detective; 'but it's only brag; there isn't a link missing in the chain of evidence against Fitzgerald, so I defy him to do his worst.'

At eight o'clock on that night the soft-footed and soft-voiced detective presented himself at Calton's office, and found the lawyer impatiently waiting for him. Kilsip closed the door softly, and then taking a seat opposite to Calton, waited for him to speak. The lawyer, however, first handed him a cigar, and then producing a bottle of whisky and two glasses from some mysterious recess, he filled one and pushed it towards the detective. Kilsip accepted these little attentions with the utmost gravity, yet they were not without their effect on him, as the keen-eyed lawyer saw. Calton was a great believer in diplomacy, and never lost an opportunity of inculcating it into young men starting in life.

'Diplomacy,' said Calton, to one young aspirant for legal honours, 'is the oil we cast on the troubled waters of social, professional, and political life; and if you can, by a little tact, manage mankind, you are pretty certain to get on in this world.' Of course, he practised what he preached, and knowing that Kilsip had that feline nature which likes to be stroked and made much of, he paid him these little attentions, which he well knew would make the detective willing to do everything in his power to help him. Calton also knew the dislike that Kilsip entertained for Gorby, and so, by dexterous management, he calculated upon twisting him, clever as he was, round his finger, and as subsequent events showed, he had not reckoned wrongly. Having thus got him into a sympathetic frame of mind, and in a humour to bend his best energies to the work he wanted him to do, Calton started the conversation.

'I suppose,' he said, leaning back in his chair, and watching the wreaths of blue smoke curling from his cigar, 'I suppose you know all the ins and the outs of the hansom cab murder?'

'I should rather think so,' said Kilsip, with a curious light in his queer eyes. 'Why, Gorby does nothing but brag about it, and his smartness in catching the supposed murderer!'

'Aha!' said Calton, leaning forward, and putting his arms on the table. 'Supposed murderer. Eh! Does that mean that he hasn't been convicted by a jury, or do you think that Fitzgerald is innocent?'

Kilsip stared hard at the lawyer, in a vague kind of way, slowly rubbing his hands together.

'Well,' he said at length, in a deliberate manner, 'before I got your note, I was convinced Gorby had got hold of the right man, but when I heard that you wanted to see me, and knowing you are defending the prisoner, I guessed that you must have found something in his favour which you want me to look after.'

'Right!' said Calton, laconically.

'As Mr Fitzgerald said he met Whyte at the corner and hailed the cab —' went on the detective.

'How do you know that?' interrupted Calton, sharply.

'Gorby told me.'

'How the devil did he find out?' cried the lawyer, with genuine surprise.

'Because he is always poking and prying about,' said Kilsip, forgetting, in his indignation, that such poking and prying formed part of detective business. 'But at any rate,' he went on quickly, 'if Mr Fitzgerald did leave Mr Whyte, the only chance he's got of proving his innocence is that he did not come back, as the cabman alleged.'

'Then, I suppose, you think that Fitzgerald will prove an *alibi*,' said Calton.

'Well, sir,' answered Kilsip, modestly, 'of course you know more about the case than I do, but that is the only defence I can see he can make.'

'Well, he's not going to put in such a defence.'

'Then he must be guilty,' said Kilsip, promptly.

'Not necessarily,' returned the barrister, dryly.

'But if he wants to save his neck, he'll have to prove an *alibi*,' persisted the other.

'That's just where the point is,' answered Calton. 'He doesn't want to save his neck.'

Kilsip, looking rather bewildered, took a sip of whisky, and waited to hear what Mr Calton had to say on the subject.

'The fact is,' said Calton, lighting a fresh cigar, 'he's got some extraordinary idea in his head about keeping where he was on that night a secret.'

'I understand,' said Kilsip, gravely nodding his head. 'Women?'

'Nothing of the sort,' retorted Calton, hastily. 'That's what I thought at first, but I was wrong; he went to see a dying woman who wanted to tell him something.'

'What about?'

'That's just what I can't tell you,' answered Calton quickly. 'It must have been something important, for she sent for him in great haste — and he was by her bedside between the hours of one and two on Friday morning.'

'Then he did not return to the cab?'

'No, he did not, he went to keep his appointment, but, for some reason or another, won't tell where this appointment was. I went to his rooms today and found this half-burnt letter, asking him to come.'

Calton handed the letter to Kilsip, who placed it on the table and examined it carefully.

'This was written on Thursday,' said the detective.

'Of course — you can see that from the date; and Whyte was murdered on Friday, the 27th.'

'It was written at something Villa, Toorak,' pursued Kilsip, still examining the paper. 'Oh! I understand, he went down there.'

'Hardly,' retorted Calton in a sarcastic tone. 'He couldn't very well go down there, have an interview, and be back in East Melbourne in one hour — the cabman Royston can prove that he was at Russell Street at one o'clock, and his landlady that he entered his lodging in East Melbourne at two — no, he wasn't at Toorak.'

'When was this letter delivered?'

'Shortly before twelve o'clock, at the Melbourne Club, by a girl, who, from what the waiter saw of her, appears to be a disreputable individual — you will see it says bearer will wait him at Bourke Street, and as another street is mentioned, and as Fitzgerald, after leaving Whyte, went down Russell Street to keep his appointment, the most logical conclusion is that the bearer of the letter waited for him at the corner of Bourke and Russell Streets. Now,' went on the lawyer, 'I want to find out who the girl that brought the letter is!'

'But how?'

'God bless my soul, Kilsip! How stupid you are,' cried Calton, his irritation getting the better of diplomacy. 'Can't you understand — that paper came from one of the back slums — therefore it must have been stolen.'

A sudden light flashed into Kilsip's eyes.

'Talbot Villa, Toorak,' he cried quickly, snatching up the letter again, and examining it with great attention, 'where that burglary took place.'

'Exactly,' said Calton, smiling complacently. 'Now do you understand what I want — you must take me to the crib in the back slums where the articles stolen from the house in Toorak were hidden. This paper' — pointing to the letter — 'is part of the swag left behind, and must have been used by someone there. Brian Fitzgerald obeyed the directions given in the letter, and he was there at the time of the murder.'

'I understand,' said Kilsip, with a gratified purr. 'There were four men engaged in that burglary, and they hid the swag at

Mother Guttersnipe's crib, in a lane off Little Bourke Street — but hang it, a swell like Mr Fitzgerald, in evening dress, couldn't very well have gone down there unless —'

'He had someone with him well-known in the locality,' finished Calton, rapidly. 'Exactly, that woman who delivered the letter at the Club guided him. Judging from the waiter's description of her appearance, I should think she was pretty well known about the slums.'

'Well,' said Kilsip, rising and looking at his watch, 'it is now nine o'clock, so if you like we will go to the old hag's place at once — dying woman,' he said, as if struck by a sudden thought, 'there was a woman died there about four weeks ago.'

'Who was she?' asked Calton, who was putting on his overcoat.

'Some relation of Mother Guttersnipe's, I fancy,' answered Kilsip, as they left the office. 'I don't know exactly what she was — she was called the "Queen," and a precious handsome woman she must have been — came from Sydney about three months ago, and from what I can make out, was not long from England, died of consumption on the Thursday night before the murder.'

'Then she must have been the woman who wrote the letter.'

'No doubt of it,' replied Kilsip; 'but if Fitzgerald was there on that night, we can get plenty of witnesses to prove an *alibi*. I am sure of two at least, Mother Guttersnipe and her granddaughter, Sal.'

But Mr Calton was not listening — as he stepped along beside his companion, he was thinking —

'What on earth could a woman just from England living in a Melbourne back slum, have to tell Fitzgerald about Madge Frettlby?'

XV
A Woman of the People

Bourke Street is always more crowded than Collins Street, especially at night. The theatres are there, and of course there is invariably a large crowd collected under the electric lights. Fashion does not come out after dark to walk about the streets, but prefers to roll along in her carriage; therefore the block in Bourke Street at night is slightly different from that of Collins Street in the day. The restless crowd which jostles and pushes along the pavements is grimy in the main, but the grimyness is lightened in many places by the presence of the ladies of the *demi-monde*, who flaunt about in gorgeous robes of the brightest colours. These gay-plumaged birds of ill-omen collect at the corners of the streets, and converse loudly with their male acquaintances till desired by some white-helmeted policeman to move on, which they do, after a good deal of unnecessary chatter. Round the doors of the hotels a number of ragged and shabby-looking individuals collect, who lean against the walls criticising the crowd, and waiting till some of their friends ask them to have a glass, a request they obey with suspicious alacrity. Further on, a crowd of horsey-looking men are standing under the Opera House verandah, and one hears nothing but sporting talk about the Cup, and odds being given and taken on the cracks of the day. Then here and there are ragged street Arabs, selling matches and newspapers; and against the verandah post, in the full blaze of the electric light, leans a weary, draggled-looking woman, one arm clasping a baby to her breast, and the other holding a pile of newspapers, while she drones out in a hoarse voice, ' '*Erald*, third 'dition, one penny!' until the ear wearies of the constant repetition. Cabs rattle incessantly along the street; here, a fast-looking hansom, with a rakish horse, bearing some gilded youth to his Club — there, a dingy-looking vehicle, drawn by a lank quadruped, which straggles blindly down the street. Alternating with these, carriages dash along with their well-groomed horses, and within, the vision of bright eyes, white dresses, and the sparkle of diamonds. Then, further up, just on the verge of the pavement, a band, consisting of three violins and a harp, is stationed, which is playing a German waltz to an admiring crowd of attentive spectators. If there is one thing which the Melbourne folk love more than another, it is music, their fondness for which is only equalled by their admiration for horse-racing. Any street band which plays at all decently, may be sure of a good audience, and a substantial remuneration for their playing. Some writer has described Melbourne as Glasgow, with the sky of Alexandria; and certainly the beautiful climate of Australia, so Italian in its brightness, must have a great effect on the nature of such an adaptable race as the Anglo-Saxon. In spite of the dismal prognostications of Marcus Clarke regarding the future Australian, whom he describes as being 'a tall, coarse, strong-jawed, greedy, pushing, talented man, excelling in swimming and horsemanship,' it is more likely that he will be a cultured, indolent individual, with an intense appreciation of the arts and sciences, and a dislike to hard work and utilitarian principles. Climatic influence should be taken into account with regard to the future Australian, and our posterity will be no more like us than the luxurious Venetians resembled their hardy forefathers, who first started to build on those lonely sandy islands of the Adriatic.

This was the conclusion Mr Calton arrived at as he followed his guide through the crowded streets, and saw with what deep interest the crowd listened to the rhythmic strains of Strauss and the sparkling melodies of Offenbach. The brilliantly lit street, with the never-ceasing stream of people pouring along; the shrill cries of the street Arabs, the rattle of vehicles, and the fitful strains of music, all made up a scene which fascinated him, and he could have gone on wandering all night, watching the myriad phases of human character constantly passing before his eyes. But his guide, with whom familiarity with the proletarians had, in a great measure, bred indifference, hurried him away to Little Bourke Street, where the narrowness of the street, with the high buildings on each side, the dim light of the sparsely scattered gas lamps, and the few ragged-looking figures slouching along, formed a strong contrast to the brilliant and crowded scene they had just left. Turning off Little Bourke Street, the detective led the way down a dark lane, which felt like a furnace, owing to the heat of the night; but, on looking up, Calton caught a glimpse of the blue sky far above, glittering with stars, which gave him quite a sensation of coolness.

'Keep close to me,' whispered Kilsip, touching the barrister on the arm; 'we may meet some nasty customers about here.'

Mr Calton, however, did not need such a warning, for the neighbourhood through which they were passing was so like that of the Seven Dials in London, that he kept as closely to the side of his guide as did Dante to that of Virgil in the Infernal Regions. It was not quite dark, for the atmosphere had that luminous kind of haze so observable in Australian twilights, and this weird light was just sufficient to make the darkness visible. Kilsip and the barrister kept for safety in the middle of the alley, so that no one could spring upon them unaware, and they could see sometimes on the one side, a man cowering back into the black shadow, or on the other, a woman with disordered hair and bare bosom, leaning out of a window trying to get a breath of fresh air. There were also some children playing in the dried-up gutter, and their shrill young voices came echoing strangely through the gloom, mingling with a bacchanalian sort of song a man was singing, as he slouched along unsteadily over the rough stones. Now and then a mild-looking string of Chinamen stole along, clad in their dull-hued blue blouses, either chattering shrilly, like a lot of parrots, or moving silently down the alley with a stolid Oriental apathy on their yellow faces. Here and there came a stream of warm light through an open door, and within, the Mongolians were gathered round the gambling tables, playing fan-tan, or else leaving the seductions of their favourite pastime, and gliding soft-footed to the many cook-shops, where enticing-looking fowls and turkeys already cooked were awaiting purchasers. Kilsip, turning to the left, led the barrister down another and still narrower lane, the darkness and gloom of which made the lawyer shudder, as he wondered how human beings could live in them.

'It is like walking in the valley of the shadow of death,' he muttered to himself, as they brushed past a woman who was crouching down in a dark corner, and who looked up at them with an evil scowl on her white face. And, indeed, it was not unlike the description in Bunyan's famous allegory, what with the semi-darkness, the wild lights and shadows, and the vague undefinable forms of men and women flitting to and fro in the dusky twilight.

At last, to Calton's relief, for he felt somewhat bewildered by the darkness and narrowness of the lanes through which he had been taken, the detective stopped before a door, which he opened, and stepping inside, beckoned to the barrister to follow. Calton did so, and found himself in a low, dark, ill-smelling passage, at the end of which they saw a faint light. Kilsip caught his companion by the arm and guided him carefully along the passage. There was much need of this caution, for Calton could feel that the rotten boards were full of holes, into which one or the other of his feet kept slipping from time to time, while he could hear the rats squeaking and scampering away on all sides. Just as they got to the end of this tunnel, for it could be called nothing else, the light suddenly went out, and they were left in complete darkness.

'Light that,' cried the detective in a peremptory tone of voice. 'What do you mean by dowsing the glim?'

Thieves argot was, evidently, well understood here, for there was a shuffle in the dark, a muttered voice, and then someone lit the candle with a match. This time Calton saw the light was held by an elfish-looking child, with a scowling white face, and tangled masses of black hair, which hung over her eyes. She was crouching down on the floor, against the damp wall, and looked up at the detective defiantly, yet with a certain fear in her eyes, as though she were a wild animal, cowed against her will.

'Where's Mother Guttersnipe?' asked the detective sharply, touching her with his foot, an indignity she resented with a malignant glance, and arose quickly to her feet.

'Upstairs,' she replied, jerking her head in the direction of the right wall, in which Calton, his eyes being more accustomed to the flickering light of the candle, could see a gaping black chasm, which he presumed was the stair alluded to. 'You won't get much out of her tonight — she's a-goin' to start 'er booze, she is.'

'Never mind what she's doing,' said Kilsip, sharply, 'take me to her at once.'

The girl gave him a sullen look, and with reluctant feet led the way into the black chasm and up the stairs, which were so shaky that Calton was in terror lest they should be precipitated into unknown depths. He held on firmly to his companion's arm, as they toiled slowly up the broken steps, and at last stopped at a door, through the cracks of which a faint glimmer of light could be seen. Here the girl gave a shrill whistle, and the door opened as if by magic. Still preceded by their elfish guide, Calton and the detective stepped through the doorway, and a curious scene was presented to their view. It was a small, square room, with a low roof, from which the paper, mildewed and torn, hung in tatters; on the left hand, at the far end, was a kind of low stretcher, upon which a woman, almost naked, was lying, amid a heap of frowsy greasy clothes. She appeared to be ill, for she kept her head tossing from side to side restlessly, and every now and then sang snatches of old songs in a shrill, cracked voice. In the centre of the room was a rough deal table, upon which stood a guttering tallow candle, which but faintly illuminated the scene, and a half empty, square bottle of Schnapps, with a broken cup beside it. In front of these signs of festivity sat an old woman with a pack of cards spread out before her, and from which she had evidently been telling the fortune of a villainous-looking young man who had opened the door, and who stood looking at the detective with no very friendly expression of countenance. He was dressed in a greasy brown velvet coat, much patched, and a black wide-a-wake hat, which was pulled down over his eyes. He looked like one of those Italians who retail ice-cream on the street, or carry round organs with monkeys on them, and his expression was so scowling and vindictive that the barrister thought it was not very hard to tell his ultimate destiny — Pentridge, or the gallows.

As they entered, the fortune-teller raised her head, and, shading her eyes with one skinny hand, looked curiously at the newcomers. Calton thought he had never seen such a repulsive-looking old crone; and, indeed, she was worthy of the pencil of Doré to depict, such was the grotesque ugliness which she exhibited. Her face was seamed and lined with innumerable wrinkles, clearly defined by the dirt which was in them; bushy grey eyebrows, drawn frowningly over two piercing black eyes, whose light was undimmed by age; a hook nose, like the beak of a bird of prey, and a thin-lipped mouth, with two long yellow tusks sticking out like those of a wild boar. Her hair was very luxurious and almost white, and was tied up in a great bunch by a greasy bit of black ribbon. As to her chin, Calton, when he saw it wagging to and fro, involuntarily quoted Macbeth's lines about the witches —

'Ye should be women
And yet your beards forbid me to interpret
That ye are so.'

And, indeed, she was no bad representative of the weird sisters.

This lady looked viciously at them when they entered, and demanded sulkily — 'What the 'ell they wanted?'

'Want your booze,' cried the child, with an elfish laugh, as she shook back her tangled hair.

'Get out, you whelp,' croaked the old hag, shaking one skinny fist at her, 'or I'll tear your heart out, cuss you.'

'Yes, she can go,' said Kilsip, nodding to the girl, 'and you can clear, too,' he added, sharply, turning to the young man, who still stood holding the door open. At first he seemed inclined to dispute the detective's order, but ultimately obeyed him, muttering, as he went out, something about 'the bloomin' cheek of showin' swells cove's cribs.' The child followed him out, her exit being accelerated by Mother Guttersnipe, who, with a rapidity only attained by long practice, seized the shoe off one of her feet, and flung it at the head of the rapidly retreating girl.

'Wait till I ketches yer, Lizer,' she shrieked, with a volley of curses, 'I'll break yer 'ead, blarst ye!'

Lizer responded with a shrill laugh of disdain, and vanished through the shaky door, which she closed after her.

When she had disappeared Mother Guttersnipe took a drink out of the broken cup, and, gathering all her greasy cards together in a business-like way, looked insinuatingly at Calton, with a suggestive leer.

'It's the future ye want unveiled, dearie?' she croaked, rapidly shuffling the cards; 'an' old mother 'ull tell —'

'No she won't,' interrupted the detective, sharply. 'I've come on business.'

The old woman started at this, and looked keenly at him from under her bushy eyebrows.

'What 'av the boys been up to now?' she asked, harshly. 'There ain't no swag 'ere this time, blarst ye.'

Just then the sick woman, who had been restlessly tossing on the bed, commenced singing a snatch of the quaint old ballad of Barbara Allen —

> 'Oh, mither, mither, mak' my bed,
>   An' mak' it saft an' narrow;
> Since my true love died for me today,
>   I'll die for him tomorrow.'

'Shut up, cuss you!' yelled Mother Guttersnipe, viciously, 'or I'll knock yer bloomin' 'ead orf,' and she seized the square bottle as if to carry out her threat; but, altering her mind, she poured some of its contents into the cup, and drank it off with avidity.

'The woman seems ill,' said Calton, casting a shuddering glance at the stretcher.

'So she are, d— her!' growled Mother Guttersnipe, angrily. 'She ought to be in Yarrer Bend, she ought, instead of stoppin' 'ere, an' singin' them beastly things, which makes my blood run cold. Just 'ear 'er,' she said, viciously, as the sick woman broke out once more —

'Oh, little did my mither think,
When first she cradled me,
I'd die sa far away fra home,
Upon the gallows tree.'

'Yah!' said the old woman, hastily, drinking some more gin out of the cup. 'She's allays a-talkin' of dyin' an' gallers, as if they were nice things to jawr about.'

'Who was that woman who died here three or four weeks ago?' asked Kilsip, sharply.

' 'Ow the 'ell should I know,' retorted Mother Guttersnipe, sullenly. 'I didn't kill 'er, did I? It were the brandy she drank; she was allays drinkin', cuss 'er.'

'Do you remember the night she died?'

'No, I don't,' answered the beldame, frankly. 'I were drunk — blind, bloomin', blazin' drunk — s'elp me G—.'

'You're always drunk,' said Kilsip.

'What if I am?' snarled the woman, seizing her bottle. 'You don't pay fur it. Yes, I'm drunk. I'm allays drunk. I was drunk last night, an' the night before, an' I'm a-goin' to git drunk tonight' — with an impressive look at the bottle — 'an' tomorrow night, an' I'll keep it up till I'm rottin' in the grave, blarst an' cuss ye.'

Calton shuddered, so full of hatred and suppressed malignity was her voice, but the detective merely shrugged his shoulders.

'More fool you,' he said, briefly. 'Come now, on the night the "Queen," as you call her, died, there was a gentleman came to see her?'

'So she said,' retorted Mother Guttersnipe; 'But, lor', I dunno anythin', I were drunk.'

'Who said — the "Queen?" '

'No, my gran'darter, Sal. The "Queen," sent 'er to fetch the toff to see 'er cut 'er lucky. Wanted 'im to look at 'is work I s'pose, cuss 'im; and Sal prigged some paper from my box,' she shrieked, indignantly; 'prigged it w'en I were too drunk to stop 'er?'

The detective glanced at Calton, who nodded to him with a gratified expression on his face. They were right as to the paper having been stolen from the Villa at Toorak.

'You did not see the gentleman who came?' said Kilsip, turning again to the old hag.

'Not I, cuss you,' she retorted, politely. ' 'E came about 'arf-past one in the morning, an' you don't expects we can stop up all night, blarst ye.'

'Half-past one o'clock,' repeated Calton, quickly. 'The very time. Is this true?'

'Wish I may die if it ain't,' said Mother Guttersnipe, graciously. 'My gran'darter Sal kin tell ye.'

'Where is she?' asked Kilsip, sharply.

At this the old woman threw back her head, and howled in a dismal manner.

'She's 'ooked it,' she wailed, drumming on the ground with her feet. 'Gon' an' left 'er pore old gran' an' joined the army, cuss 'em, a-comin' round an' a-spilin' business.'

Here the woman on the bed broke out again —

'Since the flowers o' the forest are a' wed awa'.'

'Fur G—'s sake 'old yer jawr,' yelled Mother Guttersnipe, rising, and making a dart at the bed. 'I'll choke the life out of ye, s'elp me. D'y want me to murder ye, singin' 'em blarsted funeral things?'

Meanwhile the detective was talking rapidly to Mr Calton.

'The only person who can prove Mr Fitzgerald was here between one and two o'clock,' he said quickly, 'is Sal Rawlins, as everyone else seems to have been drunk or asleep. As she has joined the Salvation Army, I'll go to the barracks the first thing in the morning and look for her.'

'I hope you'll find her,' answered Calton, drawing a long breath. 'A man's life hangs on her evidence.'

They turned to go, Calton having first given Mother Guttersnipe some loose silver, which she seized on with an avaricious clutch.

'You'll drink it, I suppose?' said the barrister, shrinking back from her.

'Werry likely,' retorted the hag, with a repulsive grin, tying the money up in a piece of her dress, which she tore off for the purpose. 'I'm a forting to the public 'ouse, I am, an' it's the on'y pleasure I 'ave in my life, cuss it.'

The sight of money had a genial effect on her nature, for she held the candle at the head of the stairs, as they went down, so that they should not break their heads. As they arrived safely, they saw the light vanish, and heard the sick woman singing, 'The Last Rose of Summer,' and then a volley of curses from Mother Guttersnipe.

The street door was open, and, after groping their way along the dark passage, with its pitfalls, they found themselves in the open street.

'Thank heaven we are safely out of that den!' said Calton, taking off his hat, and drawing a long breath.

'At all events, our journey has not been wasted,' said the detective, as they walked along. 'We've found out where Mr Fitzgerald was the night of the murder, so he will be safe.'

'That depends upon Sal Rawlins,' answered Calton, gravely; 'but come, let us have a glass of brandy, for I feel quite ill after my experience of low life.'

XVI
Missing

The next day Kilsip called at Calton's office late in the afternoon, and found the lawyer eagerly expecting him. The detective's face, however, looked rather dismal, and Calton was not reassured by its expression.

'Well!' he said, impatiently, when Kilsip had closed the door and taken his seat. 'Where is she?'

'That's just what I want to know,' answered the detective, coolly; 'I went to the Salvation Army headquarters and made enquiries about her. It appears that she had been in the Army as a hallelujah lass, but got tired of it in a week, and went off with a friend of hers to Sydney. She carried on her old life of dissipation, but, ultimately, her friend got sick of her, and the last thing they heard about her was that she had taken up with a Chinaman in one of the Sydney slums. I telegraphed at once to Sydney, and got a reply that there was no person of the name of Sal Rawlins known to the Sydney police, but they said they would make enquiries, and let me know the result.'

'Ah! She has, no doubt, changed her name,' said Calton, thoughtfully, stroking his chin. 'I wonder what for?'

'Wanted to get rid of the Army, I expect,' answered Kilsip, dryly. 'The straying lamb did not care about being hunted back to the fold.'

'And when did she join the Army?'

'The very day after the murder.'

'Rather sudden conversion?'

'Yes, but she said the death of the woman on Thursday night had so startled her, that she went straight off to the Army to get her religion properly fixed up.'

'The effects of fright, no doubt,' said Calton, dryly. 'I've met a good many examples of these sudden conversions, but they never last long as a rule — it's a case of the devil was sick, the devil a monk would be, more than anything else. Good looking?'

'So-so, I believe,' replied Kilsip, shrugging his shoulders. 'Very ignorant — could neither read nor write.'

'That accounts for her not asking for Fitzgerald when she called at the Club — she probably did not know whom she had been sent for. It will resolve itself into a question of identification, I expect. However, if the police can't find her, we will put an advertisement in the papers offering a reward, and send out handbills to the same effect. She must be found. Brian Fitzgerald's life hangs on a thread, and that thread is Sal Rawlins.'

'Yes!' assented Kilsip, rubbing his hands together. 'Even if Mr Fitzgerald acknowledges that he was at Mother Guttersnipe's on the night in question, she will have to prove that he was there, as no one else saw him.'

'Are you sure of that?'

'As sure as anyone can be in such a case. It was a late hour when he came, and everyone seems to have been asleep except the dying woman and Sal; and as one is dead, the other is the only person that can prove that he was there at the time when the murder was being committed in the hansom.'

'And Mother Guttersnipe?'

'Was drunk, as she acknowledged last night. She thought that if a gentleman did call it must have been the other one.'

'The other one?' repeated Calton, in a puzzled voice. 'What other one?'

'Oliver Whyte.'

Calton arose from his seat with a blank air of astonishment. 'Oliver Whyte!' he said, as soon as he could find his voice. 'Was he in the habit of going there?'

Kilsip curled himself up in his seat like a sleek cat, and pushing forward his head till his nose looked like the beak of a bird of prey, looking keenly at Calton.

'Look here, sir,' he said, in his low, purring voice, 'There's a good deal in this case which don't seem plain — in fact, the further we go into it, the more mixed up it seems to get. I went to see Mother Guttersnipe this morning, and she told me that Whyte had visited the "Queen" several times while she lay ill, and seemed to be pretty well acquainted with her.'

'But who the devil is this woman they call the "Queen?" ' said Calton, irritably. 'She seems to be at the bottom of the whole affair — every path we take leads to her.'

'I know hardly anything about her,' replied Kilsip, 'except that she was a good-looking woman, of about forty-nine — she came out from England to Sydney a few months ago, then on to here — how she got to Mother Guttersnipe's I can't find out, though I've tried to pump that old woman, but she's as close as wax, and it's my belief she knows more about this dead woman than she chooses to tell.'

'But what could she have told Fitzgerald to make him act in this silly manner. A stranger who comes from England, and dies in a Melbourne slum, can't possibly know anything about Miss Frettlby.'

'Not unless Miss Frettlby was secretly married to Whyte,' suggested Kilsip, 'and the "Queen" knew it.'

'Nonsense,' retorted Calton, sharply. 'Why, she hated him and loves Fitzgerald; besides, why on earth should she marry secretly, and make a confidant of a woman in one of the lowest parts of Melbourne? At one time her father wanted her to marry Whyte, but she made such strong opposition, that he eventually gave his consent to her engagement with Fitzgerald.'

'And Whyte?'

'Oh, he had a row with Mr Frettlby, and left the house in a rage. He was murdered the same night, for the sake of some papers he carried.'

'Oh, that's Gorby's idea,' said Kilsip, scornfully, with a vicious snarl.

'And it's mine too,' answered Calton, firmly. 'Whyte had some valuable papers, which he always carried about with him. The woman who died evidently told Fitzgerald that he did, as I gathered as much from an accidental admission he made.'

Kilsip looked puzzled.

'I must confess that it is a riddle,' he said at length; 'but if Mr Fitzgerald would only speak, it would clear everything up.'

'What about who murdered Whyte?'

'Well, it might not go so far as that, but it might supply the motive for the crime.'

'I dare say you are right,' answered Calton, thoughtfully, as the detective rose and put on his hat. 'But it's no use. Fitzgerald, for some reason or another, has evidently made up his mind not to speak, so our only hope in saving him lies in finding this girl.'

'If she's anywhere in Australia you may be sure she'll be found,' answered Kilsip, confidently, as he took his departure. 'Australia isn't so over-crowded as all that.'

If Sal Rawlins was in Australia, she certainly must have been in some remote spot, for in spite of all efforts she could not be found anywhere. Whether she was alive or dead was an open question, for she seemed to have vanished as completely as if the earth had swallowed her up. The last seen of her was in a Sydney den, with a Chinaman, whom she afterwards left, and since then had neither been seen nor heard of. Notices were put in the papers, both in Australia and New Zealand, offering large rewards for her discovery, but nothing came of them. As she was unable to read herself, she would, of course, be ignorant that she was wanted, and if, as Calton had surmised, she had changed her name, no one else would tell her about it, unless she happened to hear it by chance. Altogether, it seemed as if there was no hope except the forlorn one of Sal turning up of her own accord. If she came back to Melbourne she would be certain to go to her grandmother's place, as she had no motive in keeping away from it; so Kilsip kept a sharp watch on the house, much to Mrs Rawlins' disgust, for, with true English pride, she objected to this system of espionage.

'Blarst 'im,' she croaked over her evening drink, to an old crone, as withered and evil looking as herself, 'why, in G—'s name, can't 'e stop in 'is own bloomin' 'ouse, an' leave mine alone — a-coming round 'ere a-pokin' and pryin' and a-perwenting people from earnin' their livin' an' a-gittin' drunk wen they ain't well, cuss 'im.'

'What do 'e want?' asked her friend, rubbing her weak old knees.

'Wants, cuss 'im — 'e wants 'is d—d throat cut,' said Mother Guttersnipe, viciously. 'An' s'elp me G—, I'll do for 'im some night w'en 'e's a watchin' round 'ere as if it were Pentridge — 'e can git what he can out of that whelp as ran away, cuss 'er; but I knows suthin' 'e don't know, blarst 'im.' She ended with a senile laugh, and her companion having taken advantage of the long speech to drink some gin out of the broken cup, Mother Guttersnipe seized the unfortunate old creature by the hair, and in spite of her feeble cries, banged her head against the wall.

'I'll have the perlice in at yer,' whimpered the assaulted one, as she tottered as quickly away as her rheumatics would let her. 'See if I don't.'

'Go to 'ell,' retorted Mother Guttersnipe, indifferently, as she filled herself a fresh cup. 'You come a-falutin' round 'ere agin priggin' my drinks, cuss you, an' I'll cut yer throat an' wring yer wicked old 'ead orf, blarst you.'

The other gave a howl of dismay at hearing this pleasant proposal to end her, and tottered out as quickly as possible, leaving Mother Guttersnipe in undisputed possession of the field.

Meanwhile Calton had seen Brian several times, and used every argument in his power to get him to tell everything, but he maintained an obstinate silence, or merely answered, 'It would only break her heart.'

He admitted to Calton, after a good deal of questioning, that he had been at Mother Guttersnipe's on the night of the murder. After he had left Whyte by the corner of the Scotch Church, as the cabman — Royston — had stated, he had gone along Russell Street, and met Sal Rawlins near the Unicorn Hotel. She had taken him to Mother Guttersnipe's, where he had seen the dying woman, who had told him something he could not reveal.

'Well,' said Mr Calton, after hearing the admission, 'you might have saved us all this trouble by admitting this before, and yet kept your secret, whatever it may be. Had you done so, we might have got a hold of Sal Rawlins before she left Melbourne; but now it's only a chance whether she turns up or not.'

Brian did not answer to this; and, in fact, hardly seemed to be thinking of what the lawyer was saying; but just as Calton was leaving, he asked —

'How is Madge?'

'How can you expect her to be?' said Calton, turning angrily on him. 'She is very ill, owing to the worry she has been in over this affair.'

'My darling! My darling!' cried Brian, in agony, clasping his hands above his head. 'I only did it to save you.'

Calton approached him, and laid his hand lightly on his shoulder.

'My dear fellow,' he said, gravely, 'the confidences between lawyer and client are as sacred as those between priest and penitent. You must tell me this secret which concerns Miss Frettlby so deeply.'

'No,' said Brian, firmly, 'I will never reveal what that cursed woman told me. When I would not tell you before, in order to save my life, it is not likely I am going to do so now, when I have nothing to gain and everything to lose by telling it.'

'I will never ask you again,' said Calton, rather annoyed, as he walked to the door. 'And as to this accusation of murder, if I can find this girl, you are safe.'

When the lawyer left the gaol, he went to the Detective Office to see Kilsip, and ascertain if there was any news of Sal Rawlins; but, as usual, there was none.

'It is fighting against Fate,' he said, sadly, as he went away; 'his life hangs on a mere chance.'

The trial was fixed to come off in September, and, of course, there was great excitement in Melbourne over the matter. Great, therefore, was the disappointment when it was discovered that the prisoner's counsel had applied for an adjournment of the trial till October, on the ground that an important witness for the defence could not be found.

XVII
The Trial

In spite of the utmost vigilance on the part of the police, and the offer of a large reward, both by Calton, on behalf of the accused, and by Mr Frettlby, the much desired Sal Rawlins still remained hidden. The millionaire had maintained a most friendly attitude towards Brian throughout the whole affair. He refused to believe him guilty, and when Calton told him of the defence of proving an *alibi* by means of Sal Rawlins, he immediately offered a large reward, which was enough in itself to set every person with any time on their hands hunting for the missing witness. All Australia and New Zealand rang with the extremely plebeian name of Sal Rawlins, the papers being full of notices offering rewards; and handbills of staring red letters were posted up in all railway stations, in conjunction with Lewis's Egg Powder and some one else's Pale Ale. She had become famous without knowing it, unless, indeed, she had kept herself concealed on purpose; but this was hardly probable, as there was no apparent motive for her doing so. If she was above ground she must certainly have seen the handbills, if not the papers; and, though not being able to read, could hardly help hearing something about the one topic of conversation throughout Australia. Notwithstanding all this, Sal Rawlins was still undiscovered, and Calton, in despair, began to think that she must be dead. But Madge, though at times her courage gave way, was still hopeful.

'God will not permit such a judicial crime to be committed as the murder of an innocent man,' she declared.

Mr Calton, to whom she said this, shook his head, doubtfully. 'God has permitted it to take place before,' he answered, softly; 'and we can only judge the future by the past.'

At last, the day of the long-expected trial came, and as Calton sat in his office looking over his brief, a clerk entered and told him

Mr Frettlby and his daughter wished to see him. When they came in, the barrister saw that the millionaire looked haggard and ill, and there was a look of worry on his face.

'There is my daughter, Calton,' he said, after hurried greetings had been exchanged. 'She wants to be present in Court during Fitzgerald's trial, and nothing I can say will dissuade her.'

Calton turned, and looked at the girl in some surprise.

'Yes!' she answered, meeting his look steadily, though her face was very pale; 'I must be there. I shall go mad with anxiety unless I know how the trial goes on.'

'But think of the disagreeable amount of attention you will attract,' urged the lawyer.

'No one will recognise me,' she said calmly; 'I am very plainly dressed, and I will wear this veil;' and, drawing one from her pocket, she went over to a small looking-glass which was hanging on the wall and tied it on her face.

Calton looked in a perplexed manner at Mr Frettlby.

'I'm afraid you must consent,' he said.

'Very well,' replied the other, almost sternly, while a look of annoyance passed over his face. 'I will leave her in your charge.'

'And you?'

'I'm not coming,' answered Frettlby, quickly, putting on his hat. 'I don't care about seeing a man whom I have had at my dinner-table in the prisoner's dock, much as I sympathise with him. Good-day;' and with a curt nod he took his leave.

When the door closed on her father, Madge placed her hand on Calton's arm.

'Any hope?' she whispered, looking at him through the black veil.

'The merest chance,' answered Calton, putting his brief into his bag. 'We have done everything in our power to discover this girl, but without effect. If she does not come at the eleventh hour I'm afraid Brian Fitzgerald is a doomed man.'

Madge fell on her knees, with a stifled cry.

'Oh, God of Mercy,' she cried, raising her hands as if in prayer, 'save him. Save my darling, and let him not die for the crime of another. God —'

She dropped her face in her hands and wept convulsively, as the lawyer touched her lightly on the shoulder.

'Come!' he said, kindly. 'Be the brave girl you were, and we may save him yet. The hour is darkest before the dawn, you know.'

Madge dried her tears, and followed the lawyer to the cab, which was waiting for them at the door. They drove quickly up to the Court, and Calton put her in a quiet place, where she could see the dock, and yet be unobserved by the people in the body of the Court. Just as he was leaving her she touched his arm.

'Tell him,' she whispered, in a trembling voice; 'tell my darling I am here.'

Calton nodded, and hurried away to put on his wig and gown, while Madge looked hurriedly round the Court from her point of vantage. It was crowded with fashionable Melbourne of both sexes, and they were all talking together in subdued whispers. The popular character of the prisoner, his good looks, and engagement to Madge Frettlby, together with the extraordinary circumstances of the case, had raised public curiosity to the highest pitch, and, consequently, everybody who could possibly manage to gain admission was there. Felix Rolleston had secured an excellent seat beside the pretty Miss Featherweight, whom he admired so much, and he was chattering to her with the utmost volubility.

'Puts me in mind of the Coliseum and all that sort of thing, you know,' he said, putting up his eye-glass and staring round. 'Butchered to make a Roman holiday, by Jove.'

'Don't say such horrid things, you frivolous creature,' simpered Miss Featherweight, using her smelling-bottle. 'We are all here out of sympathy for that poor dear Mr Fitzgerald.'

The mercurial Felix, who had more cleverness in him than people gave him credit for, smiled outright at this eminently feminine way of covering an overpowering curiosity.

'Ah, yes,' he said lightly; 'exactly! I dare say Eve only ate the apple because she didn't like to see such a lot of good fruit go to waste.'

Miss Featherweight looked at him doubtfully, as though she was not quite certain if he was in jest or earnest, but just as she was about to reply that she thought it wicked to make jokes on the Bible, the judge entered, and all the Court arose to receive him. When the prisoner was brought in, there was a great flutter among the ladies, and some of them even had the bad taste to produce opera-glasses. Brian noticed this, and he flushed up to the roots of his fair hair, for he felt his degradation acutely. He was an intensely proud man, and to be placed in the criminal dock with a lot of frivolous people, who had called themselves his friends, looking at him as though he were a new actor or a wild animal, was galling in the extreme. He was dressed in black, and looked pale and worn, but all the ladies declared that he was as good-looking as ever, and they were sure he was innocent.

The jury were sworn in, and the Crown Prosecutor arose to deliver his opening address. As all present in the Court only knew the facts of the case through the medium of the newspapers, and floating rumours, each of which contradicted the other, they were unaware of the true history of the events which had led to Fitzgerald's arrest, and they therefore prepared to listen to the speech with profound attention. The ladies ceased to talk, the men to stare round, and nothing could be seen but row after row of eager and attentive faces, hanging on the words that issued from the lips of the Crown Prosecutor. He was not a great orator, but he spoke clearly and distinctly, and every word could be heard in the dead silence.

He gave a rapid sketch of the crime, which was merely a repetition of what had been published in the newspapers, and then proceeded to enumerate the witnesses who could prove the prisoner guilty. He would call the landlady of the deceased to show that ill-blood existed between the prisoner and the murdered man, and that the accused had called on the deceased a week prior to the committal of the crime, and threatened his life. (There was great excitement at this, and several ladies decided, on the spur of the moment, that the horrid man was guilty, but the majority of the female spectators still refused to believe in the guilt of such a good-looking young fellow.) He would call a witness who could prove that Whyte was drunk on the night of the murder, and went along Russell Street, in the direction of Collins Street; the cabman Royston could swear to the fact that the prisoner had hailed the cab, and after going away for a short time, returned and entered the cab with the deceased. He would also prove that the prisoner left the cab at the Grammar School, in the St Kilda Road, and on the arrival of the cab at the junction, he discovered the deceased had been murdered. The cabman Rankin would prove that he drove the prisoner from the St Kilda Road to Powlett Street in East Melbourne, where he got out, and he would call the prisoner's landlady to prove that the prisoner resided in Powlett Street, and that on the night of the murder he had not reached home till shortly after two o'clock. He would also call the detective, who had charge of the case, to prove the finding of a glove belonging to the deceased in the pocket of the coat which the prisoner wore on the night of the murder; and the doctor who had examined the body of the deceased would give evidence that the death was caused by inhalation of chloroform. As he had now fully shown the chain of evidence which he proposed to prove, he would call the first witness, Malcolm Royston.

Royston, on being sworn, gave the same evidence as he had given at the inquest, from the time that the cab was hailed up to his arrival at the St Kilda Police Station with the dead body of Whyte. In the cross-examination, Calton asked him if he was prepared to swear that the man who hailed the cab, and the man who got in with the deceased, were one and the same person.

WITNESS: I am.

CALTON: You are quite certain?

WITNESS: Yes; quite certain.

CALTON: Do you then recognise the prisoner as the man who hailed the cab?

WITNESS (hesitatingly): I cannot swear to that. The gentleman who hailed the cab had his hat pulled down over his eyes, so that I could not see his face; but the height and general appearance of the prisoner are the same.

CALTON: Then it is only because the man who got into the cab was dressed like the prisoner on that night that you thought they were both the same?

WITNESS: It never struck me for a minute that they were not the same; besides, he spoke as if he had been there before. I said — 'Oh, you've come back,' and he said — 'Yes; I'm going to take him home,' and got into my cab.

CALTON: Did you notice any difference in his voice?

WITNESS: No; except that the first time I saw him he spoke in a loud voice and the second time he came back, very low.

CALTON: You were sober, I suppose?

WITNESS (indignantly): Yes; quite sober.

CALTON: Ah! You did not have a drink, say at the Oriental Hotel, which, I believe, is near the rank where your cab stands?

WITNESS (hesitating): Well, I might have had a glass.

CALTON: So you might; you might have had several.

WITNESS (sulkily): Well, there's no law against a cove feeling thirsty.

CALTON: Certainly not; and I suppose you took advantage of the absence of such a law.

WITNESS (defiantly): Yes, I did.

CALTON: And you were elevated?

WITNESS: Yes; on my cab. — (Laughter).

CALTON (severely): You are here to give evidence, sir, not to make jokes, however clever they may be. Were you, or were you not, slightly the worse for drink?

WITNESS: I might have been.

CALTON: So you were in such a condition that you did not observe very closely the man who hailed you?

WITNESS: No, I didn't — there was no reason why I should — I didn't know a murder was going to be committed.

CALTON: And it never struck you it might be a different man?

WITNESS: No, I thought it was the same man the whole time.

This closed Royston's evidence, and Calton sat down very dissatisfied at not being able to elicit anything more definite from him. One thing appeared clear, that someone must have dressed himself to resemble Brian, and spoke in a low voice, because he was afraid of betraying himself.

Clement Rankin, the next witness, deposed to having picked up the prisoner on the St Kilda Road, between one and two on Friday morning, and driven him to Powlett Street, East Melbourne. In the cross-examination, Calton elicited one point in the prisoner's favour.

CALTON: Is the prisoner the same gentleman you drove to Powlett Street?

WITNESS (confidently): Oh, yes.

CALTON: How do you know? Did you see his face?

WITNESS: No, his hat was pulled down over his eyes, and I could only see the ends of his moustache and his chin, but he carried himself the same as the prisoner, and his moustache is the same light colour.

CALTON: When you drove up to him on the St Kilda Road, where was he, and what was he doing?

WITNESS: He was near the Grammar School, walking quickly in the direction of Melbourne, and was smoking a cigarette.

CALTON: Had he gloves on?

WITNESS: Yes, one on the left hand, the other was bare.

CALTON: Did he wear any rings on the right hand?

WITNESS: Yes, a large diamond one on the forefinger.

CALTON: Are you sure?

WITNESS: Yes, because I thought it a curious place for a gentleman to wear a ring, and when he was paying me my fare, I saw the diamond glitter on his finger in the moonlight.

CALTON: That will do.

The counsel for the defence was pleased with this bit of evidence, as Fitzgerald detested rings and never wore any; so he made a note of the matter on his brief.

Mrs Hableton, the landlady of the deceased, was then called, and deposed that Oliver Whyte had lived with her for nearly two months. He seemed a quiet enough young man, but often came home drunk. The only friend she knew he had was a Mr Moreland, who was often with him. On the 14th July, the prisoner called to see Mr Whyte, and they had a quarrel. She heard Whyte say, 'She is mine, you can't do anything with her,' and the prisoner answered, 'I can kill you, and if you marry her I will do so in the open street.' She had no idea at the time of the name of the lady they were talking about.

There was a great sensation in the court at these words, and half the people present looked upon such evidence as being sufficient in itself to prove the guilt of the prisoner.

In cross-examination, Calton was unable to shake the evidence of the witness, as she merely reiterated the same statements over and over again.

The next witness was Mrs Sampson, who crackled into the witness box dissolved in tears, and gave her answers in a piercingly shrill tone of anguish. She stated that the prisoner was in the habit of coming home early, but on the night of the murder, had come in shortly before two o'clock.

CROWN PROSECUTOR (referring to his brief): You mean after two.

WITNESS: 'Avin' made a mistake once, by saying five minutes after two to the policeman as called hisself a insurance agent, which 'e put the words into my mouth, I ain't a goin' to do so again, it bein' five minutes afore two, as I can swear to.

CROWN PROSECUTOR: You are sure your clock was right?

WITNESS: It 'adn't bin, but my nevy bein' a watchmaker, called unbeknown to me, an' made it right on Thursday night, which it was Friday mornin' when Mr Fitzgerald came 'ome.

Mrs Sampson bravely stuck to this statement, and ultimately left the witness box in triumph, the rest of her evidence being comparatively unimportant as compared with this point of time. The witness Rankin, who drove the prisoner to Powlett Street (as sworn to by him) was recalled, and gave evidence that it was two o'clock when the prisoner got down from his cab in Powlett Street.

CROWN PROSECUTOR: How do you know that?

WITNESS: Because I heard the post office clock strike.

CROWN PROSECUTOR: Could you hear it at East Melbourne?

WITNESS: It was a very still night, and I heard the chimes and then the hour strike quite plainly.

This conflicting evidence as to time was a strong point in Brian's favour. If, as the landlady stated, on the authority of the kitchen clock, which had been put right on the day previous to the murder, Fitzgerald had come into the house at five minutes to two, he could not possibly be the man who had alighted from Rankin's cab at two o'clock at Powlett Street.

The next witness was Dr Chinston, who swore to the death of the deceased by means of chloroform administered in a large quantity, and he was followed by Mr Gorby, who deposed as to the finding of the glove belonging to the deceased in the pocket of the prisoner's coat.

Roger Moreland, an intimate friend of the deceased, was next called. He stated that he had known the deceased in London, and had met him in Melbourne. He was with him a great deal. On the night of the murder he was in the Orient Hotel in Bourke Street. Whyte came in, and was greatly excited. He was in evening dress, and wore a light coat. They had several drinks together, and then went up to an hotel in Russell Street, and had some more drinks there. Both witness and deceased were intoxicated. Whyte took off his light coat, saying he felt warm, and went out shortly afterwards, leaving witness asleep in the bar. He was awoken by the barman, who wanted him to leave the hotel. He saw that Whyte had left his coat behind him, and took it up with the intention of giving it to him. As he stood in the street someone snatched the coat from him, and made off with it. He tried to follow the thief, but he could not do so, being too intoxicated. He then went home, and to bed, as he had to leave early for the country in the morning. In cross-examination:

CALTON: When you went into the street, after leaving the hotel, did you see the deceased?

WITNESS: No, I did not; but I was very drunk, and unless deceased had spoken to me, would not have noticed him.

CALTON: What was deceased excited about when you met him?

WITNESS: I don't know. He did not say.

CALTON: What were you talking about?

WITNESS: All sorts of things. London principally.

CALTON: Did the deceased mention anything about papers?

WITNESS (surprised): No, he did not.

CALTON: Are you sure?

WITNESS: Quite sure.

CALTON: What time did you get home?

WITNESS: I don't know; I was too drunk to remember.

This closed the case for the Crown, and as it was now late, the Court was adjourned till the next day. The Court was soon emptied of the busy, chattering crowd, and Calton, on looking over his notes, found that the result of the first day's trial was two points in favour of Fitzgerald. First: The discrepancy of time in the evidence of Rankin and the landlady, Mrs Sampson. Second: The evidence of the cabman, Royston, as to the wearing of a ring on the forefinger of the right hand by the man who murdered Whyte, whereas the prisoner never wore rings.

These were slender proofs of innocence to put against the overwhelming mass of evidence in favour of the prisoner's guilt. The opinions of all were pretty well divided, some being in favour and others against, when suddenly an event happened which surprised everyone. All over Melbourne extras were posted, and the news passed from lip to lip like wildfire — 'Return of the Missing Witness, Sal Rawlins!'

XVIII
Sal Rawlins Tells All She Knows

And, indeed, such was the case. Sal Rawlins had made her appearance at the eleventh hour, to the heartfelt thankfulness of Calton, who saw in her an angel from heaven, sent to save the life of an innocent man.

It was at the conclusion of the trial, and, together with Madge, he had gone down to his office, when his clerk entered with a telegram. The lawyer tore it open, and, with a silent look of pleasure on his face, handed the telegram to Madge. She, womanlike, being more impulsive, gave a cry when she read it, and, falling on her knees, thanked God for having heard her prayers, and saved her lover's life.

'Take me to her at once,' she implored the lawyer, being anxious to hear from Sal Rawlins' own lips the joyful words which would save Brian from a felon's death.

'No, my dear,' answered Calton, firmly, but kindly. 'I can hardly take a lady to where Sal Rawlins lives. You will know all to-morrow, but, meanwhile, you must go home and get some sleep.'

'And you will tell him?' she whispered, clasping her hands on Calton's arm.

'At once,' he answered promptly. 'And I will see Sal Rawlins to-night, and hear what she has to say. Rest content, my dear,' he added, as he placed her in the carriage, 'he is perfectly safe now.'

Brian heard the good news with a deep feeling of gratitude, knowing that his life was safe, and that he could still keep his secret. It was the natural revulsion of feeling after the unnatural life he had been leading since his arrest. When one is young and healthy, and has all the world before him, it is a terrible thing to contemplate with serenity a sudden death. And yet, in spite of his joy at being delivered from the hangman's rope, there mingled with his delight the horror of that secret which the dying woman had told him with such malignant joy.

'Why did she tell me? Oh, why did she tell me?' he cried, wringing his hands, as he paced restlessly up and down his dark cell. 'It would have been better for her to have died in silence, and not bequeathed me this legacy of sorrow.'

He was so greatly disturbed over the matter that the gaoler, seeing his haggard face next morning, muttered to himself that 'He war blest if the swell warn't sorry he war safe.'

So, while Brian was pacing up and down his cell during the weary watches of the night, Madge, in her own room, was kneeling beside her bed and thanking God for His great mercy; while Calton, the good fairy of the two lovers, was hurrying towards the humble abode of Mrs Rawlins, familiarly known as Mother Guttersnipe. Kilsip was beside him, and they were talking eagerly about the providential appearance of the invaluable witness.

'What I like,' observed Kilsip, in his soft, purring tone, 'is the sell it will be for that Gorby. He was so certain that Mr Fitzgerald was the man, and when he gets off tomorrow he will be in a rage.'

'Where was Sal the whole time?' asked Calton, absently, not thinking of what the detective was saying.

'Ill,' answered Kilsip. 'After she left the Chinaman she went into the country, caught cold by falling into some river, and then ended up by getting brain fever. Some people found her, took her in, and nursed her. When she got well she came back to her grandmother's.'

'But why didn't the people who nursed her tell her she was wanted? They must have seen the papers.'

'Not they,' retorted the detective. 'They knew nothing.'

'Vegetables!' muttered Calton, contemptuously. 'How can people be so ignorant? Why, all Australia has been ringing with the case. At any rate, it's money out of their pocket. Well?'

'There's nothing more to tell,' said Kilsip, 'except that she turned up tonight at five o'clock, looking more like a corpse than anything else.'

When they entered the squalid, dingy passage that led to Mother Guttersnipe's abode, they saw a faint light streaming down the stair. As they climbed up the shaky stair, they could hear the rancorous voice of the old hag pouring forth alternate blessings and curses on her prodigal offspring, and the low tones of a girl's voice in reply. On entering the room Calton saw that the sick woman who had been lying in the corner on the occasion of his last visit was gone. Mother Guttersnipe was seated in front of the deal table, with a broken cup and her favourite bottle of spirits before her. She was evidently going to have a night of it, in order to celebrate Sal's return, and had commenced early, so as to lose no time. Sal herself was seated on a broken chair, and leaned wearily against the wall. She stood up as Calton and the detective entered, and they saw she was a tall, slender woman of about twenty-five, not bad-looking, but with a pallid and haggard face, which showed how ill she had been. She was dressed in a kind of tawdry blue dress, much soiled and torn, and had an old tartan shawl over her shoulders, which she drew tightly across her breast as the strangers entered. Her grandmother, who looked more weird and grotesquely horrible than ever, saluted Calton and the detective on their entrance with a shrill yell, and a volley of choice language.

'Oh, ye've come agin, blarst ye,' she screeched, raising her skinny arms, 'to take my gal away from 'er pore old gran'mother, as nussed 'er, cuss her, when 'er own mother had gone a-gallivantin' with swells. I'll 'ave the lawr of ye both, s'elp me G—, I will.'

Kilsip paid no attention to this outbreak of the old fury, but turned to the girl.

'This is the gentleman who wants to speak to you,' he said, gently, making the girl sit on the chair again, for indeed she looked too ill to stand. 'Just tell him what you told me.'

' 'Bout the "Queen," sir?' said Sal, in a low, hoarse voice, fixing her wild eyes on Calton. 'If I'd only known as you was a-wantin' me I'd 'ave come afore.'

'Where were you?' asked Calton, in a pitying tone.

'Noo South Wales,' answered the girl, with a shiver. 'The cove as I went with t' Sydney left me — yes, left me to die like a dog in the gutter.'

'Blarst 'im!' croaked the old woman in a sympathetic manner, as she took a drink from the broken cup.

'I tooked up with a Chinerman,' went on her grand-daughter, wearily, 'an' lived with 'im for a bit — it's orful, ain't it?' she said, with a dreary laugh, as she saw the disgust on the lawyer's face. 'But Chinermen ain't bad; they treat a pore girl a dashed sight better nor a white cove does. They don't beat the life out of 'em with their fists, nor drag 'em about the floor by the 'air.'

'Cuss 'em!' croaked Mother Guttersnipe, drowsily, 'I'll tear their 'earts out.'

'I think I must have gone mad, I must,' said Sal, pushing her tangled hair off her forehead, 'for arter I left the Chiner cove, I went on walkin' and walkin' right into the bush, a-tryin' to cool my 'ead, for it felt on fire like. I went into a river an' got wet, an' then I took my 'at an' boots orf an' lay down on the grass, an' then the rain comed on, an' I walked to a 'ouse as was near, where they tooked me in. Oh, sich kind people,' she sobbed, stretching out her hands, 'that didn't badger me 'bout my soul, but gave me good food to eat. I gave 'em a wrong name. I was so 'fraid of that Army a-findin' me. Then I got ill, an' know'd nothin' for weeks. They said I was orf my chump. An' then I came back 'ere to see gran'.'

'Cuss ye,' said the old woman, but in such a tender tone that it sounded like a blessing; then, rather ashamed of the momentary emotion, she hastily wound up, 'Go to 'ell.'

'And did the people who took you in never tell you anything about the murder?' asked Calton.

Sal shook her head.

'No, it were a long way in the country, and they never know'd anythin', they didn't.'

'Ah! That explains it,' muttered Calton to himself. 'Come now,' he said cheerfully, 'tell me all that happened on the night you brought Mr Fitzgerald to see the "Queen." '

'Who's 'e?' asked Sal, puzzled.

'Mr Fitzgerald, the gentleman you brought the letter for to the Melbourne Club.'

'Oh, 'im?' said Sal, a sudden light breaking over her wan face. 'I never know'd his name afore.'

Calton nodded, complacently.

'I knew you didn't,' he said, 'that's why you didn't ask for him at the Club.'

'She never told me 'is name,' said Sal, jerking her head in the direction of the bed.

'Then who did she ask you to bring to her?' asked Calton, eagerly.

'No one,' replied the girl. 'This was the way of it. On that night she was orfil ill, an' I sat beside 'er while gran' was asleep.'

'I was drunk, blarst ye,' broke in gran', fiercely, 'None of yer d—d lies; I was blazin' drunk, glory rallelujah.'

'An' ses she to me, she ses,' went on the girl, indifferent to her grandmother's interruption, ' "Get me some paper an' a pencil, an' I'll write a note to 'im, I will." So I goes an' gits 'er what she arsks fur out of gran's box.'

'Stole it, blarst ye,' shrieked the old hag, shaking her fist.

'Hold your tongue,' said Kilsip, in a peremptory tone.

Mother Guttersnipe burst into a volley of oaths, and having run rapidly through all she knew, subsided into a sulky silence.

'She wrote on it,' went on Sal, 'an' then arsked me to take it to the Melbourne Club an' give it to 'im. Ses I, "Who's 'im?" Ses she, "It's on the letter; don't you arsk no questions an' you won't 'ear no lies, but give it to 'im at the Club, an' wait for 'im at the corner of Bourke Street and Russell Street." So out I goes, and gives it to a cove at the Club, an' then 'e comes along, an' ses 'e "Take me to 'er," and I tooked 'im.'

'And what like was the gentleman?'

'Oh, werry good lookin',' said Sal. 'Werry tall, with yeller 'air an' moustache. He 'ad party clothes on, an' a masher coat, an' a soft 'at.'

'That's Fitzgerald right enough,' muttered Calton. 'And what did he do when he came?'

'He goes right up to 'er, and she ses, "Are you 'e?" and 'e ses, "I am." Then ses she, "Do you know what I'm a-goin' to tell you?" an' 'e says, "No." Then she ses, "It's about 'er;" and ses 'e, lookin' very white, " 'Ow dare you 'ave 'er name on your vile lips?" an' she gits up an' screeches, "Turn that gal out, an' I'll tell you;" an' 'e takes me by the arm, an' ses 'e, " 'Ere git out," and I gits out, an' that's all I knows.'

'And how long was he with her?' asked Calton, who had been listening attentively.

' 'Bout arf-a-hour,' answered Sal. 'I takes 'im back to Russell Street 'bout twenty-five minutes to two, 'cause I looked at the clock on the post office, an' 'e gives me a sov, an' then he goes a-tearin' up the street like anything.'

'Take him about twenty minutes to walk to East Melbourne,' said Calton to himself. 'So he must just have got in at the time Mrs Sampson said. He was in with the "Queen" the whole time, I suppose?' he asked, looking keenly at Sal.

'I was at that door,' said Sal, pointing to it, 'an' 'e couldn't 'ave got out unless I'd seen 'im.'

'Oh, it's all right,' said Calton, nodding to Kilsip, 'there won't be any difficulty in proving an *alibi*. But I say,' he added, turning to Sal, 'what were they talking about?'

'I dunno,' answered Sal. 'I was at the door, an' they talks that quiet I couldn't 'ear 'em. Then he sings out, "My G—, it's too horrible!" an' I 'ear 'er a larfin' like to bust, an' then 'e comes to me, and ses, quite wild like, "Take me out of this 'ell!" an' I tooked 'im.'

'And when you came back?'

'She was dead.'

'Dead?'

'As a blessed door-nail,' said Sal, cheerfully.

'An' I never know'd I was in the room with a blarsted corpse,' wailed Mother Guttersnipe, waking up. 'Cuss 'er, she was allays a-doin' contrary things.'

'How do you know?' said Calton, sharply, as he rose to go.

'I know'd 'er longer nor you, cuss ye,' croaked the old woman, fixing one evil eye on the lawyer; 'an' I know what you'd like to know; but ye shan't, ye shan't.'

Calton turned from her with a shrug of his shoulders.

'You will come to the Court tomorrow with Mr Kilsip,' he said to Sal, 'and tell what you have just now told me.'

'It's all true, s'elp me,' said Sal, eagerly; ' 'e was 'ere all the time.'

Calton stepped towards the door, followed by the detective, when Mother Guttersnipe arose.

'Where's the money for finin' 'er?' she screeched, pointing one skinny finger at Sal.

'Well, considering the girl found herself,' said Calton, dryly, 'the money is in the bank, and will remain there.'

'An' I'm to be done out of my 'ard-earned tin, s'elp me?' howled the old fury. 'Cuss ye, I'll 'ave the lawr of ye, and get ye put in quod.'

'You'll go there yourself if you don't take care,' said Kilsip, in his soft, purring tones.

'Yah!' shrieked Mother Guttersnipe, snapping her fingers at him. 'What do I care about yer d—d quod? Ain't I bin in Pentrig', an' it ain't 'urt me, it ain't? I'm as lively as a gal, blarst ye, and cuss ye.'

And the old fury, to prove the truth of her words, danced a kind of war dance in front of Mr Calton, snapping her fingers and yelling out curses, as an accompaniment to her ballet. Her luxurious white hair got loose, and streamed out during her gyrations, and what with her grotesque looks and the faint light of the candle, she looked a gruesome spectacle. Calton, remembering the tales he had heard of the women of Paris, at the revolution, and the way they danced 'La Carmagnole,' thought that Mother Guttersnipe would have been in her element in that sea of blood and turbulence. He, however, merely shrugged his shoulders, and walked out of the room, as with a final curse, delivered in a hoarse voice, Mother Guttersnipe sank exhausted on the floor, and yelled for gin.

XIX
The Verdict of the Jury

It is needless to say that the court next morning was crowded, and numbers were unable to gain admission. The news that Sal Rawlins, who alone could prove the innocence of the prisoner, had been found, and would appear in court that morning, had spread like wildfire, and the acquittal of the prisoner was confidently expected by a large number of sympathising friends, who seemed to have sprung up on all sides, like mushrooms, in a single night. There were, of course, plenty of cautious people left who waited to hear the verdict of the jury before giving their opinion, and who still believed him guilty. But the unexpected appearance of Sal Rawlins had turned the great tide of public feeling in favour of the prisoner, and many who had been loudest in their denunciations of Fitzgerald, were now more than half convinced of his innocence. Pious clergymen talked in an incoherent way about the finger of God and the innocent not suffering unjustly, which was a case of counting unhatched chickens, as the verdict had yet to be given.

Felix Rolleston awoke, and found himself famous in a small way. Out of good-natured sympathy, and a spice of contrariness, he had declared his belief in Brian's innocence, and now, to his astonishment, found that his view of the matter was likely to be a correct one. He received so much praise on all sides for his presumed cleverness, that he soon began to think that he had believed in Fitzgerald's innocence by a calm course of reasoning, and not because of a desire to differ from everyone else in their opinion of the case. After all, Felix Rolleston is not the only man who has been astonished to find greatness thrust upon him, and come to believe himself worthy of it. He was a wise man, however, and while in the full tide of prosperity seized the flying moment, and proposed to Miss Featherweight, who, after some hesitation, agreed to endow him with herself and her thousands. She decided that her future husband was a man of no common intellect, seeing that he had long ago arrived at a conclusion which the rest of Melbourne were only beginning to discover now, so she determined that, as soon as she assumed marital authority, Felix, like Strephon in 'Iolanthe,' should go into Parliament, and with her money and his brains she might some day be the wife of a premier. Mr Rolleston had no idea of the political honours which his future spouse intended he should have, and was seated in his old place in the court, talking about the case.

'Knew he was innocent, don't you know,' he said, with a complacent smile. 'Fitzgerald's too jolly good-looking a fellow, and all that sort of thing, to commit murder.'

Whereupon a clergyman, happening to overhear the lively Felix make this flippant remark, disagreed with it entirely, and preached a sermon to prove that good looks and crime were closely connected, and that both Judas Iscariot and Nero were beauty-men.

'Ah,' said Calton, when he heard the sermon, 'if this unique theory is a true one, what a truly pious man that clergyman must be!' which allusion to the looks of the reverend gentleman was rather unkind, as he was by no means bad looking. But then Calton was one of those witty men who would rather lose a friend than suppress an epigram.

When the prisoner was brought in a murmur of sympathy ran through the crowded court, so ill and worn out he looked; but Calton was puzzled to account for the expression of his face, so different from that of a man whose life had been saved, or, rather, was going to be saved, for in truth it was a foregone conclusion.

'You know who stole those papers,' he thought, as he looked at Fitzgerald, keenly, 'and the man who did so is the murderer of

Whyte.'

The judge having entered, and the court being opened, Calton arose to make his speech, and stated in a few words the line of defence he intended to take.

He would first call Albert Dendy, a watchmaker, to prove that on Thursday night, at eight o'clock in the evening, he had called at the prisoner's lodgings while the landlady was out, and while there had put the kitchen clock right, and had regulated the same. He would also call Felix Rolleston, a friend of the prisoner's, to prove that the prisoner was not in the habit of wearing rings, and frequently expressed his detestation of such a custom. Sebastian Brown, a waiter at the Melbourne Club, would be called to prove that on Thursday night a letter was delivered to the prisoner at the Club by one Sarah Rawlins, and that the prisoner left the Club shortly before one o'clock on Friday morning. He would also call Sarah Rawlins, to prove that she had delivered a note to Sebastian Brown for the prisoner, at the Melbourne Club, at a quarter to twelve on Thursday night, and that at a few minutes past one o'clock on Friday morning she had conducted the prisoner to a slum off Little Bourke Street, and that he was there between one and two on Friday morning, the hour at which the murder was alleged to have taken place. This being his defence to the charge brought against the prisoner, he would call Albert Dendy.

Albert Dendy, duly sworn, stated —

I am a watchmaker, and carry on business in Fitzroy. I remember Thursday, the 26th of July last. On the evening of that day I called at Powlett Street, East Melbourne, to see my aunt, who is the landlady of the prisoner. She was out at the time I called, and I waited in the kitchen till her return. I looked at the kitchen clock to see if it was too late to wait, and then at my watch. I found that the clock was ten minutes fast, upon which I put it right, and regulated it properly.

CALTON: At what time did you put it right?

WITNESS: About eight o'clock.

CALTON: Between that time and two in the morning, was it possible for the clock to gain ten minutes?

WITNESS: No, it was not possible.

CALTON: Would it gain at all?

WITNESS: Not between eight and two o'clock — the time was

not long enough.

CALTON: Did you see your aunt that night?

WITNESS: Yes, I waited till she came in.

CALTON: And did you tell her you had put the clock right?

WITNESS: No, I did not; I forgot all about it.

CALTON: Then she was still under the impression that it was ten minutes fast?

WITNESS: Yes, I suppose so.

After Dendy had been cross-examined, Felix Rolleston was called, and deposed as follows:

I am an intimate friend of the prisoner. I have known him for five or six years, and I never saw him wearing a ring during that time. He has frequently told me he did not care for rings, and would never wear them.

In cross-examination:

CROWN PROSECUTOR: You have never seen the prisoner wearing a diamond ring?

WITNESS: No, never.

CROWN PROSECUTOR: Have you ever seen any such ring in his possession?

WITNESS: No, I have seen him buying rings for ladies, but I never saw him with any ring such as a gentleman would wear.

CROWN PROSECUTOR: Not even a seal ring.

WITNESS: No, not even a seal ring.

Sarah Rawlins was then placed in the witness-box, and, after having been sworn, deposed —

I know the prisoner. I delivered a letter, addressed to him at the Melbourne Club, at a quarter to twelve o'clock on Thursday, 26th July. I did not know what his name was. He met me shortly after one, at the corner of Russell and Bourke Streets, where I had been told to wait for him. I took him to my grandmother's place, in a lane off Little Bourke Street. There was a dying woman there, who had sent for him. He went in and saw her for about twenty minutes, and then I took him back to the corner of Bourke and Russell Streets. I heard the three-quarters strike shortly after I left him.

CROWN PROSECUTOR: You are quite certain that the prisoner was the man you met on that night?

WITNESS; Quite certin, s'elp me G—.

Crown Prosecutor: And he met you a few minutes past one o'clock?

Witness: Yes, 'bout five minutes — I 'eard the clock a-strikin' one just afore he came down the street, and when I leaves 'im agin, it were about twenty-five to two, 'cause it took me ten minits to git 'ome, and I 'eard the clock go three-quarters, jest as I gets to the door.

Crown Prosecutor: How do you know it was exactly twenty-five to two when you left him?

Witness: 'Cause I sawr the clocks — I left 'im at the corner of Russell Street, and comes down Bourke Street, so I could see the Post Orffice clock as plain as day, an' when I gets into Swanston Street, I looks at the Town 'All premiscus like, and see the same time there.

Crown Prosecutor: And you never lost sight of the prisoner the whole time?

Witness: No, there was only one door by the room, an' I was a-sittin' outside it, an' when he comes out he falls over me.

Crown Prosecutor: Were you asleep?

Witness: Not a blessed wink.

Calton then directed Sebastian Brown to be called, who deposed —

I know the prisoner. He is a member of the Melbourne Club, at which I am a waiter. I remember Thursday, 26th July. On that night the last witness came with a letter to the prisoner. It was about a quarter to twelve. She just gave it to me, and went away. I delivered it to Mr Fitzgerald. He left the Club at about ten minutes to one.

This closed the evidence for the defence, and after the Crown Prosecutor had made his speech, in which he pointed out the strong evidence against the prisoner, Calton arose to address the jury. He was a fine speaker, and made a splendid defence. Not a single point escaped him, and that brilliant piece of oratory is still remembered and spoken of admiringly in the purlieus of Temple Court and Chancery Lane.

He began by giving a vivid description of the circumstances of the murder — of the meeting of the murderer and his victim in Collins Street East — the cab driving down to St Kilda — the getting out of the cab of the murderer after committing the crime

— and the way in which he had secured himself against pursuit. Having thus enchained the attention of the jury by the graphic manner in which he described the crime, he pointed out that the evidence brought forward by the prosecution was purely circumstantial, and that they had utterly failed to identify the man who entered the cab with the prisoner in the dock. The supposition that the prisoner and the man in the light coat, being one and the same person, rested solely upon the evidence of the cabman, Royston, who, although not intoxicated, was, judging from his own statements, not in a fit state to distinguish between the man who hailed the cab and the man who got in. The crime was committed by means of chloroform; therefore, if the prisoner was guilty, he must have purchased the chloroform in some shop, or obtained it from some friends. At all events, the prosecution had not brought forward a single piece of evidence to show how and where the chloroform was obtained. With regard to the glove belonging to the murdered man found in the prisoner's pocket, he picked it up off the ground at the time when he first met Whyte, when the deceased was lying drunk near the Scotch Church. Certainly there was no evidence to show that the prisoner had picked it up before the deceased entered the cab; but, on the other hand, there was no evidence to show that it had been picked up in the cab. It was far more likely that the glove, and especially a white glove, would be picked up under the light of the lamp near the Scotch Church, where it was easily noticeable, than in the darkness of a cab, where there was very little room, and where it would be quite dark, as the blinds were drawn down. The cabman, Royston, swore positively that the man who got out of his cab on the St Kilda Road wore a diamond ring on the forefinger of his right hand, and the cabman, Rankin, swore to the same thing about the man who got out at Powlett Street. Against this could be placed the evidence of one of the prisoner's most intimate friends — one who had seen him almost daily for the last five years, and he had sworn positively that the prisoner never was in the habit of wearing rings. The cabman Rankin had also sworn that the man who entered his cab on the St Kilda Road alighted at Powlett Street, East Melbourne, at two o'clock on Friday morning, as he heard that hour strike from the Post Office clock, whereas the evidence of the prisoner's landlady showed plainly that he entered the house five minutes previously, and her evidence was further supported by that of the watchmaker, Dendy. Mrs Sampson saw the hand of her kitchen clock point to five minutes to two, and, thinking it was ten minutes slow, told the detective the prisoner did not enter the house till five minutes past two, which would just give the man who alighted from the cab, presuming him to have been the prisoner, sufficient time to walk up to his lodgings. The evidence of the watchmaker, Dendy, however, showed clearly that he had put the clock right at the hour of eight on Thursday night; that it was impossible for it to gain ten minutes before two on Friday morning, and, therefore, the time, five minutes to two, seen by the landlady was the correct one, and the prisoner was in the house five minutes before the other man alighted from the cab in Powlett Street. These points in themselves were sufficient to show that the prisoner was innocent, but the evidence of the woman Rawlins must prove conclusively to the jury that the prisoner was not the man who committed the crime. The witness Brown had proved that the woman Rawlins had delivered a letter to him, which he gave to the prisoner, and that the prisoner left the Club, personally, to keep the appointment spoken of in the letter, which letter, or, rather, the remains of it, had been put in evidence. The woman Rawlins swore that the prisoner met her at the corner of Russell and Bourke Streets, and had gone with her to one of the back slums, there to see the writer of the letter. She also proved that at the time of the committal of the crime the prisoner was still in the back slum, by the bed of the dying woman, and, there being only one door to the room, could not possibly have left without the witness seeing him. The woman Rawlins further proved that she left the prisoner at the corner of Bourke and Russell Streets at twenty-five minutes to two o'clock, which was five minutes before Royston drove his cab up to the St Kilda Police Station, with the dead body inside. Finally, the woman Rawlins proved her words by stating she saw both the Post Office and Town Hall clocks; and supposing the prisoner started from the corner of Bourke and Russell Streets, as she says he did, he would reach East Melbourne in twenty minutes, which made it five minutes to two on Friday morning, the time at which, according to the landlady's statement, he entered the house. All the evidence given by the different witnesses agreed completely, and formed a chain which showed the whole of the prisoner's movements at the time of the committal of the murder. Therefore, it was absolutely impossible that the murder could have been committed by the man in the dock. The strongest piece of evidence brought forward by the prosecution was that of the witness Hableton, who swore that the prisoner used threats against the life of the deceased. But the language used was merely the outcome of a passionate Irish nature, and was not sufficient to prove the crime to have been committed by the prisoner. The defence which the prisoner set up was that of an *alibi*, and the evidence of the witnesses for the defence proved conclusively that the prisoner could not, and did not, commit the murder. Finally, Calton wound up his elaborate and exhaustive speech, which lasted for over two hours, by a brilliant peroration, calling upon the jury to base their verdict upon the plain facts of the case, and if they did so they could hardly fail in bringing in a verdict of 'Not guilty.'

When Calton sat down a subdued murmur of applause was heard, which was instantly suppressed, and the judge began to sum up, which he did strongly in favour of Fitzgerald. The jury then retired, and immediately there was a dead silence in the crowded court — an unnatural silence, such as must have fallen on the blood-loving Roman populace when they saw the Christian martyrs kneeling on the hot yellow sands of the arena, and watched the long, lithe forms of lion and panther creeping stealthily towards their prey. The hour being late the gas had been lighted, and there was a sickly glare through the wide hall, which added to the singularity of the scene. Fitzgerald had been taken out of the court on the retiring of the jury, but the spectators stared steadily at the empty dock, which seemed to enchain them by some indescribable fascination. They conversed among themselves only in whispers, until even the whispering ceased, and nothing could be heard but the steady ticking of the clock, and now and then the quick-drawn breath of some timid onlooker. Suddenly a woman, whose nerves were over-strung, shrieked, and the cry rang weirdly through the crowded hall. She was taken out, and again there was silence, every eye being now fixed on the door through which the jury would re-issue with their verdict of life or death. The hands of the clock moved slowly round — a quarter — a half — three-quarters — and then the hour sounded with a silvery ring which startled everyone. Madge, sitting with her hands tightly clasped together, began to fear that her highly-strung nerves would give way.

'My God,' she muttered softly to herself; 'will this suspense never end?'

Just then the door opened, and the jury re-entered. The prisoner was again placed in the dock, and the judge again resumed his seat, this time with the black cap in his pocket, as everyone guessed.

The usual formalities were gone through, and when the foreman of the jury stood up every neck was craned forward, and every ear was on the alert to catch the words that fell from his lips. The prisoner flushed a little, and then grew pale as death, giving a quick, nervous glance at the quiet figure in black, of which he could just catch a glimpse. Then came the verdict, sharp and decisive, 'NOT GUILTY.'

On hearing this a cheer went up from everyone in the court, so strong was the sympathy with Brian.

In vain the crier of the court yelled, 'Order!' until he was red in the face. In vain the judge threatened to commit all present for contempt of court — his voice being inaudible, it did not matter much — the enthusiasm could not be restrained, and it was five minutes before order was obtained. The judge, having recovered his composure, delivered his judgment, and discharged the prisoner, in accordance with the verdict. Calton had won many cases, but it is questionable if he had ever heard a verdict which gave him so much satisfaction as that which proclaimed Fitzgerald innocent.

And Brian, stepping down from the dock a free man, passed through a crowd of congratulating friends to a small room off the court, where a woman was waiting for him — a woman who clung round his neck, and sobbed out —

'My darling! My darling! I knew that God would save you.'

XX
The *Argus* Gives its Opinion

The morning after the trial was concluded the following article in reference to the matter appeared in the *Argus*:

'During the past three months we have frequently in our columns commented on the extraordinary case which is now so widely known as "The Hansom Cab Tragedy." We can safely say that it is the most remarkable case which has ever come under the notice of our Criminal Court, and the verdict given by the jury yesterday has enveloped the matter in a still deeper mystery. By a train of strange coincidences, Mr Brian Fitzgerald, a young squatter, was suspected of having murdered Whyte, and had it not been for the timely appearance of the woman Rawlins who turned up at the eleventh hour, we feel sure that a verdict of guilty would have been given, and an innocent man would have suffered punishment for the crime of another. Fortunately for the prisoner, and for the interests of justice, his counsel, Mr Calton, by unwearied diligence, was able to discover the last witness, and prove an *alibi*. Had it not been for this, in spite of the remarks made by the learned counsel in his brilliant speech yesterday, which resulted in the acquittal of the prisoner, we question very much if the rest of the evidence in favour of the accused would have been sufficient to persuade the jury that he was an innocent man. The only points in favour of Mr Fitzgerald were the inability of the cabman Royston to swear to him as the man who had got into the cab with Whyte, the wearing of a diamond ring on the forefinger of the right hand (whereas Mr Fitzgerald wears no rings), and the difference in time sworn to by the cabman Rankin and the landlady. Against these points, however, the prosecution placed a mass of evidence, which seemed to conclusively prove the guilt of the prisoner; but the appearance of Sal Rawlins in the witness-box put an end to all doubt. In language which could not be mistaken for anything else than the truth, she positively swore that Mr Fitzgerald was in one of the slums off Bourke Street between the hours of one and two on Friday morning, at which time the murder was committed. Under these circumstances, the jury unanimously agreed in the verdict, "Not guilty," and the prisoner was forthwith acquitted. We have to congratulate his counsel, Mr Calton, for the able speech he made for the defence, and also Mr Fitzgerald, for his providential escape from a dishonourable and undeserved punishment. He leaves the court without a stain on his character, and with the respect and sympathy of all Australians, for the courage and dignity with which he comported himself throughout, while resting under the shadow of such a serious charge.

'But now that it has been conclusively proved that he is innocent, the question arises in everyone's mind, "Who is the murderer of Oliver Whyte?" The man who committed this dastardly crime is still at large, and, for all we know, may be in our midst. Emboldened by the impunity with which he has escaped the hands of justice, he may be walking securely down our streets, and talking of the very crime of which he is the perpetrator. Secure in the thought that all traces of him have been lost for ever, from the time he alighted from Rankin's cab, at Powlett Street, he has likely ventured to remain in Melbourne, and, for all that anyone knows, may have been in the court during the late trial. Nay, this very article, for which his crime has furnished the necessity of its being written, may meet his eye, and he may rejoice at the futile efforts which have been made to find him. But let him beware, Justice is not blind, but blind-folded, and when he least expects it, she will tear the bandage from her keen eyes, and drag him forth to the light of day to receive the reward of his deed. Owing to the strong evidence against Fitzgerald, that is the only direction in which the detectives have hitherto looked, but baffled on one side, they will look on the other, and this time may be successful.

'That such a man as the murderer of Oliver Whyte should be at large is a matter of danger, not only to individual citizens, but to the community at large; for it is a well-known fact that a tiger who once tastes human blood never overcomes his craving for it; and, without doubt, the man who so daringly and coolly murdered a drunken, and therefore defenceless man, will not hesitate about committing a second crime. The present feeling of all classes in Melbourne must be one of terror, that such a man should be at large, and must, in a great measure, resemble the fear which filled everyone's heart in London when the Marr murders were committed, and it was known that the murderer had escaped. Anyone who has read De Quincy's graphic description of the crime perpetrated by Williams must tremble to think that such another devil incarnate is in our midst. It is an imperative necessity that such a feeling should be done away with. But how is this to be managed? It is one thing to speak, and another to act. There seems to be no possible clue discoverable at present which can lead to the discovery of the real murderer. The man in the light coat who got out of Rankin's cab at Powlett Street, East Melbourne (designedly, as it now appears, in order to throw suspicion on Fitzgerald), has vanished as completely as the witches in Macbeth, and left no trace behind. It was two o'clock in the morning when he left the cab, and, in a quiet suburb like East Melbourne, no one would be about, so that he could easily escape unseen. There seems to be only one chance of ever tracing him, and that is to be found in the papers which were stolen from the pocket of the dead man. What they were, only two persons knew, and one knows now. The first two were Whyte and the woman who was called "The Queen," and both of them are now dead. The other who knows now is the man who committed the crime. There can be no doubt in the minds of our readers that these papers were the motive of the crime, as no money was taken from the pockets of the deceased. The fact, also, that the papers were carried in a pocket made inside the waistcoat of the deceased shows that they were of value.

'Now, the reason we think that the dead woman knew of the existence of these papers is simply this. It appears that she came out from England with Whyte as his mistress, and after staying some time in Sydney came on to Melbourne. How she came into such a foul and squalid den as that she died in, we are unable to say, unless, seeing that she was given to drink, she was taken up drunk by some Samaritan of the slums, and carried to Mrs Rawlins' humble abode. Whyte visited her there frequently, but appears to have made no attempt to remove her to a better place, alleging as his reason that the doctor said she would die if taken into the air. Our reporter learned from one of the detectives that the dead woman was in the habit of talking to Whyte about certain papers, and on one occasion was overheard to say to him, "They'll make your fortune if you play your cards well." This was told to the detective by the woman Rawlins, to whose providential appearance Mr Fitzgerald owes his escape. From this it can be gathered that the papers — whatever they might be — were of value, and sufficient to tempt another to commit a murder in order to obtain them. Whyte, therefore, being dead, and his murderer escaped, the only way of discovering the secret which lies at the root of this tree of crime, is to find out the history of the woman who died in the slum. Traced back for some years, circumstances may be discovered which will reveal what these papers contained, and once that is found, we can confidently say that the murderer will soon be discovered. This is the only chance of finding out the cause and the author of this mysterious murder; and if it fails, we fear the hansom cab tragedy will have to be relegated to the list of those undiscovered crimes, and the assassin of Whyte will have no other punishment than the remorse of his own conscience.'

XXI
Three Months Afterwards

A hot December day, with a cloudless blue sky, and a sun blazing down on the earth, clothed in all the beauty of summer garments. Such a description of snowy December must sound strange to English ears, and a hot Christmas day must strike them as being as fantastic as the play in a Midsummer's Night Dream did to Demetrius, when he remarked of it, 'This is hot ice, and wondrous cold fire.' But here in Australia is the realm of topsy-turveydom, and many things, like dreams, go by contraries. Here black swans are an established fact, and the proverb concerning them, when they were considered as mythical a bird as the Phoenix, has been rendered null and void by the discoveries of Captain Cook. Out here ironwood sinks and pumice stone floats, which must strike the curious spectator as a queer freak on the part of Dame Nature. At home the Edinburgh mail bears the hardy traveller to a cold climate, with snowy mountains and wintry blasts; but here the further north one goes the hotter it gets, till it terminates in Queensland, where the heat is so great that a profane traveller of an epigrammatic turn of mind once fittingly called it, 'An amateur hell.' But however contrary, as Mrs Gamp would say, Nature may be in her dealings, the English race out in this great continent are much the same as in the old country — John Bull, Paddy, and Sandy, all being of a conservative turn of mind, and with strong opinions as to the keeping up of old customs. Therefore, on a hot Christmas day, with the sun one hundred odd in the shade, Australian revellers sit down to the roast beef and plum pudding of old England, which they eat contentedly as the orthodox thing, and on New Year's eve the festive Celt repairs to the doors of his 'freends' with a bottle of whisky and a cheering verse of Auld Lang Syne. However, it is these peculiar customs that give an individuality to a nation, and John Bull abroad loses none of his insular obstinacy, and keeps his Christmas in the old fashion, and wears his clothes in the new fashion, without regard to heat or cold. A nation that never surrenders to the fire of an enemy cannot be expected to give in to the fire of the sun, but if some ingenious mortal would only invent some light and airy costume, after the fashion of the Greek dress, and Australians would consent to adopt the same, life in Melbourne and her sister cities would be much cooler than it is at present.

Madge was thinking somewhat after this fashion as she sat on the wide verandah, in a state of exhaustion from the heat, and stared out at the wide plains lying parched and arid under the blazing sun. There was a dim kind of haze rising from the excessive heat, hanging midway between heaven and earth, and through its tremulous veil the distant hills looked aeriel and unreal. Just before her was the garden, which made her hot to look at, so vivid were the colours of the flowers. Great bushes of oleanders, with their bright pink blossoms, luxurious rose trees, with their yellow, red and white flowers, and all along the border a rainbow of many-coloured flowers, with such brilliant tints that the eye ached to see them in the hot sunshine, and turned restfully to the cool green of the trees which encircled the lawn. In the centre was a round pool, surrounded by a ring of white marble, and containing a still sheet of water, which flashed like a mirror in the blinding light. The homestead of Yabba Yallook station was a long low house, with no upstairs, and with a wide verandah running nearly round it. Cool green blinds were hung between the pillars to keep out the sun, and all along were scattered lounging chairs of basket-work, with rugs, novels, empty soda-water bottles, and all the other evidences that Mr Frettlby's guests had been wise, and stayed inside during the noonday heat. Madge was seated in one of these comfortable chairs, and divided her attention between the glowing beauty of the world outside, which she could see through a narrow slit in the blind, and a new novel from Mullen's lying open on her knee. This latter did not interest her much, and no wonder, being one of the polyglot productions of the present day, which contains quotations from the language of every nation under the sun, and where the characters speak in a barbarous jangle of English and French, with an occasional scrap of German thrown in. The powerful and flexible English tongue, which was sufficient for the brilliant thoughts of Macaulay and Addison, is much despised by many of our modern novelists, who express themselves in a foolish mixture of French and English, which is as irritating as it is pedantic. With one of these literary curiosities on her knee, it is not surprising that Miss Frettlby let 'Tristan, a Romance by Zoe,' fall unheeded on the ground, and gave herself up to her own sad thoughts. She was not looking well, for the trial through which she had passed had been very great, and had left its impress of sorrow on her beautiful face. In her eyes, too, usually so calm, there was a troubled look, as, leaning her head upon her hands, she thought of the bitterness of the past year.

After Brian's acquittal of the murder of Oliver Whyte, she had been taken by her father up to the station, in the hope that it would restore her to health. The mental strain which had been on her during the trial had nearly brought on an attack of brain fever, but here, far from the excitement of town life, in the quiet seclusion of the country, she had recovered her health, but not her spirits. Women are more impressionable than men, and it is, perhaps, for this reason that they age quicker. A trouble which would pass lightly over a man, leaves an indelible mark on a woman, both physically and mentally, and the terrible episode of Whyte's murder had changed Madge from a bright and merry girl into a grave and beautiful woman. Ah! Sorrow is a potent enchantress, and once she touches the heart, life can never be the same again, for we never more surrender ourselves entirely to the pleasures of life, but find that many things which we have longed for, when obtained, are but dead-sea fruit. Sorrow is the veiled Isis of the world, and once we penetrate her mystery and see her deeply furrowed face and mournful eyes, the magic light of romance dies away from the world, and we see the hard, bitter facts of life in their harsh nakedness. This was the way Madge felt, and she saw the world now, not as the fantastic fairyland of her girlish dreams, but as the sorrowful vale of tears through which we must all walk till we reach the 'Promised Land.' And Brian, he also had undergone a change, for there were a few white hairs now amid his curly, chestnut locks, and his character, from being gay and bright, had become moody and irritable. After the trial he had left town immediately, in order to avoid meeting with his friends, and had gone up to his station, which was next to that of the Frettlbys'. There he worked hard all day, and smoked hard all night, thinking over the cursed secret which the dead woman had told him, and which threatened to overshadow his life. Every now and then he rode over and saw Madge, but only when he knew her father was away in Melbourne, for he seemed to have taken a dislike to the millionaire, which Madge could not help condemning as unjust, remembering how her father had stood beside him in his trouble. But there was another reason why Brian kept aloof from Yabba Yallook Station, and that was, he did not wish to meet any of the gay society which was there, knowing that since his trial he was an object of curiosity and sympathy to everyone — a position which was very galling to his proud nature. At Christmas time Mr Frettlby had asked a lot of people up from Melbourne, and though Madge would rather have been left alone, yet she could not refuse her father, and had to play hostess with a smiling brow and aching heart. Felix Rolleston, who a month since had joined the noble army of benedicts, was there with Mrs Rolleston, *née* Miss Featherweight, who ruled him with a rod of iron. Having bought Felix with her money, she had determined to make good use of him, and, being ambitious to shine in Melbourne society, had insisted upon Felix studying politics, so that when the next general election came round he could enter Parliament. Felix had rebelled at first, but ultimately gave way, as he found that when he had a good novel concealed among his parliamentary papers time passed quite pleasantly, and he got the reputation of a hard worker at little cost. They had brought up Julia with them, and this young person had made up her mind to become the second Mrs

Frettlby. She had not received much encouragement, but, like the English at Waterloo, did not know when she was beaten, and carried on the siege of Mr Frettlby's heart in an undaunted manner. Dr Chinston had come up for a little relaxation, and never gave a thought to his anxious patients or the many sick-rooms he was in the habit of visiting. A young English fellow, called Peterson, who amused himself by travelling; an old colonist, full of reminiscences of the old days, when, 'by gad, sir, we hadn't a gas lamp in the whole of Melbourne,' and several other people, completed the party. They had all gone off to the billiard-room, and left Madge in her comfortable chair, half asleep.

Suddenly, she started as she heard a step behind her, and turning, saw Sal Rawlins, in the neatest of black gowns, with a coquettish white cap and apron, and an open book. The fact is, Madge had been so delighted with Sal for saving Brian's life that she had taken her into her service as maid. Mr Frettlby had offered strong opposition at first that a fallen woman like Sal should be near his daughter; but Madge determined to rescue the unhappy girl from the life of sin she was leading, and so at last he reluctantly consented. Brian, too, had objected, but ultimately yielded, as he saw that Madge had set her heart on it. Mother Guttersnipe objected at first, characterising the whole affair as 'blarsted 'umbug,' but she, likewise, gave in, and Sal became maid to Miss Frettlby, who immediately set to work to remedy Sal's defective education by teaching her to read. The book she held in her hand was a spelling-book, and this she handed to Madge.

'I think I knows it now, Miss,' she said, respectfully, as Madge looked up with a smile.

'Do you, indeed?' said Madge, gaily. 'You will be able to read in no time, Sal.'

'Read this?' said Sal, touching 'Tristan: A Romance, by Zoe.'

'Hardly!' said Madge, picking it up, with a look of contempt. 'I want you to learn English, and not a confusion of tongues like this thing. But it's too hot to do lessons, Sal,' she went on, leaning back in her seat, 'so get a chair and talk to me.'

Sal complied, and Madge looked out on to the brilliant flower-beds, and at the black shadow of the tall witch elm which grew on one side of the lawn. She wanted to ask a certain question of Sal, and did not know how to do it. The moodiness and irritability of

Brian had troubled her very much of late, and, with the quick instinct of her sex, she ascribed it indirectly to the woman who had died in the back slum. Anxious to share his troubles and lighten his burden, she determined to ask Sal about this mysterious woman, and find out, if possible, what secret had been told to Brian which affected him so deeply.

'Sal,' she said, after a short pause, turning her clear grey eyes on the woman, 'I want to ask you something.'

The other shivered and turned pale.

'About — about that?'

Madge nodded.

Sal hesitated for a moment, and then flung herself at the feet of her mistress.

'I will tell you,' she cried. 'You have been kind to me, an' have a right to know. I will tell you all I know.'

'Then,' asked Madge, firmly, as she clasped her hands tightly together, 'who was this woman whom Mr Fitzgerald went to see, and where did she come from?'

'Gran' an' me found her one evenin' in Little Bourke Street,' answered Sal, 'just near the theatre. She was quite drunk, an' we took her home with us.'

'How kind of you,' said Madge.

'Oh, it wasn't that,' replied the other, dryly. 'Gran' wanted her clothes; she was awful swell dressed.'

'And she took the clothes — how wicked!'

'Anyone would have done it down our way,' answered Sal, indifferently; 'But Gran' changed her mind when she got her home. I went out to get some gin for Gran', and when I came back she was huggin' and kissin' the woman.'

'She recognised her?'

'Yes, I s'pose so,' replied Sal, 'an' next mornin', when the lady got square, she made a grab at Gran', an' hollered out, "I was comin' to see you." '

'And then?'

'Gran' chucked me out of the room, an' they had a long jaw; and then, when I come back, Gran' tells me the lady is a-goin' to stay with us 'cause she was ill, and sent me for Mr Whyte.'

'And he came?'

'Oh, yes — often,' said Sal. 'He kicked up a row when he first turned up, and when he found she was ill, sent a doctor; but it warn't no good. She was two weeks with us, and then died the mornin' she saw Mr Fitzgerald.'

'I suppose Mr Whyte was in the habit of talking to this woman?'

'Lots,' returned Sal; 'but he always turned Gran' an' I out of the room afore he started.'

'And' — hesitating — 'did you ever overhear one of these conversations?'

'Yes — one,' answered the other, with a nod. 'I got riled at the way he cleared us out of our own room; and once, when he shut the door and Gran' went off to get some gin, I sat down at the door and listened. He wanted her to give up some papers, an' she wouldn't. She said she'd die first; but at last he got 'em, and took 'em away with him.'

'Did you see them?' asked Madge, as the assertion of Gorby that Whyte had been murdered for certain papers flashed across her mind.

'Rather,' said Sal, 'I was lookin' through a hole in the door, an' she takes 'em from under her piller, an' 'e takes 'em to the table, where the candle was, an' looks at 'em — they were in a large blue envelope, with writing on it in red ink — then he put 'em in his pocket, and she sings out: "You'll lose 'em," an' 'e says: "No, I'll always 'ave 'em with me, an' if 'e wants 'em 'e'll have to kill me fust afore 'e gits 'em." '

'And you did not know who the man was to whom the papers were of such importance?'

'No, I didn't; they never said no names.'

'And when was it Whyte got the papers?'

'About a week before he was murdered,' said Sal, after a moment's thought. 'An' after that he never turned up again. She kept watchin' for him night an' day, an' 'cause he didn't come, got mad at him. I hear her sayin', "You think you've done with me, my gentleman, an' leaves me here to die, but I'll spoil your little game," an' then she wrote that letter to Mr Fitzgerald, an' I brought him to her, as you know.'

'Yes, yes,' said Madge, rather impatiently. 'I heard all that at the trial, but what conversation passed between Mr Fitzgerald and this woman. Did you hear it?'

'Bits of it,' replied the other. 'I didn't split in Court, 'cause I thought the lawyer would be down on me for listening. The fust thing I heard Mr Fitzgerald sayin' was, "You're mad — it ain't true," an' she ses, "S'elp me G— it is, Whyte's got the proof," an' then he sings out, "My poor girl," and she ses, "Will you marry her now?" and ses he, "I will, I love her more than ever;" and then she makes a grab at him, and says, "Spile his game if you can," and ses he, "What's yer name," and she says —'

'What?' asked Madge, breathlessly.

'Rosanna Moore!'

There was a sharp exclamation as Sal said the name, and, turning round quickly, Madge found Brian standing beside her, pale as death, with his eyes fixed on the woman, who had risen to her feet.

'Go on!' he said sharply.

'That's all I know,' she replied, in a sullen tone.

Brian gave a sigh of relief.

'You can go,' he said, slowly; 'I wish to speak with Miss Frettlby alone.'

Sal looked at him for a moment, and then glanced at her mistress, who nodded to her as a sign that she might withdraw. She picked up her book, and with another sharp inquiring look at Brian, turned and walked slowly into the house.

XXII
A Daughter of Eve

After Sal had vanished into the house, Brian sank into a chair beside Madge, with a weary sigh. He was in riding dress, which became his stalwart figure well, and looked remarkably handsome — but ill and worried.

'What on earth were you asking that girl about?' he said abruptly, taking his hat off, and tossing it and his gloves on to the floor.

Madge flushed crimson for a moment, and then taking Brian's two strong hands in her own, looked steadily into his frowning face.

'Why don't you trust me?' she asked, in a quiet tone.

'But it is not necessary that I should,' he answered moodily. 'The secret that Rosanna Moore told me on her death-bed is nothing that would benefit you to know.'

'Is it about me?' she persisted.

'It is, and it is not,' he answered, epigrammatically.

'I suppose that means that it is about a third person, and concerns me,' she said calmly, releasing his hands.

'Well, yes,' impatiently striking his boot with his riding whip. 'But it is nothing that can harm you as long as you do not know it, but God help you should anyone tell it to you, for it would embitter your life.'

'My life being so very sweet now,' answered Madge, with a slight sneer. 'You are trying to put out a fire by pouring oil on it, and what you say only makes me more determined to learn what it is.'

'Madge, I implore you not to persist in this foolish curiosity,' he said, almost fiercely, 'it will only bring you misery.'

'If it concerns me I have a right to know it,' she answered curtly. 'When I marry you how can we be happy together, with the shadow of a secret between us?'

Brian rose, and leaned against the verandah post, with a dark frown on his face.

'Do you remember that verse of Browning's,' he said, coolly —

' "Where the apple reddens
  Never pry,
Lest we lose our Edens,
  Eve and I."

'Singularly applicable to our present conversation, I think.'

'Ah,' she said, her pale face flushing with anger, 'you want me to live in a fool's paradise, which may end at any moment.'

'That depends upon yourself,' he answered, coldly. 'I never roused your curiosity by telling you that there was a secret, but betrayed it inadvertently to Calton's cross-questioning. I tell you candidly that I did learn something from Rosanna Moore, and it concerns you, but only indirectly through a third person. But it would do no good to reveal it, and would ruin both our lives.'

She did not answer, but looked straight before her into the glowing sunshine.

Brian fell on his knees beside her, and stretched out his hands with an entreating gesture.

'Oh, my darling,' he cried sadly, 'cannot you trust me? The love which has stood such a test as yours cannot fail like this. Let me bear the misery of knowing it alone, without blighting your young life with the knowledge of it. I would tell you if I could, but, God help me, I cannot — I cannot,' and he buried his face in his hands.

Madge closed her mouth firmly, and touched his comely head with her cool, white fingers. There was a struggle going on in her breast between her feminine curiosity and her love for the man at her feet — the latter conquered, and she bowed her head over his.

'Brian,' she whispered softly, 'let it be as you wish. I will never again try and learn this secret, since you do not desire it.'

He arose to his feet, and caught her in his strong arms, with a glad smile.

'My dearest!' he said, kissing her passionately, and then for a few moments neither of them spoke. 'We will begin a new life,' he said, at length. 'We will put the sad past away from us, and only think of it as a dream.'

'But this secret will still fret you,' she murmured.

'It will wear away with time and with change of scene,' he answered sadly.

'Change of scene!' she repeated in a startled tone. 'Are you going away?'

'Yes; I have sold my station, and will leave Australia for ever during the next three months.'

'And where are you going?' asked the girl, rather bewildered.

'Anywhere,' he said, a little bitterly. 'I am going to follow the example of Cain, and be a wanderer on the face of the earth!'

'Alone!'

'That is what I have come to see you about,' said Brian, looking steadily at her. 'I have come to ask you if you will marry me at once, and we will leave Australia together.'

She hesitated.

'I know it is asking a great deal,' he said, hurriedly, 'to leave your friends, your position, and' — with hesitation — 'your father; but think of my life without you — think how lonely I shall be wandering round the world by myself; but you will not desert me now I have so much need of you — you will come with me and be my good angel in the future as you have been in the past?'

She put her hand on his arm, and looking at him with her clear, grey eyes, said — 'Yes!'

'Thank God for that,' said Brian, reverently, and there was again a silence.

Then they sat down and talked about their plans, and built castles in the air, after the fashion of lovers.

'I wonder what papa will say?' observed Madge, idly twisting her engagement ring round and round.

Brian frowned, and a dark look passed over his face.

'I suppose I must speak to him about it?' he said at length, reluctantly.

'Yes, of course!' she replied, lightly. 'It is merely a formality; still, one that must be observed.'

'And where is Mr Frettlby?' asked Fitzgerald, rising.

'In the billiard-room,' she answered, as she followed his example. 'No!' she continued, as she saw her father step on to the verandah. 'Here he is.'

Brian had not seen Mark Frettlby for some time, and was astonished at the change which had taken place in his appearance. Formerly, he had been as straight as an arrow, with a stern, fresh-coloured face; but now he had a slight stoop, and his face looked old and withered. His thick, black hair was streaked here and there with white, and the only thing unchanged about him were his eyes, which were as keen and bright as ever. Remembering how old his own face looked, and how altered Madge was, now seeing her father, he wondered if this sudden change was traceable to the same source, namely, the murder of Oliver Whyte. Mr Frettlby's face looked sad and thoughtful as he came along; but, catching sight of his daughter, a smile of affection broke over it.

'My dear Fitzgerald,' he said, holding out his hand; 'this is indeed a surprise! When did you come over?'

'About half-an-hour ago,' replied Brian, reluctantly, taking the extended hand of the millionaire. 'I came to see Madge, and have a talk with you.'

'Ah! That's right,' said the other, putting his arm round his daughter's waist. 'So that's what has brought the roses to your face, young lady?' he went on, pinching her cheek playfully. 'You will stay to dinner, of course, Fitzgerald?'

'Thank you, no!' answered Brian, hastily, 'my dress —'

'Nonsense,' interrupted Frettlby, hospitably; 'we are not in Melbourne, and I am sure Madge will excuse your dress. You must stay.'

'Yes, do,' said Madge, in a beseeching tone, touching his hand lightly. 'I don't see so much of you that I can let you off with half-an-hour's conversation.'

Brian seemed to be making a violent effort.

'Very well,' he said, in a low voice; 'I will stay.'

'And now,' said Frettlby, in a brisk tone, as he sat down; 'the important question of dinner being settled, what is it you want to see me about? — Your station?'

'No!' answered Brian, leaning against the verandah post, while Madge slipped her hand through his arm, 'I have sold it.'

'Sold it!' echoed Frettlby, aghast. 'What for?'

'I felt restless, and wanted a change.'

'Ah! A rolling stone,' said the millionaire, shaking his head, 'gathers no moss, you know.'

'Stones don't roll of their own accord,' replied Brian, in a gloomy tone. 'They are impelled by a force over which they have no control.'

'Oh, indeed!' said the millionaire, in a joking tone. 'And may I ask what is your propelling force?'

Brian looked at the old man's face with such a steady gaze that the latter's eyes dropped after an uneasy attempt to return it.

'Well,' he said, impatiently, looking at the two tall young people standing before him. 'What do you want to see me about?'

'Madge has agreed to marry me at once, and I want your consent.'

'Impossible!' said Frettlby, curtly.

'There is no such a word as impossible,' retorted Brian, coolly, thinking of the famous remark in *Richelieu*. 'Why should you refuse? I am rich now.'

'Pshaw!' said Frettlby, rising impatiently. 'It's not money I'm thinking about — I've got enough for both of you; but I cannot live without Madge.'

'Than come with us?' said his daughter, kissing him.

Her lover, however, did not second the invitation, but stood moodily twisting his tawny moustache, and staring out into the garden in an absent sort of manner.

'What do you say, Fitzgerald?' said Frettlby, who was eyeing him keenly.

'Oh, delighted, of course,' answered Brian, confusedly.

'In that case,' returned the other, coolly, 'I will tell you what we will do. I have bought a steam yacht, and she will be ready for sea about the end of January. You will marry my daughter at once, and go round New Zealand for your honeymoon. When you return, if I feel inclined, and you two turtle-doves don't object, I will join you, and we will make a tour of the world.'

'Oh, how delightful,' cried Madge, clasping her hands. 'I am so fond of the ocean — with a companion, of course,' she added, with a saucy glance at her lover.

Brian's face had brightened considerably, for he was a born sailor, and a pleasing yachting voyage in the blue waters of the Pacific, with Madge as his companion, was, to his mind, as near Paradise as any mortal could get.

'And what is the name of the yacht?' he asked, with deep interest.

'Her name,' repeated Mr Frettlby, hastily. 'Oh, a very ugly name, and which I intend to change. At present she is called the "Rosanna." '

'Rosanna!'

Brian and his betrothed both started at this, and the former stared curiously at the old man, wondering at the coincidence between the name of the yacht and that of the woman who died in the Melbourne slum.

Mr Frettlby flushed a little when he saw Brian's eye fixed on him with such an enquiring gaze, and arose with an embarrassed laugh.

'You are a pair of moon-struck lovers,' he said, gaily, taking an arm of each, and leading them into the house; 'but you forget dinner will soon be ready.'

XXIII
Across the Walnuts and the Wine

Moore, sweetest of bards, sings —

> 'Oh, there's nothing half so sweet in life
> As love's young dream.'

But he evidently made this assertion in his callow days, and before he had learned the value of a good digestion. To a young and fervid youth, love's young dream is, no doubt, very charming, lovers, as a rule, having a small appetite; but to a man who has seen the world, and drank deeply of the wine of life, there is nothing half so sweet in the whole of his existence as a good dinner. 'A hard heart and a good digestion will make any man happy.' This remark was made by Tallyrand, a cynic if you like, but a man who knew the temper of his day and generation. Ovid wrote about the art of love — Brillat Savarin, of the art of dining; yet, ten to one, the gastronomical treatise of the brilliant Frenchman is more widely read than the passionate songs of the Roman poet. Who does not value that hour as the sweetest in the whole twenty-four when, seated at an artistically laid table, with delicately cooked viands, good wines, and pleasant company, all the cares and worries of the day give place to a delightful sense of absolute enjoyment? Dinner with the English people is generally a very dreary affair, and there is a heaviness about the whole thing which communicates itself to the guests, who eat and drink with a solemn persistence, as though they were occupied in fulfilling some sacred rite. But there are men — alas! few and far between — who possess the rare art of giving good dinners — good in the sense of sociality as well as of cookery. Mark Frettlby was one of these rare individuals — he had an innate genius for getting pleasant people together, who, so to speak, dovetailed into one another. He had an excellent cook, and his wines were irreproachable, so that Brian, in spite of his worries, was glad that he had accepted the invitation. The bright gleam of the silver, the glitter of glass, and the perfume of flowers, all collected under the subdued crimson glow of a pink-globed lamp, which hung from the ceiling, could not but give him a pleasurable sensation.

On one side of the dining-room there were French windows opening on to the verandah, and beyond appeared the vivid green of the trees, and the dazzling colours of the flowers, somewhat tempered by the soft hazy glow of the twilight. Brian had made himself as respectable as possible, under the odd circumstances of dining in his riding-dress, and sat next to Madge, contentedly sipping his wine, and listening to the pleasant chatter which was going on around him. Felix Rolleston was in great spirits, the more so as Mrs Rolleston was at the further end of the table, hidden from his view by an epergne of fruit and flowers. Julia Featherweight sat near Mr Frettlby, and chatted to him so persistently that he wished she would become possessed of a dumb devil. Dr Chinston and Paterson were seated on the other side of the table, and the old colonist, whose name was Valpy, had the post of honour, on Mr Frettlby's right hand. The conversation had turned on to the subject, ever green and fascinating, of politics, and Mr Rolleston thought it was a good opportunity to air his views as to the Government of the Colony, and to show his wife that he really meant to obey her wish, and become a power in the political world.

'By Jove, you know,' he said, with a wave of his hand, as though he were addressing the House; 'the country is going to the dogs, and all that sort of thing. What we want is a man like Beaconsfield.'

'Ah! But you can't pick up a man like that every day,' said Frettlby, who was listening with an amused smile to Rolleston's disquisitions.

'Rather a good thing, too,' observed Dr Chinston, dryly. 'Genius would become too common.'

'Well, when I am elected,' said Felix, who had his own views, which modesty forbade him to publish, on the subject of the coming colonial Disraeli, 'I will probably form a party.'

'To advocate what?' asked Paterson, curiously.

'Oh, well, you see,' hesitated Felix, 'I haven't drawn up a programme yet, so can't say at present.'

'Yes, you can hardly give a performance without a programme,' said the doctor, taking a sip of wine, and then everybody laughed.

'And on what are your political opinions founded?' asked Mr Frettlby, absently, without looking at Felix.

'Oh, you see, I've read the Parliamentary reports and Constitutional history, and — and Vivian Grey,' said Felix, who began to feel himself somewhat at sea.

'The last of which is what the author called it, a *lusus naturae*,' observed Chinston. 'Don't erect your political schemes on such bubble foundations as there are in that novel, for you won't find a Marquis Carabas out here.'

'Unfortunately, no!' observed Felix, mournfully; 'but we may find a Vivian Grey.'

Everyone smothered a smile, the allusion was so patent.

'Well, he didn't succeed in the end,' cried Paterson.

'Oh course he didn't,' retorted Felix, disdainfully; 'he made an enemy of a woman, and a man who is such a fool as to do that deserves to fall.'

'You have an excellent opinion of our sex, Mr Rolleston,' said Madge, with a wicked glance at the wife of that gentleman, who was listening complacently to her husband's aimless chatter.

'No better than they deserve,' replied Rolleston, gallantly.

'But you have never gone in for politics, Mr Frettlby?'

'Who? — I — no,' said the host, rousing himself out of the brown study into which he had fallen. 'I'm afraid I'm not sufficiently patriotic, and my business did not permit me.'

'And now?'

'Now,' echoed Mr Frettlby, glancing at his daughter, 'I am going to travel.'

'The jolliest thing out,' said Paterson, eagerly. 'One never gets tired of seeing the queer things there are in the world.'

'I've seen queer enough things in Melbourne in the early days,' said the old colonist, with a wicked twinkle in his eyes.

'Oh!' cried Julia, putting her hands up to her ears, 'don't tell me them, for I'm sure they're naughty.'

'We weren't saints then,' said Old Valpy, with a senile chuckle.

'Ah, then, we haven't changed much in that respect,' retorted Frettlby, dryly.

'You talk of your theatres now,' went on Valpy, with the garrulousness of old age; 'why, you haven't got a dancer like Rosanna.'

Brian started on hearing this name again, and he felt Madge's cold hand touch his.

'And who was Rosanna?' asked Felix, curiously, looking up.

'A dancer and burlesque actress,' replied Valpy, vivaciously, nodding his old head. 'Such a beauty; we were all mad about her — such hair and eyes. You remember her, Frettlby?'

'Yes,' answered the host, in a curiously dry voice.

As the conversation seemed to be getting too much of the after-dinner style, Madge arose, and all the other ladies followed her example. The ever polite Felix held the door open for them, and received a bright smile from his wife for, what she considered, his brilliant talk at the dinner table. Brian sat still, and wondered why Frettlby changed colour on hearing the name — he supposed that the millionaire had been mixed up with the actress, and did not care about being reminded of his early indiscretions — and, after all, who does?

'She was as light as a fairy,' said Valpy, with a wicked chuckle.

'What became of her?' asked Brian, abruptly.

Mark Frettlby looked up suddenly, as Fitzgerald asked this question.

'She went to England in 1858,' said the aged one. 'I'm not quite sure if it was July or August, but it was 1858.'

'You will excuse me, Valpy, but I hardly think that these reminiscences of a ballet-dancer are amusing,' said Frettlby, curtly, pouring himself out a glass of wine. 'Let us drop the subject.'

When a man expresses a wish at his own table, it is hardly the proper thing for anyone to go contrary to it, but Brian felt strongly inclined to pursue the conversation. Politeness, however, forbade him to make any further remark, and he consoled himself with the reflection that, after dinner, he would ask old Valpy about the ballet-dancer whose name caused Mark Frettlby to exhibit such strong emotion. But, to his annoyance, when the gentlemen went into the drawing-room, Frettlby took the old colonist off to his study, where he sat with him the whole evening, talking over old times.

Fitzgerald found Madge seated at the piano, in the drawing-room, playing one of Mendelssohn's Songs without Words.

'What a dismal thing that is you are playing, Madge,' he said lightly, as he sank into a seat beside her. 'It is more like a funeral than anything else.'

'Gad, so it is,' said Felix, who came up at this moment. 'I don't care myself about "Op. 84" and all that classical humbug. Give me something light — "Belle Helene," with Emelie Melville, and all that sort of thing.'

'Felix!' said his wife, in a stern tone.

'My dear,' he answered, recklessly, rendered bold by the champagne he had taken, 'you observed —'

'Nothing particular,' answered Mrs Rolleston, glancing at him with a stony eye, 'except that I consider Offenbach low.'

'I don't,' said Felix, sitting down to the piano, from which Madge had just risen, 'and to prove he ain't, here goes.'

He ran his fingers lightly over the keys, and dashed into a brilliant Offenbachian galop, which had the effect of waking up the people in the drawing-room, who felt sleepy after dinner, and sent the blood tingling through their veins. When they were thoroughly roused, Felix, now that he had an appreciative audience, for he was by no means an individual who believed in wasting his sweetness on the desert air, prepared to amuse them.

'You haven't heard the last new song by Frosti, have you?' he asked, after he had brought his galop to a conclusion.

'Is that the composer of "Inasmuch" and "How so?" ' asked Julia, clasping her hands. 'I do love his music, and the words are so sweetly pretty.'

'Infernally stupid, she means,' whispered Paterson to Brian. 'They've no more meaning in them than the titles.'

'Sing us the new song, Felix,' commanded his wife, and her obedient husband obeyed her. It was entitled, 'Somewhere,' words by Vashti, music by Paola Frosti, and was one of those extraordinary compositions which may mean anything — that is, if the meaning can be discovered. Felix had a nice voice, though not very strong, and the music was pretty, while the words were mystical. The first verse was as follows:

A flying cloud, a breaking wave,
   A faint light in a moonless sky:
A voice that from the silent grave
   Sounds sad in one long bitter cry.
I know not, sweet, where you may stand,
   With shining eyes and golden hair,
Yet I know, I will touch your hand
   And kiss your lips somewhere —

Somewhere! Somewhere! —
  When the summer sun is fair,
Waiting me, on land or sea,
  Somewhere, love, somewhere!

The second verse was very similar to the first, and when Felix finished a murmur of applause broke from every one of the ladies.

'How sweetly pretty,' sighed Julia. 'Such a lot in it.'

'But what is its meaning?' asked Brian, rather bewildered.

'It hasn't got one,' replied Felix, complacently. 'Surely you don't want every song to have a moral, like a book of Aesop's Fables?'

Brian shrugged his shoulders, and turned away with Madge.

'I must say I agree with Fitzgerald,' said the doctor, quickly. 'I like a song with some meaning in it. The poetry of the one you sang is as mystical as Browning, without any of his genius to redeem it.'

'Philistine,' murmured Felix, under his breath, and then vacated his seat at the piano in favour of Julia, who was going to sing a ballad called 'Going Down the Hill,' which had been the rage in Melbourne musical circles during the last two months.

Meanwhile, Madge and Brian were walking up and down in the moonlight. It was an exquisite night, with a cloudless blue sky glittering with stars, and a great yellow moon in the west. Madge seated herself on the side of the marble ledge which girdled the still pool of water in front of the house, and dipped her hand into the cool water. Brian leaned against the trunk of a great magnolia tree, whose glossy green leaves and great creamy blossoms looked fantastic in the moonlight. In front of them was the house, with the ruddy lamp-light streaming through the wide windows, and they could see the guests within, excited by the music, waltzing to Rolleston's playing, and their dark figures kept passing and repassing the windows while the charming music of 'Bid Me Good-bye and Go' waltz mingled with their merry laughter.

'Looks like a haunted house,' said Brian, thinking of Poe's weird poem; 'but such a thing is impossible out here.'

'I don't know so much about that,' said Madge, gravely, lifting up some water in the palm of her hand, and letting it stream back like diamonds in the moonlight. I knew a house in St Kilda which was haunted.'

'By what?' asked Brian, sceptically.

'Noises!' she answered, solemnly.

Brian burst out laughing and startled a bat, which flew round and round in the silver moonlight, and whirred away into the shelter of a witch elm.

'Rats and mice are more common here than ghosts,' he said, lightly. 'I'm afraid the inhabitants of your haunted house were fanciful.'

'So you don't believe in ghosts?'

'There's a Banshee in our family,' said Brian, with a gay smile, 'who is supposed to cheer our death-beds with her howlings; but as I've never seen the lady myself, I'm afraid she's a Mrs Harris.'

'It's aristocratic to have a ghost in a family, I believe,' said Madge; 'that is the reason we colonials have none.'

'Ah, but you will have,' he answered with a careless laugh. 'There are, no doubt, democratic as well as aristocratic ghosts; but, pshaw!' he went on, impatiently, 'what nonsense I talk. There are no ghosts, except of a man's own raising. The ghosts of a dead youth — the ghosts of past follies — the ghosts of what might have been — these are the spectres which are more to be feared than those of the churchyard.'

Madge looked at him in silence, for she understood the meaning of that passionate outburst — the secret which the dead woman had told him, and which hung like a shadow over his life. She arose quietly and took his arm. The light touch roused him, and a faint wind sent an eerie rustle through the still leaves of the magnolia, as they walked back in silence to the house.

XXIV
Brian Receives a Letter

Notwithstanding the hospitable invitation of Mr Frettlby, Brian refused to stay at Yabba Yallook that night, but after saying good-bye to Madge, mounted his horse and rode slowly away in the moonlight. He felt very happy as, letting the reins lie on his horse's neck, he gave himself up unreservedly to his thoughts. *Atra Cura* certainly did not sit behind the horseman on this night; and

Brian, to his surprise, found himself singing 'Kitty of Coleraine,' as he rode along in the silver moonlight. And was he not right to sing when the future seemed so bright and pleasant? Oh, yes! They would live on the ocean, and she would find how much pleasanter it was on the restless water, with their solemn sense of mystery, than on the crowded land.

'Was not the sea
Made for the free —
Land for courts and slaves alone?'

Moore was certainly correct in making such a statement, and she would find out when, with a fair wind and the white sails set, they would plough the blue New Zealand waters. And then they would go home to Ireland to the ancestral home of the Fitzgeralds, where he would lead her in under the arch, with '*Cead mille failthe*' on it, and everyone blessing the fair young bride. Why should he trouble himself about the crime of another? No! He had made a resolve, and intended to keep it; he would put this secret with which he had been entrusted behind his back, and would wander about the world with Madge and — her father. He felt a sudden chill come over him as he murmured the last words to himself — 'her father.'

'I'm a fool,' he said, impatiently, as he gathered up the reins, and spurred his horse into a canter. 'It can make no difference to me as long as Madge remains ignorant; but to sit beside him, to eat with him, to have him always present like a skeleton at a feast — God help me!'

He urged his horse into a gallop, and as he thundered over the turf, with the fresh, cool night wind blowing keenly against his face, he felt a sense of relief, as though he were leaving some dark spectre behind. On he galloped, with the blood throbbing in his young veins, over miles of plain, with the dark-blue, star-studded sky above, and the pale moon shining down on him — past a silent shepherd's hut, which stood near a wide creek, and then splashing through the cool water, which wound away through the dark plain like a thread of silver in the moonlight — then, again, the wide, grassy plain, dotted here and there with tall clumps of shadowy trees, and on either side he could see the sheep scurrying away like fantastic spectres — on — on — ever on, until his own homestead appears, and he sees the star-like light shining brightly in the distance — a long avenue of tall trees, over whose wavering shadows his horse thundered, and then the wide grassy space in front of the house, with the clamorous barking of dogs. A groom, roused by the clatter of hoofs up the avenue, comes round the side of the house, and Brian leaps off his horse, and flinging the reins to the man, walked into his own room. There he finds a lighted lamp, brandy and soda on the table, and a packet of letters and newspapers. He flung his hat on the sofa, and opened the window and door, so as to let in the cool breeze; then pouring himself out a glass of brandy and soda, he turned up the lamp, and prepared to read his letters. The first he took up was from a lady. 'Always a she correspondent for me,' says Isaac Disraeli, 'provided she does not cross.' Brian's correspondent did not cross, but notwithstanding this, after reading half a page of small talk and scandal, he flung the letter on the table with an impatient ejaculation. The other letters were principally business ones, but the last one proved to be from Calton, and Fitzgerald opened it with a sensation of pleasure. Calton was a capital letter-writer, and his epistles had done much to cheer Fitzgerald in the dismal period which succeeded his acquittal of Whyte's murder, and when he was in danger of getting into a morbid state of mind. Brian, therefore, poured himself out some more brandy and soda, and, lying back in his chair, prepared to enjoy himself.

'My dear Fitzgerald,' wrote Calton, in his peculiarly clear handwriting, which was such an exception to the usual crabbed hieroglyphics of his brethren of the bar, 'while you are enjoying the cool breezes and delightful freshness of the country, here am I, with numerous other poor devils, cooped up in this hot and dusty city. How I wish I were with you in the land of Goschen, by the rolling waters of the Murray, where everything is bright and green, and unsophisticated — the two latter terms are almost identical — instead of which my view is bounded by bricks and mortar, and the muddy waters of the Yarra have to do duty for your noble river. Ah! I too have lived in Arcadia, but I don't now; and even if some power gave me the choice to go back again, I am not sure that I would accept. Arcadia, after all, is a lotos-eating Paradise of blissful ignorance, and I love the world with its pomps, vanities, and wickedness. While you, therefore, oh Corydon — don't be afraid, I'm not going to quote Virgil — are studying Nature's book, I am deep in the musty leaves of Themis' volume, but I dare say that the great mother teaches you much better things than her artificial daughter does me. However, you remember that pithy proverb, 'When one is in Rome, one must not speak ill of the Pope,' so, being in the legal profession, I must respect its muse. I suppose when you saw that this letter came from a law office, you wondered what the deuce a lawyer was writing to you for, and my handwriting, no doubt, suggested a writ — pshaw! I am wrong there, you are past the age of writs — not that I hint that you are old, by no means — you are just at that appreciative age when a man enjoys life most, when the fire of youth is tempered by the experience of age, and one knows how to enjoy to the utmost the good things of this world, *videlicet* — love, wine, and friendship. I am afraid I am growing poetical, which is a bad thing for a lawyer, for the flower of poetry cannot flourish in the arid wastes of the law. On reading what I have written, I find I have been as discursive as Praed's Vicar, and as this letter is supposed to be a business one, I must deny myself the luxury of following out a train of idle ideas, and write sense. I suppose you still hold the secret which Rosanna Moore entrusted you with — ah! you see I know her name, and why? — simply because, with the natural curiosity of the human race, I have been trying to find out who murdered Oliver Whyte, and as the *Argus* very cleverly pointed out Rosanna Moore as likely to be at the bottom of the whole affair, I have been learning her past history. The secret of Whyte's murder, and the reason for it, is known to you, but you refuse, even in the interests of justice, to reveal it — why, I don't know; but we all have our little faults, and from an amiable though mistaken sense of — shall I say duty? — you refuse to deliver up the man whose cowardly crime so nearly cost you your life.

'After your departure from Melbourne everyone said, "The hansom cab tragedy is at an end, and the murderer will never be discovered." I ventured to disagree with the wiseacres who made such a remark, and asked myself, "Who was this woman who died at Mother Guttersnipe's?" Receiving no satisfactory answer from myself, I determined to find out, and took steps accordingly. In the first place, I learned from Roger Moreland, who, if you remember, was a witness against you at the trial, that Whyte and Rosanna Moore had come out to Sydney in the John Elder about a year ago as Mr and Mrs Whyte. I need hardly say that they did not think it needful to go through the formality of marriage, as such a tie might have been found inconvenient on some future occasion. Moreland knew nothing about Rosanna Moore, and advised me to give up the search, as, coming from a city like London, it would be difficult to find anyone that knew her there. Notwithstanding this, I telegraphed home to a friend of mine, who is a bit of an amateur detective, "Find out the name and all about the woman who left England in the John Elder on the 21st day of August, 18—, as wife of Oliver Whyte." *Mirabile dictu*, he found out all about her, and knowing, as you do, what a maelstrom of humanity London is, you must admit my friend was clever. It appears, however, that the task I set him to do was easier than he expected, for the so-called Mrs Whyte was rather a notorious individual in her own way. She was a burlesque actress at the Frivolity Theatre in London, and, being a very handsome woman, had been photographed innumerable times. Consequently, when she very foolishly went with Whyte to choose a berth on board the boat, she was recognised by the clerks in the office as Rosanna Moore, better known as Musette of the Frivolity. Why she ran away with Whyte I cannot tell you. With reference to men understanding women, I refer you to Balzac's remark anent the same. Perhaps Musette got weary of St John's Wood and champagne suppers, and longed for the purer air of her native land. Ah! You open your eyes at this latter statement — you are surprised — no, on second thoughts you are not, because she told you herself that she was a native of Sydney, and had gone home in 1858, after a triumphant career of acting in Melbourne. And why did she leave the applauding Melbourne public and the flesh-pots of Egypt? You know this also. She ran away with a rich young squatter, with more money than morals, who happened to be in Melbourne at the time. She seems to have had a weakness for running away. But why she chose Whyte to go with this time puzzles me. He was not rich, not particularly good-looking, had no position, and a bad temper. How do I know all these traits of Mr Whyte's character, morally and socially? Easily enough; my omniscient friend found them all out. Mr Oliver Whyte was the son of a London tailor, and his father being well off, retired into private life, and ultimately went the way of all flesh. His son, finding himself with a capital income, and a pretty taste for amusement, cut the shop of his late lamented parent, found out that his family had come over with the Conqueror — Glanville de Whyte helped to sew the Bayeux tapestry, I suppose — and graduated at the Frivolity Theatre as a masher. In common with the other gilded youth of the day, he worshipped at the gas-lit shrine of Musette, and the goddess, pleased with his incense, left her other admirers in the lurch, and ran off with fortunate Mr Whyte. As far as this goes there is nothing to show why the murder was committed. Men do not perpetrate crimes for the sake of light o' loves like Musette, unless, indeed, some wretched youth embezzles money to buy his divinity jewellery. The career of Musette, in London, was simply that of a clever member of the *demi-monde*, and, as far as I can learn, no one was so much in love with her as to commit a crime for her sake. So far so good; the motive of the crime must be found in Australia. Whyte had spent nearly all his money in England, and, consequently, Musette and her lover arrived in Sydney with comparatively little cash. However, with an Epicurean-like philosophy, they enjoyed themselves on what little they had, and then came to Melbourne, where they stayed at a second-rate hotel. Musette, I may tell you, had one special vice, a common one — drink. She loved champagne, and drank a good deal of it. Consequently, on arriving in Melbourne, and finding that a new generation had arisen, which knew not Joseph — I mean Musette — she drowned her sorrows in the flowing bowl, and went out after a quarrel with Mr Whyte, to view Melbourne by night — a familiar aspect to her, no doubt. What took her to Little Bourke Street I don't know. Perhaps she got lost — perhaps it had been a favourite walk of hers in the old days; to all events she was found dead drunk in that unsavoury locality by Sal Rawlins. I know this is so, because Sal told me so herself. Sal acted the part of the good Samaritan — took her to the squalid den she called home, and there Rosanna Moore fell dangerously ill. Whyte, who had missed her, found out where she was, and that she was too ill to be removed. I presume he was rather glad to get rid of such an encumbrance, so went back to his lodgings at St Kilda, which, judging from the landlady's story, he must have occupied for some time, while Rosanna Moore was drinking herself to death in a quiet hotel. Still he does not break off his connection with the dying woman; but one night is murdered in a hansom cab, and that same night Rosanna Moore dies. So, from all appearance, everything is ended; not so, for before dying Rosanna sends for Brian Fitzgerald at his club, and reveals to him a secret which he locks up in his own heart. The writer of this letter has a theory — a fanciful one, if you will — that the secret told to Brian Fitzgerald contains the mystery of Oliver Whyte's death. Now then, have I not found out a good deal without you, and do you still decline to reveal the rest? I do not say you know who killed Whyte, but I do say you know sufficient to lead to the detection of the murderer. If you tell me, so much the better, both for your own sense of justice and for your peace of mind; if you do not — well, I shall find it out without you. I have taken, and still take, a great interest in this strange case, and I have sworn to bring the murderer to justice; so I make this last appeal to you to tell me what you know. If you refuse, I will set to work to find out all about Rosanna Moore prior to her departure from Australia in 1858, and I am certain sooner or later to discover the secret which led to Whyte's murder. If there is any strong reason why it should be kept silent, I perhaps, will come round to your view, and let the matter drop; but if I have to find it out myself, the murderer of Oliver Whyte need expect no mercy at my hands. So think over what I have said; if I do not hear from you within the next week, I will regard your decision as final, and pursue the search myself.

'I am sure, my dear Fitzgerald, you will find this letter too long, in spite of the interesting story it contains, so I will have pity on you, and draw to a close. Remember me to Miss Frettlby and to her father. With kind regards to yourself, I remain, yours very truly, DUNCAN CALTON.'

When Fitzgerald had finished the last of the closely-written sheets, he let the letter fall from his hands, and, leaning back in his chair, stared into the dawning light outside with a haggard face. He arose after a few moments, and, pouring himself out a glass of brandy, drank it feverishly. Then mechanically lighting a cigar, he stepped out of the door into the fresh beauty of the dawn. There was a soft crimson glow in the east, which announced the approach of the sun, and he could hear the chirping of the awakening birds in the trees. But Brian did not see the marvellous breaking of the dawn, but stood staring at the red light flaring in the east, and thinking of Calton's letter.

'I can do no more,' he said, bitterly, leaning his head against the wall of the house. 'There is only one way of stopping Calton, and that is by telling him all. My poor Madge! My poor Madge!'

A soft wind arose, and rustled among the trees, and there appeared great shafts of crimson light in the east; then, with a sudden blaze, the sun peered over the brim of the wide plain. The warm yellow rays touched lightly the comely head of the weary man, and, turning round, he held up his arms to the great luminary, as though he were a fire worshipper.

'I accept the omen of the dawn,' he cried, 'for her life and for mine.'

XXV
What Dr Chinston Said

His resolution taken, Brian did not let the grass grow under his feet, but rode over in the afternoon to tell Madge of his intended departure.

The servant told him she was in the garden, so he went there, and, guided by the sound of merry voices, and the silvery laughter of pretty women, soon found his way to the lawn tennis ground. Madge and her guests were all there, seated under the shade of a great witch elm, and watching, with great interest, a single-handed match being played between Rolleston and Peterson, both of whom were capital players. Mr Frettlby was not present, as he was inside writing letters, and talking with old Mr Valpy, and Brian gave a sigh of relief as he noted his absence. Madge caught sight of him as he came down the garden path, and flew quickly towards him with outstretched hands, as he took his hat off.

'How good of you to come,' she said, in a delighted tone, as she took his arm; 'and on such a hot day.'

'Yes, it's something fearful in the shade,' said pretty Mrs Rolleston, with a laugh, putting up her sunshade.

'Pardon me if I think the contrary,' replied Fitzgerald, bowing, with an expressing look at the charming group of ladies under the great tree.

Mrs Rolleston blushed and shook her head.

'Ah! It's easy seen you come from Ireland, Mr Fitzgerald,' she observed, as she resumed her seat. 'You are making Madge jealous.'

'So he is,' answered Madge, with a gay laugh. 'I shall certainly inform Mr Rolleston about you, Brian, if you make these gallant remarks.'

'Here he comes, then,' said her lover, as Rolleston and Peterson, having finished their game, walked off the tennis ground, and joined the group under the tree. Though in tennis flannels, they both looked remarkably warm, and, throwing his racket down, Mr Rolleston followed its example with a sigh of relief.

'Thank goodness it's over, and that I have won,' he said, wiping his heated brow; 'galley slaves couldn't have worked harder than we have done, while all you idle folks sat *sub tegmine fagi*.'

'Which means?' asked his wife, lazily.

'That onlookers see most of the game,' answered her husband, impudently.

'I suppose that's what you call a free and easy translation,' said Peterson, laughing. 'Mrs Rolleston ought to give you something for your new and original adaptation of Virgil.'

'Let it be iced then,' retorted Rolleston, lying full length on the ground, and staring up at the blue of the sky as seen through the network of leaves. 'I always like my "something" iced.'

'It's a way you've got,' said Madge, with a laugh, as she gave him a glass filled with some sparkling, golden coloured liquor, with a large lump of ice clinking musically against the side of it.

'He's not the only one who's got that way,' said Peterson, gaily, when he had been supplied with a similar drink.

'It's a way we've got in the army,
It's a way we've got in the navy,
It's a way we've got in the 'Varsity.'

'And so say all of us,' finished Rolleston, noisily, and holding out his glass to be replenished; 'I'll have another, please. Whew, it is hot.'

'What, the drink?' asked Julia, with a giggle.

'No — the day,' answered Felix, making a face at her. 'It's the kind of day one feels inclined to adopt Sydney Smith's advice, by getting out of one's skin, and letting the wind whistle through one's bones.'

'With such a hot wind blowing,' said Peterson, gravely, 'I'm afraid they'd soon be broiled bones.'

'Go, giddy one,' retorted Felix, throwing his hat at him, 'or I'll drag you into the blazing sun, and make you play another game.'

'Not I,' replied Peterson, coolly. 'Not being a salamander, I'm hardly used to your climate yet, and there is a limit even to lawn tennis;' and turning his back on Rolleston, he began to talk to Julia Featherweight.

Meanwhile, Madge and her lover, leaving all this frivolous chatter behind them, were walking slowly towards the house, and Brian was telling her of his approaching departure, but not his reasons for going.

'I got a letter last night,' he said, turning his face away from her; 'and, as it's about some important business, I must start at once.'

'I don't think it will be long before we follow,' answered Madge, thoughtfully. 'Papa leaves here at the end of the week.'

'Why?'

'I'm sure I don't know,' said Madge, petulantly; 'he is so restless, and never seems to settle down to anything. He says for the rest of his life he is going to do nothing but wander all over the world.'

There suddenly flashed across Fitzgerald's mind a line from Genesis, which seemed singularly applicable to Mr Frettlby — 'A fugitive and a vagabond thou shalt be in the earth.'

'Everyone gets these restless fits sooner or later,' he said, idly. 'In fact,' with an uneasy laugh, 'I believe I'm in one myself.'

'That puts me in mind of what I heard Dr Chinston say yesterday,' she said. 'This is the age of unrest, as electricity and steam have turned us all into Bohemians.'

'Ah! Bohemia is a pleasant place,' said Brian absently, unconsciously quoting Thackeray, 'but we all lose our way to it late in life.'

'At that rate we won't lose our way to it for some time,' she said laughing, as they stepped into the drawing-room, so cool and shady, after the heat and glare outside.

As they entered Mr Frettlby arose out of a chair near the window, and appeared to have been reading as he held a book in his hand.

'What! Fitzgerald,' he exclaimed, in a hearty tone, as he held out his hand; 'I am glad to see you.'

'I let you know I am living, don't I?' replied Brian, his fair face flushing as he reluctantly took the proffered hand. 'But the fact is I have come to say good-bye for a few days.'

'Ah! Going back to town I suppose,' said Mr Frettlby, lying back in his chair, and playing with his watch chain. 'I don't know that you are wise, exchanging the clear air of the country for the dusty atmosphere of Melbourne.'

'Yet Madge tells me you are going back,' said Brian, idly toying with a vase of flowers on the table.

'Depends upon circumstances,' replied Midas carelessly. 'I may and I may not. You go on business, I presume?'

'Well, the fact is Calton —' Here Brian stopped suddenly, and bit his lip with vexation, for he had not intended to mention the lawyer's name.

'Yes?' said Mr Frettlby, interrogatively, sitting up quickly, and looking keenly at Brian.

'Wants to see me about business,' he finished, awkwardly.

'Connected with the sale of your station, I suppose,' said Frettlby, still keeping his eyes on the young man's face. 'Can't have a better man. Calton's an excellent man of business.'

'A little too excellent,' replied Fitzgerald, ruefully, 'he's a man that can't leave well alone.'

'*A propos* of what?'

'Oh, nothing,' answered Fitzgerald, hastily, and just then his eyes met those of Frettlby. The two men looked at one another steadily for a moment, but in that short space of time a single name flashed through their brains — that name was Rosanna Moore. Mr Frettlby was the first to lower his eyes, and break the magnetism.

'Ah, well,' he said, lightly, as he rose from his chair, and held out his hand, 'if you are two weeks in town call at St Kilda, and it's more than likely you will find us there.'

Brian shook hands in silence, and watched him pick up his hat, and move on to the verandah, and then out into the hot sunshine.

'He knows,' he muttered involuntarily.

'Know what, sir?' said Madge, who came silently behind him, and slipped her arm through his. 'That you are hungry, and want something to eat before you leave us?'

'I don't feel hungry,' said Brian, as they walked towards the door.

'Nonsense,' answered Madge, merrily, who, like Eve, was on hospitable thoughts intent. 'I'm not going to have you appear in Melbourne a pale, fond lover, as though I were treating you badly. Come sir — no,' she continued, putting up her hand as he tried to kiss her, 'business first, pleasure afterwards,' and they went into the dining-room laughing.

Mark Frettlby wandered down to the lawn tennis ground, thinking of the look he had seen in Brian's eyes. He shivered for a moment in the hot sunshine, as though it had grown suddenly chill.

'Someone stepping across my grave,' he murmured to himself, with a cynical smile. 'Bah! How superstitious I am, and yet — he knows, he knows!'

'Come on, sir,' cried Felix, who had just caught sight of him, 'a racket awaits you.'

Frettlby woke with a start, and found himself near the lawn tennis ground, and Felix at his elbow, smoking a cigarette.

He roused himself with a great effort, and tapped the young man lightly on the shoulder.

'What?' he said with a forced laugh, 'do you really expect me to play lawn tennis on such a day? You are mad.'

'I am hot, you mean,' retorted the imperturbable Rolleston, blowing a wreath of smoke.

'That's a foregone conclusion,' said Dr Chinston, who came up at that moment.

'Such a charming novel,' cried Julia, who had just caught the last remark.

'What is?' asked Peterson, rather puzzled.

'Howell's book, "A Foregone Conclusion," ' said Julia, also looking puzzled. 'Weren't you talking about it?'

'I'm afraid this talk is getting slightly incoherent,' said Felix, with a sigh. 'We all seem madder than usual today.'

'Speak for yourself,' said Chinston, indignantly, 'I'm as sane as any man in the world.'

'Exactly,' retorted the other, coolly, 'that's what I say, and you, being a doctor, ought to know that every man and woman in the world is more or less mad.'

'Where are your facts?' asked Chinston, smiling.

'My facts are all visible ones,' said Felix, gravely pointing to the company. 'They're all crooked on some point or another.'

There was a chorus of indignant denial at this, and then everyone burst out laughing at the extraordinary way in which Mr Rolleston was arguing.

'If you go on like that in the House,' said Frettlby, amused, 'you will, at all events, have an entertaining Parliament.'

'Ah! They'll never have an entertaining Parliament till they admit ladies,' observed Peterson, with a quizzical glance at Julia.

'It will be a Parliament of love then,' retorted the doctor, dryly, 'and not medieval either.'

While everyone was laughing at this remark, Frettlby took the doctor's arm, and walked away with him. 'I want you to come up to my study, doctor,' he said, as they strolled towards the house, 'and examine me.'

'Why, don't you feel well?' said Chinston, as they entered the house.

'Not lately,' replied Frettlby. 'I'm afraid I've got heart disease.'

The doctor looked sharply at him, and then shook his head.

'Nonsense,' he said, cheerfully, 'it's a common delusion with people that they have heart disease, and in nine cases out of ten it's all imagination; unless, indeed,' he added, waggishly, 'the patient happens to be a young man.'

'Ah! I suppose you think I'm safe as far as that goes,' said Frettlby, as they entered the study; 'and what did you think of Rolleston's argument about people being mad?'

'It was amusing,' replied Chinston, taking a seat, Frettlby doing the same. 'That's all I can say about it, though, mind you, I think there are more mad people at large than the world is aware of.'

'Indeed!'

'Yes; Do you remember that horrible story of Dickens', in the "Pickwick Papers," about the man who was mad, and knew it, yet successfully concealed it for years? Well, I believe there are many people like that in the world, people whose lives are one long struggle against insanity, and yet who eat, drink, talk, and walk with the rest of their fellow-men, evidently as gay and light-hearted as they are.'

'How extraordinary.'

'Half the murders and suicides are done in temporary fits of insanity,' went on Chinston, 'and if a person broods over anything, his incipient madness is sure to break out sooner or later; but, of course, there are cases where a perfectly sane person may commit a murder on the impulse of the moment, but I regard such persons as mad for the time being; but, again, a murder may be planned and executed in the most cold-blooded manner.'

'And in the latter case,' said Frettlby, without looking at the doctor, and playing with the paper knife, 'do you regard the murderer as mad?'

'Yes, I do,' answered the doctor, bluntly. 'He is as mad as a person who kills another because he supposes he has been told by God to do so — only there is method in his madness. For instance, I believe that hansom cab murder, in which you were mixed up —'

'D— it, sir! I wasn't mixed up in it,' interrupted Frettlby, pale with anger.

'Beg pardon,' said Chinston, coolly, 'a slip of the tongue; I was thinking of Fitzgerald. Well, I believe that crime to have been premeditated, and that the man who committed it was mad. He is, no doubt, at large now, walking about and conducting himself as sanely as you or I, yet the germ of insanity is there, and sooner or later he will commit another crime.'

'How do you know it was premeditated?' asked Frettlby, abruptly.

'Anyone can see that,' answered the other. 'Whyte was watched on that night, and when Fitzgerald went away the other was ready to take his place, dressed the same.'

'That's nothing,' retorted Frettlby, looking at his companion sharply. 'There are dozens of men in Melbourne who wear evening dress, light coats and soft hats — in fact, I generally wear them myself.'

'Well, that might have been a coincidence,' said the doctor, rather disconcerted; 'but the use of chloroform puts the question beyond a doubt; people don't usually carry chloroform about with them.'

'I suppose not,' answered the other, and then the matter dropped.

Chinston made an examination of Mark Frettlby, and when he had finished, his face was very grave, though he laughed at the millionaire's fears.

'You're all right,' he said, gaily. 'Action of the heart a little weak, that's all — only,' impressively, 'avoid excitement — avoid excitement.'

Just as Frettlby was putting on his coat, a knock came to the door, and Madge entered.

'Brian is gone,' she began. 'Oh, I beg your pardon, doctor — but is papa ill?' she asked with sudden fear.

'No, child, no,' said Frettlby, hastily, 'I'm all right; I thought my heart was affected, but it isn't.'

'Not a bit of it,' answered Chinston, reassuringly. 'All right — only avoid excitement.'

But when Frettlby turned to go to the door, Madge, who had her eyes fixed on the doctor's face, saw how grave it was.

'There is danger?' she said, touching his arm as they paused for a moment at the door.

'No! No!' he answered, hastily.

'Yes, there is,' she persisted. 'Tell me the worst, it is best for me to know.'

The doctor looked at her in some doubt for a few moments, and then placed his hand on her shoulder. 'My dear young lady,' he said gravely, 'I will tell you what I have not dared to tell your father.'

'What?' she asked in a low voice, her face growing pale.

'His heart is affected.'

'And there is great danger?'

'Yes, great danger. In the event of any sudden shock —' he hesitated.

'Yes —'

'He would probably drop down dead.'

'My God!'

XXVI
Kilsip has a Theory of his Own

Mr Calton sat in his office reading a letter he had just received from Fitzgerald, and it seemed to give him great satisfaction, judging from the complacent smile on his face. 'I know,' wrote Brian, 'that now you have taken up the affair, you will not stop until you find everything out, so, as I want the matter to rest as at present, I will anticipate you, and reveal all. You were right in your conjecture that I knew something likely to lead to the detection of Whyte's murderer; but when I tell you my reasons for keeping such a thing secret, I am sure you will not blame me. Mind you, I do not say that I know who committed the murder; but I have suspicions — very strong suspicions — and I wish to God Rosanna Moore had died before she told me what she did. However, I will tell you all, and leave you to judge as to whether I was justified in concealing what I was told. I will call at your office some time next week, and then you will know everything that Rosanna Moore told me; but once that you are possessed of the knowledge you will pity me.'

'Most extraordinary,' mused Calton, leaning back in his chair, as he laid down the letter. 'I wonder if he's going to tell me that he killed Whyte after all, and that Sal Rawlins perjured herself to save him! No, that's nonsense, or she'd have turned up in better time, and wouldn't have risked his neck up to the last moment. Though I make it a rule never to be surprised at anything, I expect what Brian Fitzgerald tells me will startle me considerably. I've never met with such an extraordinary case, and from all appearances the end isn't reached yet. After all,' said Mr Calton, thoughtfully, 'truth is stranger than fiction.'

Here a knock came to the door, and in answer to an invitation to enter, it opened, and Kilsip glided into the room.

'You're not engaged, sir?' he said, in his soft, low voice.

'Oh, dear, no,' answered Calton, carelessly; 'come in — come in!'

Kilsip closed the door softly, and gliding along in his usual velvet-footed manner, sat down in a chair near Calton's, and placing his hat on the ground, looked keenly at the barrister.

'Well, Kilsip,' said Calton, with a yawn, playing with his watch chain, 'any good news to tell me?'

'Well, nothing particularly new,' purred the detective, rubbing his hands together.

'Nothing new, and nothing true, and no matter,' said Calton, quoting Emerson. 'And what have you come to see me about?'

'The Hansom Cab Murder,' replied the other quietly.

'The devil!' cried Calton, startled out of his professional dignity. 'And have you found out who did it?'

'No!' answered Kilsip, rather dismally; 'but I've got an idea.'

'So had Gorby,' retorted Calton, dryly, 'an idea that ended in smoke. Have you any practical proofs?'

'Not yet.'

'That means you are going to get some?'

'Well, if possible.'

'Much virtue in "if," ' quoted Calton, picking up a pencil, and scribbling idly on his blotting paper. 'And to whom does your suspicion point?'

'Aha!' said Mr Kilsip, cautiously.

'Don't know him,' answered the other, coolly; 'family name Humbug, I presume. Bosh! Whom do you suspect?'

Kilsip looked round cautiously, as if to make sure they were alone, and then said, in a stage whisper —

'Roger Moreland!'

'That was the young man that gave evidence as to how Whyte got drunk?'

Kilsip nodded.

'Well, and how do you connect him with the murder?'

'Do you remember in the evidence given by the cabmen, Royston and Rankin, they both swore that the man who was with Whyte on that night wore a diamond ring on the forefinger of the right hand?'

'What of that? Nearly every second man in Melbourne wears a diamond ring.'

'But not on the forefinger of the right hand.'

'Oh! And Moreland wears a ring in that way?'

'Yes!'

'Merely a coincidence. Is that all your proof?'

'All I can obtain at present.'

'It's very weak,' said Calton, scornfully.

'The weakest proofs may form a chain to hang a man,' observed Kilsip, sententiously.

'Moreland gave his evidence clearly enough,' said Calton, rising, and walking up and down. 'He met Whyte; they got drunk together. Whyte went out of the hotel, and shortly afterwards Moreland followed with the coat, which was left behind by Whyte, and then someone snatched it from him.'

'Ah, did they?' interrupted Kilsip, quickly.

'So Moreland says,' said Calton, stopping short. 'I understand; you think Moreland was not so drunk as he says, and after following Whyte outside, put on his coat, and got into the cab with him.'

'That is my theory.'

'It's ingenious enough,' said the barrister; 'but why should Moreland murder Whyte? What motive had he?'

'Those papers —'

'Pshaw! Another idea of Gorby's,' said Calton, angrily. 'How do you know there were any papers?'

The fact is, Calton did not intend Kilsip to know that Whyte really had papers until he heard what Fitzgerald had to tell him.

'And another thing,' said Calton, resuming his walk, 'if your theory is correct, which I don't think it is, what became of Whyte's coat? Has Moreland got it?'

'No, he has not,' answered the detective, decisively.

'You seem very positive about it,' said the lawyer, after a moment's pause. 'Did you ask Moreland about it?'

A reproachful look came into Kilsip's white face.

'Not quite so green,' he said, forcing a smile. 'I thought you'd a better opinion of me than that, Mr Calton. Ask him? — no.'

'Then how did you find out?'

'The fact is, Moreland is employed as a barman in the Kangaroo Hotel.'

'A barman!' echoed Calton; 'and he came out here as a gentleman of independent fortune. Why, hang it, man, that in itself is sufficient to prove that he had no motive to murder Whyte. Moreland pretty well lived on Whyte, so what could have induced him to kill his golden goose, and become a barman — pshaw! The idea is absurd.'

'Well, you may be right about the matter,' said Kilsip, rather angrily; 'and if Gorby makes mistakes I don't pretend to be infallible. But, at all events, when I saw Moreland in the bar he wore a silver ring on the forefinger of his right hand.'

'Silver isn't a diamond.'

'No; but it shows that was the finger he was accustomed to wear his ring on. When I saw that I determined to search his room. I managed to do so while he was out, and found —'

'A mare's nest?'

Kilsip nodded.

'And so your castle of cards falls to the ground,' said Calton, jestingly. 'Your idea is absurd. Moreland no more committed the murder than I did. Why, he was too drunk on that night to do anything.'

'Humph — so he says.'

'Well, men don't calumniate themselves for nothing.'

'It was a lesser danger to avert a greater one,' replied Kilsip, coolly. 'I am sure that Moreland was not drunk on that night. He only said so to escape awkward questions as to his movements. Depend upon it he knows more than he lets out.'

'Well, and how do you intend to set about the matter?'

'I shall start looking for the coat first.'

'Ah! You think he has hidden it?'

'I am sure of it. My theory is this. When Moreland got out of the cab at Powlett Street —'

'But he didn't,' interrupted Calton, angrily.

'Let us suppose, for the sake of argument, that he did,' said Kilsip, quietly. 'I say when he left the cab he walked up Powlett Street, turned to the left down George Street, and walked back to town through the Fitzroy Gardens, then, knowing that the coat was noticeable, he threw it away, or rather, hid it, and walked out of the Gardens through the town —'

'In evening dress — more noticeable than the coat.'

'He wasn't in evening dress,' said Kilsip, quietly.

'No more he was,' observed Calton, eagerly, recalling the evidence at the trial. 'Another blow to your theory. The murderer was in evening dress — the cabman said so.'

'Yes; because he had seen Mr Fitzgerald in evening dress a few minutes before, and thought that he was the same man who got into the cab with Whyte.'

'Well, what of that?'

'If you remember, the second man had his coat buttoned up. Moreland wore dark trousers — at least, I suppose so — and, with the coat buttoned up, it was easy for the cabman to make the mistake, believing, as he did, that it was Mr Fitzgerald.'

'That sounds better,' said Calton, thoughtfully. 'And what are you going to do?'

'Look for the coat in the Fitzroy Gardens.'

'Pshaw! A wild goose chase.'

'Possibly,' said Kilsip, as he arose to go.

'And when shall I see you again?' said Calton.

'Oh, tonight,' said Kilsip, pausing at the door. 'I had nearly forgotten, Mother Guttersnipe wants to see you.'

'Why? What's up?'

'She's dying, and wants to tell you some secret.'

'Rosanna Moore, by Jove!' said Calton. 'She'll tell me something about her. I'll get to the bottom of this yet. All right, I'll be here at eight o'clock.'

'Very well, sir!' and the detective glided out.

'I wonder if that old devil knows anything?' said Calton to himself, as he resumed his seat. 'She might have overheard some conversation between Whyte and his mistress, and is going to split. Well, I'm afraid when Fitzgerald does confess I will know all about it beforehand.'

XXVII
Mother Guttersnipe Joins the Majority

Punctual to his appointment, Kilsip called at Calton's office at eight o'clock, in order to guide him through the squalid labyrinths of the slums, and found the barrister waiting impatiently for him. The fact is, Calton had got it into his head that Rosanna Moore was at the bottom of the whole mystery, and every new piece of evidence he discovered went to confirm this belief. When Rosanna Moore was dying, she might have confessed something to Mother Guttersnipe, which would hint at the name of the murderer, and he had a strong suspicion that the old hag had received hush-money in order to keep quiet. Several times before Calton had been on the point of going to her and trying to get the secret out of her — that is, if she knew it; but now fate appeared to be playing into his hands, and a voluntary confession was much more likely to be a true one than when dragged piecemeal from unwilling lips. Consequently, when Kilsip made his appearance, Calton was in a perfect fever of excitement, which he concealed under a calm exterior.

'I suppose we'd better go at once,' he said to Kilsip, as he lit a cigar. 'That old hag may go off at any moment.'

'She might,' assented Kilsip, doubtfully; 'but I wouldn't be a bit surprised if she pulled through. Some of these old women have nine lives like a cat.'

'Not improbable,' retorted Calton, as they passed into the brilliantly lighted street; 'her nature seemed to me to be essentially feline. But tell me,' he went on, 'what's the matter with her — old age?'

'Partly; drink also, I think,' answered Kilsip. 'Besides, her surroundings are not very healthy, and her dissipated habits have pretty well settled her.'

'It isn't anything catching, I hope,' cried the barrister, with a shudder, as they passed into the crowd of Bourke Street.

'Don't know, sir, not being a doctor,' answered the detective, stolidly.

'Oh!' ejaculated Calton, in dismay.

'It will be all right, sir,' said Kilsip, reassuringly; 'I've been there dozens of times, and I'm all right.'

' dare say,' retorted the barrister; 'but I may go there once and catch it, whatever it is.'

'Take my word, sir, it's nothing worse nor old age and drink.'

'Has she a doctor?'

'Won't let one come near her — prescribes for herself.'

'Gin, I suppose? Humph! Much nicer than the usual run of medicines.'

They went into Little Bourke Street, and after going through the narrow and dark lanes, which now seemed quite familiar to Calton, reached Mother Guttersnipe's den, for in truth it could be called nothing else. After climbing the rickety stairs, which groaned and creaked beneath their weight, they entered the room, and found Mother Guttersnipe lying on the bed in the corner, and the elfish child with the black hair playing cards with a slatternly-looking girl at the deal table by the faint light of a tallow candle. They both sprang to their feet as the strangers entered, and the elfish child pushed a broken chair in a sullen manner towards Mr Calton, while the other girl shuffled into a far corner of the room, and crouched down there like a dog. The noise of their entry awoke the hag from an uneasy slumber into which she had fallen, and sitting up in bed, she huddled the clothes round her, and presented such a gruesome spectacle that Calton involuntarily recoiled. Her white hair was all unbound, and hung in tangled masses over her shoulders in snowy profusion. Her face, parched and wrinkled, with the hooked nose, and beady black eyes, like those of a mouse, was poked forward, and her skinny arms, bare to the shoulder, were waving wildly about as she grasped at the bedclothes with her claw-like hands. The bottle of square and the broken cup lay beside her, and filling herself a dram, she lapped it up greedily. Some of it went the wrong way, and she was seized with a paroxysm of coughing, which lasted till the elfish child shook her up, and took the cup from her.

'Greedy old beast,' muttered this amiable infant, peering into the cup, 'ye'd drink the Yarrer dry, I b'lieve.'

'Go t' 'ell,' muttered the old woman, feebly. 'Who's they, Lizer?' she said, shading her eyes with one trembling hand, while she looked at Calton and the detective.

'The perlice cove an' the swell,' said Lizer, suddenly. 'Come to see yer turn up yer toes.'

'I ain't dead yet, ye whelp,' snarled the hag with sudden energy; 'an' if I gits up I'll turn up yer blarsted toes, cuss ye.'

Lizer gave a shrill laugh of disdain, and Kilsip stepped forward.

'None of this,' he said, sharply, taking Lizer by one thin shoulder, and pushing her over to where the other girl was crouching; 'stop there till I tell you to move.'

Lizer tossed back her tangled black hair, and was about to make some impudent reply, when the other girl, who was older and wiser, put out her hand, and pulled her down beside her.

Meanwhile, Calton was addressing himself to the old beldame in the corner.

'You wanted to see me?' he said gently, for, notwithstanding his repugnance to her, she was, after all, a woman, and dying.

'Yes, blarst ye,' croaked Mother Guttersnipe, lying down, and pulling the greasy bedclothes up to her neck. 'You ain't a parson?' with sudden suspicion.

'No, I am a lawyer.'

'I ain't a-goin' to have the cussed parsons a-prowlin' round 'ere,' growled the old woman, viciously. 'I ain't a-goin' to die yet, cuss ye; I'm goin' to get well an' strong, an' 'ave a good time of it.'

'I'm afraid you won't recover,' said Calton, gently. 'You had better let me send for a doctor.'

'No, I sha'n't,' retorted the hag, aiming a blow at him with all her feeble strength. 'I ain't a-goin' to have my inside spil'd with salts and senner. I don't want neither parsons nor doctors, I don't. I wouldn't 'ave a lawyer, only I'm a-thinkin' of makin' my will, I am, blarst it.'

'Mind I gits the watch,' yelled Lizer, from the corner. 'If you gives it to Sal I'll tear her eyes out.'

'Silence!' said Kilsip, sharply, and, with a muttered curse, Lizer sat back in her corner.

'Sharper than a serpent's tooth, she are,' whined the old woman, when quiet was once more restored. 'That young devil 'ave fed at my 'ome, an' now she turns, cuss her.'

'Well — well,' said Calton, rather impatiently, 'what is it you wanted to see me about?'

'Don't be in such a 'urry,' said the hag, with a scowl, 'or I'm blamed if I tell you anything, s'elp me G—'.

She was evidently growing very weak, so Calton turned to Kilsip and told him in a whisper to get a doctor. The detective scribbled a note on some paper, and, giving it to Lizer, ordered her to take it. At this, the other girl arose, and, putting her arm in that of the child's, they left together.

'Them two young 'usseys gone?' said Mother Guttersnipe. 'Right you are, for I don't want what I've got to tell to git into the noospaper, I don't.'

'And what is it?' asked Calton, bending forward.

The old woman took another drink of gin, and it seemed to put life into her, for she sat up in the bed, and commenced to talk rapidly, as though she were afraid of dying before her secret was told.

'You've been 'ere afore,' she said, pointing one skinny finger at Calton, 'and you wanted to find out all about 'er; but you didn't, blarst ye. She wouldn't let me tell, for she was always a proud jade, a-flouncin' round while 'er pore mother was a-starvin'.'

'Her mother! Are you Rosanna Moore's mother?' cried Calton, considerably astonished.

'May I die if I ain't,' croaked the hag. ' 'Er pore father died of drink, cuss 'im, an' I'm a-follerin' 'im to the same place in the same way. You weren't about town in the old days, or you'd a-bin after her, blarst ye.'

'After Rosanna?'

'The werry girl,' answered Mother Guttersnipe. 'She were on the stage, she were, an' my eye, what a swell she were, with all the coves a-dyin' for 'er, an' she dancin' over their black 'earts, cuss 'em; but she was allays good to me till 'e came.'

'Who came?'

' 'E!' yelled the old woman, raising herself on her arm, her eyes sparkling with vindictive fury. ' 'E, a-comin' round with di'monds and gold, and a-ruin' my pore girl; an' how 'e's 'eld 'is bloomin' 'ead up all these years as if he were a saint, cuss 'im — cuss 'im!'

'Who does she mean?' whispered Calton to Kilsip.

'Mean!' screamed Mother Guttersnipe, whose sharp ears had caught the muttered question. 'Why, Mark Frettlby!'

'Good God!' Calton rose up in his astonishment, and even Kilsip's inscrutable countenance displayed some surprise.

'Aye, 'e were a swell in them days,' pursued Mother Guttersnipe, 'and 'e comes a-philanderin' round my gal, blarst 'im, an' seduces 'er, and leaves 'er an' the child to starve, like a black-'earted villain as 'e were.'

'The child! Her name?'

'Bah,' retorted the hag, with scorn, 'as if you didn't know my gran'darter Sal.'

'Sal, Mark Frettlby's child?'

'Yes, an' as pretty a girl as the other, tho' she 'appened to be born on the wrong side of the 'edge. Oh, I've seen 'er a-sweepin' along in 'er silks an' satins as tho' we were dirt — an' Sal 'er 'alf sister — cuss 'er.'

Exhausted by the efforts she had made, the old woman sank back in her bed, while Calton sat in a dazed manner, thinking over the astounding revelation that had just been made. That Rosanna Moore should turn out to be Mark Frettlby's mistress he hardly wondered at; after all, he was but a man, and in his young days had been no better and no worse than the rest of his friends. Rosanna Moore was pretty, and was evidently one of those women who — rakes at heart — prefer the untrammelled freedom of being a mistress to the sedate bondage of a wife. In questions of morality, so many people live in glass houses, that there are few nowadays who can afford to throw stones, so Calton did not think any the worse of Frettlby for his youthful follies. But what he did wonder at, was that Frettlby should be so heartless as to leave his child to the tender mercies of an old hag like Mother Guttersnipe. It was so entirely different from what he knew of the man, that he was inclined to think it was some trick of the old woman's.

'Did Mr Frettlby know Sal was his child?' he asked.

'Not 'e,' snarled Mother Guttersnipe, in an exultant tone. ' 'E thought she was dead, 'e did, arter Roseanner gave him the go-by.'

'And why did you not tell him?'

''Cause I wanted to break 'is 'eart, if 'e 'ad any,' said the old beldame, vindictively. 'Sal was a-goin' to 'ell as fast as she could till she was tuk from me. If she had gone and got into quod I'd 'ave gone to 'im, and said, "Look at yer darter! 'Ow I've ruined her as you did mine." '

'You old devil,' said Calton, revolted at the malignity of the scheme. 'You sacrificed an innocent girl for this.'

'None of yer preachin',' retorted the hag sullenly; 'I ain't bin brought up for a saint, I ain't — an' I wanted to pay 'im out, blarst 'im — 'e paid me well to 'old my tongue about my darter, an' I've got it 'ere,' laying her hand on the pillow, 'All gold, good gold — an' mine, cuss me.'

Calton arose, he felt quite sick at this exhibition of human depravity, and longed to be away. As he was putting on his hat, however, the two girls entered with the doctor, who nodded to Kilsip, cast a sharp scutinising glance at Calton, and then walked over to the bed. The two girls went back to their corner, and waited in silence for the end. Mother Guttersnipe had fallen back in the bed, with one claw-like hand clutching the pillow, as if to protect her beloved gold, and over her face a deadly paleness was spreading, which told the practised eye of the doctor that the end was near. He knelt down beside the bed for a moment, holding the candle to the dying woman's face. She opened her eyes, and muttered drowsily —

'Who's you, go t'ell,' but then she seemed to grasp the situation again, and she started up with a shrill yell, which made the hearers shudder, it was so weird and eerie.

'My money!' she yelled, clasping the pillow in her skinny arms. 'It's all mine, ye shan't have it — blarst ye.'

The doctor arose from his knees, and shrugged his shoulders. 'Not worthwhile doing anything,' he said, coolly, 'she'll be dead soon.'

The old woman, mumbling over her pillow, caught the word, and burst into tears.

'Dead! Dead! My poor Rosanna, with 'er golden 'air, always lovin' 'er pore mother till 'e took 'er away, an' she came back to die — die — ooh!'

Her voice died away in a long melancholy wail, that made the two girls in the corner shiver, and put their fingers in their ears.

'My good woman,' said the doctor, bending over the bed, 'would you not like to see a minister?'

She looked at him with her bright, beady eyes, already somewhat dimmed with the mists of death, and said, in a harsh, low whisper — 'Why?'

'Because you have only a short time to live,' said the doctor gently. 'You are dying.'

Mother Guttersnipe sprang up, and seized his arm with a scream of terror.

'Dyin', dyin' — no! no!' she wailed, clawing his sleeve. 'I ain't fit to die — cuss me; save me — save me; I don't know where I'd go to, s'elp me — save me.'

The doctor tried to remove her hands, but she held on with wonderful tenacity.

'It is impossible,' he said, briefly.

The hag fell back in her bed.

'I'll give you money to save me,' she shrieked; 'good money — all mine — all mine. See — see — 'ere — suverains,' and, tearing her pillow open, she took out a canvas bag, and from it poured a gleaming stream of gold. Gold — gold — it rolled all over the bed, over the floor, away into the dark corners, yet no one touched it, so enchained were they by the horrible spectacle of the dying woman clinging to life. She clutched up some of the shining pieces, and held them up to the three men as they stood silently beside the bed, but her hands trembled so that sovereigns kept falling from them on the floor, with metallic clinks.

'All mine — all mine,' she shrieked, loudly. 'Give me my life — gold — money — cuss ye — I sold my soul for it — save me — give me my life,' and, with trembling hands, she tried to force the gold on them. They did not say a word, but stood silently looking at her, while the two girls in the corner clung together, and trembled with fear.

'Don't look at me — don't,' cried the hag, falling down again amid the shining gold. "Ye want me to die, blarst ye — I shan't — I shan't — give me my gold,' clawing at the scattered sovereigns. 'I'll take it with me — I shan't die — G—, G—' whimpering. 'I ain't done nothin' — let me live — give me a Bible — save me, G— cuss it — G—, G—,' and she fell back on the bed, a corpse.

The faint light of the candle flickered on the shining gold, and the dead face, framed in tangled white hair; while the three men, sick at heart, turned away in silence to seek assistance, with that wild cry still ringing in their ears —

'G— save me, G—!'

XXVIII
Mark Frettlby has a Visitor

According to the copy books of our youth, 'Procrastination is the thief of time,' and, certainly, Brian found that the remark was a true one. He had been nearly a week in town, yet could not make up his mind to go and see Calton, and though morning after morning he set out with the determination to go straight to Chancery Lane, yet he never arrived there. He had gone back to his lodgings in East Melbourne, and passed his time either in the house or in taking long walks in the gardens, or along the banks of the muddy Yarra. When he did go into town, on business connected with the sale of his station, he drove there and back in a hansom, for he had a curious shrinking against seeing any of his friends. He quite agreed with Byron's remark about 'D—d good-natured friends,' and was determined that he would not meet or talk with people, whose every word and action would imperceptibly remind him of the disgrace which had fallen on him of standing in the criminal dock. Even when walking by the Yarra he had a sort of uneasy feeling that he was looked upon as an object of curiosity, and as being very handsome, many people turned and looked at him, he attributed their admiration to a morbid desire for seeing a man who had nearly been hanged for murder.

As soon as his station was sold, and he married to Madge, he determined to leave Australia, and never set foot on it again. But until he could leave the place he saw no one, nor mixed with his former friends, so great was his dread at being stared at. Mrs Sampson, who had welcomed him back with shrill exclamations of delight, was loud in his expressions of disapproval as to the way he was shutting himself up.

'Your eyes bein' 'ollow,' said the sympathising cricket, 'it is nat'ral as it's want of air, which my 'usband's uncle, being a druggist, an' well-to-do, in Collingwood, ses as 'ow a want of ox-eye-gent, being a French name, as 'e called the atmispeare, were fearful for pullin' people down, an' makin' 'em go off their food, which you hardly eats anythin', an' not bein' a butterfly it's expected as your appetite would be larger.'

'Oh, I'm all right,' said Brian, absently, lighting a cigarette, and only half listening to his landlady's garrulous chatter, 'but if anyone calls tell them I'm not in. I don't want to be bothered by visitors.'

'Bein' as wise a thing as Solomon ever said,' answered Mrs Sampson, energetically, 'which, no doubt, 'e was in good 'ealth when seein' the Queen of Sheber, as is necessary when anyone calls, and no feelin' disposed to speak, which I'm often that way myself on occasions, my sperits bein' low, as I've 'eard tell soder water 'ave that effect on 'em, which you takes it with a dash of brandy, tho' to be sure that might be the cause of your want of life, and — drat that bell,' she finished, hurrying out of the room as the front door bell sounded, 'which my legs is a-givin' way under me thro' being' overworked.'

Meanwhile, Brian sat and smoked contentedly, much relieved by the departure of Mrs Sampson, with her constant chatter, but he soon heard her mount the stairs again, and she entered the room with a telegram, which she handed to her lodger.

' 'Opin' it don't contain bad noose,' she said, as she retreated to the door again, 'which I don't like 'em, 'avin' 'ad a shock in early life thro' one 'avin' come unexpected, as my uncle's grandfather were dead, 'avin' perished of consumption, our family all being disposed to the disease — and now, if you'll excuse me, sir, I'll get to my dinner, bein' in the 'abit of takin' my meals reg'lar, and I studies my inside carefully, bein' easily upset, thro' which I never could be a sailor.'

Mrs Sampson, having at last exhausted herself, went out of the room, and croaked loudly down the stairs, leaving Brian to read his telegram. Tearing open the red marked envelope, it turned out to be from Madge, saying that they had come back to town, and asking him down to dinner that evening. Fitzgerald folded up the telegram, then rising from his seat, walked moodily up and down the room with his hands in his pockets.

'So he is there,' said the young man aloud; 'and I shall have to meet him and shake hands with him, knowing all the time what he is. If it were not for Madge I'd leave this cursed place at once, but after the way she stood by me in my trouble, I should be a coward if I did so.'

It was as Madge had predicted — her father was unable to stay long in one place, and had come back to Melbourne a week after Brian had arrived. The pleasant party at the station was broken up, and, like the graves of a household, the guests were scattered far and wide. Peterson had left for New Zealand *en route* for the wonders of the Hot Lakes, and the old colonist was about to start for England in order to refresh his boyish memories. Mr and Mrs Rolleston had come back to Melbourne, where the wretched Felix was compelled once more to plunge into politics, and Dr Chinston had resumed his usual routine of fees and patients.

Madge was glad to be back in Melbourne once more, as now that her health was restored she began to have a craving for the excitement of town life. It is now more than three months since the murder, and the nine days' wonder was a thing of the past. The possibility of a war with Russia was now the one absorbing topic of the hour, and the colonies were busy preparing for the attacks of a possible enemy. As the Spanish Kings had drawn their treasures from Mexico and Peru, so might the White Czar lay violent hands on the golden stores of Australia, but here there were no uncultured savages to face, but the sons and grandsons of men who had dimmed the glories of the Russian arms at Alma and Balaclava. So in the midst of stormy rumours of wars the tragic fate of Oliver Whyte was quite forgotten. After the trial, everyone, including the detective office, had given up the matter, and mentally relegated it to the list of undiscovered crimes. In spite of the utmost vigilance, nothing new had been discovered, and it seemed likely that the assassin of Oliver Whyte would remain a free man. There were only two people in Melbourne who still held the contrary opinion, and they were Calton and Kilsip. Both these men had sworn to discover this unknown murderer, who struck his cowardly blow in the dark, and though there seemed no possible chance of success, yet they worked on. Kilsip suspected Roger Moreland, the boon companion of the dead man, but his suspicions were vague and uncertain, and there seemed little hope of verifying them. The barrister did not as yet suspect any particular person, though the death-bed confession of Mother Guttersnipe had thrown a new light on the subject, but he thought that when Fitzgerald told him the secret which Rosanna Moore had confided to his keeping, the real murderer would soon be discovered, or, at least, some clue would be found that would lead to his detection. So, as the matter stood at the time of Mark Frettlby's return to Melbourne, Mr Calton was waiting for Fitzgerald's confession before making a move, while Kilsip worked stealthily in the dark, trying to get evidence against Moreland.

On receiving Madge's telegram, Brian determined to go down in the evening, but not to dinner, so he sent a reply to Madge to that effect. He did not want to meet Mark Frettlby, but did not, of course, tell this to Madge, so she had her dinner by herself, as her father had gone in to his club, and the time of his return was uncertain. After dinner, she wrapped a light cloak round her, and went out on to the verandah to wait for her lover. The garden looked charming in the moonlight, with the black, dense cypress tress standing up against the sky, and the great fountain splashing cool and silvery. There was a heavily-foliaged oak just by the gate, and she strolled down the path, and stood under it in the shadow, listening to the whisper and rustle of its multitudinous leaves. It is curious the unearthly glamour which moonlight seems to throw over everything, and though Madge knew every flower, tree, and shrub in the garden, yet they all looked weird and fantastical in the cold, white light. She went up to the fountain, and seating herself on the edge, amused herself by dipping her hand into the chilly water, and letting it fall, like silver rain, back into the basin. While thus engaged, she heard the iron gate open and shut with a clash, and springing to her feet, saw a gentleman coming up the path in a light coat and soft wide-awake hat.

'Oh, it's you at last, Brian?' she cried, as she ran down the path to meet him. 'Why did you not come before?'

'Not being Brian, I can't say,' answered her father's voice.

Madge burst out laughing.

'What an absurd mistake,' she cried. 'Why, I thought you were Brian.'

'Indeed!'

'Yes; in that hat and coat I couldn't tell the difference in the moonlight.'

'Oh,' said her father, with a laugh, pushing his hat back, 'moonlight is necessary to complete the spell, I suppose?'

'Of course,' answered his daughter. 'If there was no moonlight, alas for lovers!'

'Alas, indeed!' echoed her father. 'They would become as extinct as the moa; but where are your eyes, Puss, when you take an old man like me for your gay young Lochinvar?'

'Well, really, papa,' answered Madge, deprecatingly, 'You do look so like him in that coat and hat that I could not tell the difference till you spoke.'

'Nonsense, child,' said Frettlby, roughly, 'you are fanciful;' and turning on his heel, he walked rapidly towards the house, leaving Madge staring after him in astonishment, as well she might, for her father had never spoken to her so roughly before. Wondering at the cause of his sudden anger, she stood spell-bound, until there came a step behind her, and a soft, low whistle. She turned with a scream, and saw Brian smiling at her.

'Oh, it's you,' she said, with a pout, as he caught her in his arms and kissed her.

'Only me,' said Brian, ungrammatically; 'disappointing, isn't it?'

'Oh, fearfully,' answered the girl, with a gay laugh, as arm-in-arm they walked towards the house. 'But do you know I made such a curious mistake just now; I thought papa was you.'

'How strange,' said Brian, absently, for indeed he was admiring her charming face, which looked so pure and sweet in the moonlight.

'Yes, wasn't it?' she replied. 'He had on a light coat and a soft hat, just like you wear sometimes, and as you are both the same height, I took you for one another.'

Brian did not answer, but there was a cold feeling at his heart as he saw a possibility of his worst suspicions being confirmed, for just at that moment there came into his mind the curious coincidence of the man who got into the hansom cab being dressed the same as he was. What if — 'Nonsense,' he said, aloud, rousing himself out of the train of thought the resemblance had suggested.

'I'm sure it isn't,' said Madge, who had been talking about something else for the last five minutes. 'You are a very rude young man.'

'I beg your pardon,' said Brian, waking up. 'You were saying —'

'That the horse is the most noble of all animals — Exactly.'

'I don't understand —' began Brian, rather puzzled.

'Of course you don't,' interrupted Madge, petulantly; 'considering I've been wasting my eloquence on a deaf man for the last ten minutes, and very likely lame as well as deaf.' And to prove the truth of the remark, she ran up the path with Brian after her. He had a long chase of it, for Madge was nimble and better acquainted with the garden than he was, but at last he caught her just as she was running up the steps into the house, and then — history repeats itself.

They went into the drawing-room and found that Mr Frettlby had gone up to his study, and did not want to be disturbed. Madge sat down to the piano, but before she struck a note, Brian took both her hands prisoners.

'Madge,' he said, gravely, as she turned round, 'what did your father say when you made that mistake?'

'He was very angry,' she answered. 'Quite cross; I'm sure I don't know why.'

Brian sighed as he released her hands, and was about to reply when the visitors' bell sounded, they heard the servant answer it, and then someone was taken upstairs to Mr Frettlby's study.

When the footman came in to light the gas, Madge asked who it was that had come to the door.

'I don't know, Miss,' he answered; 'he said he wanted to see Mr Frettlby particularly, so I took him up to the study.'

'But I thought that papa said he was not to be disturbed?'

'Yes, Miss, but the gentleman had an appointment with him.'

'Poor papa,' sighed Madge, turning again to the piano. 'He has always got such a lot to do.'

Left to themselves, Madge began playing Waldteufel's last new valse, a dreamy, haunting melody, with a touch of sadness in it, and Brian, lying lazily on the sofa, listened. Then she sang a gay little French song about Love and a Butterfly, with a mocking refrain, which made Brian laugh.

'A memory of Offenbach,' he said, rising and coming over to the piano. 'We certainly can't touch the French in writing these airy trifles.'

'They're unsatisfactory, I think,' said Madge, running her fingers over the keys; 'they mean nothing.'

'Of course not,' he replied, 'but don't you remember that De Quincy says there is no moral either big or little in the Iliad, so these light chansons are something similar.'

'Well, I think there's more music in Barbara Allan than all those frothy things,' said Madge, with fine scorn. 'Come and sing it.'

'A five-act funeral, it is,' groaned Brian, as he rose to obey; 'let's have Garry Owen instead.'

Nothing else, however, would suit the capricious young person at the piano, so Brian, who had a pleasant voice, sang the quaint old ditty of cruel Barbara Allan, who treated her dying love with such disdain.

'Sir John Graham was an ass,' said Brian, when he had finished; 'or, instead of dying in such a silly manner, he'd have married her right off, without asking her permission.'

'I don't think she was worth marrying,' replied Madge, opening a book of Mendelssohn's duets; 'or she wouldn't have made such a fuss over her health not being drunk.'

'Depend upon it, she was a plain woman,' remarked Brian, gravely, 'and was angry because she wasn't toasted among the rest of the country belles. I think the young man had a narrow escape myself — she'd always have reminded him about that unfortunate oversight.'

'You seem to have analysed her nature pretty well,' said Madge, a little dryly; 'however, we'll leave the failings of Barbara Allan alone, and sing this.'

This was Mendelssohn's charming duet, 'Would that my Love,' which was a great favourite of Brian's. They were in the middle of it when suddenly Madge stopped, as she heard a loud cry, evidently proceeding from her father's study. Recollecting Dr Chinston's warning, she ran out of the room, and upstairs, leaving Brian rather puzzled by her unceremonious departure, for though he had heard the cry, yet he did not attach much importance to it.

Madge knocked at the study door, and then she tried to open it, but it was locked.

'Who's there?' asked her father, sharply, from inside.

'Only me, papa,' she answered. 'I thought you were —'

'No! No — I'm all right,' replied her father, quickly. 'Go down stairs, I'll join you shortly.'

Madge went back to the drawing-room only half satisfied with the explanation. She found Brian waiting at the door, with rather an anxious face.

'What's the matter?' he asked, as she paused a moment at the foot of the stairs.

'Papa says nothing,' she replied, 'but I am sure he must have been startled, or he would not have cried out like that.'

She told him what Dr Chinston had said about the state of her father's heart, a recital which shocked Brian greatly. They did not return to the drawing-room, but went out on to the verandah, where, after wrapping a cloak around Madge, Fitzgerald lit a cigarette. They sat down at the far end of the verandah somewhat in the shadow, and could see the hall door wide open, and a warm flood of mellow light pouring therefrom, and beyond the cold white moonshine. After about a quarter of an hour, Madge's alarm about her father having somewhat subsided, they were chatting on indifferent subjects, when a man came out of the hall door, and paused for a moment on the steps of the verandah. He was dressed in rather a fashionable suit of clothes, but, in spite of the heat of the night, had a thick white silk scarf round his throat.

'That's rather a cool individual,' said Brian, removing his cigarette from between his lips. 'I wonder what — Good God!' he cried, rising to his feet as the stranger turned round to look at the house, and took off his hat for a moment — 'Roger Moreland.'

The man started, and looked quickly round into the dark shadow of the verandah where they were seated, then, putting on his hat, ran quickly down the path, and they heard the gate clang after him.

Madge felt a sudden fear at the expression on Brian's face, as revealed by a ray of moonlight streaming full on it.

'Who is Roger Moreland?' she asked, touching his arm — 'Ah! I remember,' with sudden horror, 'Oliver Whyte's friend.'

'Yes,' in a hoarse whisper, 'and one of the witnesses at the trial.'

XXIX
Mr Calton's Curiosity is Satisfied

There was not much sleep for Brian that night. He left Madge almost immediately, and went home, but did not go to bed. He felt too anxious and ill at ease to sleep, and passed the greater part of the night walking up and down his room, occupied with his own sad thoughts. He was wondering in his own mind as to what could be the meaning of Roger Moreland's visit to Mark Frettlby. All the evidence that he had given at the trial was that he had met Whyte, and had been drinking with him during the evening. Whyte then went out, and that was the last Moreland had seen of him. Now, the question was, 'What did he go to see Mark Frettlby for?' He had no acquaintance with him, and yet he called by appointment. It is true he might have been in poverty, and the millionaire being well-known as an extremely generous man, Moreland might have called on him to get money. But then the cry which Frettlby had given after the interview had lasted a short time proved that he had been startled. Madge had gone upstairs and found the door locked, her father refusing her admission. Now, why was he so anxious Moreland should not be seen by anyone? That he had made some startling revelation was certain, and Fitzgerald felt sure that it was in connection with the hansom cab murder case. He wearied himself with conjectures about the matter, and towards daybreak threw himself, dressed as he was, on the bed, and slept heavily till twelve o'clock the next day. When he arose and looked at himself in the glass, he was startled at the haggard and worn appearance of his face. The moment he was awake his mind went back to Mark Frettlby and the visit of Roger Moreland.

'The net is closing round him,' he murmured to himself. 'I don't see how he can escape. Oh! Madge! Madge! If I could only spare you the bitterness of knowing what you must know, sooner or later, and that other unhappy girl — the sins of the fathers will be visited on the children — God help them.'

He had his bath, and, after dressing himself, went into his sitting-room, where he had a cup of tea, which refreshed him considerably. Mrs Sampson came crackling merrily upstairs with a letter, and gave vent to an exclamation of surprise, on seeing his altered appearance.

'Lor, sir!' she exclaimed, 'What 'ave you bin a-doin' — me knowin' your 'abits know'd as you'd gone to bed, not to say as it's very temptin' in this 'ot weather, but with excuses, sir, you looks as you 'adn't slept a blessed wink.'

'No more I have,' said Brian, listlessly holding out his hand for the letter. 'I was walking up and down my room all last night — I must have walked miles.'

'Ah! 'ow that puts me in mind of my pore 'usband,' chirped the cricket; 'bein' a printer, and accustomed like a howl to the darkness, when 'e was 'ome for the night 'e walked up and down till 'e wore out the carpet, bein' 'an expensive one, as I 'ad on my marriage, an' the only way I could stop 'im was by givin' 'im something soothin', which you, sir, ought to try — whisky 'ot, with lemon and sugar — but I've 'eard tell as chloroform —'

'No, d— it,' said Brian, hastily, startled out of his politeness, 'I've had enough of that.'

'Achin' teeth, no doubt,' said the landlady, going to the door, 'which I'm often taken that way myself, decayed teeth runnin' in the family, tho', to be sure, mine are stronger than former, a lodger of mine 'avin' bin a dentist, an' doin' them beautiful, instead of payin' rent, not 'avin' ready cash, his boxes bein' filled with bricks on 'is departure from the 'ouse.'

As Brian did not appear particularly interested in these domestic reminiscences, and seemed as if he wanted to be left alone, Mrs Sampson, with a final crackle, went down stairs and talked with a neighbour in the kitchen, as to the desirability of drawing her money out of the Savings Bank, in case the Russians should surprise and capture Melbourne.

Brian, left alone, stared out of the window at the dusty road and the black shadows cast by the tall poplars in front of the house.

'I must leave this place,' he said to himself; 'every chance remark seems to bear on the murder, and I'm not going to have it constantly by my side like the skeleton at the feast.'

He suddenly recollected the letter which he held in his hand, and which he now looked at for the first time. It proved to be from Madge, and tearing it hastily open, he read it.

'I cannot understand what is the matter with papa,' she wrote. 'Ever since that man Moreland left last night, he has shut himself up in his study, and is writing there hour after hour. I went up this morning, but he would not let me in. He did not come down to breakfast, and I am getting seriously alarmed. Come down tomorrow and see me, for I am anxious about his state of health, and I am sure that Moreland told him something which has upset him.'

'Writing,' said Brian, as he put the letter in his pocket, 'what about, I wonder? Perhaps he is thinking of committing suicide! If so, I for one will not stop him. It is a horrible thing to do, but it would be acting for the best under the circumstances.'

In spite of his determination to see Calton and tell all, Fitzgerald did not go near him that day. He felt ill and weary, the want of sleep, and mental worry, telling on him fearfully, and he looked ten years older than he did before the murder of Whyte. It is trouble which draws lines on the smooth forehead and furrows round the mouth. If a man has any mental worry, his life becomes a positive agony to him. Mental tortures are quite as bad as physical ones, if not worse. The last thing before dropping off to sleep is the thought of trouble, and with the first faint light of dawn, it returns and hammers all day at the weary brain. But while a man can sleep, life is rendered at least endurable; and of all the blessings which Providence has bestowed, there is none so precious as that same sleep, which, as wise Sancho Panza says, 'Wraps every man like a cloak.' Brian felt the need of rest, so sending a telegram to Calton to call on him in the morning, and another to Madge, that he would be down to luncheon next day, he stayed inside all day, and amused himself with smoking and reading. He went to bed early, and succeeded in having a sound sleep, so when he awoke next morning, he felt considerably refreshed and reinvigorated.

He was having his breakfast at half-past eight, when he heard the sound of wheels, and immediately afterwards a ring at the bell. He went to the window, and saw Calton's trap was at the door, while the owner was shortly afterwards shown into the room.

'Well, you are a nice fellow,' cried Calton, after greetings were over. 'Here I've been waiting for you with all the patience of Job, thinking you were still up country.'

'Will you have some breakfast?' asked Brian, laughing at his indignation.

'What have you got?' said Calton, looking over the table. 'Ham and eggs. Humph! Your landlady's culinary ideas are very limited.'

'Most landladies' ideas are,' retorted Fitzgerald, resuming his breakfast. 'Unless Heaven invents some new animal, lodgers will go on getting beef and mutton, alternated with hash, until the end of the world.'

'When one is in Rome, one mustn't speak ill of the Pope,' answered Calton, with a grimace. 'Do you think your landlady could supply me with brandy and soda?'

'I think so,' answered Fitzgerald, rising, and ringing the bell; 'but isn't it rather early for that sort of thing?'

'There's a proverb about glass houses,' said Calton, severely, 'which applies to you in this particular instance.'

Whereupon Fitzgerald laughed, and Calton having been supplied with what he required, prepared to talk business.

'I need hardly tell you how anxious I am to hear what you've got to say,' he said, leaning back in his chair, 'but I may as well tell you that I am satisfied that I know half your secret already.'

'Indeed!' Fitzgerald looked astonished, 'in that case, I need not —'

'Yes you need,' retorted Calton. 'I told you I only know half.'

'Which half?'

'Hum — rather difficult to answer — however, I'll tell you what I know, and you can supply all deficiencies. I am quite ready — go on — stop —' he arose and closed the door carefully. 'Well,' resuming his seat, 'Mother Guttersnipe died the other night.'

'Is she dead?'

'As a door-nail,' answered Calton calmly. 'And a horrible death-bed it was — her screams ring in my ears yet — but before she died she sent for me, and said —'

'What?'

'That she was the mother of Rosanna Moore.'

'Yes!'

'And that Sal Rawlins was Rosanna's child.'

'And the father?' said Brian, in a low voice.

'Was Mark Frettlby.'

'Ah!'

'And now what have you to tell me?'

'Nothing!'

'Nothing,' echoed Calton, surprised, 'then this is what Rosanna Moore told you when she died?'

'Yes!'

'Then why have you made such a mystery about it?'

'You ask that,' said Fitzgerald, looking up, in surprise. 'If I had told it, don't you see what difference it would have made to Madge?'

'I'm sure I don't,' retorted the barrister, completely mystified. 'I suppose you mean Frettlby's connection with Rosanna Moore; well, of course, it was not a very creditable thing for her to have been Frettlby's mistress, but still —'

'His mistress?' said Fitzgerald, looking up sharply; 'then you don't know all.'

'What do you mean — was she not his mistress?'

'No — his wife!'

Calton sprang to his feet, and gave a cry of surprise.

'His wife!'

Fitzgerald nodded.

'Why, Mother Guttersnipe did not know this — she thought Rosanna was his mistress.'

'He kept his marriage secret,' answered Brian, 'and as his wife ran away with someone else shortly afterwards, he never revealed it.'

'I understand now,' said the barrister, slowly. 'For if Mark Frettlby was lawfully married to Rosanna Moore — Madge is illegitimate.'

'Yes, and she now occupies the place which Sal Rawlins — or rather Sal Frettlby — ought to.'

'Poor girl,' said Calton, a little sadly. 'But all this does not explain the mystery of Whyte's murder.'

'I will tell you that,' said Fitzgerald, quickly. 'When Rosanna left her husband, she ran away to England with some young fellow, and when he got tired of her she returned to the stage, and became famous as a burlesque actress, under the name of Musette. There she met Whyte, as your friend found out, and they came out here for the purpose of extorting money from Frettlby. When they arrived in Melbourne, Rosanna let Whyte do all the business, and kept herself quiet. She gave her marriage certificate to Whyte, and he had it on him the night he was murdered.'

'Then Gorby was right,' interposed Calton, eagerly. 'The man to whom those papers were valuable did murder Whyte!'

'Can you doubt it? And that man was —'

'Not Mark Frettlby?' burst out Calton. 'In God's name, not Mark Frettlby?'

Brian nodded, 'Yes, Mark Frettlby!'

There was a silence for a few moments, Calton being too much startled by the revelation to say anything.

'When did you discover this?' he asked, after a pause.

'At the time you first came to see me in prison,' said Brian. 'I had no suspicion till then; but when you said Whyte was murdered for the sake of certain papers — knowing what they were and to whom they were valuable — I immediately guessed that Mark Frettlby had killed Whyte in order to obtain them, and keep his secret.'

'There can be no doubt of it,' said the barrister, with a sigh. 'So this is the reason Frettlby wanted Madge to marry Whyte — her hand was to be the price of his silence. When he withdrew his consent, Whyte threatened him with exposure. I remember he left the house in a very excited state on the night he was murdered. Frettlby must have followed him up to town, got into the cab with him, and after killing him with chloroform, took the marriage certificate from his secret pocket, and escaped.'

Brian rose to his feet, and walked rapidly up and down the room.

'Now you can understand what a hell my life has been for the last few months,' he said, 'knowing that he had committed the crime; and yet I had to sit with him, eat with him, and drink with him, with the knowledge that he was a murderer, and Madge — Good God — Madge, his daughter!'

Just then a knock came to his door, and Mrs Sampson entered with a telegram, which she handed to Brian. He tore it open as she withdrew, and glancing over it, gave a cry of horror, and let it flutter to his feet.

Calton turned rapidly on hearing his cry, and seeing him fall into a chair with a ghastly white face, snatched up the telegram and read it. When he did so, his face grew as pale and startled as Fitzgerald's, and lifting his hand, he said solemnly —

'It is the judgment of God!'

XXX
Nemesis

Men, according to the old Greek, 'were the sport of the gods' who, enthroned on high Olympus, put evil desires into the hearts of mortals; and when evil actions were the outcome of evil thoughts, amused themselves by watching the ineffectual efforts made by their victims to escape a relentless deity called Nemesis, who exacted a penalty for their evil deeds. It was no doubt very amusing — to the gods, but it is questionable if the men found it so. They had their revenge, however, for weary of plaguing puny mortals, who whimpered and cried when they saw they could not escape, the inevitable Nemesis turned her attention from actors to spectators, and made a clean sweep of the whole Olympian hierarchy. She smashed their altars, pulled down their statues, and after she had completed her malicious work, found that she had, vulgarly speaking, been cutting off her nose to spite her face, for she, too, became an object of derision and disbelief, and was forced to retire to the same obscurity to which she had relegated the other deities. Men, however, found out that she had not been altogether useless as a scapegoat upon which to lay the blame of their own shortcomings, so they created a new deity called Fate, and laid any misfortune which happened to them to her charge. Her worship is still very popular, especially among lazy and unlucky people, who never bestir themselves on the ground that whether they do so or not their lives are already settled by Fate. After all, the true religion of Fate has been preached by George Eliot, when she says that our lives are the outcome of our actions. Set up any idol you please upon which to lay the blame of unhappy lives and baffled ambitions, but the true cause is to be found in men themselves. Every action, good or bad, which we do has its corresponding reward, and Mark Frettlby found it so, for the sins of his youth were now being punished in his old age. No doubt he had sinned gaily enough in that far-off time when life's cup was still brimming with wine, and no asp hid among the roses; but Nemesis had been an unseen spectator of all his thoughtless actions, and now came to demand her just dues. He felt somewhat as Faust must have felt when Mephistopheles suggested a visit to Hades, in repayment of those years of magic youth and magic power. So long ago it seemed since he had married Rosanna Moore, that he almost persuaded himself that it had been only a dream — a pleasant dream, with a disagreeable awakening. When she had left him he had tried to forget her, recognising how unworthy she was of a good man's love. He heard that she had died in a London hospital, and with a passionate sigh for a perished love, had dismissed her from his thoughts for ever. His second marriage had turned out a happy one, and he regretted the death of his wife deeply. Afterwards, all his love centred in his daughter, and he thought he would be able to spend his declining years in peace. This, however, was not to be, and he was thunderstruck when Whyte arrived from England with the information that his first wife still lived, that the daughter of Mark Frettlby was illegitimate. Sooner than this, Frettlby agreed to anything; but Whyte's demands became too exorbitant, and he refused to comply with them. On Whyte's death he again breathed freely, when suddenly a second possessor of his fatal secret started up in the person of Roger Moreland. As the murder of Duncan had to be followed by that of Banquo, in order to render Macbeth safe, so he foresaw that while Roger Moreland lived his life would be one long misery. He knew that the friend of the murdered man would be his master, and would never leave him during his life, while after his death he would probably publish the whole ghastly story, and defame the memory of the widely-respected Mark Frettlby. What is it that Shakespeare says? —

> 'Good name in man or woman
> Is the immediate jewel of their souls.'

And after all these years of spotless living and generous use of his wealth, was he to be dragged down to the depths of infamy and degradation by a man like Moreland? Already, in fancy, he heard the jeering cries of his fellow-men, and saw the finger of scorn point at him — he, the great Mark Frettlby, who was famous throughout Australia for his honesty, integrity, and generosity. No, it could not be, and yet this would surely happen unless he took means to prevent it.

The day after he had seen Moreland, and knew that his secret was no longer safe, since it was in the power of a man who might reveal it at any moment in a drunken fit, or out of sheer maliciousness, he sat at his desk writing. After a time he laid down his pen, and taking up a portrait of his dead wife which stood just in front of him, he stared at it long and earnestly. As he did so, his mind went back to the time when he had first met and loved her. Even as Faust had entered into the purity and serenity of Gretchen's chamber, out of the coarseness and profligacy of Auerbach's cellar, so he, leaving behind him the wild life of his youth, had entered into the peace and quiet of a domestic home. The old feverish life with Rosanna Moore, seemed to be as unsubstantial and chimerical, as, no doubt, his union with Lillith after he met Eve, seemed to Adam in the old Rabbinical legend. There seemed to be only one way open to him, by which he could escape the relentless fate which dogged his steps. He would write a confession of everything from the time he had first met Rosanna, and then — death. He would cut the Gordian knot of all his difficulties, and then his secret would be safe — safe — no, it could not be while Moreland lived. When he was dead Moreland would see Madge and embitter her life with the story of her father's sins — yes — he must live to protect her, and drag his weary chain of bitter remembrance through life, always with that terrible sword of Damocles hanging over him. But still, he would write out his confession, and after his death, whenever it may happen, it might help if not altogether to exculpate, at least to secure some pity for a man who had been hardly dealt with by Fate. His resolution taken, he put it into force at once, and sat all day at his desk filling page after page with the history of his past life, which was so bitter to him. He started at first languidly, and as in the performance of an unpleasant but necessary duty. Soon, however, he became interested in it, and took a peculiar pleasure in putting down every minute circumstance which made the case stronger against himself. He dealt with it, not as a criminal, but as a prosecutor, and painted his conduct as much blacker than it really had been. Towards the end of the day, however, after reading over the earlier sheets, he experienced a revulsion of feeling, seeing how severe he had been on himself, so he wrote a defence upon his conduct, showing that fate had been too strong for him. It was a weak argument to bring forward, but still he felt it was the only one that he could make. It was quite dark when he had finished, and while sitting in the twilight, looking dreamily at the sheets scattered all over his desk, he heard a knock at the door, and heard his daughter's voice asking if he was coming to dinner. All day long he had closed his door against everyone, but now his task being ended, he collected all the closely written sheets together, placed them in a drawer of his escritoire, which he locked, and then opened the door.

'Dear papa,' cried Madge as she entered rapidly, and threw her arms around his neck, 'what have you been doing here all day by yourself?'

'Writing,' returned her father laconically, as he gently removed her arms.

'Why, I thought you were ill,' she answered, looking at him apprehensively.

'No, dear,' he replied, quietly. 'Not ill, but worried.'

'I knew that dreadful man who came last night had told you something to worry you. Who was he?'

'Oh! A friend of mine,' answered Frettlby, with hesitation.

'What — Roger Moreland?'

Her father started.

'How do you know it was Roger Moreland?'

'Oh! Brian recognised him as he went out.'

Mark Frettlby hesitated for a few moments, and then busied himself with the papers on his desk, as he replied in a low voice —

'You are right — it was Roger Moreland — he is very hard up, and as he was a friend of poor Whyte's, asked me to assist him, which I did.'

He hated to hear himself telling such a deliberate falsehood, but there was no help for it — Madge must never know the truth as long as he could conceal it.

'Just like you,' said Madge, kissing him lightly with filial pride. 'The best and kindest of men.'

He shivered slightly as he felt her caress, and thought how she would recoil from him did she know all. 'After all,' says some cynical writer, 'the illusions of youth are mostly due to the want of experience.' Madge, ignorant in a great measure of the world, cherished her pleasant illusions, though many of them had been destroyed by the trials of the past year, and her father longed to keep her in this frame of mind.

'Now go down to dinner, my dear,' he said, leading her to the door. 'I will follow soon.'

'Don't be long,' replied his daughter, 'or I shall come up again,' and she ran down the stairs, her heart feeling strangely light.

Her father looked after her until she vanished, then heaving a regretful sigh returned to his study, and taking out the scattered papers fastened them together, and endorsed them, 'My Confession.' He then placed them in an envelope, sealed it, and put it back in the desk. 'If all that is in that packet were known,' he said aloud, as he left the room, 'what would the world say?'

That night he was singularly brilliant at the dinner table. Generally a very reticent and grave man, on this night he laughed and talked so gaily that the very servants noticed the change. The fact was he felt a sense of relief at having unburdened his mind, and felt as though by writing out that confession he had laid the spectre which had haunted him for so long. His daughter was delighted at the change in his spirits, but the old Scotch nurse, who had been in the house since Madge was a baby, shook her head —

'He's fey,' she said gravely. 'He's no lang for the warld.' Of course she was laughed at — people who believe in presentiments generally are — but, nevertheless, she held firmly to her opinion.

Mr Frettlby went to bed early that night, as the excitement of the last few days and the feverish gaiety in which he had lately indulged proved too strong for him. No sooner had he laid his head on his pillow than he dropped off to sleep at once, and forgot in placid slumber the troubles and worries of his waking hours.

It was only nine o'clock, so Madge stayed by herself in the great drawing-room, and read a new novel, which was then creating a sensation, and was called 'Sweet Violet Eyes.' It belied its reputation, however, for it was very soon thrown on the table with a look of disgust, and rising from her seat Madge walked up and down the room, and wished some good fairy would hint to Brian that he was wanted. If man is a gregarious animal, how much more, then, is a woman! This is not a conundrum, but a simple truth. 'A female Robinson Crusoe,' says a writer who prided himself upon being a keen observer of human nature — 'a female Robinson Crusoe would have gone mad for want of something to talk to.' This remark, though severe, nevertheless contains several grains of truth, for women, as a rule, talk more than men. They are more sociable, and a Miss Misanthrope, in spite of Justin M'Carthy's, is unknown — at least in civilised communities. Miss Frettlby, being neither misanthropic nor dumb, began to long for someone to talk to, and, ringing the bell, ordered Sal to be sent in. The two girls had become great friends, and Madge, though two years younger than the other, assumed the *rôle* of mentor, and under her guidance Sal was rapidly improving. It was a strange irony of fate which brought together these two children of the same father, each with such different histories — the one reared in luxury and affluence, never having known want; the other dragged up in the gutter, all unsexed and besmirched by the life she had led. 'The whirligig of time brings in its revenges,' and it was the last thing in the world Mark Frettlby would have thought of seeing: Rosanna Moore's child, whom he fancied dead, under the same roof as his daughter Madge.

On receiving Madge's message Sal came to the drawing-room, and the two were soon chatting amicably together. The drawing-room was almost in darkness, only one lamp being lighted. Mr Frettlby very sensibly detested gas, with its glaring light, and had nothing but lamps in his drawing-room. Away at the end of the apartment, where Sal and Madge were seated, there was a small table, on which stood a large lamp, with an opaque globe, which, having a shade over it, threw a soft and subdued circle of light round the table, leaving the rest of the room in a kind of semi-darkness. Near this sat Madge and Sal, talking gaily, and away up on the left-hand side they could see the door open, and a warm flood of light pouring in from the hall.

They had been talking together for some time, when Sal's quick ear caught a footfall on the soft carpet, and, turning rapidly, she saw a tall figure advancing down the room. Madge saw it too, and started up in surprise on recognising her father. He was clothed in his dressing-gown, and carried some papers in his hand.

'Why, papa,' said Madge, in surprise, 'I —'

'Hush!' whispered Sal, grasping her arms. 'He's asleep.'

And so he was. In accordance with the dictates of the excited brain, the weary body had risen from the bed and wandered about the house. The two girls, drawing back into the shadow, watched him with bated breath as he came slowly down the room. In a few moments he was within the circle of light, and, moving noiselessly along, he laid the papers he carried on the table. They were in a large blue envelope, much worn, with writing in red ink on it. Sal recognised it at once as the one she had seen the dead woman with, and with an instinctive feeling that there was something wrong, tried to draw Madge back as she watched her father's action with an intensity of feeling which held her spell-bound. Frettlby opened the envelope, and took therefrom a yellow, frayed piece of paper, which he spread out on the table. Madge bent forward to see it, but Sal, with sudden terror, drew her back.

'For God's sake no,' she cried.

But it was too late; Madge had caught sight of the names on the paper — 'Marriage — Rosanna Moore — Mark Frettlby' — and the whole awful truth flashed upon her. These were the papers Rosanna Moore had handed to Whyte. Whyte had been murdered by the man to whom the papers were of value —

'God! My father!'

She staggered blindly forward, and then, with one piercing shriek, fell to the ground. In doing so, she struck against her father, who was still standing beside the table. Awakened suddenly, with that wild cry in his ears, he opened his eyes wide, put out feeble hands, as if to keep something back, and with a strangled cry fell dead on the floor beside his daughter. Sal, horror-struck, did not lose her presence of mind, but, snatching the papers off the table, she thrust them into her pocket, and then shrieked aloud for the servants. But they, already attracted by Madge's wild cry, came hurrying in, to find Mark Frettlby, the millionaire, lying dead, and his daughter lying in a faint beside her father's corpse.

XXXI
Hush-money

As soon as Brian received the telegram which announced the death of Mark Frettlby, he put on his hat, stepped into Calton's trap, and drove along to the St Kilda station in Flinders Street with that gentleman. There Calton dismissed his trap, sending a note to his clerk with the groom, and went down to St Kilda with Fitzgerald. On arrival they found the whole house perfectly quiet and orderly, owing to the excellent management of Sal Rawlins. She had taken the command in everything, and although the servants, knowing her antecedents, were disposed to resent her doing so, yet such was her administrative powers and strong will, that they obeyed her implicitly. Mark Frettlby's body had been taken up to his bedroom, Madge had been put to bed, and Dr Chinston and Brian sent for. When they arrived they could not help expressing their admiration at the capital way in which Sal Rawlins had managed things.

'She's a clever girl that,' whispered Calton to Fitzgerald. 'Curious thing she should have taken up her proper position in her father's house. Fate is a deal cleverer than we mortals think her.'

Brian was about to reply when Dr Chinston entered the room. His face was very grave, and Fitzgerald looked at him in alarm.

'Madge — Miss Frettlby,' he faltered.

'Is very ill,' replied the doctor; 'has an attack of brain fever. I can't answer for the consequences yet.'

Brian sat down on the sofa, and stared at the doctor in a dazed sort of way. Madge dangerously ill — perhaps dying. What if she did die, and he lost the true-hearted woman who stood so nobly by him in his trouble?

'Cheer up,' said Chinston, patting him on the shoulder; 'while there's life there's hope, and whatever human aid can do to save her will be done.'

Brian grasped the doctor's hand in silence, his heart being too full to speak.

'How did Frettlby die?' asked Calton.

'Heart disease,' said Chinston. 'His heart was very much affected, as I discovered a week or so ago. It appears he was walking in his sleep, and entering the drawing-room, he alarmed Miss Frettlby, who screamed, and must have touched him. He awoke suddenly, and the natural consequences followed — he dropped down dead.'

'What alarmed Miss Frettlby?' asked Brian, in a low voice, covering his face with his hand.

'The sight of her father walking in his sleep, I suppose,' said Chinston, buttoning his glove; 'and the shock of his death which took place indirectly through her, accounts for the brain fever.'

'Madge Frettlby is not the woman to scream and waken a somnambulist,' said Calton, decidedly, 'knowing as she did the danger. There must be some other reason.'

'This young woman will tell you all about it,' said Chinston, nodding towards Sal, who entered the room at this moment. 'She was present, and since then has managed things admirably; and now I must go,' he said, shaking hands with Calton and Fitzgerald. 'Keep up your heart, my boy; I'll pull her through yet.'

After the doctor had gone, Calton turned sharply to Sal Rawlins, who stood waiting to be addressed.

'Well,' he said, briskly, 'can you tell us what startled Miss Frettlby?'

'I can, sir,' she answered quietly. 'I was in the drawing-room when Mr Frettlby died — but — we had better go up to the study.'

'Why?' asked Calton, in surprise, as he and Fitzgerald followed her upstairs.

'Because, sir,' she said, when they had entered the study and she had locked the door, 'I don't want any one but yourselves to know what I tell you.'

'More mystery,' muttered Calton, as he glanced at Brian, and took his seat at the escritoire.

'Mr Frettlby went to bed early last night,' said Sal, calmly, and Miss Madge and I were talking together in the drawing-room, when he entered, walking in his sleep, and carrying some papers —'

Both Calton and Fitzgerald started, and the latter grew pale.

'He came down the room, and spread out a paper on the table where the lamp was. Miss Madge bent forward to see what it was. I tried to stop her, but it was too late. She gave a scream, and fell on the floor. In doing so she happened to touch her father. He awoke, and fell down dead.'

'And the papers?' asked Calton, uneasily.

Sal did not answer, but producing them from her pocket, laid them in his hands.

Brian bent forward, as Calton opened the envelope in silence, but both gave vent to an exclamation of horror at seeing the certificate of marriage which they knew Rosanna Moore had given to Whyte. Their worst suspicions were confirmed, and Brian turned away his head, afraid to meet the barrister's eye. The latter folded up the papers thoughtfully, and put them in his pocket.

'You know what these are?' he asked Sal, eyeing her keenly.

'I could hardly help knowing,' she answered; 'it proves that Rosanna Moore was Mr Frettlby's wife, and —' she hesitated.

'Go on,' said Brian, in a harsh tone, looking up.

'And they were the papers she gave Mr Whyte.'

'Well!'

Sal was silent for a moment, and then looked up with a flush.

'You needn't think I'm going to split,' she said, indignantly, recurring to her Bourke Street slang in the excitement of the moment. 'I know what you know, but s'elp me G— I'll be silent as the grave.'

'Thank you,' said Brian, fervently, taking her hand; 'I know you love her too well to betray this terrible secret.'

'I would be a nice un', I would,' said Sal, with scorn, 'after her lifting me out of the gutter, to round on her — a poor girl like me, without a friend or a relative, now Gran's dead.'

Calton looked up quickly. It was plain Sal was quite ignorant that Rosanna Moore was her mother. So much the better; they would keep her in ignorance, perhaps not altogether, but it would be folly to undeceive her at present.

'I'm goin' to Miss Madge now,' she said, going to the door, 'and I won't see you again; she's getting light-headed, and might let it out; but I'll not let anyone in but myself,' and so saying, she left the room.

'Cast thy bread upon the waters,' said Calton, oracularly. 'The kindness of Miss Frettlby to that poor waif is already bearing fruit — gratitude is the rarest of qualities, rarer even than modesty.'

Fitzgerald made no answer, but stared out of the window, and thought of his darling lying sick unto death, and he could do nothing to save her.

'Well,' said Calton, sharply.

'Oh, I beg your pardon,' said Fitzgerald, turning in confusion. 'I suppose the will must be read, and all that sort of thing.'

'Yes,' answered the barrister, 'I am one of the executors.'

'And the others?'

'Yourself and Chinston,' answered Calton; 'so I suppose,' turning to the desk, 'we can look at his papers, and see that all is straight.'

'Yes, I suppose so,' replied Brian, mechanically, his thoughts far away, and then he turned again to the window. Suddenly Calton gave vent to an exclamation of surprise, and, turning hastily, Brian saw him holding a thick roll of papers in his hand, which he had taken out of the drawer.

'Look here, Fitzgerald,' he said, greatly excited, 'here is Frettlby's confession — look!' and he held it up.

Brian sprang forward in astonishment. So at last the hansom cab mystery was to be cleared up. These sheets, no doubt, contained the whole narration of the crime, and how it was committed.

'We will read it, of course,' he said, hesitating, half hoping that Calton would propose to destroy it at once.

'Yes,' answered Calton; 'the three executors must read it, and then — we will burn it.'

'That will be the better way,' answered Brian, gloomily. 'Frettlby is dead, and the law can do nothing in the matter, so it would be best to avoid the scandal of publicity. But why tell Chinston?'

'We must,' said Calton, decidedly. 'He will be sure to gather the truth from Madge's ravings, and may as well know all. He is quite safe, and will be silent as the grave. But I am more sorry to tell Kilsip.'

'The detective? Good God, Calton, surely you will not do so!'

'I must,' replied the barrister, quietly. 'Kilsip is firmly persuaded that Moreland committed the crime, and I have the same dread of his pertinacity as you had of mine. He may find out all.'

'What must be, must be,' said Fitzgerald, clenching his hands. 'But I hope no one else will find out this miserable story. There's Moreland, for instance.'

'Ah, true!' said Calton, thoughtfully. 'He called and saw Frettlby the other night, you say?'

'Yes. I wonder what for?'

'There is only one answer,' said the barrister, slowly. 'He must have seen Frettlby following Whyte when he left the hotel, and wanted hush-money.'

'I wonder if he got it,' observed Fitzgerald.

'Oh, I'll soon find that out,' answered Calton, opening the drawer again, and taking out the dead man's cheque-book. 'Let me see what cheques have been drawn lately.'

Most of the blocks were filled up for small amounts, and one or two for a hundred or so. Calton could find no large sum such as Moreland would have demanded, when, at the very end of the book, he found a cheque torn off, leaving the block-slip quite blank.

'There you are,' he said, triumphantly holding out the book to Fitzgerald. 'He wasn't such a fool as to write in the amount on the block, but tore the cheque out, and wrote in the sum required.'

'And what's to be done about it?'

'Let him keep it, of course,' answered Calton, shrugging his shoulders. 'It's the only way to secure his silence.'

'I expect he cashed it yesterday, and is off by this time,' said Brian, after a moment's pause.

'So much the better for us,' said Calton, grimly. 'But I don't think he's off, or Kilsip would have let me know. We must tell him, or he'll get everything out of Moreland, and the consequences would be that all Melbourne will know the story; whereas, by showing him the confession, we get him to leave Moreland alone, and thus secure silence in both cases.'

'I suppose we must see Chinston?'

'Yes, of course. I will telegraph to him and Kilsip to come up to my office this afternoon at three o'clock, and then we will settle the whole matter.'

'And Sal Rawlins?'

'Oh! I quite forgot about her,' said Calton, in a perplexed voice. 'She knows nothing about her parents, and, of course, Mark Frettlby died in the belief that she was dead.'

'We must tell Madge,' said Brian, gloomily. 'There is no help for it. Sal is by rights the heiress to the money of her dead father.'

'That depends upon the will,' replied Calton, dryly. 'If it specifies that the money is left to 'my daughter, Margaret Frettlby,' Sal Rawlins can have no claim; and if such is the case, it will be no good telling her who she is.'

'And what's to be done?'

'Sal Rawlins,' went on the barrister, without noticing the interruption, 'has evidently never given a thought to her father or mother, as the old hag, no doubt, swore they were dead. So I think it will be best to keep silent — that is, if no money is left to her, and, as her father thought her dead, I don't think there will be any. In that case, it would be best to settle an income on her. You can easily find a pretext, and let the matter rest.'

'But suppose, in accordance with the wording of the will, she is entitled to all the money?'

'In that case,' said Calton, gravely, 'there is only one course open — she must be told everything, and the dividing of the money left to her generosity. But I don't think you need be alarmed, I'm pretty sure Madge is the heiress.'

'It's not the money I think about,' said Brian, hastily. 'I'd take Madge without a penny.'

'My boy,' said the barrister, placing his hand kindly on Brian's shoulder, 'when you marry Madge Frettlby, you will get what is better than money — a heart of gold.'

XXXII
De Mortuis Nil Nisi Bonum

'Nothing is certain but the unforseen;' so says a French proverb, and judging from the unexpected things which daily happen to us, it is without doubt a very true one. If anyone had told Madge Frettlby one day that she would be stretched on a bed of sickness the next, and would be quite oblivious of the world and its doings, she would have laughed the prophet to scorn. Yet it was so, and she was tossing and turning on a bed of pain to which the couch of Procustes was one of roses. Sal sat beside her, ever watchful of her wants, and listened through the bright hours of the day, or the still ones of the night, to the wild and incoherent words which issued from her lips. She kept incessantly calling on her father to save himself, and then would talk about Brian, and sing snatches of song, or sobbed out broken sentences about her dead mother, until the heart of the listener ached to hear her. No one was allowed into the room except Sal, and when Dr Chinston heard the things she was saying, although used to such cases, he recoiled.

'There is blood on your hands,' cried Madge, sitting up in bed, with her hair all tangled and falling over her shoulders; 'red blood, and you cannot wash it off. Oh, Cain! God save him! Brian, you are not guilty; my father killed him. God! God!' and she fell back on her disordered pillows weeping bitterly.

'What does she mean?' asked the doctor, startled by her last words.

'Nothing,' answered Sal, curtly, going to the bed.

Dr Chinston did not say anything, but shortly afterwards took his leave, after telling Sal on no account to let anyone see the patient.

' 'Tain't likely,' said Sal, in a disgusted tone, as she closed the door after him. 'I'm not a viper to sting the bosom as fed me,' from which it may be gathered she was advancing rapidly in her education.

Meanwhile Dr Chinston had received Calton's telegram, and was considerably astonished thereat. He was still more so when, on arriving at the office at the time appointed, he found Calton and Fitzgerald were not alone, but a third man whom he had never seen was with them. This latter Calton introduced to him as Mr Kilsip, of the detective office, a fact which began to make the worthy doctor uneasy, as he could not divine the meaning of the presence of a detective. However, he made no remark, but took the seat handed to him by Mr Calton and prepared to listen. Calton locked the door of the office, and then went back to his desk, having the other three seated before him in a kind of semi-circle.

'In the first place,' said Calton to the doctor, 'I have to inform you that you are one of the executors under the will of the late Mr Frettlby, and that is why I asked you to come here today. The other executors are Mr Fitzgerald and myself.'

'Oh, indeed,' murmured the doctor, politely.

'And now,' said Calton, looking at him, 'do you remember the hansom cab murder, which caused such a sensation some months ago?'

'Yes, I do,' replied the doctor, rather astonished; 'but what has that to do with the will?'

'Nothing to do with the will,' answered Calton, gravely, 'but the fact is, Mr Frettlby was implicated in the affair.'

Dr Chinston glanced enquiringly at Brian, but that gentleman shook his head.

'It's nothing to do with my arrest,' he said, sadly.

Madge's words, uttered in her delirium, flashed across the doctor's memory.

'What do you mean?' he gasped, pushing back his chair. 'How was he implicated?'

'That I cannot tell you,' answered Calton, 'until I read his confession.'

'Ah!' said Kilsip, becoming very attentive.

'Yes,' said Calton, turning to Kilsip, 'Your hunt after Moreland is a wild goose chase, for the murderer of Oliver Whyte is discovered.'

'Discovered!' cried Kilsip and the doctor in one breath.

'Yes, and his name is Mark Frettlby.'

Kilsip shot a glance of disdain out of his bright black eyes, and gave a low laugh of disbelief, but the doctor pushed back his chair furiously, and arose to his feet.

'This is monstrous,' he cried, in a rage. 'I won't sit still and hear this accusation against my dead friend.'

'Unfortunately, it is too true,' said Brian, sadly.

'How dare you say so?' said Chinston, turning angrily on him. 'And you going to marry his daughter!'

'There is only one way to settle the question,' said Calton, coldly. 'We must read his confession.'

'But why the detective?' asked the doctor, ungraciously, as he took his seat reluctantly.

'Because I want him to hear for himself that Mr Frettlby committed the crime, and that he may keep it quiet.'

'Not till I've arrested him,' said Kilsip, determinedly.

'But he's dead,' said Brian.

'I'm speaking of Roger Moreland,' retorted Kilsip. 'For he and no other murdered Oliver Whyte.'

'That's a much more likely story,' Chinston said.

'I tell you no,' said Calton, vehemently. 'God knows I would like to preserve Mark Frettlby's good name, and it is with this object I have brought you all together. I will read the confession, and when you know the truth, I want you all to keep silent about it, as Mark Frettlby is dead, and the publication of his crime can do no good to anyone.'

'I know,' resumed Calton, addressing the detective, 'that you are fully convinced in your own mind that you are right and I am wrong, but what if I tell you that Mark Frettlby died holding those very papers for the sake of which the crime was committed?'

Kilsip's face lengthened considerably.

'What were the papers?'

'The marriage certificate of Mark Frettlby and Rosanna Moore, the woman who died in the back slum.'

Kilsip was seldom astonished, but he was this time, while Dr Chinston fell back in his chair and looked at the barrister with a dazed sort of expression.

'And what's more,' went on Calton, triumphantly, 'do you know that Moreland went to Frettlby two nights ago and obtained a certain sum for hush-money?'

'What!' cried Kilsip.

'Yes, Moreland, in coming out of the hotel, evidently saw Frettlby, and threatened to expose him unless he paid for his silence.'

'Very strange,' murmured Kilsip, to himself, with a disappointed look on his face. 'But why did Moreland keep still so long?'

'I cannot tell you,' replied Calton, 'but, no doubt, the confession will explain all.'

'Then for heaven's sake read it,' broke in Dr Chinston, impatiently. 'I'm quite in the dark, and all your talk is Greek to me.'

'One moment,' said Kilsip, dragging a bundle from under his chair, and untying it. 'If you are right, what about this?' and he held up a light coat, very much soiled and weather-worn.

'Whose is that?' asked Calton, startled. 'Not Whyte's?'

'Yes, Whyte's,' repeated Kilsip, with great satisfaction. 'I found it in the Fitzroy Gardens, near the gate that opens to George Street, East Melbourne. It was up in a fir-tree.'

'Then Mr Frettlby must have got out at Powlett Street, and walked down George Street, and then through the Fitzroy Gardens into town,' said Calton.

Kilsip took no heed of the remark, but took a small bottle out of the pocket of the coat and held it up.

'I also found this,' he said.

'Chloroform,' cried everyone, guessing at once that it was the missing bottle.

'Exactly,' said Kilsip, replacing it. 'This was the bottle which contained the poison used by — by — well, call him the murderer. The name of the chemist being on the label, I went to him and found out who bought it. Now, who do you think?' with a look of triumph.

'Frettlby,' said Calton, decidedly.

'No, Moreland!' burst out Chinston, greatly excited.

'Neither,' retorted the detective, calmly. 'The man who purchased this was Oliver Whyte himself.'

'Himself?' echoed Brian, now thoroughly surprised, as, indeed, were all the others.

'Yes. I had no trouble in finding out that, thanks to the "Poisons Act." As I knew no one would be so foolish as to carry chloroform about in his pocket for any length of time, I mentioned the day of the murder as the probable date it was bought. The chemist turned up his book, and found that Whyte was the purchaser.'

'And what did he buy it for?' asked Chinston.

'That's more than I can tell you,' said Kilsip, with a shrug of his shoulders. 'It's down in the book as being bought for medicinal uses, which may mean anything.'

'The law requires a witness,' observed Calton, cautiously. 'Who was the witness?'

Again Kilsip smiled triumphantly.

'I think I can guess,' said Fitzgerald. 'Moreland?'

Kilsip nodded.

'And I suppose,' remarked Calton, in a slightly sarcastic tone, 'that is another of your proofs against Moreland. He knew that Whyte had chloroform on him, therefore he followed him that night and murdered him?'

'Well, I —'

'It's a lot of nonsense,' said the barrister, impatiently. 'There's nothing against Moreland to implicate him. If he killed Whyte, what made him go and see Frettlby?'

'But,' said Kilsip, sagely nodding his head, 'if, as Moreland says, he had Whyte's coat in his possession before the murder, how is it that I should discover it afterwards up a fir-tree in the Fitzroy Gardens, with an empty chloroform bottle in the pocket.'

'He may have been an accomplice,' suggested Calton.

'What's the good of all this conjecturing?' said Chinston, impatiently, now thoroughly tired of the discussion. 'Read the confession, and we will soon know the truth, without all this talk.'

Calton assented, and all having settled themselves to listen, he began to read what the dead man had written.

XXXIII
The Confession

'What I am now about to write is set forth by me so that the true circumstances connected with the "Hansom Cab Tragedy," which took place in Melbourne in 18—, may be known. I owe a confession, particularly to Brian Fitzgerald, seeing that he was accused of the crime. Although I know he was rightfully acquitted of the charge, yet I wish him to know all about the case, though I am convinced, from his altered demeanour towards me, that he is better acquainted with it than he chooses to confess. In order to account for the murder of Oliver Whyte, I must go back to the beginning of my life in this colony, and show how the series of events began which culminated in the committal of the crime.

'Should it be necessary to make this confession public, in the interests of justice, I can say nothing against such a course being taken; but I would be grateful if it could be suppressed, both on account of my good name and of my dear daughter Margaret, whose love and affection has so soothed and brightened my life.

'If, however, she should be informed of the contents of these pages, I ask her to deal leniently with the memory of one who was sorely tried and tempted.

'I came to the colony of Victoria, or, rather, as it was called then, New South Wales, in the year 18—. I had been in a merchant's office in London, but not seeing much opportunity for advancement, I looked about to see if I could better myself. I heard of this new land across the ocean, and though it was not then the El Dorado which it afterwards turned out, and, truth to tell, had rather a shady name, owing to the transportation of convicts, yet I longed to go there and start a new life. Unhappily, however, I had not the means to go, and saw nothing better before me than the dreary life of a London clerk, as it was impossible that I could save out of the small salary I got. Just at this time, however, an old maiden aunt of my mother's died and left a few hundred pounds to me, so, with this, I came out to Australia, determined to become a rich man. I stayed some time in Sydney, and then came over to Port Phillip, now so widely known as Marvellous Melbourne, where I intended to pitch my tent. I saw that it was a young and rising colony, though, of course, coming as I did, before the days of the gold diggings, I never dreamt it would spring up, as it had done since, to a nation. I was careful and saving in those days, and, indeed, I think it was the happiest time of my life.

'I bought land whenever I could scrape the money together, and, at the time of the gold rush, was considered well-to-do. When, however, the cry that gold had been discovered was raised, and the eyes of all the nations were turned to Australia, with her glittering treasures, men poured in from all parts of the world, and the "Golden Age" commenced. I began to get rich rapidly, and was soon pointed out as the wealthiest man in the Colonies. I bought a station, and, leaving the riotous, feverish Melbourne life, went to live on it. I enjoyed myself there, for the wild, open-air life had great charms for me, and there was a sense of freedom to which I had hitherto been a stranger. But man is a gregarious animal, and I, growing weary of solitude and communings with Mother Nature, came down on a visit to Melbourne, where, with companions as gay as myself, I spent my money freely, and, as the phrase goes, saw life. After confessing that I loved the pure life of the country, it sounds strange to say that I enjoyed the wild life of the town, but I did. I was neither a Joseph nor a St Anthony, and I was delighted with Bohemia, with its good fellowship and charming suppers, which took place in the small hours of the morning, when wit and humour reigned supreme. It was at one of these suppers that I first met Rosanna Moore, the woman who was destined to curse my existence. She was a burlesque actress, and all the young fellows in those days were madly in love with her. She was not exactly what was called beautiful, but there was a brilliancy and fascination about her which few could resist. On first seeing her I did not admire her much, but laughed at my companions as they raved about her. On becoming personally acquainted with her, however, I found that her powers of fascination had not been over-rated, and ended by falling desperately in love with her. I made enquiries about her private life, and found that it was irreproachable, as she was guarded by a veritable dragon of a mother, who would let no one approach her daughter. I need not tell about my courtship, as these phases of a man's life are generally the same, but it will be sufficient to prove the depth of my passion for her when I at length determined to make her my wife. It was on condition, however, that the marriage should be kept secret until such time as I should choose to reveal it. My reason for such a course was this, my father was still alive, and he, being a rigid Presbyterian, would never have forgiven me for having married a woman of the stage; so, as he was old and feeble, I did not wish him to learn that I had done so, fearing that the shock would be too much for him in his then present state of health. I told Rosanna I would marry her, but wanted her to leave her mother, who was a perfect fury, and not an agreeable person to live with. As I was rich, young, and not bad looking, Rosanna consented, and, during an engagement she had in Sydney, I went over there and married her. She never told her mother she had married me, why, I do not know, as I never laid any restriction on her doing so. The mother made a great noise over the matter, but I gave Rosanna a large sum of money for her, and this the old harridan accepted, and left for New Zealand. Rosanna went with me to my station, where we lived as man and wife, though, in Melbourne, she was supposed to be my mistress. At last, feeling degraded in my own eyes as to the way I was living to the world, I wanted to reveal our secret, but this Rosanna would not consent to. I was astonished at this, and could never discover the reason, but in many ways Rosanna was an enigma to me. She then grew weary of the quiet country life, and longed to return to the glitter and glare of the footlights. This I refused to let her do, and from that moment she took a dislike to me. A child was born, and for a time she was engrossed with it, but soon wearied of the new plaything, and again pressed me to allow her to return to the stage. I again refused, and we became estranged from one another. I grew gloomy and irritable, and was accustomed to take long rides by myself, frequently being away for days. There was a great friend of mine who owned the next station, a fine, handsome young fellow, called Frank Kelly, with a gay, sunny disposition, and a wonderful flow of humour. When he found I was so much away, thinking Rosanna was only my mistress, he began to console her, and succeeded so well that one day, on my return from a ride, I found she had fled with him, and had taken the child with her. She left a letter saying that she had never really cared for me, but had married me for my money — she would keep our marriage secret, and was going to return to the stage. I followed my false friend and false wife down to Melbourne, but arrived too late, as they had just left for England. Disgusted with the manner in which I had been treated, I plunged into a whirl of dissipation, trying to drown the memory of my married life. My friends, of course, thought that my loss amounted to no more than that of a mistress, and I soon began myself to doubt that I had ever been married, so far away and visionary did my life of the year previous seem. I continued my fast life for about six months, when suddenly I was arrested upon the brink of destruction by — an angel. I say this advisedly, for if ever there was an angel upon earth, it was she who afterwards became my wife. She was the daughter of a doctor, and it was her influence which drew me back from the dreary path of profligacy and dissipation which I was then leading. I paid her great attention, and we were, in fact, looked upon as good as engaged, but I knew that I was still linked to that accursed woman, and could not ask her to be my wife. At this second crisis of my life Fate again intervened, for I received a letter from England, which informed me that Rosanna Moore had been run over in the streets of London, and had died in a hospital. The writer was a young doctor, who had attended her, and I wrote home to him, begging him to send out a certificate of her death, so that I might be sure she was no more. He did so, and also enclosed an account of the accident, which had appeared in a newspaper. Then, indeed, I felt that I was free, and closing, as I thought, for ever the darkest page of my life's history, I began to look forward to the future. I married again, and my domestic life was a singularly happy one. As the colony grew greater, with every year I became even more wealthy than I had been, and was looked up to and respected by my fellow-citizens. When my dear daughter Margaret was born, I felt that my cup of happiness was full, but suddenly I received a disagreeable reminder of the past. Rosanna's mother made her appearance one day — a disreputable-looking creature, smelling of gin, and in whom I could not recognise the respectably-dressed woman who used to accompany Rosanna to the theatre. She had spent long ago all the money I had given her, and had sank lower and lower, until she now lived in a slum off Little Bourke Street. I made enquiries after the child, and she told me it was dead. Rosanna had not taken it to England with her, but had left it in her mother's charge, and, no doubt, neglect and want of proper nourishment was the cause of its death. There now seemed to be no link to bind me to the past with the exception of the old hag, who knew nothing about the marriage. I did not attempt to undeceive her, but agreed to allow her enough to live on if she promised never to trouble me again, and to keep quiet about everything which had reference to my connection with her daughter. She promised readily enough, and went back to her squalid dwelling in the slums, where, for all I know, she still lives, as money has been paid to her regularly every month by my solicitors. I heard nothing more about the matter, and now felt quite satisfied that I had heard the last of Rosanna. As years rolled on, things prospered with me, and so fortunate was I in all speculations that my luck became proverbial. Then, alas! When all things seemed to smile upon me, my wife died, and the world has never seemed the same to me since. I, however, had my dear daughter to console me, and in her love and affection I became reconciled to the loss of my wife. A young Irish gentleman, called Brian Fitzgerald, came out to Australia, and I soon saw that my daughter was in love with him, and that he reciprocated that affection, whereat I was glad, as I have always esteemed him highly. I looked forward to their marriage, when suddenly a series of events occurred, which must be fresh in the memory of those who read these pages. Mr Oliver Whyte, a gentleman from London, called on me and startled me with the news that my first wife, Rosanna Moore, was still living, and that the story of her death had been an ingenious fabrication in order to deceive me. She had met with an accident, as stated in the newspaper, and had been taken to a hospital, where she recovered. The young doctor, who had sent me the certificate of her death, had fallen in love with her and wanted to marry her, and had told me that she was dead in order that her past life might be obliterated. The doctor, however, died before the marriage, and Rosanna did not trouble herself about undeceiving me. She was then acting on the burlesque stage under the name of "Musette," and seemed to have gained an unenviable notoriety by her extravagance and infamy. Whyte met her in London, and she became his mistress. He seemed to have had a wonderful influence over her, for she told him all her past life, and about her marriage with me. Her popularity being on the wane in London, as she was now growing old, and had to make way for younger actresses, Whyte proposed that they should come out to the Colonies and extort money from me, and he had come to me for that purpose. The villain told me all this in the coolest manner, and I, knowing he held the secret of my life, was unable to resent it. I refused to see Rosanna, but told Whyte I would agree to his terms, which were, first, a large sum of money was to be paid to Rosanna, and, secondly, Whyte wanted to marry my daughter. I, at first, absolutely declined to sanction the latter proposal, but as he threatened to publish the story, and that meant the proclamation to the world of my daughter's illegitimacy, I at last agreed, and he began to pay his addresses to Madge. She, however, refused to marry him, and told me she was engaged to Fitzgerald, so, after a severe struggle with myself, I told Whyte that I would not allow him to marry Madge, but would give him whatever sum he liked to name. On the night he was murdered he came to see me, and showed me the certificate of marriage between myself and Rosanna Moore. He refused to take a sum of money, and said unless I consented to his marriage with Madge he would publish the whole affair. I implored him to give me time to think, so he said he would give me two days, but no more, and left the house, taking the marriage certificate with him. I was in despair, and saw that the only way to save myself was to obtain possession of the marriage certificate and deny everything. With this idea in my mind I followed him up to town and saw him meet Moreland, and drink with him. They went into the hotel in Russell Street, and when Whyte came out, at half-past twelve, he was quite intoxicated. I saw him go along to the Scotch Church, near the Bourke and Wills' monument, and cling to the lamp-post at the corner. I thought I would then be able to get the certificate from him, as he was so drunk, when I saw a gentleman in a light coat — I did not know it was Fitzgerald — come up to him and hail a cab for him. I saw there was nothing more to be done at that time, so, in despair, went home and waited for the next day, in fear lest he should carry out his determination. Nothing, however, turned up, and I was beginning to think that Whyte had abandoned his purpose, when I heard that he had been murdered in the hansom cab. I was in great fear lest the marriage certificate would be found on him, but as nothing was said about it I began to wonder. I knew he had it on him, so came to the conclusion that the murderer, whoever he was, had taken it from the body, and would sooner or later come to me to extort money, knowing that I dare not denounce him. Fitzgerald was arrested, and afterwards acquitted, so I began to think that the certificate had been lost, and my troubles were at an end. However, I was always haunted by a dread that the sword was hanging over my head, and would fall sooner or later. I was right, for two nights ago Roger Moreland, who was an intimate friend of Whyte's, called on me and produced the marriage certificate, which he offered to sell to me for five thousand pounds. In horror, I accused him of murdering Whyte, which he denied at first, but afterwards acknowledged, stating that I dare not betray him for my own sake. I was nearly mad with the horror I was placed in, either to denounce my daughter as illegitimate or let a murderer escape the penalty of his crime. At last I agreed to keep silent, and handed him a cheque for five thousand pounds, receiving in return the marriage certificate. I then made Moreland swear to leave the colony, which he readily agreed to do, saying Melbourne was dangerous. When he left I reflected upon the awfulness of my position, and had almost determined to commit suicide, but, thank God, I saved myself from that crime. I wrote out this confession in order that after my death the true story of the murder of Whyte may be known, and that anyone who may hereafter be accused of the murder may not be wrongfully punished. I have no hopes of Moreland ever receiving the penalty of his crime, as when this is open all trace of him will, no doubt, be lost. I will not destroy the marriage certificate, but place it with these papers, so that the truth of my story can be seen. In conclusion, I would ask forgiveness of my daughter Margaret for my sins, which have been visited on her, but she can see for herself that circumstances were too strong for me. May she forgive me, as I hope God in his infinite mercy will, and may she come sometimes and pray over my grave, nor thank too hardly upon her dead father.'

XXXIV
The Hands of Justice

Calton's voice faltered a little when he read those last sad words, and he laid the manuscript down on the table, amid a dead silence, which was first broken by Brian.

'Thank God,' he said, reverently, 'thank God that he was innocent of the crime!'

'So,' said Calton, a little cynically, 'the riddle which has perplexed us so long is read, and the Sphinx is silent for evermore.'

'I knew he was incapable of such a thing,' cried Chinston, whom emotion had hitherto kept silent.

Meanwhile Kilsip listened to these eulogistic remarks on the dead man, and purred to himself, in a satisfied sort of way, like a cat who has caught a mouse.

'You see, sir,' he said, addressing the barrister, 'I was right after all.'

'Yes,' answered Calton, frankly, 'I acknowledge my defeat, but now —'

'I'm going to arrest Moreland right off,' said Kilsip.

There was a silence for a few moments, and then Calton spoke again.

'I suppose it must be so — poor girl — poor girl.'

'I'm very sorry for the young lady myself,' said the detective in his soft, low voice, 'but you see I cannot let a dangerous criminal escape for a mere matter of sentiment.'

'Of course not,' said Fitzgerald, sharply. 'Moreland must be arrested right off.'

'But he will confess everything,' said Calton, angrily, 'and then everyone will know about this first marriage.'

'Let them,' retorted Brian, bitterly. 'As soon as she is well enough we will marry at once, and leave Australia for ever.'

'But —'

'I know her better than you do,' said the young man, doggedly; 'and I know she would like an end made of this whole miserable business at once. Arrest the murderer, and let him suffer for his crime.'

'Well, I suppose it must be so,' said Chinston, with a sigh, 'but it seems very hard that this slur should be cast upon Miss Frettlby.' Brian turned a little pale.

'The sins of the father are generally visited upon the children by the world,' he said, bitterly. 'But after the first pain is over, in new lands among new faces, she will forget the bitter past.'

'Now that it is settled Moreland is to be arrested,' said Calton, 'how is it to be done? Is he still in Melbourne?'

'Rather,' said Kilsip, in a satisfied tone; 'I've had my eye on him for the last two months, and someone is watching him for me now — trust me, he can't move two steps without my knowing it.'

'Ah, indeed!' said Calton quickly. 'Then do you know if he has been to the bank and cashed that cheque for five thousand, which Frettlby gave him?'

'Well, now,' observed Kilsip, after a pause, 'do you know you rather startled me when you told me he had received a cheque for that amount.'

'Why?'

'It's such a large one,' replied the detective, 'and had I known what sum he had paid into his account I should have been suspicious.'

'Then he has been to the bank?'

'To his own bank, yes. He went there yesterday afternoon at two o'clock — that is the day after he got it — so it would be sent round to Mr Frettlby's bank, and would not be returned till next day, and as he died in the meanwhile I expect it hasn't been honoured, so Mr Moreland won't have his money yet.'

'I wonder what he'll do,' said Chinston.

'Go the manager and kick up a row,' said Kilsip, coolly, 'and the manager will no doubt tell him he'd better see the executors.'

'But, my good friend, the manager doesn't know who the executors are,' broke in Calton, impatiently. 'You forget the will has yet to be read.'

'Then he'll tell him to go to the late Mr Frettlby's solicitors. I suppose he knows who they are,' retorted Kilsip.

'Thinton and Tarbit,' said Calton, musingly, 'but it's questionable if Moreland would go to them.'

'Why shouldn't he, sir?' said Kilsip, quickly. 'He does not know anything about this,' laying his hand on the confession, 'and as the cheque is genuine enough he won't let five thousand pounds go without a struggle.'

'I'll tell you what,' observed Calton, after a few moments of reflection, 'I'll go across the way and telephone to Thinton and Tarbit, and when he calls on them they can send him up to me.'

'A very good idea,' said Kilsip, rubbing his hands, 'and then I can arrest him.'

'But the warrant?' interposed Brian, as Calton arose and put on his hat.

'Is here,' said the detective, producing it.

'By Jove, you must have been pretty certain of his guilt,' remarked Chinston, dryly.

'Of course I was,' retorted Kilsip, in a satisfied tone of voice. 'When I told the magistrate where I found the coat, and reminded him of Moreland's acknowledgment at the trial, that he had it in his possession before the murder, I soon got him to see the necessity of having Moreland arrested.'

'Half-past four,' said Calton, pausing for a moment at the door and looking at his watch. 'I'm afraid it's rather late to catch Moreland today; however, I'll see what Thinton and Tarbit know,' and he went out.

The rest sat waiting his return, and chatted about the curious end of the hansom cab mystery, when, in about ten minutes, Calton rushed in hurriedly and closed the door after him quickly.

'Fate is playing into our hands,' he said, as soon as he recovered his breath. 'Moreland called on Thinton and Tarbit, as Kilsip surmised, and as neither of them were in, said he would call again before five o'clock. I told the clerk to bring him up to me at once, so he may be here at any moment.'

'That is, if he's fool enough to come,' observed Chinston.

'Oh, he'll come,' said the detective, confidently, rattling a pair of handcuffs together. 'He is so satisfied that he has made things safe that he'll walk right into the trap.'

It was getting a little dusk, and the four men were greatly excited, though they concealed it under an assumed nonchalance.

'What a situation for a drama,' said Brian.

'Only,' said Chinston, quietly, 'it is as realistic as in the old days of the Coliseum, where the actor who played Orpheus was torn to pieces by bears at the end of the play.'

'His last appearance on any stage, I suppose,' said Calton, a little cruelly, it must be confessed.

Meanwhile, Kilsip remained seated in his chair, humming an operatic air and chinking the handcuffs together, by way of accompaniment. He felt intensely pleased with himself, the more so, as he saw that by this capture he would be ranked far above Gorby. 'And what would Gorby say? — Gorby, who had laughed at all his ideas as foolish, and who had been quite wrong from the first. If only —'

'Hush!' said Calton, holding up his finger, as steps were heard echoing on the flags outside. 'Here he is, I believe.'

Kilsip arose from his chair, and, stealing softly to the window, looked cautiously out. Then he turned round to those inside and, nodding his head, slipped the handcuffs into his pocket. Just as he did so, there was a knock at the door, and, in response to Calton's invitation to enter, Thinton and Tarbit's clerk came in with Roger Moreland. The latter faltered a little on the threshold, when he saw Calton was not alone, and seemed half inclined to retreat. But, evidently, thinking there was no danger of his secret being discovered, he pulled himself together, and advanced into the room in an easy and confident manner.

'This is the gentleman who wants to know about the cheque, sir,' said Thinton and Tarbit's clerk to Calton.

'Oh, indeed,' answered Calton, quietly. 'I am glad to see him; you can go.'

The clerk bowed and went out, closing the door after him. Moreland took his seat directly in front of Calton, and with his back to the door. Kilsip, seeing this, strolled across the room in a nonchalant manner, while Calton engaged Moreland in conversation, and quietly turned the key.

'You want to see me, sir?' said Calton, resuming his seat.

'Yes; that is alone,' replied Moreland, uneasily.

'Oh, these gentlemen are all my friends,' said Calton, quietly; 'anything you may say is quite safe.'

'That they are your friends, and are quite safe, is nothing to me,' said Moreland, insolently. 'I wish to speak to you in private.'

'Don't you think you would like to know my friends?' said Calton, coolly taking no notice of his remark.

'D— your friends, sir!' cried Moreland, furiously, rising from his seat.

Calton laughed, and introduced Mr Moreland to the others.

Dr Chinston, Mr Kilsip, and — Mr Fitzgerald.'

'Fitzgerald,' gasped Moreland, growing pale. 'I — I — what's that?' he shrieked, as he saw Whyte's coat, all weather-stained, lying on a chair near him, and which he immediately recognised.

'That is the rope that's going to hang you,' said Kilsip, quietly, coming behind him, 'for the murder of Oliver Whyte.'

'Trapped, by G—!' shouted the wretched man, wheeling round, so as to face Kilsip. He sprang at the detective's throat, and they both rolled together on the floor, but the latter was too strong for him, and, after a sharp struggle, he succeeded in getting the handcuffs on Moreland's wrists. The others stood around perfectly quiet, knowing that Kilsip required no assistance. Now that there was no possibility of escape, Moreland seemed to become resigned, and rose sullenly off the floor.

'By G—! I'll make you pay for this,' he hissed between his

teeth, with a white despairing face. 'You can't prove anything.'

'Can't we?' said Calton, touching the confession. 'You are wrong. This is the confession of Mark Frettlby made before he died.'

'It's a d—d lie.'

'A jury will decide that,' said the barrister, dryly. 'Meanwhile you will pass the night in the Melbourne Gaol.'

'Ah! Perhaps they'll give me the same cell as you occupied,' said Moreland, with a hard laugh, turning to Fitzgerald. 'I should like it for its old associations.'

Brian did not answer him, but picking up his hat and gloves, prepared to go.

'Stop!' cried Moreland, fiercely. 'I see that it's all up with me, so I'm not going to lie like a coward. I've played for a big stake and lost, but if I hadn't been such a fool, I'd have cashed that cheque next morning, and been far away by this time.'

'It would certainly have been wiser,' said Calton.

'After all,' said Moreland nonchalantly, taking no notice of his remark, 'I don't know that I'm sorry about it. I've had a hell upon earth since I killed Whyte.'

'Then you acknowledge your guilt?' said Brian, quietly.

Moreland shrugged his shoulders.

'I told you I wasn't a coward,' he answered, coolly. 'Yes, I did it; it was Whyte's own fault. When I met him that night he told how Frettlby wouldn't let him marry his daughter, but said that he'd make him, and showed me the marriage certificate. I thought if I could only get it I'd make a nice little pile out of Frettlby over it; so when Whyte went on drinking I did not. After he had gone out of the hotel, I put on his coat, which he left behind. I saw him standing near the lamp-post, and Fitzgerald come up and then leave him. When you came down the street,' he went on, turning to Fitzgerald, 'I shrank back into the shadow, and when you passed I ran up to Whyte as the cabman was putting him into the hansom. He took me for you, so I didn't undeceive him, but I swear I had no idea of murdering Whyte when I got into the cab. I tried to get the papers, but he wouldn't let me, and commenced to sing out. Then I thought of the chloroform in the pocket of his coat, which I was wearing. I pulled it out, and found that the cork was loose. Then I took out Whyte's handkerchief, which was also in the coat, and emptied the bottle on it, and put it back in my pocket. I again tried to get the papers, without using the chloroform, but couldn't, so I clapped the handkerchief over his mouth, and he went off after a few minutes, and I got the papers. I thought he was only insensible, and it was only when I saw the newspapers that I knew he was dead. I stopped the cab in St Kilda Road, got out and caught another cab, which was going to town. Then I got out at Powlett Street, took off the coat, and carried it over my arm. I went down George Street, towards the Fitzroy Gardens, and having hid the coat up a tree, where I suppose you found it,' to Kilsip, 'I walked home — so I've done you all nicely, but —'

'You're caught at last,' finished Kilsip, quietly.

Moreland fell down in a chair, with an air of utter weariness and lassitude.

'No man can be stronger than Destiny,' he said, dreamily. 'I have lost and you have won; so life is a chess board, after all, and we are the puppets of Fate.'

He refused to utter another word; so leaving Calton, and Kilsip with him, Brian and the doctor went out and hailed a cab. It drove up to the entrance of the court, where Calton's office was, and then Moreland, walking as if in a dream, left the room, and got into the cab, followed by Kilsip.

'Do you know,' said Chinston, thoughtfully, as they stood and watched the cab drive off, 'do you know what the end of that man will be?'

'It requires no prophet to foretell that,' said Calton, dryly. 'He will be hanged.'

'No, he won't,' retorted the doctor. 'He will commit suicide.'

XXXV

'The Love that Lives'

There are certain periods in the life of men when Fate seems to have done her worst, and any further misfortunes which may befall are accepted with a philosophical resignation, begotten by the very severity of previous trials. Fitzgerald was in this state of mind — he was calm, but it was the calmness of despair — the misfortunes of the past year seemed to have come to a climax, and he looked forward to the publication of the whole bitter story with an indifference that surprised himself. His own name, and that of Madge and her dead father, would be on every tongue, yet he felt perfectly callous to whatever might be said on the subject. As long as Madge recovered, and they could go away to another part of the world, leaving Australia, with its bitter memories behind — he did not care. Moreland would suffer the bitter penalty of his crime, and then nothing more would ever be heard of the matter. It would be better for the whole story to be told, and momentary pain endured, than to go on striving to hide the infamy and shame which might be discovered at any moment. Already the news was all over Melbourne that the murderer of Oliver Whyte had been captured, and that his confession would bring to light certain startling facts concerning the late Mark Frettlby. Brian well knew that the world winked at secret vices as long as there was an attempt at concealment, though it was cruelly severe on those which were brought to light, and that many whose lives might be secretly far more culpable than poor Mark Frettlby's, would be the first to slander the dead man. The public curiosity, however, was destined never to be gratified, for the next day it became known that Roger Moreland had hanged himself in his cell during the night, and had left no confession behind him.

When Brian heard this, he breathed a heartfelt prayer of thanks for his deliverance, and went to see Calton, whom he found at his chambers, in deep conversation with Chinston and Kilsip. They all came to the conclusion that as Moreland was now dead, nothing could be gained by publishing the confession of Mark Frettlby, so agreed to burn it, and when Fitzgerald saw in the heap of blackened paper in the fireplace all that remained of the bitter story, he felt a weight lifted off his heart. The barrister, Chinston, and Kilsip, all promised to keep silent on the subject, and they kept the promise nobly, for nothing was ever known of the circumstances which led to the death of Oliver Whyte, and it was generally supposed that it must have been caused by some quarrel between the dead man and his friend, Roger Moreland.

Fitzgerald, however, did not forget the good service that Kilsip had done him, and gave him a sum of money which made him independent for life, though he still followed his old profession of a detective from sheer love of excitement, and was always looked upon with admiration as the man who had solved the mystery of the famous hansom cab murder. Brian, after several consultations with Calton, at last came to the conclusion that it would be no use to reveal to Sal Rawlins the fact that she was Mark Frettlby's daughter, as by the will the money was clearly left to Madge, and such a revelation could bring her no pecuniary benefit, while her bringing up unfitted her for the position; so a yearly income, more than sufficient for her wants, was settled upon her, and she was allowed to remain in ignorance of her parentage. The influence of Sal Rawlins' old life, however, was very strong on her, and she devoted herself to the task of saving her fallen sisters. Knowing as she did, all the intricacies of the slums, she was enabled to do an immense amount of good, and many an unhappy woman was saved from the squalor and hardship of a gutter life by the kind hand of Sal Rawlins.

Felix Rolleston became a member of Parliament, where his speeches, if not very deep, were at least amusing; and while in the House always behaved like a gentleman, which could not be said about all his parliamentary colleagues.

Madge slowly recovered from her illness, and as she had been explicitly named in the will as heiress to Mark Frettlby's great wealth, she placed the management of her estates in the hands of Mr Calton, who, with Thinton and Tarbit, acted as her agents in Australia. On her recovery she learned the story of her father's early marriage, but both Calton and Fitzgerald were silent about the fact of Sal Rawlins being her half-sister, as such a relation could do no good, and would only create a scandal, as no explanation could be given except the true one. Shortly afterwards Madge married Fitzgerald, and both of them only too gladly left Australia, with all its sorrows and bitter memories.

Standing with her husband on the deck of one of the P and O steamers, as it ploughed the blue waters of Hobson's Bay into foam, they both watched Melbourne as it gradually faded from their view, under the glow of the sunset. They could see the two great domes of the Exhibition, and the Law Courts, and also Government House, with its tall tower rising from the midst of the green trees. In the background was a bright crimson sky, barred with masses of black clouds, and over all the great city hung a cloud of smoke like a pall.

The flaring red light of the sinking sun glared angrily on the heavy waters, and the steamer seemed to be making its way through a sea of blood. Madge, clinging to her husband's arm, felt her eyes fill with tears, as she saw the land of her birth receding slowly.

'Good-bye,' she murmured, softly. 'Good-bye for ever.'

'You do not regret?' he said, bending his head.

'Regret, no,' she answered, looking at him with loving eyes. 'With you by my side, I fear nothing. Surely our hearts have been tried in the furnace of affliction, and our love has been chastened and purified.'

'We are sure of nothing in this world,' replied Brian, with a sigh. 'But after all the sorrow and grief of the past, let us hope that the future will be peace.'

'Peace!'

A white winged sea gull arose suddenly from the crimson waters, and circled rapidly in the air above them.

'A happy omen,' she said, looking up fondly to the grave face of her husband, 'for your life and for mine.'

He bent down and kissed her.

The great steamer moved slowly out to sea, and as they stood on the deck, hand clasped in hand, with the fresh salt breeze blowing keenly in their faces, it bore them away into the placid beauty of the coming night, towards the old world and the new life.

FINIS